ROCKED STARR

ROCKED STARR

what really happens to a fallen star

COLLEN DIXON

Published by
The FIN Group Publishers
12138 Central Avenue, Suite 293
Mitchellville, MD 20721
301.758.8700

First Printing, March 2010

Library of Congress Cataloging-in-Publication Data: 2010920526

Rocked Starr
The FIN Group Publishers
p.
Includes bibliographical references and index.

ISBN 978-0-9710566-6-4 (SC)
ISBN 978-0-9710566-7-1 (HC)

Book and cover design by Burtch Hunter Design ~ www.burtchhunter.com

Hardcover: $29.95 US / $34.00 Canada
Softcover: $17.95 US / $21.00 Canada

This book is dedicated to all of the "Starrs" in the world.
The entertainers, the performers, the singers, the dancers . . .
those who dare to share their talents with the world, and often succumb to it.
Keep the faith, and know that there are some of us who can admire
and support you, without requiring that you destroy you.

BIGGIE . . . TUPAC . . . AALIYAH . . . LEFT EYE
R.I.P.

ROCKED STARR

chapter zero

SHE HANDED *him the brand new Canon Sure Shot™. It was a precious gift, one of the best she'd ever received. Although it was only a point and click camera with a built-in flash, it was far better than any other one she'd ever owned.*

"Come on, take my picture, Boo," she said, a smile radiating from her face.

The man, "Boo," reluctantly held the camera up, asking, "Just look through here, right?" Taking pictures was her thing, not his.

"Yeah, then just push the button," she said and then struck a quick pose. He snapped the picture, the bulb flashing brightly.

"Can we move this along? This ain't no photo shoot an' I ain't got all day, people," a man's voice snapped from the darkened theater.

"Oh, okay," she said, and motioned for Boo to move to the wings. "Go on over there," she said, pointing toward the side of the stage.

"Sure, good luck, baby," he whispered, and pecked her on the cheek. "Knock 'em out the box." He hurried over to edge of the stage, disappearing in the darkness that surrounded the platform.

She stood in the lone spotlight, looked down, and moved a little more toward its center. Cupping her hand over her eyes, she sought direction from an audience she could not see. "Is this cool? Is this where you want me to be?"

"Yeah, uh, look down, aiight? You see the mark? Stand on it." The man's

voice was gruff and commanding, slicing through the dark air. "Don't she know nothin'? Damn!" he snickered to his sidekick.

Onstage, the woman heard only her directions. She found her mark and took a deep breath. Wiggling her fingers, she adjusted her glittery jacket, and patted down the front of her tight-fitting jeans. For the millionth time that day, she worried about her new partials and about her decision to wear them tonight. They made her look better, but they also made her nervous. What if they fell out while she was singing?

Hell, the partials were the least of her worries. Her whole life was riding on what happened in the next few minutes. This was her chance, probably her only chance, and she didn't want to blow it. Not like she had blown so very much of her life.

Her feet shifted. She was hit with the sudden urge to pee. Her bladder was screaming, but she squeezed her eyes and her legs tightly. The feeling finally passed. Then she wanted a hit, a drink, or something to calm her nerves, but she was clean and determined to stay that way. She suddenly got an itch, and wanted to scratch, but she resisted. She rubbed her face, and took another deep breath. She wasn't going to let that monkey get another free ride on her back.

She got it together, silently outtalking the voices raging in her head. "You can do this," she thought. "You gonna do this." Projecting a confidence she did not feel, she called out to her man. "Hey Boo, get me from the side, okay?"

He emerged from the shadows, and strutted across the stage. After a quick peek at the view finder, he snapped the shutter. "Got it, baby."

"Aiight, now. That's enough! You come here to sing or take pictures? Time is money, money is time, goddammit. Man, you get off that stage an' let her do her thing or we outta here." The man's voice, teeming with impatience, was harsh and cutting.

Boo gave her a quick thumbs up sign and hurried back offstage. Again, she was alone in the spotlight. The glare of which prevented her from seeing anything else. She, however, knew who was out there. The ones who mattered. The ones who held her future in their hands.

She closed her eyes and said a quick prayer. She hadn't talked to God in a long time, but she hoped that He'd hear her. This was the opportunity she'd been waiting for since she was old enough to talk. She took a deep breath, and let out a note. It was a little off, a little rusty. "Wait, wait a minute. Hold up.

Imma get this."

"Go 'head, try again," said the man in the dark.

She glanced over to the side of the stage. She couldn't see Boo. Where was he? Had she been a fool to trust him again? "That motherfucker. Imma show him. Once I get this deal, he'll see how he fucked up with me again," she thought.

"Okay, I'm ready," she yelled.

She spread her fingers out and cleared her throat again. Her warm-ups had been good, so she knew she could do it. This time her voice didn't fail her. Despite the years of smoking and abusing drugs, she still had voice. She still had song. She would not be denied.

With each note she became more and more sure of herself, and as she finished Chaka Khan's, "Through the Fire," a capella and without benefit of a microphone, she really felt like she had been through the fire.

Then she waited, standing alone on the empty stage of the Carter Barron, hands clasped tightly together, trying not to notice the chill in the fall air. It seemed like an eternity while she waited for judgment to be passed. The voices in the crowd were muffled, and then the man spoke.

"Yeah, uh, ya know what? I think Imma pass on that. I don't think you got what I'm lookin' for."

An enraged Boo hollered, "Say what?" from the corner, and took a step forward. Before his second step, he was knocked unconscious by a blow that came out of nowhere.

Her heart dropped when she heard his voice and then the "thud" from him dropping to the floor. He hadn't left her. But what happened? She then squinted into the light. "What was that noise? What's going on? What you mean? You said this was a done deal!" She turned to find her man. "Boo, where you at?"

"Oh, it's done, aiight. As done as it's gonna get," the man said. It sounded like he was getting closer to her, that he was approaching the stage.

"Naw, naw uh. You ain't gonna renege on me. I know 'bout you. I ain't to be played with. You'll see. Fuck with me, will you. I'll tear your little playhouse down. Watch me. Boo! Where you at? Boo!" Her voice was elevated and desperate.

Still unable to make out any movement in the dark, her cries for Boo masked the sound of the heavy footsteps that were drawing nearer and nearer. She jumped back when the mysterious man from the audience entered her spotlight, his face finally within view.

"You threatnin' me?"

"I'm promisin' you," she said. "An' my man is gonna help me keep that promise. Boo!" she screamed into the darkness. "Where you at? What the fuck! What the hell's goin' on?"

The man from the audience held his arms out, as if to take in the whole arena. "This is yo' tribute, Miss Lady. Ya had ya moment to shine, ya moment in the spotlight. That's what ya wanted, right?"

"No, nigga. You promised me a contract. An' if I don't get it, Imma blow your spot up."

The mystery man took a long look at her, chuckled in amusement, and snapped his fingers. Immediately, a large man moved out of the shadows behind her and, in a swift movement, pinned her thin arms to her sides. His other hand formed a tight seal on her mouth. She strained furiously, trying to wrest herself from his iron grip, but she was no match for him.

"Oh yeah, ya gonna blow somethin' up, aiight, but it ain't gonna be my spot."

The man reached in his pocket, pulled out a syringe, and plucked the needle. "Hold that bitch still," he said. "She wanna be a star? Okay, Imma put her ass on a rocket so she can fly out to the galaxy. I'm 'bout to give her the high of her fuckin' life. Yeah, ya gonna enjoy this trip, trick. Except this time, there ain't gonna be no comin' back. There ain't gonna be no fuckin' encore. A shame 'bout that, bitch— ya voice ain't half bad."

THE HOUSE lights were brought down, and darkness swept the packed hall. Except for the emergency lights that illuminated the aisles, the only other light in the cavernous space zeroed in on the sinewy, vibrantly dressed woman with a classic Fender guitar swung across her hips. As the crowd quieted in response, her nimble fingers created a haunting instrumental. She played to and for her adoring fans, strumming the strings in a poignant series of musical rifts. Completely absorbed in the music and the moment, she, as always, gave all she had: her lilting voice blending with the Fender in perfect harmony.

This was the last of three sold-out performances at D.C.'s Constitution Hall. As her voice filled the 3,000-seat venue, the standing-room-only crowd whistled and called out to their beloved young diva.

Camara loved it. There was something about performing that invigorated and energized her. Every time she stood on a stage, it was like the first time. But Cam never displayed nervous energy. Or revealed her mojo. Trident wintergreen gum. She always kept a piece tucked in the back of her mouth, between her teeth and gums. A nervous habit, she didn't actually chew it, it was just there. An unusual habit, but it worked for Cam. It kept her pipes moist and relaxed, and the blood flowing. Two factors that enabled her to adhere to the grueling performance schedule she had been on for the past year.

For her second encore, Cam belted out a beautiful fusion-rendition of the first chorus of *Superstar*, a Grammy-award winning song of The Carpenters and Luther Vandross. It was an expert arrangement that Cam herself had crafted.

Even though her voice was clearly straining, she refused to stop. A part of her never, ever wanted to stop. Singing was her life. It was the air she breathed. The ground she walked on. She and song were as one. As her voice dipped and soared, the crowd stood to its feet.

"Go girl!"

"Do your thing!"

"You better sing that shit, Baby Girl!"

Cam smiled and dropped her head. As was her habit at the end of every performance, she reached one hand to her neck, to touch the small diamond cross she was never without. With her clear skin, minimal makeup, and freshly cut pixie hairstyle, she looked like a little girl. And she felt like one too. Like a child basking in the adulation and attention of her parents. Except these parents were her fans. And she wanted to give them all that she had. To prove that she was worthy of their love.

Tears sprang to her eyes when she thought about how her fans had dug deep in their pockets, put on their best outfits, and braved the cold to come and see her. She had to find the strength to give them her best. It didn't matter if she was singing before royalty or before the disenfranchised youth at her children's foundation, she always felt humbled and honored that there were people who wanted to hear her sing.

As she took what she hoped would be her final bow of the evening, Camara remembered the words of her vocal coach, Deidre Holmes. Last year, on Cam's 21st birthday, Deidre had warned her to take better care of her voice.

"You can't keep pushing your chords like you do. It just isn't healthy," Dee had said, peering over her reading glasses. "Your voice box is like a good man. You think he'll always be around, no matter how bad you treat 'em. You pretend not to notice when things start to change, when he starts showing up late, or when he starts actin' different. Then one day, he doesn't show up at all. And sometimes he never comes back. And then you wonder why. So, don't let that happen to you." Dee yanked a tissue from her pocket, and held it under Cam's chin. "Now, spit that gum out," she said, slitting her eyes at Cam.

Cam pretended to be absorbed in the sheet music she was scanning, and cradled a cup of hot tea in her hands. "I don't have any gum, Dee." She opened her mouth and showed her, confident Dee would never see it. "I'm okay, Dee. And I'm being very careful. But, I have to learn this music, don't I? And I want to be the best vocalist, well, performer there is. I don't want people to think that I'm just some studio singer who needs a whole lot of production because I can't carry a note. You know how rumors get started."

Dee sighed. "No one would ever mistake you for a studio voice, Cam. And being the best is an admirable goal. And learning and being willing to take instruction is always a good thing too. But you're taking chances, Cam, serious chances." She removed the music from Cam's hands. "You can't tell me that your throat isn't hurting. I hear it in your pitch. It sounds strained whenever you get in the G-minor range."

Forcing a smile, Cam turned away and sipped her hot tea before returning to the podium where she stood and sang. Dee said that standing improved the performance of the diaphragm, and trained the singer to project better and stronger.

Outside of her Aunt Mary who had raised her, Dee was one of the few adults Cam actually trusted. Recommended by Sheila, her church choir director, Cam and Dee had developed a strong bond. First as student and teacher, then as student and mentor, and, finally, as friends. Cam had acquired most of the people in her close-knit management team the same way: through church and community relationships. Her accountant, Richard Samuels, was a church trustee, and her attorney was a deacon named Cecil Owens. They were both upstanding members of the church and the community, and Deacon Owens had been involved with the family's legal matters for years.

Both had proven very trustworthy. They took time and care to explain things to Aunt Mary and Cam, and helped them navigate the treacherous waters of the entertainment industry. They respected Cam's privacy, to the extent that when Deacon Owens needed special expertise, he kept it in the family, asking advice only from his nephew, Kevin Owens. As Cam's career grew, and she moved from church performances to studios and concert halls, it became apparent to all that she needed a more seasoned manager than her Aunt Mary. Hence, Victor "Vic" Burton entered her guarded inner circle on the recommendation of Kevin Owens. Vic, a seasoned industry vet, had worked with both established and upcoming artists, and seemed to be working to provide a solid foundation for the rising star.

Cam's inner circle was extremely important to her. And it was important that Aunt Mary felt comfortable working with whoever she had on her team. And that level of comfort was even more critical now that Aunt Mary was less involved with her daily career, and unable to travel with Cam as she had in the past. Through Vic, her management team became larger and much better structured. He hired Allison as her personal assistant and publicist, Torrie as her personal stylist, and Necy as her hairstylist.

Trust did not come easily for Cam, and initially, relying on complete strangers had been difficult for her, a trait she had carried since childhood. However, as the days on tour grew into weeks and months, an easy camaraderie developed between the women, and strong threads of friendship wove them together as each did what they did best for Cam.

Cam's Aunt Mary was actually her grandmother Chloe's baby sister. Chloe Addison and her husband Odell had taken in Mary after their mother died, like good Southern folk often did. They looked out for one another. Took care of their own.

Mary was only a few years older than Chloe's daughter, Faith, but she had an old soul. She was reliable and dependable, but more than a little naïve. Some thought she might be a little slow, because of the way she trusted people and acted like she was still in North Carolina. She'd run barefoot down the streets of Deanwood like she was skipping through a sweet-smelling country honeysuckle-filled field. Many times, Chloe got on her sister for the backwards way she behaved, never knowing that in the long run, it would be Mary's spirit that would one day save Chloe's entire family.

In their two-story row house in Northeast DC, Chloe and Odell were strict but kind, raising Mary, and their own children, Faith and Odell "OJ" Junior, in a house brimming with love and laughter. A creative child, Faith loved nature and taking pictures with her little Brownie camera. The National Arboretum was one of her favorite places to visit, and she never tired of looking at the flowers and trees. Her numerous photo albums, filled with fading black and white and colored snapshots, were her most valuable possessions. No matter what she did or where she went, Faith always took her camera. And her pictures.

The family attended church faithfully, and Mary, Faith, and OJ were active in a number of youth activities at First Baptist. In fourth grade, Faith, along with Mary, joined the church choir, and it was discovered that she could sing like a caged bird. In fact, she was often the soloist. Nearly every Sunday, a burgundy and white-robed Faith commanded the choir stand, where she would clutch the microphone and sing Walter Hawkins' version of *"Oh Happy Day."*

Nearly the same age, her Aunt Mary was happy to bask in Faith's shadow, content shaking the tambourine and rocking with the rest of the choir. Chloe and Odell could hardly contain their pride. The whole congregation could see that Faith had the heart and soul of a great singer, that she was destined to become the next Tramaine Hawkins or Shirley Caesar.

As a teen, however, Faith became increasingly rebellious. When OJ left to join the army, Faith became even more incorrigible; even Mary's calming presence had no influence on her. Church became unimportant to her; she walked away from the choir and into the music of the street. An old story, but Chloe and Odell were taken by surprise when Faith started lying, sneaking around, drinking, and experimenting with drugs, mostly weed. Mostly she smoked reefer, nothing stronger. Until that *"Love Boat"* cruised into the city.

"Love Boat" or *"Lovely"* was weed dipped in PCP or Angel Dust. The effects were like nothing anyone had ever seen before. Behaviors

changed. Moods swung. It was also nicknamed *"Butt Naked,"* for most people that smoked it ended up stripping off their clothes, wherever they were, and ran naked in the streets. Thankfully, Faith was one of the few that the Love Boat didn't victimize, but she did smoke more than her fair share of weed. Her drug use and fast times on the street changed her. She stopped taking pictures, stopped caring about anything but getting high, and became increasingly out of control and unmanageable. Eventually, at 16, Faith announced she was pregnant, and that the baby's father was one of the neighborhood hustlers, Charlie "Carlos" Bonds.

He was nicknamed Carlos because he fancied himself Puerto Rican or West Indian, with smooth, buttery brown skin and "good" hair. Looks aside, he seemed to bring out the worst in Faith, and theirs was an extremely volatile relationship. She would often come home with bruises that she claimed were accidental, but Mary and Chloe knew better. They could see she was sliding down a slippery slope, and no matter what they said or did, Faith seemed determined to fall. And fall hard.

Chloe, reeling with shame, was supportive of Faith during her pregnancy, escorting her to the doctor, making sure she took her prenatal vitamins, and praying for a healthy grandchild who would not be born addicted to drugs. Despite all of their best efforts, they couldn't stop Faith from dropping out of school. This, coupled with the pregnancy, really broke Mary, Chloe, and Odell's collective hearts.

Mary stood by her niece, and, when her little daughter arrived, helped her nurse and care for her newborn. Although they made it clear that Carlos was not welcome in their home, Mary and Faith became close again. Faith named her beautiful daughter Camara, because she was as pretty as a picture; a beauty in an otherwise ugly world.

And Camara was her world. Faith snapped pictures of everything her little one did, whether it was laughing or crying or getting her diaper changed. The old Faith was back. She began working on a photo album of Cam, and to her it was the most valuable thing on earth. She wanted to do right by her daughter, and decided to leave Carlos alone so she could focus on her child. She vowed to straighten out her life. Faith even recommitted herself to Christ, and had Camara christened at the church

where she had once led the choir. For the ceremony, Faith even found the
money to buy a tiny diamond cross to place around her baby's neck.

Mary, Chloe, and Odell were overjoyed and did all they could for Faith
and little Camara. They believed in her and believed she wanted to
change. However, shortly after Cam's christening, Faith hooked up with
Carlos again, and left the family home to "make it" on the streets of DC.
Little Cam was left with photo albums and a sense of abandonment.

Mary became little Cam's surrogate mother, due largely in part to
Chloe's declining health, Odell's losing battle with emphysema, and both
of their irreparably injured hearts.

OJ came home "a little touched" in the late mid 1980s, discharged
from the Army with what would later be known as post-traumatic stress
syndrome. He returned with no tangible skills, only a fierce appetite for
narcotics. The family dynamics were challenging for the Addison clan,
but Mary held them together. She worked several jobs after Chloe's debil-
itating battle with "sugar" prevented her from working, and Odell became
bedridden. Somehow, Mary even managed to keep OJ from stealing all of
their belongings so he could hock them to support his habit.

The light in the otherwise bleak household was little Cam. Her existence revolved around the few toys she had, going to school, and going to
church. No matter how much she worked, Mary kept Cam in church nearly every evening, and every Sunday. For a while, Faith came to the house
every time she remembered she had a daughter. As time wore on, her visits were less and less frequent, until she finally just stopped coming. It was
then that Mary decided not to talk about Faith or Carlos to Cam.

Cam couldn't recall ever seeing her father, and only heard his name
mentioned once or twice as a child, usually in a heated conversation
between her mother and her aunt. She was an obedient, quiet child who
listened intently to her aunt and did everything she was told. She was
afraid to ask about her parents, especially her mother. She knew not to
ask about her father, and somehow, Cam blamed herself for her mother
not being there. Was her birth the reason her mother had run and stayed

away? Cam carried this guilty burden deep within herself.

When the thick braided little Cam overheard the adults having hushed conversations about "Faith," she often wondered why her mother wasn't around. And sometimes, Uncle OJ would pass through, and rant and rave about seeing Faith down on 14th Street, which would cause both her grandmother and aunt to sob like wounded spirits. Several times, Faith actually did turn up, usually after a frantic phone call from jail. She would be begging to be bailed out and vowing to do better. And as always, her family came to her rescue. Chloe entrusted her faith and confidence to the one attorney she knew from church, Deacon Cecil Owens. And despite her shame and sometimes inability to pay, Deacon Owens always came through for Chloe and the disappointment that was her daughter. The good deacon kept the family's calamities to himself, and it was a thoughtful, albeit legal, action that Chloe, Mary, and eventually Cam, really appreciated. Faith's comings and goings were a revolving door process that existed during Cam's entire childhood. But, during her stays, she always added more pictures to Cam's photo album. Those photos were a mainstay in Cam's life, often providing the confirmation that despite her mother's actions, she still loved her.

So, when the time came to engage an attorney for better circumstances, like when Cam's career began taking off, Deacon Owens was the only one the family trusted to handle her affairs. Her family might have been short on funds, but they were long in gratitude and loyalty.

Cam became even more reclusive after her grandfather passed, and OJ stole most of his father's insurance money. Grief and stress weakened Chloe even more, and Mary had to work longer hours to keep the taxman from taking her sister's home. A gospel music lover and a good steward, Mary channeled her energy into nurturing Cam, so she would develop and grow into a healthy child. She couldn't fathom the thought of Cam falling by the wayside like her mother, so Mary did all she could to insulate her from the perils of the world.

She encouraged the painfully shy Cam to sing in the cherub choir, even though the little tyke really didn't want to. But, it was good for her. It gave her some much needed socialization skills, even though Cam seemed content to hang in the shadows of the older children as they sang solos and performed for the congregation.

But it was during these times that Cam honed her craft. She found an acceptance in singing that was missing from her life. When she sang, it didn't matter whose little girl she was, or what her circumstances were. She could transform herself, and find comfort in the words of the hymns. Cam learned how to harmonize, even though she really didn't know what she was doing, and quietly expanded her range. It wasn't until the tone-deaf musical director Mr. Mathis fell ill, and his younger protégée, Sheila Jenkins, took over, that anyone even realized that Cam could really sing.

When Sheila took over the choir, she instituted a very rudimentary work ethic. She had each of the children sing a solo. When Cam reached for the microphone and proceeded to rip it, Sheila knew a star was born. When Mary heard that Cam had been selected to perform a solo, she tried to prevent her from singing, because it brought back too many memories of Faith. She was concerned that being in the spotlight, even if it was for the Lord, would prove too much for little Cam.

For a while, Sheila tried to comply with Mary's request, but even she felt that Mary shouldn't impose her superstitions and misgivings on a gifted child like Cam. Finally, one Sunday, Reverend Moore stepped in at the altar call, and requested that Cam sing *"His Eye is on the Sparrow,"* and the whole congregation nearly fell out or caught the Holy Ghost. Even Mary was forced to admit that Cam had a God-given talent that was too large to be contained, and she eventually acquiesced.

Cam's vocal ability brought her great recognition in the DC area. She was billed as a natural phenom, and was responsible for First Baptist winning back-to-back citywide and regional choir competitions. As she grew older, she was often featured as a soloist. Mary, though still uncomfortable about Cam's burgeoning acclaim, fully supported her surrogate daughter and was always front and center at any local event. Sometimes she was late, and came dressed in her Marriott hotel maid's uniform. But she was there. And it meant the world to Cam to know that her Aunt Mary was in her corner. Even when she really didn't have one to be in.

chapter two

THE ROAR from the crowd brought Cam back into the present.

"Go on, girl. Take your time!" Some man shouted. It was if he felt her pain.

"Sing that shit, Baby Girl!" Another voice, teeming with adoration and emotion, screamed.

Cam squinted, her eyes brimming with tears. She had lapsed for almost two minutes, yet the audience thought that it was part of the act. She rose to her feet, and her eyes caught a glimpse of the stage lights as they hit the chrome on a wheelchair. Even in the darkened crowd, Cam saw the awestruck expression of one of her biggest fans, and president of one of her fan clubs, wheelchair-bound Rashad Givens.

Rashad was a bright, charismatic young man, who was actually graduating early from high school and planning to attend Morehouse College. Cam had met him a few years ago, when he waited at the stage door with flowers, proclaiming to be her number one fan. They often communicated via email, and Rashad had formed his own fan club and created a fan website in her honor. Given that he couldn't travel a great deal, he made sure to attend Cam's concerts whenever she had one near him in the ATL.

She drew inspiration from Rashad's spirit, who stressed that he wasn't "handicapped," but "handi-capable." His bright personality and relentless commitment to being accepted for the person he was really captured Cam's heart and helped her better appreciate the beauty of all of God's creatures. It also spurred her to form a youth foundation for underprivileged and handi-capable kids, and she named Rashad to the board of advisors.

When she and Rashad had touched base a few months ago, she mentioned that the DC concert was going to be one of her last for a while. Rashad had promised that he would come, and he did. She made sure that he would be seated in the front, so he would know how special he was to her. Since he had traveled all the way from Atlanta to see her, she wouldn't disappoint him. She smiled at him and with all of her strength, she belted out the last line of *"Superstar."*

After, she broke the news to the audience: she'd be taking off for a while to rest her voice and regroup. Then, when she asked them if they'd remember her in a few months, the crowd exploded again.

"I love you," she said, her voice choking. "I always will. I really, really, mean it. And I'll be back, real soon. I promise. Thank you, and good night." Cam released her gum from its secret place, left her Fender guitar silent on a chair in the spotlight, and walked backwards off the stage, waving until out of sight. As her faithful bodyguard Big Mac and his minions parted the backstage crowd, Cam rushed through the swarm of props and cheers from her back-up dancers and musicians, and ran into the arms of her stage manager Manny, who drew her into his burly chest.

Wynton "Manny" Andrews was a middle-aged, veteran music industry road manager, with many years of managing volatile, narcissistic entertainers. With his large, rotund midsection, and salt and pepper hair, Manny looked old, but could hang with the best of them. He had been there and done that with many pros, and the musicians and backup dancers would often tease him about being old enough to tour with Jesus. But that was all right. He'd cuss them out, keep it moving, and always had Cam's back. He liked to drink and tell jokes, but he always kept it cute when it came to Cam. His flask remained hidden until the last detail of the tour was finalized, and then Manny would get ghost.

Montel "Big Mac" McIntyre was Cam's head of security. A big, broad, ex-Green Beret and martial arts expert, Big Mac was no joke. He was built like Tiny Lister, but was strikingly handsome. The color of burnished tan, his hair was cut razor close, and he was clean shaven, with full, deep-set eyes. He always wore shades and his earpiece, and he was the one Cam relied on most.

"You did great, Baby Girl. Just great. It was outta sight, Cam. Off the chain," Manny said, and rubbed her aching shoulders.

Cam could barely speak. Manny had always treated her like a surrogate daughter, and now she thought about how much she was going to miss him. She just nodded and sobbed. "Thank you, Manny. Thanks so much for everything."

Manny misted over, wiped his eyes and lifted Cam's chin. "You're welcome, Cam. I should be thanking you for allowing me the opportunity to work with you. You've been the greatest thing to hit this industry in a long time. A breath of fresh air in a world of stale, fake-ass, posers." Manny hunched his shoulders, and then quickly glanced from side to side. "Well, I guess I'd better shut the hell up. Shit, I might have to work for one of them wannabes one day."

The normally silent Big Mac grunted. "Not me, man. I ain't workin' for nobody but Cam. I'll go back to tossin' niggas out the titty bars first."

They all laughed, and tears welled again in Cam's eyes. She pressed her face into Manny's chest. Despite her ability to charm millions of adoring fans, Cam was still very much the shy, naïve girl from her youth. "I appreciate what you've done for me. Just being here for me has been such a blessing." Cam's voice was muffled, but Manny heard and felt every word she said.

Manny pulled her from his chest, and touched his forehead to hers. "You're a wonder, girl. Girl Wonder. Just get you some time off, get your head right, and you'll be back and hotter than ever. Like fiyah."

A stiff finger poked Cam in the shoulder, and it jarred her back to reality. Standing with her hands thrust on her hips, Shaye, one of Cam's backup singers, had a sour expression on her otherwise attractive face.

"Heywood's checkin' for you. I suggest you get at him with a quick-ness."

"We'll be right there," Big Mac said, and dropped his massive arms to his side.

Cam's eyes flashed, while Manny's rolled. "Um, thanks, Shaye," Cam said.

Shaye sucked her teeth then turned her stocking feet towards the dressing rooms. "No biggie. I'm just passin' on a message. *Hmmph*. Like I'm the damned errand girl." She sauntered off into the crowd before Cam could even ask where Heywood was.

"See? That's what I'm talkin' about. That's the type of head-trips we got walkin' around here, Cam. She gotta lotta damned nerve. You're the reason she's even eatin' today, an' she got the nerve to have an attitude. Wit' you of all people. Talkin' 'bout biting the hand that feeds yo' hungry ass. Damn.

"Everybody's tryin' to be a superstar. She don't have what it takes to even *think* about tryin' to be a headliner. And that's showmanship. And some class. Shoot. The first thing that girl needs is to stop bein' so damned rude, and go to charm school or somethin'. You can tell she ain't got no home trainin'," Manny said, his leathery face balled up in a scowl.

"Later for that tired-assed, big-backed broad," a deep, sultry voice spoke. It was Sonya, a tall, thick, mocha colored sister with spiked, reddish brown twists. She was also one of Cam's backup singers, and one of her few friends. Plus, she had a major crush on Big Mac.

Sonya waded through the crowd and came up and grabbed Cam by the waist, and winked at Big Mac. "She's just hatin', that's all. Don't even sweat it, Cam. You were slammin' tonight, girl," she said with a wink. "Never better. And you know I'd let 'cha know if you weren't on point."

Her thick New York accent rang, and she spoke almost like she was singing. She twirled around Cam. "Come on, girlfriend. Let's go get changed so we can get somethin' to eat. I know you must be starved. We can hit Gladys Knight and Ron Winans's Chicken and Waffles. I know they're still open."

Cam, who never ate before a performance, was starved. She reluctantly released herself from Manny's embrace, and brushed him across the cheek. "I'll see you later, Manny."

Manny smiled. "Not if I see you first, Baby Girl. Be easy."

With Big Mac leading, Cam and Sonya linked their arms and made their way through the packed backstage until they reached Cam's dressing room. Big Mac slipped into the dressing room, while the other guards stationed themselves around Cam and Sonya. Big Mac always conducted the security sweeps of Cam's dressing rooms himself. He would never allow anyone else to do such a critical task, and it helped. One time, there was a concert hall staff member, buck naked, waiting in the closet of Cam's room when she appeared at Radio City Music Hall last year. Big Mac had more fun tossing that poor man out on his butt cheeks.

Big Mac stuck his head out of the door, and then signaled the all clear. Whispering into his earpiece, he motioned for the other guards to position themselves in various areas of the hallway, and to prepare the exit for Cam's departure. Posting himself at the door, he held it open for Cam and Sonya to enter.

"I don't get it, Sonya. I don't know why Shaye's so hostile toward me all the time."

Sonya placed her hands on her hips, and tilted her head toward Cam. "Cam, you need to stop. You know Shaye's been buckin' to be in the spotlight since before you even started on the hip-hop scene. You know that. And now that you're taking your little break, she's really turning up the heat on trying to go solo. She's been putting that demo of hers in anyone's face that'll listen. She's a shady heifer. That should really be her stage name. '*Shaye-dee.*'"

Cam shook her head. "I know. And I wish her luck." Cam sighed. "Why is it that we all can't do what it is that's gonna make us happy, without feeling like you gotta cut somebody else down to do it? She's a talented girl, and if she wants a solo career, I hope she gets it. And does well for herself."

"Well, that's a lot more than anyone else would wish for her, Cam. But, Shaye's too gully for all of that. Too low down. Too cutthroat. She's determined she's gonna make it. No matter what. Even if it means— well, never mind."

"If it means what?" Cam's eyes questioned Sonya.

"Never mind, Cam. You just focus on getting yourself some rest. Don't sweat that Shaye bullshit."

Cam sighed and reiterated her earlier sentiments, wishing Shaye the best. "I'm sure she'll do well."

"Like I said, later for that backstabbin' broad. Now, go get changed and chill out for a minute. I'll be right back, okay?" Sonya said. "I just gotta go grab my stuff from my room, and I'll be back to scoop you up in a few. Everybody wants you to come down and hang out before you go, okay?"

The 'everybody' Sonya was referring to were the other background singers. Probably not Shaye, but members of Cam's band, the crew, and some of the dancers. The thought that her peeps wanted to chill with her made Cam smile, and Sonya returned the warmth.

"Girlfriend, you were bangin' tonight. And you were movin' an' groovin', too. You had those steps down pat, Cam. And see, you thought you wouldn't be able to hang. Girl, you betta stop trippin' and underestimating yourself. I knew you'd be a beast tonight!"

Cam really appreciated Sonya's support, and she thanked her for it.

"No sweat, Cam. I just wanna make sure you gig me when you come back. *Psych!*" Sonya cut her eye at Big Mac. "But I tell you what you can do for a sista. I need to borrow Big Mac for a minute. I think I'm gonna need some security to get to my dressing room. You think you can help a sista out?"

Big Mac smirked, and Cam smiled as she watched Sonya saunter down the crowded corridor. As she reached for the doorknob to her dressing room, Cam paused, finally feeling the full impact of her resolution to leave this all behind for a while. She hadn't thought about the goodbyes or the see you laters. Or about how she might lose good folks like Sonya to the next big thing. But, she had to do it. She ran her fingers along the wood-grained door, and shook her head. Despite what she was giving up, she had no real regrets. If she had anything to do with it, it was going to be a long time before she entered another dressing room.

chapter three

FOR MONTHS, Cam had been trying to take some time off. She was becoming disillusioned with the business; the ruthless, nonstop, phony music business, and she wanted to get away from it. Far away from it. She had evolved from a young musical prodigy who started off singing gospel, and who had actually won on *"Showtime at the Apollo,"* to a major recording star. But, it had been an arduous journey.

From the beginning, Cam had been determined to succeed, and to be the best all-around entertainer she could be. While growing up, Aunt Mary had allowed her to take ballet classes, but no modern dance. The ballet kept her lithe and limber, but her lack of exposure to modern dance was challenging. To overcome her shyness about her body, she worked with the best choreographers to learn the latest dance moves and how to force her body to flow in suggestive ways that went against her church upbringing.

Determined to build up her stamina and lungs, she also embarked on a grueling fitness regime with an authentic boot camp instructor and Big Mac. So far, her weight had not been an issue, but crafting an exceptional endurance level was. She was a talented machine.

Cam always felt that her music was a blessing and a curse. Her love of music and her musical capabilities came naturally; she always felt closer to her mom when she was singing. On the other hand, it was and always would be a painful reminder of her mother.

★

When Cam was 14 years old and gaining a reputation on the gospel circuit, she appeared at a benefit concert at Metropolitan Baptist Church. It was there that she met and witnessed a phenom in the making, a young singer named James Troutman.

Jamie, as he was better known, was lighting up the circuit. She had heard of him and his talent, by being in DC together, but she had never had a chance to meet him. As luck or fate would have it, Cam and Aunt Mary had bumped into Jamie's manager as they were entering the rear of the church, and he had offered to introduce them. His manager was carrying a vase overflowing with red roses, and led them to one of the choir's dressing rooms where Jamie was running through his selections.

His manager placed the flowers on a table, and introduced Cam and Aunt Mary to Jamie and his mother. Even though he was warming up, Jamie stopped and greeted her as if he had known her all of his life.

"Hey girl. I was hopin' that I'd get a chance to meet you, Camara. Can I call you Cam?" he asked, and gave her a big hug. He even greeted Aunt Mary with a very polite, "Hello, Ma'am."

He was dressed in all white, just like a little angel. Suit, shirt, tie, handkerchief, socks, and even his shoes were pearly white. Cam was nervous, but couldn't help but smile. Oddly enough, she felt like she was in the presence of greatness, even though Jamie was her own age.

"I've heard so much about you," he said, with a big grin. Slightly stocky, Jamie was a rich cocoa brown color, and his face shined with a fresh coat of Vaseline. He was really cute, with big, bright, flashy eyes, perfect white teeth, and a thick, curly Gerri curl. Yes, sir. He was really cute. Almost too cute. "I didn't know you were so pretty," he said, and his mother cut her eyes at him.

"I've heard a lot about you too, Jamie," Cam said, and blushed. "I've always wanted to meet you."

"Well, we've met," he said with a wink. "And now don't forget," he said, stressing the rhyme. "That we've got to stay in touch," he said, and touched Cam's arm. "'Cause we are too much." He giggled and turned toward his mother, a portly, womanly version of Jamie. She was also decked out in white, including thick white stockings that made swishing sounds when she walked, her thighs rubbing together. She didn't appear too amused by Jamie's little ditty.

He ignored her lack of enthusiasm. "Hey ma, can you give Camara my number? Please?"

"Okay, James. We'd better ask her aunt if that's okay."

Aunt Mary nodded, and Jamie's mother continued. "You don't have to worry about Jamie, he's a good boy," she said, and jotted the number down and handed it to Aunt Mary. "We're sorry," she said. "But, I need to get him ready."

Aunt Mary rested her hands on Cam's shoulders and nudged her slightly. "We understand. We need to get ready too."

Jamie winked at Cam again, and gave her another hug. "Knock 'em dead, Cam." He reached over and picked out one of the flowers and handed it to Cam. "These are my favorite," he said, and sniffed the remaining roses. "I've always loved roses. Especially the red ones. They're beautiful. Just like you."

Cam was stunned. She didn't know boys liked flowers. There was something different about Jamie that made her like him even more. Jamie, though only a year older than Cam, was a seasoned showman. He knew how to draw in a crowd. Cam watched in the wings as they introduced Jamie to the packed house, the audience crackling in anticipation. Only a teenager, he already had the powerful voice of a man. He started singing *"How I Got Over,"* from the other side of the stage without a microphone, and the house went up. He was totally engaged in his performance, and whether he was moved by the Holy Ghost or by his own star power, he was a force to be reckoned with. And even Cam recognized that he would go far.

Cam's performance was excellent that evening too, with someone in the audience snapping lots of pictures. As she exited the stage to the sounds of a cheering, spirit-filled audience, a visibly nervous Aunt Mary met her with a towel and a room temperature bottle of water.

"Cam," she said, nervously glancing over her shoulder, as she handed Cam the bottle. Aunt Mary mopped Cam's face with the towel, and then placed the towel on Cam's shoulder. Slipping her arm through Cam's arm, Aunt Mary started guiding her through the crowd toward the room where her clothes were. "Someone, well, someone's here to see you. But, if you're not feeling up to it, she'll have to understand."

"Who is it?" Cam asked.

A camera flashed in her face, temporarily blinding her. "It's me, Baby Girl!" screamed a rail thin woman with beaded braids and cracking gum. She was holding a disposable camera as she darted out of the shadows, nearly knocking Aunt Mary over.

Cam glanced at her aunt and then at the woman. "Mommy?"

"Yes, baby. It's me," she grinned, displaying yellow, mosaic teeth. She grabbed Cam away from Aunt Mary, and drew her into her sunken arms.

She was twitching a little, and the smell of stale cigarettes and mothballs radiated from her clothes, but Cam didn't care. She melted into her mother's arms like a toddler taking her first steps. She clung to her, for it had been many months since she had seen her mother.

"Faith," Aunt Mary snapped. "I thought I told you to wait until I had a chance to talk to Camara." She spoke in a tone that Cam had rarely heard, and it startled her.

"Oh, Mary. Lighten up," said Faith, popping her gum and rubbing Cam's back. "I knew my baby girl was gonna wanna see her momma." She smiled at her aunt, turned to Cam, and pinched her cheeks.

"We got lots to talk about, don't we Cammy baby? You are doin' so well, you got a voice like I used to have. That was before," she cleared her throat, "Before I started smokin' so much. Now, don't you ever do that, you hear? Smokin' will mess you up."

Aunt Mary grunted and crossed her arms. "There are many things that'll mess you up, Camara. Now, Faith. It's good to see you. I am surprised, though, that you'd come to the church. What's going on?"

Faith scratched her face and toyed with Cam's pigtails. "What's goin' on is that I'm here to see my child. *My* daughter. I'm gonna spend some time with her, and she's gonna spend some time wit' me. That's all."

Aunt Mary gently touched Cam's arm and told her to go and get changed so that they could leave.

"You're still gonna be here, aren't you mommy? When I come back?" Cam asked as she reluctantly left the boney arms of her mother.

"I ain't goin' no where, Punkin. No where."

As soon as Cam left the room, Aunt Mary lit into Faith. "Faith, what are you doing here? Half high. And in a church of all places. Why did you come here? Just to disrupt and destroy your child's life for the umpteenth time?"

Faith continued popping her gum, and glared at her aunt with a defiant expression. "That's my child, an' I have a right to be wit' her."

"Why now? *Hmmph.* There has to be something in it for you."

"It is. My child. An' why you got her dressin' like she's a toddla'? Like some little kid. Hell, she's damn near 15 years old."

"Hush your mouth, Faith. This is the Lord's house, and you in here cursing. You should be ashamed of yourself," Mary said, and shook her head.

"What I am is back in my child's life, an' here to stay. You hear me? Now deal with it."

And stay she did. She and Cam picked up right where they had left off the last time Faith had come around. Faith did everything within her power to walk the walk, and stayed clean and sober. As Cam approached her 15th birthday, she had received her greatest gift. Her mother.

And Faith even returned to the Addison home, where her mother, Chloe, welcomed her back. It irritated Aunt Mary, but there wasn't much that she could do, except less than subtly remind Cam that she was a good girl, and that she didn't need to fall into the same trap as her mother.

When she wasn't reminding Faith of her shortcomings and fall from grace, she was also warning Faith not to bring any of her dirt home. And since she questioned Faith's sincerity, Aunt Mary was insistent that Faith never, ever break Cam's heart by discussing her father. That was a topic that was not for discussion. It was bad enough that Mary had to watch Cam deal with the hull that was her mother, but she would not stand by and watch Faith drag her further into the pit of hell by bringing that criminal father into her protected world. Incredibly, it was the one thing that Faith reluctantly agreed to. Well, partially anyway. She did want to protect her child, so she didn't bring Carlos around, but she told Cam all about him anyway.

"Your daddy was the best lookin' dude in all of Deanwood, Camara. Hell, probably even all of Northeast. He was fine. That's where you get them fine features an' that nice grade of hair," her mother said.

"His name is Charlie, but we called him Carlos. He was a good lookin' thing, that Carlos. Fine as hell. *Umph, umph, umph.*"

Camara smiled, and then looked away. "I always wanted to know about my daddy, mommy. Auntie told me never to ask about him. Why is that?"

"Well, your aunt didn't like him too tough. Said he was too pretty. An' that he was no good for it." She shook her head and sighed. "He was pretty, though. An' he knew it. An' Mary didn't like that he was so cocky with his. An' irresponsible. So, for real, she was just tryin' to look out for you. An' sometimes she gets a little carried away.
"See, your daddy's had a hard life, an' he keeps doin' things that get him in trouble. You know what jail is, right?"

Cam nodded, and her mother continued. "Well, that's where your daddy spends a lot of his time. In an' out, usually on some bullshit. It's not that he don't love you, and it's not that he don't love me. But, well, you know, it's just hard for him. An' it's been hard for me too. I mean, I've done some things I ain't proud of too, for real. But, the truth is that we both don't want to make it no harder for you by havin' him run in an' outta your life. Hell, I've been bad enough, but at least I got family to look out for you. Your Aunt Mary and Momma, well, I knew they'd take good care of you. An' now that I'm gonna get myself together, I'm gonna take good care of you too. Make up for lost time, baby. Mommy means it. I really do."

It appeared Faith really was trying to turn her life around. Her latest legal infraction had been handled by Deacon Owens's nephew, Kevin, a recent Howard Law graduate. He was able to get Faith's shoplifting charges dismissed, and tried to help get her life on the right path. Faith didn't even seem to mind the help she was being given by her family and attorney. She took a job as a stock clerk at the Safeway on Minnesota Avenue, and stayed away from her usual crowd.

She and Cam spent every available moment together. They took lots of pictures together, and even went to church, with Faith regaling in the chants and thank yous from the congregation as Cam's little light continued to shine as a soloist. They rode the Metrobus all around town, and Faith showed her all the areas she needed to stay away from, but needed to know about.

Her mother schooled her on all the things that Aunt Mary would never discuss, or even acknowledge existed. They talked about drugs and boys, because Faith didn't want Cam to get caught out there with either one of them like she had. She wanted more for her child, and she was honest and candid about it.

She even talked about Cam's father, and said that if she could get them a ride, they were going to go down to the prison in Lorton, Virginia, to see him. It bothered Faith that Cam didn't know him, and never really saw him, when he was right there in the same area. Cam, who yearned to know her father, pressed her mother for every bit of information she could get, and made her mother promise to take her to see him. Faith made it clear that seeing him was a promise that she intended to keep. And it was a promise that Cam clung to.

In the interim, they cried together. And they laughed together. And they shared a love of music. They listened to lots and lots of music. All of the types of music Aunt Mary never allowed Cam to listen to. Tucked away in Faith's former room and Cam's bedroom, they listened to 45s and albums by everyone from Luther Vandross to Prince. Anita Baker, Sade and Chaka Khan.

She and Cam even sang together, and Cam could see where her voice came from. They worked on their harmony and ran rifts, and even though Faith's voice was a shell of what it had been, she gave Cam a run for her money. She taught her, too, expanding Cam's vocal range from gospel to soul and R&B.

They confided in each other, whispering and giggling, and telling tales. More like teenaged sisters than mother and daughter, they watched Soul Train and snuck out whenever they could. One day, Faith surprised Cam, saying that they were taking a special trip. Cam was elated, thinking that she was finally going to meet her father. She was disappointed, but only briefly, when Faith told her that she had copped some tickets to a taping of Video Soul with Donnie Simpson down at BET Studios off Brentwood Road.

When she found out who the guest star was, Cam was absolutely thrilled. It was none other than Jamie Tee, the former child gospel star who had reinvented himself as the newest teen heartthrob. The "new and improved" Jamie Tee was awesome. Slimmed down from his earlier years, Jamie's body was now sleek and panther-like, and his formerly cherubic cheeks were taut and firm. Cam was amazed. Gone was the shiny curl, replaced with a closely cropped head of naturally waved hair. With a sharp and perfectly-shaved moustache, Jamie was hot and he knew it. His appeal was on lock with the young girls and even the older ladies were on him. He was constantly being linked to one beautiful songstress, actress or heiress, his single, *"Fired Up"* was getting major airplay, and the hometown loved their reborn star.

Even though there were throngs of admirers waiting to see him after the show, Jamie spotted Cam, and waded through the crowd to greet her with a big bear hug.

"You're still as pretty as a rose," Jamie whispered in her ear, causing the shy Cam to tuck her head even deeper into his shoulder.

They had talked a few times after they met at Metropolitan the first time, and that was only when Aunt Mary dialed the number and monitored their brief conversations. The fact that they had met in church didn't faze Aunt Mary. He was still a boy. A boy who probably had designs on Cam. So, the same rules applied. Cam wasn't allowed to talk to boys alone, not even him. She remembered that he had said he wanted to move into R&B, and it was obvious that that move was paying off. He told her that he had just signed a big contract with RCA, and Cam responded that she was truly excited for him and always knew he was going to be a big star.

Faith, standing on the sidelines and watching the joyous reunion of Jamie and Cam, was smiling broadly. Reuniting Cam with Jamie was a major coup for her. Not only had she been able to get Cam to see an actual television show, she had nudged her towards the spotlight where she belonged. Afterwards, on the way home, she encouraged Cam to keep in touch with Jamie, even though Aunt Mary wouldn't like it. It would be their secret. For Cam, that was more than enough.

chapter four

AFTER SEEING the success Jamie was having, Faith decided that was the path Cam needed to take. So, when Faith suggested that Cam pursue a musical career in popular music, Cam readily agreed. The decision angered Aunt Mary, and disappointed Chloe yet again. Faith argued and argued with them, trying to make them see the good that might result from a career in popular music. The money. Besides being able to pay for Chloe's medical care, Faith could also afford to go to a real rehab, and stay clean.

Mary, who was Cam's legal guardian, refused to even consider allowing Cam to sing that "evil" music. But, Faith was persistent, reminding Mary that if she tried to squash Cam's dreams, Cam might end up dejected and torn down like her. Chewed up and spit out. That gave Aunt Mary pause, but she was resilient, and still refused. Faith, however, was on a mission. She even tried to get hooked up with Jamie's management. They were interested, but not moving fast enough for the runaway train that was Faith. So, working both ends, she hedged her bets and started sneaking Cam around to local clubs for kiddie hops and showcases so she could sing R&B.

With all the tension in the Addison house, Chloe's already poor health took a turn for the worse. The family really needed money, and no one was in a position to make any besides Cam. Faith had been right. There was no choice. Cam had to use her God-given voice to save her family. And as grace or luck would have it, during one of the showcases Cam appeared in, she caught the eye of record producer and label owner Kennard Heywood, and the rest, as they say, was history. He christened Cam "Starr," and her meteoric rise to the top exceeded anyone's dreams.

During Cam's ascent, Faith was able to afford to go to a real rehabilitation center, and, as promised, remained committed to staying clean. She never strayed far from Cam, feeling like she was the best person to be with Cam because she could identify the wolves and keep them at bay when it came to her daughter. She was streetwise and protective of Cam, but Aunt Mary was still in control. She stayed right there with them, and Cam felt blessed to have both women in her life, both part of her path to success.

Heywood was relentless in pursuing Cam, and quickly signed her to his newly formed Kennetic Records, an offshoot of his notorious Kutthroat Label. Kennetic was the label that was evolving rap into hip-hop, and Heywood used Cam to sing hooks or verses on the singles of some of his most popular rappers. She quickly gained a name for herself, and a few months shy of her 17th birthday, Heywood was grooming her for huge success as a solo artist.

Cam's first album had gone platinum in less than a week of its release, and had three songs on the Billboard Top 40. She, however, barely noticed. Her mother had died unexpectedly the day before the album came out. Something had enticed Faith back into the sordid world of drugs, and on the eve of Cam's album release, she had overdosed. Faith's body was discovered behind the Carter Barron Amphitheatre, with a dirty, empty needle in her arm. The theatre was located on the Gold Coast in DC, and wasn't a known haven for drug activity.

Cam, unable to eat or sleep, asked herself repeatedly why her mother had been there. Why she had shot up, when she had never used heroin before? Why did she fall back on drugs when she had been given a second chance at life, and everything was going so well? So many unanswered questions, and the police had nothing. No witnesses, no answers. To them, Cam's mother was just another junkie who had taken one too many hits.

Heywood, however, was there for Cam. He swooped in and handled things. His fixers cleaned it up so that the general public would never know the details of how and where her mother had died. But Cam knew. And it still hurt her. It troubled her soul. She felt despondent, lost, and alone, but she surprised herself by not retreating back into her shyness safety zone. Somehow, she found the strength and determination to do what she knew she was placed on this earth to do. And that was to sing. So, she pressed on, resolute in her desire to make her mother proud.

Her mother's death thrust Cam into the headlines, and created a sympathetic buzz that softened the normally harsh blows from the critics and the media, and helped her record sales to soar. For the next three years, she wrote and worked non-stop, lighting up not only the stage, but the small and big screens as well. Cam's dreams were coming true, and she even teamed with Jamie Tee for a hot-selling duet on his third straight platinum album. But, just as her dreams were being fulfilled, so were her nightmares.

All of the highs, continuous media frenzy, and relentless attention on her life took its toll on her. Frightened of being called a flash in the pan, Cam had toiled non-stop, poring over and refining every note on her second album. And when her sophomore release dropped, she knew that she had to take a break. But, when it went platinum in its first week, and she had two singles that reached number one on the Top 40 chart, she kept going.

She received multiple Soul Train, American Music, Billboard, BET, and MTV Awards, and was even nominated in several Grammy categories. It was surreal, and whenever she felt like she couldn't go any further, she thought about disappointing the fans and persevered.

She defied the critics and haters who thought that her first two albums were flukes, and by the time she had written and composed some of the music for her third album, *"Songs from a Silent Place,"* Cam more acutely felt the need for an extended vacation. Where most aspiring and seasoned artists would've loved to have her track record, Cam just felt unfulfilled. And professionally and personally drained.

Despite all of the trappings of wealth, Cam felt dirt poor. And she wanted to do something about it before she went so far down she couldn't pull herself up again.

Her face was everywhere. National magazines wanted her to grace their covers, and *Essence, Rolling Stone, Ebony, Vibe,* and *People* magazines all carried full-length articles on Starr and her amazing success. Agents called daily with offers for guest appearances on talk shows and sitcoms. She even had a few movie scripts sent her way. Aunt Mary had become overwhelmed, and was grateful that she could rely on Vic to manage Cam's career. Even though Aunt Mary retained final signoff on anything Cam did, she was becoming further and further removed from the daily dealings. Cam believed that Vic was more than capable of doing his job, but she also sometimes felt that he was working too closely with Heywood on selecting her professional opportunities. Cam realized that she needed to take more control over her life. She was contractually obligated to Heywood, but the time was coming for her to reevaluate her contract with Vic.

Cam had never become comfortable with the fame and often found herself shocked by all of the attention her talent brought. Her closest friend in the industry was Jamie, who had reached a lofty level of success as a solo artist. He had traveled a road similar to the one Cam was on, and he was her greatest ally and support. During his ascent to fame, he had experienced many public highs, but managed to keep his lows on the low. No matter where he went or what he was doing, he made sure to stay in touch with Cam. And it was their conversations that kept her grounded and focused, as she witnessed his success and the trials and tribulations he encountered.

When the headiness of success became too overwhelming, Cam wanted to retreat back into the safety of anonymity. What kept her going was Jamie and the love of her fans, not the narcissistic ride she had embarked upon. Whenever she felt like she was on the brink of giving it all up, she would call Jamie, who would check her with a quickness.

"Get it together, Miss Girl," Jamie would screech into the phone. "You play the game, don't let the game play you," he'd say. And Jamie followed his own advice. He maintained an elaborate lifestyle, jet-setting off to exotic locales and junkets, taking gigs when he wanted to. And where he wanted.

"You have skills and talent, girlfriend. Use 'em before you get used."

"I know, Jamie. I'm just getting a little tired of it all," Cam would say.

"You should be tired, girl. Heywood works you like a slave in bondage. *Let my people go,*'" his crystal tenor voice would sing into the phone, and they would both laugh. He never disguised his disdain for Heywood, and the feeling was mutual. Cam didn't know if it had to do with the fact that Jamie never signed with or worked with Heywood, or that Heywood didn't like Jamie being close to Cam. It also didn't help that Jamie had hooked up with one of the hottest young producers on the scene, Noah Parker.

Heywood really despised Noah for some reason. While he always claimed he wasn't jealous of anyone, whenever Noah's name was mentioned, Heywood couldn't conceal his contempt. He kept it cute in front of the cameras and for the press, but behind closed doors, it was another story. "That wannabe. That fake ass, educated fool. He don't know shit except how to be lucky." Cam had witnessed Heywood's ire on several occasions, and it wasn't pretty. It was pure hateration. Whatever the cause was, Cam kept Jamie and Heywood as far apart as possible.

"Take a break. And when you take one, make it work for you. Don't be one of those studio heifers who cranks out records like a third-world country babymaker pops out brats. Do you, dammit. And be true to you. You feel me?" Jamie said.

Jamie meant every word he said. Even though he was a superstar, he wasn't caught up in the glitz and glamour. That was just how he was and had been since he was a kid. He was comfortable in front of crowds and fans, and his personality was effervescent. Jamie lived life by his own rules, and though he could, as he would say, "give good face," for the public, Cam knew that there was a part of Jamie that the world would never know or see. And she was glad that he trusted her enough to share it with her.

"You know it's not that easy, Jamie. I can't just walk away. I've got commitments I have to fulfill," Cam said.

"Everyone's got commitments, Cam. But, you ain't everybody. You are Starr. You are an enterprise. You are your business. So give 'em the business. If and when you decide to walk is up to you. An' when you decide to stroll back in is up to you too."

He paused, and Cam overheard muffled voices in the background. "Get a plan, and work your plan. You're the captain of your ship, Baby Girl. Shit, you are the ship. And the ship don't sail unless you want it to. So, do what you gotta do to be free." He paused again. "Hold on, Cam," he said, and placed his hand over the receiver. After a few moments, he returned. "Look, Baby Girl, I gotta bounce. I just found out there's a hot party going on in St. Tropez tonight, and I gotta get ready. Ya know a brotha's gots to be in the place to be."

"St. Tropez? Where are you now, boy?" Cam couldn't resist. Normally, she didn't ask, but she couldn't let him get away with dropping the French Riviera locale and not say anything.

Jamie chuckled. "I'm in London right now. I've been here for a few days, workin' a little bit and partyin' a little bit, but I'm ready to rock 'n roll. And you know my motto."

"I know."

"Have Amex Black, will travel. You just need to take some time to do some fun things too, Cam. You know what they say, don't you?"

"No, I don't, Jamie. What do they say?"

"If you're burning the candle at both ends, then you should at least be gettin' it in, lettin' it drip on somebody for a little joy and pain. Otherwise, what's the point, Baby Girl?"

Their pep talks and conversations meant the world to Cam. As Jamie's words resonated in her mind, she reaffirmed her dedication and purpose, and vowed to stay true to her craft, and not succumb to the false realities that threatened to consume her.

Always the diligent worker, Cam dutifully fulfilled her contract obligations to her label. But, when the album surpassed another milestone by remaining in the top ten for twenty weeks, she agreed to do one more concert tour. That was because Heywood had insisted. But, if Cam had anything to do with it, this was going to be the last time for a long time that Heywood got his way.

chapter five

BEFORE CAM could enter the dressing room, she saw Billy, one of the lighting technicians, approaching. Big Mac was going to wave him off, but Cam held his arm and told him it was okay.

"Excuse me, Cam," Billy said. He was standing behind a pre-teenaged girl, who was clutching a piece of paper and biting her lip.

"I hope you don't mind, but this is my niece Stephanie. She'd really like your autograph."

Stephanie danced from side to side, like she had to go to the bathroom. "Oh, uh, yes, Cam. Oooh, I'm so excited to me-me-meet you."

Cam smiled and gently held the girl by her shoulders. "That's okay, Stephanie. I'm happy to meet you too. And I'd be honored to give you my autograph."

Stephanie squealed as Cam took the paper from her hands and signed it. "Oooh, wait 'til my friends see this. My uncle told me you were really cool. I can't wait to tell my friends."

Billy nodded and grabbed his niece by the elbow. "See, Steph. I told you. She's the best."

Cam smiled brightly at them, then closed and leaned back against the dressing room door. Surveying the room, there were flowers and cards from her fan clubs, a chilled bottle of Dom Perignon, a basket of fresh exotic fruit, and several bottles of room temperature water. On her dressing table lay an open florist box with a single red rose inside, Jamie's calling card. He always sent or gave one to her, no matter where she performed. Cam smiled at the sight of the flower.

Cam's small entourage, consisting of Torrie, Necy, and Allison, waited for her on the couch. "I'll be back in a few," Cam called to them as she breezed past and headed for the shower, anxious to get out of her "work" clothes as she called them.

As she showered, Allison, ever the busy publicist, sat Indian-style on the closed toilet stool with her laptop resting on her thighs. Clicking the keys, she ticked off a list of things that Cam had to do before her descent into ambitious anonymity.

Cam had to meet with Rashad and the other members of her fan club before she left. Allison knew how important Rashad was to Cam, so it wasn't like she really had to remind her. The band and her back-up singers had a little going away planned, and were waiting in the break room for her. The interview she had with *The Washington Post* earlier that day and concert reviews were going to be posted on their website, so Allison wanted to make sure that they capitalized on it if they were good, and did some spin control in case they weren't. Allison also liked checking YouTube, Twitter, MySpace, Facebook and the some of the gossip blogs, like TheYBF.com and NecoleBitchie.com, who were sure to post concert footage or commentary on Cam's performance. It was part of her standard post-concert activities, and she really wasn't too worried about the chatter. She had no doubt that everyone would give Cam the head bob. Her reviews would most definitely be favorable.

"You ready, Cam?" Allison asked.

"As always," Cam sang out from the shower.

"Somebody posted some of your concert footage already on YouTube," Allison laughed. "They said, and I quote, 'Cam was the bomb.'"

Allison fingered the touchpad, and accessed more entries on YouTube. "There are several more videos on YouTube, Cam. They're all talkin' about how good you were."

"That's cool. Be sure to update my Twitter, MySpace and Facebook pages, will you? Please let my fans know how much I appreciate their support, okay?"

"Already done," Allison added as she clicked away on the keyboard.

"Excellent," Cam said. "So, um, what about the bloggers? I know that Sandra Rose is gonna say something hateful about me," Cam laughed.

Allison feigned ignorance. "Why you say that? Because you L-S-L-H?"

"Exactly," Cam said, and she and Allison both laughed.

"Well, let me see what ol' girl is hatin' on you about today." Allison typed in the web address, surveyed the screen, and laughed. "Yep, you were right. She commented about your light skin, long hair, and how she hated that Tiffany blue outfit you put on for your second costume change."

Cam stuck her head out of the shower. "Well, I guess she didn't notice that I got a hair cut. And, I'm not that light skinned." Cam shook her head. "I hope Torrie doesn't hear about what she said. She's still mad at Sandra Rose because she dogged out that outfit I wore to the Grammy's last year."

"Okay?" Allison agreed. "I know Torrie'll hit back at her if she finds out Sandra's talkin' greasy about that outfit you had on tonight because she helped design it."

"Oh well, it won't be the first time Torrie's had beef over something slick that was said about one of my outfits." Cam pulled her head back in the shower stall and continued washing.

"You're right. It ain't the first time, and it won't be the last," Allison said. "I just hope Torrie never runs into ol' girl. That'll be a dust up, for sure," she giggled. "Well, at least you won't have to deal with that shit for a minute."

"You know what? I really won't miss it either, Allison. I really won't. If there's one thing that I won't miss is the haters. I don't care what you do, how you look, what you wear, how you sound, someone's not going to like it," Cam said.

"I know, right? That shit really gets on my nerves. Making your haters your congratulaters is more than a notion," Allison said.

"For real, but you know what? I can't worry about that stuff. And neither should you. It's gonna be okay," Cam stuck her shower-capped head out of the shower again, and smiled at her friend and assistant.

"I have to worry about it. That's my job, remember?" Allison said, then she paused. "You know I'm gonna miss doing this kind of stuff with you, you know?"

"Huh?" Cam called out over the rush of the water. "What'd you say?"

Allison repeated herself, and again Cam stuck her head out. "What are you talking about, girl? We'll just be doing some different stuff, that's all. And you need a break just like I do. Ripping and running across the country with this tour has been outta control." Cam giggled, and shut the water off. "But, I'm not gonna lie. You made it a lot of fun for me."

"Me too," Allison said. "And you know you got a rack of scripts to go through. Ever since you did that guest appearance on *The Practice*, Hollywood has really been sweatin' you." She removed a body towel from the teak armoire and tossed to Cam. "And the scripts just aren't about you playing you, either. There are actually a few really good ones."

Drying herself off, Cam wrapped the towel around herself and stepped out of the stall onto the towel Allison had placed on the floor. "You know I'm interested, but I don't want to do anything crazy. I mean, it's comfortable playing a 'singer,' and I eventually want to move away from that, but I have to be ready. I don't want the bloggers doggin' me out about my acting skills."

"Christ, Cam. You really let those bloggers rent space in your head, don't you? You're not only worried about them doggin' you on your singing, now you're giving them the power to critique your acting?"

"That's right, Allison. You know how they are. And I need to listen to them. They know what's up, and face it, word of mouth is critical to being successful. They can make or break you. Fans let you know what they like and what they don't like. Now, I'm not listening to what everyone has to say, especially some of those websites that are nothing but a lot of negativity and foolishness. But, there are folks out there who can give you some constructive criticism. Especially those bloggers over on the Panache Report. That's what's up. So, on the real, that's why I want you to line up an acting coach for me, okay? A good one."

"Okay, Miss Perfection. I got it."

"Hey, what can I say? If I'm gonna do anything, I want to do it right."

Allison laughed and closed her laptop. "I feel you. But I also know that you just don't want anyone talking about you, sayin' you can't act."

"That might be true, and they still might say it, even after I take the lessons. But it won't be for lack of trying."

Allison smiled and hugged her damp friend. "Girlfriend, they can never say you didn't try. Or that you didn't give the best that you had, no matter what you did."

"What ya'll doin' back there? Havin' a moment?" Torrie shouted, and they all burst into laughter. As Cam went through her post bath ritual of baby oil and lightly scented shea butter, Torrie busied herself, gathering things and picking up Cam's wardrobe, while Allison again fixated on her Blackberry and laptop. Eventually, Cam emerged from the shower area fully revived, and Torrie handed her a pair of Jean-Paul Gautier jeans and a Pelle Pelle hoodie. Necy stood near the dressing table, warming up the curling irons in the steel stove to redo Cam's hair.

As Cam quickly dressed, Torrie and Allison echoed the sentiments that had been repeated since she'd left the stage.

"Girl, you were *all* that tonight," Torrie said.

"Yeah, you were. You really ripped it," Necy chimed in. "And you looked good, too. I know it's taken a minute for your fans to get used to you cutting off all of that gorgeous hair you had, but it was on point, girl.

"An' those outfits were on point. I told you they were gonna look great. And I'm glad you didn't wear something Heywood picked out for a change."

Cam and Allison glanced at each other and smiled at Torrie's comment. Allison shrugged and then nodded, and handed Cam a fresh piece of gum. "For real, Cam. Torrie is quite right on that note. I know Heywood's gettin' all into the fashion and clothing game and what not, but he really doesn't know how to dress you. And he really shouldn't even try."

Cam removed the old gum from her mouth and tossed it in the trashcan, and then shoved in the new piece. "You got my Blackberry, Allison?"

Allison leaned over and reached into Cam's handbag. She removed the device from the purse, and handed it to Cam, who was still working with Torrie for just the right look.

"Thanks," Cam said. She flicked the Blackberry on, and started mindlessly scanning for information. Anything to get her mind off of the direction the conversation was taking. And Torrie fussing with her clothes.

Torrie sucked her teeth as she adjusted the white leather Chanel belt hooked around Cam's waist. "You can't be good at everything. Now, I'm not comin' outta pocket or hatin' on a brotha. I give him his props on the music an' shit, even though he do be bitin' sometimes. You know, you not supposed to sample every damned thing all the time."

"Originality does count for somethin', doesn't it?" Necy snickered, and high-fived Allison.

"Hello?" Allison agreed.

Torrie giggled and continued talking and adjusting Cam's outfit. "He oughta be like the rest of these hip-hop moguls and let folks that have real fashion backgrounds run the shit while they just front. But not Heywood. Naw. If he can't micro-manage everything, he ain't happy."

Necy pulled out a blowdryer from her bag, "Well, I'll be happy when you finish with Miss Girl's outfit, Torrie. Are you done yet?"

Torrie smirked, and flagged Cam away. "Go on, finish our little beauty queen. I'll find her some kicks to put on."

Necy motioned for Cam to sit in the stylist chair, and nodded in agreement. As Cam sat down, still clutching her PDA, Necy kept talking, with her face toward Torrie, who was rummaging through a trunk, searching for the right pair of shoes.

"Yeah, you're right, Torrie. But, this isn't about Heywood's happiness anymore," Necy said. She turned back toward Cam and touched her shoulder. "It's all about you, girl. And I'm so happy for you. Now, let me see what's really good with this kitchen." She flung a short cape around Cam's neck, tied it, and switched on the blowdryer. She grabbed a brush, and went at the back of Cam's head.

Allison smiled and raised her voice above the buzz of the dryer. "I just can't believe you're gonna let this all go, Cam. But, I guess you need to. And really, you probably couldn't have chosen a better time. Christmas'll be here in a few weeks, so you can enjoy yourself and your fam, and see what's poppin' in the New Year."

"Huh?" Cam said. "I can't hear you."

Allison repeated what she said, nearly shouting. Then she said, "I just don't know what I'm gonna do while you're gone."

"I'll watch Big Mac for you," Torrie said with a wink and a throaty laugh. "My body needs guarding." Cam looked up and smiled.

"Yeah, you and everybody else's, okay?" Allison said.

"Okay?" Necy leered, and switched the dryer off. "I'll take that job my damned self," she cackled. She pulled a red hot iron from the stove and blew on it.

"Naw, that's okay. I'm sure Cam wants to take all of that with her," Torrie said.

Cam hadn't really thought about it. What would life be like without the constant presence of a bodyguard? Granted, she wouldn't be "faming" like she was now, but she wasn't sure if she was ready to go it all alone. She didn't think that she was any better than anyone else, but she was aware of the fact that with fame came some fans with stalkerish potential. She hadn't really thought about how she was going to maintain her security and peace of mind, so she definitely needed to give that a little more thought.

Cam giggled, and laid down her Blackberry. "Girl, you make it sound like I'm going away forever. And Big Mac's not going no where. He doesn't think I can function without him.

"Plus, I'm just taking a little time off. And trust me, I'm sure that all of you have enough to keep yourselves busy," Cam said. "Like running my foundation and making sure that the tabloids don't run my name too far into the ground while I'm gone."

"I know that's right," Allison said. "Protecting your image is a full-time job in and of itself. *Shee-it*, as straight of an arrow as your ass is, we need for them to rub a little dirt on you. Or at least a little dust or somethin'."

Necy was nearly finished curling Cam's hair. She whipped out a can of hairspray, and commenced to styling Cam's 'do with a wide-toothed comb. "Don't worry, Cam. You know we'll hold it down for you while you're out.

"But, believe me, I'm gonna be booking you up for next year. And working to make sure that folks don't forget about you, either. So, you gonna be in the rags a little bit. Whatever it takes to keep your name in folk's minds."

"And your songs in their iPods®," Torrie chimed in.

They laughed and Cam slipped her mobile unit into her pocket, and nibbled on a pomegranate while Torrie ushered Necy away from the salon chair so she could work on Cam's face. Some of the heavy stage makeup always remained on Cam, even after she showered. To remedy this, Torrie dipped her fingertips into a jar and gently applied cold cream to the face of her favorite client and friend. Using a white face cloth, she finished the job, leaving Cam's face a clean slate.

After the laughter, their mood turned slightly somber. This was the last time that they would be together for a while. The last time they were doing what had become their routine.

"On the real, aren't you scared, Cam?" Torrie nearly whispered. "I mean, you've always done this. Are you sure you really want to press pause when you're so hot? You know folks would kill to be in your spot. Especially someone like that damned Shaye. Or that Skye Bratton. Look at this shit."

Torrie reached into her hooker bag, and pulled out a copy of the *Star* magazine. After flipping through several pages, she found the article she was looking for, and held it open in front of Cam and Allison. Inside was a picture of Heywood and Skye, in deep conversation, at some party. Under the photo, the caption read:

SECRET TALKS—IS THIS ABOUT HIP-HOP OR HOOKING UP?

"This heifer can't wait to just jump on Heywood's gravy train," Torrie said.

"Choo-choo," Necy cackled. "That ain't all she's tryna jump on, I bet."

"I even heard that since you're not going to do that New Year's Hip-hop Eve Event, he's thinkin' about puttin' her on the roster. Can you believe that?" Torrie curled her lips and rolled her eyes.

Skye Bratton was one of the hot new singers who had just broken from her girl group, *TreaZure*, and was being hyped as the next great solo act. It had been rumored that Heywood was secretly behind the breakup, and was courting Skye for his label, but Cam hadn't given it much thought. But, deep down, she felt that there was more to the talk than just talk.

Even though Torrie and Allison were her girls, Cam had never revealed to them that she and Heywood were dealing. They assumed, and Allison probably really knew, but they never straight out asked Cam about it. And Cam never confirmed or denied it. And it was instances like these that she was glad that she hadn't ever admitted to being involved with him.

★

Cam yanked the paper from Torrie's hands and tossed it onto the stand. Cam stared into the mirror, and caught Torrie's concerned gaze. Even Allison had stopped doing what she was doing, and was staring at Cam too. Torrie placed a gentle hand on Cam's shoulder. "Don't worry about that bullshit, Cam. I know that Heywood has probably been tryna get at you for a while now, but you keep your head up, okay? He ain't worth it."

"I'm sayin', he's a dog," Necy said, as she started gathering up her equipment. "Believe that."

Allison laughed nervously, and launched into protect mode. "I don't think that's it, Torrie. Cam ain't checkin' for Heywood like that. You know with her, it's all about the business."

Torrie caught the hint and moved on. "My bad, you right. Ain't nobody thinkin' bout him. Cam, you just need to get away from all of this drama and mania for a minute. You just do you for a while, okay?"

Cam swallowed, and tried to smile. "I've thought about it a lot, Torrie, and this *is* what I want to do. And I'm not worried about Skye or anyone else for that matter. Heywood can devote all of his attention to her from now on. I'm not beat about it. There's enough fans and music for all of us."

"Are you sure about that, Cam?" Allison asked. "Talkin' 'bout it is one thing, but actually being able to do is another. I've seen stars go away, and when they come back, it's never the same. And they can't handle it."

"Yeah, it really crushes that ego when they come back and album sales are down and they have to play smaller venues," Necy added. "It fucks 'em up, and then they start chasing that other stuff to get that high. The 'caine. The Chronic. The Lovely. The White Lady. This that an' a third. I've seen it a thousand times. Hell, I almost got caught up in that shit myself, but I learned my lesson, for real."

chapter six

DRUGS. In the industry, at industry events, and sometimes even at business meetings, drug use was rampant. Where the rappers glorified smoking weed, there were much more troubling addictions making the rounds with celebrities. Crystal meth. X, Cocaine. Whatever you needed to stir your creative juices, get you high, numb the pain, or just take you to the next level, it was readily accessible and available. Yet Cam had never even been tempted. With her family history, there was no way she was going down the same path her uncle and mother had taken. No way. She could barely finish a strawberry daiquiri without feeling queasy and afraid she was not totally in control of herself.

Even so, she could understand how some celebrities lost touch with reality. Living the fame game was a delicate balance of the real and the unreal, where complete strangers, the fans, cried and lost control when they saw you, or sent letters declaring their undying love and dedication to you.

People would offer to do anything for you and to you. To give you anything at anytime. Folks were constantly trying to get close to you, to help themselves, not you. It took a strong person to see through it and survive it, a person strong enough to be aware of their weaknesses and surround themselves with people who were stronger than they were.

But that level of awareness was often diminished by the peripheral items that were always available. Even if you weren't into self-medicating, drugs and easy fixes always crept into your environment. The occasional glass of champagne would turn into a couple of shots of tequila. The tequila would be followed by a cigarette, and if you were too amped up to sleep, someone suggested that you take a hit from a blunt. The blunts turned into something else. Dip your blunt into cocaine or heroin, a perfect mix. Too low? Need a pick-me-up? Take this pill. Doctor prescribed. Too high? Here's something to bring you down. Mellow you out. Before you knew it, you were constantly chasing something, and either the prescription pills became your confidant, or the most important person in your entourage became the one who copped or scored for you.

Paranoia could set in. Everyone wants something from you all the time. No one even knows your real name. You're only a manufactured image that everyone feels like they know. You know you're only human, but the way people gawk and stare at you makes you feel like you're being stalked. So, when you have people come to your house to work, you tell your staff to make sure they don't look at you. And don't talk to you. If you can't feel comfortable in your own home, where can you?

But, then the bloggers and the media hear about it, and suddenly you're branded a "diva" or worse, a "bitch." Suddenly, there's an all out smear campaign on your character. People come out of the woodwork, claiming to have had a horrible encounter with you, or dropping some long lost, albeit false, piece of information about what you did in high school. You become the target of thinly veiled blind items on wicked blogs or in articles where countless anonymous sources state that they've either witnessed or been subjected to your irreverent behavior. If you defend the lies, you're branded bipolar. If you ignore them, the lies continue and get even bigger. You can't win. So, if you care, you either sink into depression and self-medicate, or really get a "don't give a fuck" attitude, and throw your cares to the wind. Either way, when you become a star, you're part of the public domain. And the same domain that made you, can dismantle and break you.

For the most part, the media was kind to Cam. There were no notably bad stories ever written about her, and Allison made sure to keep her in the best light possible. It wasn't hard, because Cam was really a decent person who hadn't gotten caught up. She didn't have outrageous concert riders that demanded that a bowl of all red M&Ms be in her dressing room before a concert. Generally speaking, the media handled her with kid gloves. Perhaps because she hadn't given them any reason not to.

True, they speculated about she and Heywood's relationship, but even he had a vested interest in ensuring that the public didn't know they were involved. For him, it was a good thing because it kept his name out there, and he always categorically denied anything other than a business relationship with Cam. He kept fixers on the payroll just to make sure the information he wanted got out there, and what he didn't want out, disappeared quickly. Personally, it always bothered Cam that Heywood was so insistent that no one know that they were involved, and made her question his motives. But professionally, it could not have been better for her and her career. She was a rare celebrity whose name had not been associated with any scandal or real dirt, and eventually, it didn't bother her that she wasn't linked to him as his lover.

Keeping secrets, promoting false images, and playing to public illusions were all part of the game. The celebrity or die game. Where everyone wanted to play, and no one ever wanted to lose. And in the end, there was rarely ever a winner.

Thankfully, Cam had been shielded from a lot of this by her upbringing, and by the protective shelter she had built around her. Cam was smart. She knew that it was only a matter of time before her business got put out on Front Street. It happened to the best of them. It was part of being a celebrity. Walking that fine line in the public eye. You had to hide or lie about who you really were, just so that the media wouldn't learn about it and use it against you. So, you lied to protect yourself, but the lies ended up hurting you too. It was the lesser of two evils, neither of which really made you feel that one was really better than the other. But Cam was going to be prepared, whenever that fate arrived on her doorstep. And with Heywood in your life, that unwanted visitor could show up at any time.

Cam struggled to smile, but couldn't. Perhaps she was being rash in her thinking, but then again, maybe she wasn't. She had never taken as much as a week off since she stopped singing gospel, and she felt the stress and strain. Even though she loved what she was doing, she didn't love how she was doing it.

She missed her Aunt Mary, who was busy taking care of Grandma Chloe. Even though her success had enabled Cam to buy a large family estate in the gated community of Woodmore, Maryland, and to employ a full-time nurse for her grandmother, she still didn't see them enough. And she wanted to spend more quality time with her family. She wanted to go home for a while, be with people she loved and trusted, and just be Cam, not Starr, for a while.

Cam reached for her friends' hands and grasped them firmly. "You know what? I'm okay if this isn't the same when I come back. In fact, I don't want it to be the same. I believe that it'll be even better, because I'll be even better by then."

"We'll all be better by then, right ladies?" cackled Necy with a wink, "You just ask my man." Laughter ruled the room again, and the girls chit-chatted while Torrie finished applying Cam's makeup, Necy packed up her gear, and Allison finished straightening the dressing room. Allison reminded Cam that her fan club was waiting for her outside by the limo, and that she would be signing autographs and posing for pictures for the website.

Another "last" for a while, but a necessary one. Her fan club would help Cam stay relevant during her absence. Allison knew that the bloggers would keep Cam's name out there.

And Cam agreed. Her fans were the most important part of her success, and she didn't want them to think that she had forgotten them. She wondered for the millionth time if she was doing the right thing, but never got to answer herself, as her thoughts were interrupted by a loud knock on the door.

She leaned back in the chair, and checked her wristwatch. It was only a few minutes past midnight, much too soon for the slow-moving Sonya to be there. "Sonya?" Cam called out. "Is that you? Come on in, girlfriend."

The door cracked open and a huge bouquet of red roses in a crystal vase slipped through. The door pushed open wide, a sullen Big Mac appeared, and then a grinning Heywood stepped in behind him. "Hey, Cam. What's up, lovely? Didn't Shaye tell you I was lookin' for ya? I was waiting outside in the limo, but you was takin' too long."

chapter seven

KENNARD HEYWOOD was one of the industry's hottest producers and record label owners. He was also a gifted songwriter, or at least he pretended to be. He was clever enough to be credited for writing many hits, even if he didn't actually do it. It was all business to him.

He wasn't an incredibly attractive man, but his substantial wealth and bravado made him one of the most sought-after men in the hip-hop world. He exuded confidence and power.

And he cleaned up nicely. He dressed extremely well, and never wore the same outfit or shoes twice. Heywood had a vast array of expensive jewelry, from diamond and platinum crusted necklaces to huge diamond rings. He was always well-groomed, and manic about cleanliness. He never shook anyone's hand, clapped anyone on the back, or touched anyone or anything if he could help it. He reveled in the limelight, and was notorious for throwing fabulous parties and being seen at all of the right places with all of the right people.

Was she in love with him? Cam wasn't sure she knew what being in love meant. She did appreciate Heywood, though. Appreciated his help with her career, appreciated that even though his language was laden with profanity, he was always mindful not to use it around her.

He was also a gentleman around her Aunt and grandmother, and it warmed Cam's heart that he could be so respectful. She had come to know a kind soul behind all of that brashness, one who treated her gently and with care with regard to her personal concerns. If he did get upset with her he would quickly apologize. Every now and then, he would show his vulnerability, especially when talking about never knowing his father, and his often strained relationship with his mother. Apparently, the only adult in his life he respected was a man named Tyrone, who had taken Heywood under his wing and treated him like a son. But, he also told Cam that Tyrone was his past, and said that was where he was going to stay. There was an inflection in his voice that let Cam know that it was not a topic for further discussion. And Cam understood.

Whenever the topic of family arose, Heywood would become quiet. The subject was absolutely off-limits during any interview, and if a reporter was bold enough to ask, he or she was immediately put on Heywood's shit-list. On the rare, private occasions he did talk about his family, Cam felt closer to knowing the "true" Heywood than ever.

While Heywood loved living in the spotlight, he was very guarded about the things that genuinely mattered to him. A study in contrasts, he possessed a lot of idiosyncrasies. For example, he pretended not to care about what the press said about him, but checked the gossip blogs on a daily basis, and even had Twitter, MySpace and Facebook pages, public and supposedly private ones that either he or his assistant Donald "Duck" Harter would update.

The media would never know that he took 3-4 showers a day, and had a thing about keeping his hands and nails clean. They would also never know other things that might be considered uncharacteristic, not hard or gangsta enough. Like how he owned a horse farm in the middle of Kentucky. Cam would never have known about it either, had she not overheard Heywood and Duck talking about it.

★

In the wee hours of the morning a few years ago, she, Heywood, and part of his production team were in a Manhattan recording studio Kennetic Records used, laying down some tracks. Cam had her headphones on, and was listening to one of her songs, trying to rework some of the runs. They had been in the studio for a while, as was customary whenever one of Heywood's artists was recording a new CD. He required his artists to be committed to working hours on end, for days straight, until he was satisfied with the product. Even Cam wasn't exempt from this requirement; even though she usually didn't take as long to complete her work as some of her other labelmates.

While Cam was working on the lyrics and arrangement, Duck came into the sound booth and started talking to Heywood, who was sitting behind the boards. One of them must have hit an intercom switch on the board, because the sound from the booth interrupted her playback, and she heard part of their conversation. Specifically, she heard Duck say that the weather was getting bad down at the farm.

"What?" Cam asked, speaking into the mic. Duck jumped and Heywood almost fell out of his chair.

"Huh?" Heywood asked, with a surprised expression.

"I can hear you," Cam said, tapping her headphones.

Heywood glared at Duck. "What the fuck's wrong wit' ya, nigga? Ya cut the intercom on."

"Oops, my bad," Duck stammered. "I musta just did it."

"Uhh, what you hear?" Heywood asked, his eyes boring holes in her from the booth.

"Something about a farm? I must be hearing things," she said.

He laughed. "Ya did, Baby Girl. Duck's in here on some of his simple-assed bullshit," Heywood said. "Do ya thing, ma. Buzz me when ya ready." He clicked the intercom off, and Cam went back to her rework.

Later that morning, when Cam asked him about it, he downplayed it. He just mentioned that he owned a small horse farm. No big deal, he said. It was one of his childhood indulgences, and one of his best kept secrets. And he wanted to keep it that way. Cam figured he was embarrassed that she knew he was involved in such a corny enterprise, when in fact she found it interesting and slightly endearing that Heywood had found a way to channel his inner child. No matter, as the farm never came up in conversation again.

Quirks and eccentricities aside, Cam was also unfortunately intimately acquainted with the other half of Heywood's Gemini twin persona. One step away from the streets, Heywood was ruthless to anyone who crossed his path. He knew how to clean it up when necessary, but his hair-trigger temper was well known, especially when it came to handling his business. He was never above checking one of his contemporaries, especially if he thought he was being disrespected.

His peers were two divergent entities. Music producers and industry figureheads in the game approached him in totally different manners. First, there were the old school, well-heeled, well-connected producers, like Fitz Bassford, who served as pseudo mentors to him. They were the ones who had put him on, shown him the ropes and given him his first gig as an intern on their labels; taking him under their wings and offering sound advice on how to get ahead, make friends, and influence people. They were the first ones to take him on the rounds, introducing him at industry parties, and giving him an opportunity to make music. They regarded his success the way a parent would regard a successful child; totally supportive and hoping that he would match or exceed their level of success.

Then there were the other old heads who seemed resentful of Heywood and his success. They might have started off as one of his mentors, but eventually ended up rivals. These people were not mesmerized by the illumination of his stardom, but waiting for his star to burn out. They smiled in his face, secretly whispering behind his back, wishing he would self-destruct. They tolerated him with detached, albeit phony indifference, and often placated him, for he was a moneymaker, and a better pseudo friend than enemy.

Younger industry tycoons either quietly challenged him or boldly picked verbal fights with him. They were the ones whose artists would take their war on wax. Diss tracks and "wars of the words" were infamous and profit-making, constantly fueled by the mounting East Coast vs. West Coast feud. It was the classic gang-bang, street fight as hip-hop artists battled back and forth, changed labels, dissed management, and shouted out their producers like Heywood and Noah. And it continued to escalate. From the CDs, to the magazines, to the smug references in interviews. And Heywood did his part to keep the fires burning. He never held his tongue. He was known for checking cats, young or old, who were in the game and posing a threat to him.

Rumors also swirled that Heywood was a little less than above board with his acts. Some disgruntled artists, including rappers, groups, and hip-hop singers, would complain to the media, and then their careers would come to an untimely end. Heywood had no shame in his game. In public, he always referred contract issues to his attorneys, or cited artistic differences as the reason some artists left his stable. He never addressed why these same artists literally disappeared from the music scene.

A few gossip sites on the Internet quoted unnamed and anonymous sources who reported that Heywood treated his artists unfairly, forcing them to sign contracts that ensured that he and his company would be the only ones to profit from their work, and forcing them to give him songwriting credit. He would lavish them with Rolexes and Benzes, and deduct their cost from any earnings. He would appear in his artists' videos and then charge them an exorbitant price for his guest appearance. They were forever steeped in debt. None of these charges were ever proven or even made public, and Heywood always sidestepped these issues in any interview, saying "business is business," or "no one held a gun to anyone's head to make 'em sign a contract." Even though it was rumored that he had, in fact, flashed a gun during negotiations at Kutthroat Records.

Heywood brushed off the rumors by saying that the sources were cowards and haters, and that everyone should be able to read a contract. However, when artists with a number one song were still broke, there obviously was a problem. When questioned, Heywood said it wasn't with him, it was with their representatives. "It ain't my job to manage them. That's what they're gettin' paid for. Real talk," he'd say. "I manage images, not insecurities. It's their management's job to manage their business, not mine."

Hearing Heywood talk like that made Cam leery, and even more determined to make sure that she wasn't being taken advantage of by him or anyone else. She trusted her management team, but then she also wanted to believe that Heywood wouldn't try to take her for bad. Especially since he claimed to care so much for her.

She wanted to believe in him, despite the rumors and obvious edge in his demeanor. She rationalized that he had to act a certain way and use his street smarts in order to stay in the game. The callousness he displayed towards others probably stemmed from his rough beginnings.

Heywood got his start as a street-corner hustler, a small-time drug runner who had a dream. He lusted after the flashy dealers who drove their smoked-out Benzes and Beamers through his Brooklyn Bed-Stuy neighborhood, and if he hadn't gotten caught as a minor, he probably would have pursued a life of crime. Once he was caught, he used his street savvy and cred from running drugs to hooking up with some of the talented up and coming rappers from his hood. He went from pushing weed to pushing underground CDs from the trunk of his hooptie. A born salesman with steely determination, he was able to parlay his skills into something legitimate, from the street corner to top of the music mountain.

According to Heywood, he had loved rap since days of the Whodini and the Sugar Hill Gang. He did the street thing for a while, then went to Howard University to get a textbook education and make some connections. He stayed for a few semesters, until he ran into an old buddy from New York who was part of the entourage of DJ Dizzy, who was performing at the University's homecoming. Heywood got bit by the hip-hop bug, quit Howard, and got a job as a hypeman for a New Jersey based hip-hop group with one album and several well-known hits.

It was then that he discovered his ear and talent as a producer, realizing that his creativity and mastery of the boards was near genius. He struck out on his own, producing a string of hits for a number of new and established groups, and eventually became renowned for having the Midas touch when it came to creating stars. His association with Cam had proven to be one of his greatest triumphs. He had personally taken her under his wing when she was making the transition from gospel ingénue to hip-hop star, and the rest was history.

Heywood was smart, a quick study, and quite business savvy. He had a huge entourage, always rolled at least 20 deep, but kept only a chosen few in his inner circle. He lived by the adage, "keep your friends close and your enemies closer," and his closest and most consistent friend was Duck.

Duck was the only one Heywood really trusted. He had teams of attorneys and business associates, but Duck was always around or no more than five minutes away. Duck tweeted for him, and scanned new talent for him too. Duck stayed logged on YouTube, keeping his ear to the ground for any breakout rappers or artists. Duck even updated the playlist on Heywood's iPod® with the latest and greatest Internet stars.

Duck also carried Heywood's untraceable cellphones and his micro-camcorder, in a briefcase that contained at least $10K in cash, and a file full of blank and completed non-disclosure agreements, or NDAs. Heywood called them N-Snips, or "no snitching papers." Heywood lived by the code that "snitches get stitches," and everyone who worked for him knew that. That was lesson number one. Heywood taught Cam the ways and means to keep your stuff on the down low. The stuff you didn't want anyone to know about.

"Whassup, Beautiful?" Heywood asked as he stepped into the room. He was dressed in a billowy white shirt with sparkling diamond cufflinks and black tailored slacks. A fluffy white chinchilla coat was draped over his broad shoulders, his ears were studded in huge two-carat diamond stud earrings, and his wrists and neck were also iced out. And from the doorway, the scent of his signature cologne filled the room.

Cam's face melted into an uneasy smile, while Torrie and Allison exchanged quick glances. "Heywood. What's up? I'm surprised to see you here."

Heywood eyed Cam's assistants, and nodded toward the hallway. "You know I wouldn't miss your last performance. Ain't that right, ladies?"

Torrie fidgeted in her make-up kit, while Allison rustled with some papers. "Yeah, uh, right, Heywood," Torrie said, her eyes averted.

"We're finished, so we were just about to leave, Heywood," Allison said, and then turned to Cam. "We'll meet you down in the break room in a few." Torrie said that she would make sure Cam's personal belongings were back at the Ritz-Carlton by the time she returned.

Whenever Cam performed in DC, she had a ritual. She stayed at home during the day of the performance, and at a hotel at night, because she didn't want to wake up her folks.

Cam pointed to her mid-sized Louis Vuitton overnight bag. "Just make sure that one gets to the hotel. The rest can be sent to my house later on."

Heywood waved a hand in Allison's direction. "Hold up. I changed Cam's hotel. Damn, girl. Ya supposed to be the assistant, an' ya ain't know that? Ya a little slow on the uptake. See, I moved Cam to the Mandarin. It's hotter than that old stuffy-assed Ritz."

"But, she was there last night. How'd you do that? Why'd you do that?" Allison's forehead wrinkled, and she placed her hands on her hips.

"Because, The Ritz ain't the business no more. That was last year's spot. She shoulda neva been there. She's supposed to be at the hot spots, not some ol' tired ass joint like that." He looked her up and down. "Ya oughta be up on basic shit like that." Heywood propped the door open, as Torrie noisily threw the last few items into her case and nodded for the others. Necy was gritting on Heywood and Allison's lips were downturned.

"He probably want her there 'cuz that's where he's stayin'," Torrie muttered under her breath.

"What you say?" Heywood smirked.

"She didn't say anything." Allison jumped in. She was young, but she was a true professional. She was smart enough to pick her battles and do what she could to help her friends. It was one of the things Cam liked about her.

"Why did you do that, Heywood? I liked the Ritz," Cam said. "It was perfectly fine."

"Well, whateva, Cam. We'll be puttin' on at the Ritz tonight. Right after we get our party on at Dream," Necy said, and then turned toward a still red-faced Torrie. "Come on girl, let's bounce." Torrie, holding her case in one hand, grabbed Cam's shoulder with her other hand. "Cam, you be easy, girl. In case I don't get a chance to tell you later, you enjoy your time away from all of this. You deserve it." She kissed Cam's cheek, and glared at Heywood as she crossed the room. "You know, you really shouldn't wear white after Labor Day."

"That's an old wives' tale, ya old wife. An' this is winter white, baby. I might have to revoke ya fashion license, since ya apparently don't know ya color palette. Get it right, Torrie. Or shut the hell up."

Allison and Necy rushed behind Torrie, and both paused to lean over and give Cam a hug. "I'll go tell Rashad and your fan club that you're running a little late, okay? You know he's about to flip over that chair if you don't hurry up," Allison said with a quick smile. "Now, do you need anything else before I go? Anything?"

Cam patted her Blackberry. "No, I'll be alright. Just go let the folks know I'll be there in a few. And until then, just enjoy yourselves. Oh, if you see Sonya out there—"

"We know, Cam. We'll tell her to keep it movin'," Necy said.

"Cool," Cam said.

"Smooches, Baby Girl," Necy said as she reached down to give Cam an air kiss on both sides of her face. She threw shade at Heywood one last time as she rolled her cases by him.

"Oh yeah, what time do you want your wake-up call?" Allison asked, as she stepped toward the door.

"She'll call you. An' it won't be too damn early," Heywood butted in, and again motioned for them to leave.

After they left, Heywood shut the door behind them, smiled, and pecked Cam on the forehead as he handed her the vase of roses. "What's goin' on in the break room?" he asked.

Cam hunched her shoulders. "Nothing special. The crew's just having a little send off for me."

Heywood grunted. "*Hmmph.* Well, they betta keep that shit short. We got stuff to do." He winked and licked his lips. His eyes fell upon the single red rose, and he smirked. "Ya know seein' ya out there lightin' that stage up makes me hot."

"Yeah, um. I hear you, Heywood. But, that's not happening."

"What? Ya got your period? Ya know that won't stop me."

Cam's stomach churned. "Yes, and yes that will stop you. Yuck."

"Ya know I'm just playin'," Heywood said.

"Yeah, I'm sure. But for real, I have to meet Rashad and my fan club before I go, too."

"Rashad? That crippled ass mutha fucka's here? What he do—roll his ass up 85 an' 95 to get here or did they Medevac his ass here? Damn! Somebody need to put a fuckin' boot on his wheels," Heywood smirked.

"Heywood! Don't talk about him like that. That's not nice, and you know it. Stop being so hateful and ignorant."

"Whateva. I ain't bein' ig'nant." He shrugged his shoulders. "If ya want to entertain Rashad the Stalker slash Stan slash chrome rollin' serial killer, then that's up to ya. Go 'head. But ya need to keep that shit short. He's a drag, for real."

Cam rolled her eyes at him. She didn't know if he was jealous or just being stupid, but Heywood knew that speaking ill about any of her friends, and especially Rashad, was straight out of line.

Heywood's voice softened. "I'm just kiddin', ma. For real, I wanted to tell ya that ya did great tonight, baby. Ya was all that. Ya know you the baddest broad in the game." He crossed the room, and leaned up against the dressing table, where he purposely crushed Jamie's flower. "Oops, my bad," he said, and held the limp flower up. "I guess you don't need this no more," he said, and then pushed the broken stem and petals into the trash can.

Cam started to say something, but figured there was no use. She watched him as he pulled off his fur and threw it on the couch before plopping down on it. Using his feet, he turned her chair toward him.

"Heywood," Cam said, with a sigh. "That was so childish. Why'd you have to ruin my flower?"

He snorted, and the softness in his voice quickly vanished. "Who gives a fuck about that damned weed? Look, I brought ya some real flowers."

Cam tried not to roll her eyes, and shook her head instead. "You just don't get it, do you? It's the thought that counts, Heywood. Plus, it was mine, and you had no right."

"Whatever."

Again, Cam sighed. "There you go with that 'whatever' again. Why do you always have to give my friends such a hard time? Because they're friends of mine? You're rude to them if they're here or not here."

Heywood twisted his face and huffed. "What? You talkin' bout that raggedy crew that just left? *Shee-it*, I told ya, Starr. They ain't ya friends. They ya employees. The goddamned hired help. Lackies. An' ya need to start treatin' 'em like that. That's why they act all high an' mighty, walkin' round wit' they asses up on they backs. Trick ass bitches. They work for *you*, therefore they can't be ya friends. Ya need to stop gettin' that shit twisted."

Cam had learned a long time ago not to disagree with Heywood. She just sighed and placed the flowers on the crowded stand. "Thanks for the roses. They're really pretty."

Heywood spun Cam's chair around, until she faced him. "Not as beautiful as you, girl." He cupped her chin and tilted her head from side to side, observing her profile. His eyes wandered down her body, and Cam bristled. She felt his breath, which was always minty fresh. Heywood hated going to the dentist, but he made sure that his breath was always on point. He kept a tin of peppermint Altoids on hand, and his staffers had to have a tin in their possession at all times. Heywood had even fired an employee who didn't have a mint when he needed it.

"Look at that face. Gorgeous. Ya coulda easily been a model, baby." He paused. "See, yo' a damned double, shit, triple threat. The whole nine. A total package. Ya got skills, personality, an' ya face is bangin'. See? I told ya 'bout hidin' behind those shades so folks can't see them million dollar eyes."

He drew closer to her face, his nose nearly touching hers. "An' ya body's slammin'. Remember when I told ya to ease up on those baggy-assed clothes an' show these niggas what ya was workin' with?" He reached over and gently pinched her thigh.

Heywood was forever complimenting Cam on her looks, but she never gave his words too much weight. They sounded artificial. Too much like mack lines, and she just wasn't buying it. Plus, looks were fleeting and she had enough sense to know that folks judged you and then sentenced you, based on your appearance. It was just a shame that inner beauty wasn't as highly regarded.

"You got talent and brains. An' you can sing, dance, an' act." He sighed, his chest heaving with drama. "We could be the bomb together, girl. I just don't understand why ya wanna keep breakin' my heart."

Cam shook her head. "Don't even go there, Heywood. You know that's not even possible."

"What ya mean? Ya tryna say I ain't got no heart?"

Cam ignored him, grabbed the *Star* magazine the girls had left near her chair, and tossed it into his lap. When Heywood saw the photo, he just grunted and smirked.

"Come on, baby. That's work. Strictly business. Nuttin' else. Ya been in the game long enough to know what ya lookin' at. I'm just givin' the paparazzi a little somethin' somethin' to chew on. Some grist. A little gristle. A bone for them dogs to gnaw on."

Cam tapped her foot against the chair. "Gnaw on? Whatever, Heywood. I hear you. You made it a point to keep our relationship on the low for 'business purposes,' but you don't have any problem being seen around town with any other chick. Especially her." Cam took the gum from her mouth and stuck it onto the magazine page, in the center of Heywood's beaming face, and he laughed.

When finally he spoke again, his voice was soft. "Come on, baby. Ya know whassup. The press loves to speculate on shit. Plus, ya know you an' I can't get down like that. I gotta help ya protect yo' rep. Ya know folks don't wanna think 'bout their Baby Girl Starr bein' wit' the likes of me. To them, I'm just a hood ass nigga still tryna earn. Still tryna get mines. Still tryna get these otha niggas to give me respect. Ya know that."

Cam frowned, but remained silent. She shot him a "You must think I'm stupid" look. As he kept speaking, the images of him partying at industry events, jetting around the world, and hosting party after party popped up into her head. Heywood loved having a camera shoved in his face, being on television, on the 'net and in magazines, and the thought of all that exposure made her wrinkle her nose. As much as she admired his hustle, other parts of him drove her crazy. And had driven her away.

"Straight up, Cam. Skye's about business. An' she's hungry. Like ya used to be. But she's a lot greedier than ya ever were." Heywood shrugged. "But, that's all. For real. She's gonna need a lot more work than ya ever did. A lot more polish. But, then again, she's willin' to put in work, I mean put in the work, 'naw mean?"

Heywood stroked his razor cut goatee, while Cam remained quiet. "Ya can't blame a brotha for being on the j-o-b, can you Cam? I'm sayin', I gotta eat too, while ya off takin' a break an' chillin'. Speakin' of which—"

"What?"

Heywood eased himself closer to Cam, and placed his legs outside of hers, pinning hers in. "We got some bizness to discuss."

"Now, Heywood? I'm beat. I can't even think right now. I just want to go say goodbye to everyone, get something to eat, and go to sleep."

"Ya got plenty of time for that, when ya take ya little sabbatical. But, before ya go ridin' off into the sunset, ya gotta do one more thing."

Cam's head immediately ached. She should've known that he had something else up his couture sleeve. "What, Heywood? I've done every-thing you asked me to do to support the album. I've done it all. What else is there for me to do?"

"I want ya to do a video for that *Hallowed Ground* joint. That's the last song on the album ya gotta do one for. An' it's gots to be hot. Like fiyah. All that. I got Art all lined up for it, an' he's cleared his schedule just for you."

Art "Artist" Payne was one of the hottest music video producers in the industry. He had done a video from Cam's first album, and it had received an MTV Award. But since Art had blown up, their schedules had always clashed. Cam knew that Heywood had to have pulled a rab-bit out of his hat to get Art nailed down.

Cam sighed. "I thought you didn't even like that song? You said it sounded too churchy, remember?"

Heywood flapped his knees, the powerful scent of his cologne filled Cam's nostrils, as he pressed Cam's legs together tightly. "I know, but I've had a revelation. Instead of goin' all churchy, an' what not, we gonna take it in the opposite direction, an' make it sexy. Give it a real wicked treat-ment. Make it real edgy. Folks won't be expectin' that."

Cam shook her head. "I don't like that, Heywood. That's not what the song's about. I'm not going to do that."

Heywood loosened his grip on Cam's legs, and grabbed the armrests on her chair. "When did you start questionin' me an' what I do, girl?"

Heywood hunched his shoulders and brushed them off. "What? Ya think ya know more about the music business than I do? Get real."

Shaking her head, Cam forced herself to look him square in the eyes. She was so close to freedom she could almost taste it. And for once, she stood up to him. "I don't think I know more about music than you, but I do know more about this, Heywood. That's not what the song's about, and I'm not going to make it wicked. That's just wrong, Heywood."

"Well, you might not have a choice, Baby Girl."

Frustration rose in Cam's lungs, but she tried not to let it show in her voice. Heywood had a bad temper, and she didn't feel like getting into it with him. "Have you talked to Vic about this? He knows I didn't want to do any more videos."

"Vic?" said Heywood. "Who's he? Face it, doll. It's in the contract. An' if Vic's supposed to be yo' manager, he oughta know whassup. He's gettin' paid enough to read the fine print. An' I don't think that he's got that many clients that he can't keep up with what ya doin'. Plus, whoever he's got ain't as important as you. Real talk."

Heywood had always dissed Cam's management team, but prior to this moment, Heywood had given Vic props. Now he was dissing him, too.

"If you don't believe me, check it. Call Vic, I'm sure he'll confirm." Cam just looked at him without blinking.

"Hey, don't get all bent out the frame about this, baby. This is business. Nothin' personal. But dig it, if I say you'll do it like that, then ya know what, ma? It'll get done like that." Heywood snapped his fingers and said, "Just like that."

chapter eight

THE VIEW from the Presidential Suite of the Mandarin Oriental Hotel was spectacular. At daybreak, it was like she could see heaven and all of God's presence in the stillness of the clear winter sky.

As Cam sat in the wingback chair, Indian-style, she chewed her gum and nestled into the thick pink terry cloth robe she always traveled with. Comforted by the momentary silence, she held a tattered composition notebook in her hands. On the cover was a simple "IV," Roman numeral four. She flipped through several dog-eared pages until she was a few pages shy of the end. On the pages were scribbled notes, pictures, and words, in various colored inks and sizes. Each contained snippets of or completed songs. The notebook was her lifeline. It was the fourth diary she had scribed since she was old enough to write. The first three music journals were locked away in a safe deposit box Cam had secured at Chevy Chase Bank in Largo. Drawing on her Aunt Mary's country smarts, she had even put the safe deposit box in her mother's name, and she was the only one with signatory access to it. She hadn't even told Allison where she had stashed them. Only Aunt Mary knew.

Although Heywood tried to pry their whereabouts from her, she refused to tell him. The main business advice Cam took from Heywood outside of how to perfect her craft was how to protect her masters. He had scoffed when she told him that she wanted them, and he convinced her to store them in the label's vaults. After a while, and much to Heywood's chagrin, Cam decided that since she owned them she wanted them in her possession.

Heywood was always offering her unsolicited advice, and when she first started out, she hung onto his every word. But, as time progressed, she became a little less starry-eyed. One evening, on the balcony of his Fifth Avenue penthouse, sipping ice cold Cristal and nibbling on gigantic hand-dipped chocolate strawberries, Heywood had broached the subject of her music books. In an instant, the perfect, romantic evening had been ruined for her. And, though she kept her thoughts to herself, Cam felt like the whole night had been a set-up; carefully engineered by him to tighten his possession of her, but also obtain her most valuable possession. Her music.

It was the evening after Cam's debut album soared up the Billboard Charts, and every radio station in the nation was playing the hot single *"SVU – Special Victim for You."*

Cam had just left the Hot 97 Radio Stations, where everyone, including Buckwild and Starr seemed in awe. As Heywood lurked in the shadows, the interview was a virtual lovefest for the new ingénue. It was a courtesy rarely extended to many artists.

After the interview and an appearance at the label's promo party at the über hot Mars 2112 Club, Heywood had swept Cam over to his home for a private celebration. Along the way, the topic of the value of her original recordings came up. And it continued until they reached Heywood's rooftop lair.

"Ya certified, Baby Girl. Ya blowin' up," Heywood said, and lifted his stem to her. "Ya really need to listen to what I'm sayin'. It was smart to retain yo' masters. That was good lookin' out. But, on the real, yo' masters are too valuable for ya to keep in some lawyer's dusty old office. They need to be stored in a climate-controlled environment, somewhere where they'll be protected from fire an' dust, ya heard? I can take care of 'em for ya."

Though the words seemed logical, something about Heywood having her masters under his control made her uncomfortable. They were hers, and she was sure they were safe and secure. Deacon Owens had made the arrangements and her sacred music was stashed in a safe location in Philadelphia. And only she and he, by proxy, had access to it.

Cam felt fortunate and blessed to have Deacon Owens as her attorney. He was old school, meticulous about details and making sure that his clients' affairs were in a pristine state. When she was just starting out in the music field, he worked with her CPA to ensure that her funds were well invested and protected, and had insisted that Cam get her personal and business affairs in order. She was fully insured with Lloyds of London, and she had recorded her will, a living will, and power of attorney.

Talk of death was nothing Aunt Mary wanted to hear, so Cam hadn't told her that she had committed all of her plans in writing. And that her will was also in that safe deposit box in Largo. It was important that she had made provisions for her family, just in case something happened to her or her livelihood. She felt better that all of her worldly possessions were bequeathed to Aunt Mary, because Cam knew that her aunt would always have her best interest at heart.

And Cam's best interest was her music. It was more important to her than money, investments, or T-bills. Outside of God and her family, it was all that really mattered. Her songs were her children, and her music was her lover; at least until she found someone special enough to share her world in that capacity. And, from the onset of their relationship, she knew that person would never be Heywood.

Heywood never let up about the masters. He went so far as to try to pry her current notebook away from her, but Cam refused to even let him see it. When she was working, she'd have Allison or Big Mac guard it for her.

Since Heywood was used to getting exactly what he wanted when he wanted it, it burned him that she was so successful in keeping her notebook away from him. And he tried every way he could to get his paws on it.

Keeping a step ahead of him was hard, because Heywood always tried to flip the script on her, and accuse her of not trusting him. To prove his trust to her, he had even showed her the location of the customized, walk-in vault in his penthouse. Just like the one from the movie *Absolute Power*, it had a two-way mirror along with some distinctive

Heywood touches, including a bidet, sink, and chaise lounge. The soundproof vault had its own hermetically sensitive ventilation and sprinkler systems, and a separate backup generator. It could also be used as a safe room, and was completely high-tech, equipped with a copier machine, several computers, video monitors, and an intercom system that allowed him to listen in on every room in the penthouse.

After seeing the vault, conveniently concealed behind a bureau and a mirror in Heywood's bedroom, Cam thanked her lucky stars that she had resisted ever sleeping with him there. It was just a feeling, and she trusted her feelings. She had never relented to his insistence or heated pursuits. To her, the two-way mirror was proof positive that Heywood was into some form of debauchery. She could see him either taping or allowing someone to watch him have sex with an unsuspecting person or persons.

The access pad was hidden behind a wall sconce, and when Heywood revealed it, he added her thumbprint to the biometric access code as further proof of his trust in her. The vault was where Heywood stored his real "ice." His million dollar platinum and diamond encrusted crosses and musical notes were hanging on black velvet stands in locked glass cases. Besides the jewelry and equipment, the vault also contained racks and racks of neatly cataloged media. There were CDs, DVDs, reel-to-reels, even VHS tapes. He had also stored books, and rows upon rows of movies, music, and files.

Cam wondered if Heywood had obsessive-compulsive disorder. On one hand, everything in certain areas of his life had to be spotless and in complete order. On the other hand, he was filthy in mind and language, and was easily able to get gully and posture with reckless abandon. He was a fixture in the chi-chi gentlemen's clubs and strip bars, making it rain on the baby oiled bodies of the exotic dancers, and probably getting lap dances and screwing all the passed around video girls he could. He was a study in contrast and complexity. No doubt. Something just wasn't right about him.

Anyway, Cam wasn't moved by the fingerprint access gesture. Even though she appreciated the things he did for her, she wasn't a fool. She knew that as soon as she left, he'd delete her access privileges. She wasn't that naïve. No matter what he said or did, she would never, ever disclose the location of either her notebooks or masters. She had learned that lesson from her grandmother and aunt: don't ever let anybody own you. And she certainly didn't want anyone, especially Heywood, to feel like he had it like that. He would never own her body, mind, or soul.

Cam's rambling thoughts were interrupted by loud snores coming from the adjoining suite. She envisioned Heywood, flat on his back, snorting like a rabid bull. His snoring was just one of many things she now found repulsive, and the list was steadily growing.

Listening for a second, she decided that his snores sounded like what a vicious battle between a rusty chainsaw and broken jackhammer would sound like. Alternating between death rattling gasps and odd buzzing noises, Cam hated every one of his sleep sounds. At first, they had been cute and quirky, but grew old quick. She had to leave the room if she wanted any sleep at all, often curling up in a chair and covering her ears with a pillow. And sometimes she'd even have to put her headphones on to drown him out. Cam chuckled to herself, thinking of how ridiculous all of this was. Soon, very soon, she would be free of Heywood and his unbearable habits. She could hardly wait.

For appearance's sake, Heywood always rented out a whole hotel floor, one that included at least three suites. The middle suite would remain empty, so he could occupy the one farthest away from Cam, yet be able to slip into her room unnoticed. The watchful eye of Cam's bodyguard Big Mac peeped that game a long time ago, but he never said anything about it.

It was good that her fan base thought of her as single and available. At first Cam believed Heywood's reasoning, and found the "hide in plain sight" games intriguing and necessary to keep the tabloids at bay. But then, as time passed, she realized that Heywood was playing the games for his own benefit. He could keep their personal lives out of the headlines, while he "hid in plain sight" with various other sexy singers, supermodels and curvaceous actresses.

From the beginning, Cam and Heywood's relationship was atypical. He was the first "man" Cam had ever been intimate with, although she had messed around a little with a kid named Robby Jackson back in the eighth grade. And under Aunt Mary's watchful eye, Cam was never able to meet or hang out with any guys until she met Heywood. She had developed a crush on Jamie, but that's all it ever was. A girlish crush. But, Heywood was a real man. And the first man she would become seriously involved with.

They were involved, and even though it wasn't a matter of public record, they were the "it" couple behind the scenes. He was her advisor, mentor, and eventually her lover, and it was a very emotional time for the relatively young Cam. She didn't have anyone to talk to about her feelings, certainly not Aunt Mary, and she found herself looking to Heywood to advise her on what to do. And how to do it.

She had trusted her trust in him. Even as their relationship evolved and she felt dishonest when she had to lie to her Aunt about being with him, she continued. She assumed that since Heywood was older he knew what he was doing, and was treating her like a woman should be treated. Or so she thought.

Inexperienced, she never questioned the lack of passion or fireworks in their relationship. Cam was never thrilled by Heywood's bedroom skills, even as she found herself more and more enamored with the man Heywood professed to be, and her emotions were sprung by the attention he showered on her. At least in private.

She blamed herself for the inadequacy of their sex life, and tried harder to be the sexy video vixen she knew he wanted and was used to being with. She read *Cosmo*, *GQ*, and numerous books on how to please her man, and eventually, her self-doubt ended when she realized that the missing link in their intimacy wasn't her. It was Heywood.

He talked a real good sex game, but he was simply lacking in that department. His shortcomings were quite noticeable, and Cam was ultra-disappointed when she remembered that Robby's penis was bigger around than Heywood's. And on top of that, twelve-year old Robby was a lot more considerate and interested in what she wanted than the thirty-ish Heywood ever was. She had never even had an orgasm with him.

Despite it all, Cam had to admit that she felt deeply and dangerously attached to Heywood. Was it love or obligation? Or was it fear? She wasn't sure, but she knew it wasn't the sex.

Sex wasn't all that to her, and she felt that as long as Heywood was happy, she'd be happy. At one time, she thought they had a future together, and he said that he even wanted to marry her. One day. Cam now knew that would never happen. There was something deep in her spirit that didn't mesh with his. There was just something about Heywood that didn't settle right with her.

Perhaps it was his inability to take no for an answer. At first Cam thought that was sexy. His take charge, hold no prisoners swagger. He protected her. When it came to business, Heywood's voice resonated above all others. When Heywood spoke, folks jumped. They deferred to him. He had confidence and power. It was intoxicating. He was both charming and lethal, lethally charming. Something about him was irresistible. And Cam, like everyone else, found it nearly impossible to say no to him.

The young Cam had been awestruck to have someone ballin' like Heywood lavish attention on her. He'd surprise her with thoughtful gifts, and even rented out all of Six Flags Great Adventure to impress her on their first "undate." And he was fun, unpredictable, and romantic. And when she shared with him that she was a virgin, he seemed to respect her status. Eventually, it became evident that the thought of being her first intrigued him, and he stepped up his efforts to win her over.

Courtesy of Heywood, her dressing and hotel rooms always overflowed with fresh long-stemmed roses, making her feel special, desired, and loved. And when she felt comfortable enough to finally sleep with him, she thought that she had it all. But, as she hit the rewind button in her mind, she slowly realized that she had mixed fantasy with reality. It was her own version of a revisionist memory.

Yes, he had routinely filled her room with flowers. And yes, he was romantic and encouraging, and smiled at her like no other man had ever smiled at her before. And Cam was barely seventeen, and though she was slim, she was curvy, and her body was a nubile fun house waiting for its first guest. Up to that point, her life had been about music and church, and Heywood had opened up a whole new intriguing world for her. And she thought that sharing his world would be magical.

Unfortunately, it was anything but that. Their first time together wasn't a fairy tale, but more like a Stephen King novel. She had actually been frightened of him.

Mr. Showman had set the stage and had all the right props, but his performance was thoroughly disappointing and completely unfulfilling. Looking back on the situation, Cam realized that she had allowed her emotions to gloss over a lot of the finer details. Details that were now her stark reality.

While Heywood wasn't a "one-minute man," he wasn't working with much and had a difficult time keeping what little he had hard. Technically, he was the only man that she had slept with, but she thought that most men were usually packing, and known for having staying power. Heywood had neither, and that blew her mind.

His attempt at foreplay was nauseating. When he had gone down on her, grunting and slurping like he was eating an overripe watermelon down to the rind, it had made her stomach bubble. And the talking. It wasn't like he was whispering sweet nothings in her ear or sharing sexy pillow talk. He was proclaiming his narcissistic conquest, running lines like, "Oooh, Daddy's gonna make you feel real good." He kept grabbing and playing with himself, but the limpness won over the stiffness. When he finally commanded his dick to stay up, he hurriedly mounted her and humped away, snarling like a rabid beast, and after a few moments, he growled in a medieval manner and collapsed over on his side. "It'll get better, Cam," he said, barely able to force the words out. "It's because ya haven't been with any niggas before. Ya too uptight. Ya gotta loosen up, learn how to take all of this. But, don't worry. I'll show ya whassup."

And in the ensuing months and years, Heywood still hadn't showed her what was up. Their bedroom interludes had become peppered with his increased weed habit, and his constant demands that she use X with him. Cam refused, but played his game. Heywood would get high, want to screw, and eventually give in to the drugs. He still talked a good game, but barely delivered. And the abrupt ending point of their infrequent and unsatisfying physical relationship came when Heywood wanted to bring another woman into their bed.

That was it for Cam. She wanted to shut down their covert relationship right along with her music career. She chose terminating their physical relationship first because it would probably be easier.

It happened several months ago, right after they left a Baby Phat fashion show, traveling, as always, in the back of a Maybach limo. Heywood had been gloating over the fact that they were able to be seen out in public, yet the media didn't know that they were involved. Also, he was happy that he had gotten plenty of face time with the cameras, and the numerous shots were certain to be posted on the web in a matter of hours.

Oddly enough, as soon as the paparazzi disappeared behind them, Heywood cursed the presence of the photographers and reporters. Then he said he wanted to go to The Spotted Pig, a known haven for photo stalkers, and Cam had had enough.

"Why would you want to go there, Heywood? Didn't we just leave the whole 'media blitz' thing back there? Why can't we just go someplace quiet and get something to eat?"

Wearing dark shades and puffing on a cigar rolled joint, or blunt, Heywood filled the back of the limo with smoke. Cam cracked the window, and he laughed until he coughed.

"Quiet?" he said, choking back a cough. "Ya wanna know what quiet is to a celebrity? Quiet is dead. As in dead career. As in no one's feelin' ya anymore. An' ya know what that means? When no one feels ya anymore, ya don't get paid."

"Is that all there is to you?" Cam asked.

"Say what? All there is to me? You think this is all for me? Baby, you got it twisted. This is all about you."

"All about me?" Cam gritted her teeth. "Yeah, right. This isn't about me, Heywood. And if it is, then I don't want it anymore."

"What ya mean?" He puffed on his joint, and glared at her.

"Don't you ever get tired of this? I do. I'm exhausted. I'm tired of being stalked like a deer in the wild. Having folks climb trees and hide behind bushes just to get a picture. I'm tired of it."

"What ya sayin', Cam?"

"I need a break." Cam's voice cracked.

"A break from what?"

Cam's voice flattened. "A break from this. All of this."

Heywood fell strangely silent, and held the burning blunt between his fingers. "All of what? All of this? What, ya mean me?"

Cam reached in the minibar and grabbed a chilled bottle of Pepsi. She held it in her hands, feeling the coldness from the beverage falling over their conversation. She was suddenly faced with having to deal with both issues at once, and she had to steady herself. "If that's what it takes, then yeah, you too. Face it, Heywood. We don't have anything anyway. If it's not work, it's something related to work. And I'm tired of it."

Heywood turned toward the window and dragged on his joint as Cam slowly opened her drink. "Ya don't mean that. Come on, Cam. Ya just talkin' crazy." He pushed his shades on top of his head, and then turned back and faced her, with a strange expression on his face and in his reddened eyes.

"I'm not. I'm serious."

"Ya mean ya ain't tryin' to be wit' me like that no more, Cam?"

Cam reached for his arm, and Heywood flexed. "This isn't about you, Heywood. For once, I need to do something for me. I have to do me. And I don't think being with you 'like that' is good for me. I need to clear my head and get my mind right. I'm worn out."

"Worn out? Why, ya ungrateful b—." He cut himself off. "I don't believe ya. After all I've done for ya. Ya know the number of chicks on the come up that want yo' spot? Ya better recognize what ya givin' up."

"Were you getting ready to call me a bitch, Heywood?" she asked, and glared at him.

He cleared his throat. "Naw, ya know ya ain't no bitch. But damn, Cam. This is a bitch move. It's like ya don't even appreciate everythin' I've done for ya."

She stared at him, and for a fleeting second, she considered having the driver stop and let her out. But, it was New York, in the wee hours of the morning, and she wasn't that crazy. Heywood sounded concerned, but probably just worried about his stacks. She now knew what he was really about, and it wasn't her.

But, she had to play it safe and bide her time. "It's not that I don't appreciate it, but it's not like you haven't gotten paid for what you've done. I just need a break. It's not like I'm dropping off the face of the earth."

"Ya might as well. No one gives up or stops doin' what they do when they as successful as you are, Cam. Whassup wit' that?"

"Nothing's up, Heywood. I told you, I just need a break. I need to do me."

After a few tense moments, Heywood shrugged his shoulders, and shoved his glasses back over his eyes. "Whatever, Cam. You do you. An' when you get finished doing you, an' ya wanna to come crawlin' back to me, ya better have some thick-assed knee-pads on, 'cause that's what it's gonna take."

★

Despite his prior rants and less than veiled threats, Heywood didn't cause too much static as Cam said goodbye to her band and fans before she left Constitution Hall. As much trash as Heywood talked, he always tried to keep it cute in front of others. But in private, he wasn't always so polite. On the ride from the hall to the hotel, he laid out his vision for the video shoot. And it wasn't a subject for debate.

"We're gonna make this shoot ya best one yet. I want you in an exotic location, somewhere like Africa. Go back to the Motherland."

"Africa? Are you kidding me?"

Heywood's jaw tightened. "Naw, I'm not kiddin'. That's gonna be hot."

Cam shook her head. "Get outta here, Heywood. There's no way. I can't go to Africa. I don't want to go there. That's too far. And what about the holidays? I do not want to spend Christmas in some foreign country. I want to be home, with my family."

Heywood cut his eye at her. "Listen, it's my dime, an' if I want ya to go to Africa, that's where ya go, Baby Girl. But, fortunately for you, an' because of the time constraints, *and* because I like ya, I'm willin' to consider some closer locations. Like the Caribbean."

Cam breathed a sigh of relief. "Where? Like the Virgin Islands or somewhere?"

"Yeah, somethin' like that. Art's checkin' out some locales and he's gonna send me what he has. He's done a lot of work down there, so he's got ideas about where we could shoot, an' he's on board to get it started. An' I want to get it crackin' on Monday."

Art "Artist" Payne was one of the hottest video directors on the scene. He was always booked months in advance, which made Cam very suspicious. "Monday? As in tomorrow? How did you get Art on such short notice?"

Heywood cleared his throat. "Uhh, he had a cancellation. One of those wack-assed heavy metal bands he was workin' wit' had some issues an' complications, so he called me an' let me know he was available. You know how I do."

"Yeah, I know how you do, Heywood, and this is just crazy. How am I gonna be ready for some video shoot by tomorrow? And you don't even know where it's gonna be? Plus, I'm tired. Bone tired. I'm gonna look like death warmed over if you put me in front of a camera."

"Aww, you'll be aiight. You can chill today an' tomorrow, an' be ready by Tuesday. Wherever I decide'll be nice. There's Aruba, Turks & Caicos, an' I heard that Antigua is pretty nice, so I'll give 'em some thought. We'll do site selections on Monday, an' ya should be good to go by Tuesday."

"We? What do you mean 'we'? Are you planning on going? Oh, I don't believe that. Since when did you ever make time for video shoots?"

"Now, you know I want this done right. I ain't gonna leave that to chance. If this is gonna be the last video you make, at least for a minute, then I wanna make sure I pee all over it."

Cam rolled her eyes at the imagery. She could see him peeing all over his pants legs instead of anything else. "I hear you, Heywood. But things don't always go as planned."

"Well, that's the plan, beautiful. I'll be down there for the shoot, an' then I'll be on my merry way. That's right. I want the whole thing wrapped by Wednesday, so if we have to do any retakes, it should be canned before the weekend. That way, you can get on wit' ya little hiatus, ya know what I'm sayin'?"

Cam fought the urge to stick her head through the limo's open sunroof and sing "Hallelujah," or just dive out of the moving vehicle. As tired and as achy as she was, the thought of finally being unbound from Heywood's chains made her feel like she could do just about anything.

"Antigua, huh? Well, what about my girls? Torrie's supposed to be in New York tomorrow. And who's going to do my hair? I gave Necy the week off. I didn't think I'd need her."

"Necy, as in yo' hairstylist? Please. Money talks, sweetie. I'll have her an' that tired assed Torrie down there by Tuesday. No sweat."

Cam sighed, but refused to allow Heywood to have the last move in this game of master manipulation.

"Heywood, listen to me. I'm not playing with you. I do this video, I'm done. It's a wrap. You're not going to come back to me next week with the remix, or some other idea. I'm done. And I don't care what's in the contract. I know you think that money talks, but guess what? I'm through listening. You feel me?"

"I feel ya. I got that. You're done. An' I'll be done wit' ya for a while too," he said, and made an "X" over the area where his heart was. "Cross my heart."

"Yeah, right. If you only had one."

"There ya go with that bullshit again. Ya got my word, Cam. This is it. You'll be free, I swear. I gotta keep it movin'. I got other things lined up."

Cam squelched her excitement. "That's cool. Now, what about the treatment? What you want to do is just not vibin' with me." Cam had always had free reign over the video treatment, and she was adamantly against the "evil" slant Heywood was proposing. She thought his idea was wack and let him know in no uncertain terms.

"Naw, now. Hold up, Cam. Ya can't have everything. Damn. Now, I'm conceding on the locale, but that's it. I ain't givin' up the concept for the video. That's a non-negotiable."

"Since when did I lose control over *my* videos? I don't like the concept, Heywood. It's going to ruin the whole song. It's too dark. My fans know that's not me. They know I don't get down like that."

Heywood's eyes rolled as he pulled a platinum cigar case and lighter from his breast pocket, opened it, and withdrew another blunt. "Step out ya comfort zone, ma. Think out the box for a minute, will ya? When ya gonna let that 'I'm a good girl' nonsense go? Ya need to cut that little church girl act loose. It's tired an' it's fuckin' old."

Cam folded her arms and looked out onto the darkened streets. "It's no act, Heywood. I'm not some dark soul, and I don't want my last video to make it seem like I am. I don't want my fans to remember me like that."

"Well, that's how it's gonna be, baby. An' this way, they'll remember somethin' about ya. An' in this business, ya want folks to remember ya. Cam, I'm serious. This'll be the final hoo-rah for yo' fans. Now, if ya don't wanna go out like this, say the word. We can always do another video. Hell, we can even do another album, an' then ya can do all the videos ya want. Just the way ya want 'em." He smirked, lit his blunt, and inhaled deeply. Nudging Cam with his elbow, he offered the joint to her.

She cracked the window and fanned the smoke away from her face. "Come on. You know I don't even get down like that."

"See? There ya go again. Go on, take it. It might loosen ya up some, an' make ya get into this video a little better." He laughed at his own joke.

"Very funny, Heywood." She moved away from him, watching the late night traffic crawl through downtown. Cam had endured a lot to get where she was, and though she was thankful, and blessed, she had to wonder if it was worth it. She had made a small fortune, and it was well-invested, thanks to Aunt Mary and her accountant. Cam knew that if she continued to be smart, she'd never have to worry about money.

But it was a rush to do what she loved doing, which was singing. It made her higher than any drug could. But, there was still an emptiness to it all. The fans were great, but they really didn't know her. They had a skewed perception of who she was, based on her talent and what they believed from the media. But, she appreciated who they were to her, and would miss the nice fans, young and old.

Young women who loved her style and her music. Who dressed like her, wore their hair like she did, and knew every word to every song she ever sang. They sang along with her, tears streaming down their faces as emoted about lost loves and broken hearts.

However, she wouldn't miss the guys who hounded her to death, writing love poems, proposing marriage, and making kissing noises at her. They made her feel disrespected. And then there were the "haters," the other industry artists like Shaye, who were always trying to take her spot. Little did they realize that Cam would give it all away if it meant never having to feel their negative vibes again.

★

Cam continued to block out the horrible noises emanating from Heywood's bedroom, and refocused on her music and the plans for her "break." Still jotting down notes in her songbook, the Dianne Reeves hit *Better Days* popped into her head, and she started humming the tune. She gave it a different run, and substituted Dianne's words with her own. The song made her think of her Aunt Mary and ailing grandmother, and how she would finally have a chance to do some of the things she wanted to do with them. Relax. Enjoy life. Laugh. Spend time together.

She would also find a place of her own. Not that she'd ever desert her family, but she wanted a place that was just for herself. Either a beach house or a cottage near a lake. It would be somewhere near her family estate, but it would be her own little sanctuary.

Her thoughts drifted back to her "break." She'd finally be able to get the pair of Cocker Spaniels she had always wanted, but never had time for. In her dreams, she had already named them: Bill and Hillary, after her favorite past and future presidents. She'd wake up in the morning, feed the dogs, fix her own coffee, sit in a porch swing, and rock as she watched the clouds part and the sun rise. She was so into her dream that she even heard the birds singing.

Cam careened back into reality when she realized the chirping noise she was hearing wasn't the birds in her dream, but the sound of her Blackberry notifying her that she had messages. She grabbed her lifeline to the outer world, and quickly read her messages.

The first one was from Jamie. It read:

"Hey beautiful. I know u slayed them last nite in DC… gud lookn out, girlfriend. Im n Dubai but will b back n LA next wk. Got stories 2 tell!!! LOL!! Ill call u. Luv u, J."

Cam smiled. She had to love Jamie and all of his comings and goings. She responded to his text with:

"Thanks, Jamie. U r always lookn out 4 a sista! LOL! Call me soon, k? Luv u 2."

She hit 'send', then scrolled down to the next message. It was from

Allison. It read:

"Hey Cam. FYI, u r booked on Flight No. 496 lvn BWI @ 7 a.m. on Monday. Fly n 2 Antigua on AA. Limo will pick u up at 5:30. Don't worry- I'll make sure ur summer clothes are flown down. Holla @ me when u get up 4 brunch @ B. Smith's. Me, Torrie & Sonya want to go get r eat on. Peace."

The smile caused by Jamie's text melted. Cam was furious. She fired off a text to Allison that she would be ready to go in a half-hour, and tried to quell her anger. Heywood had manipulated her once again. Did he ever take a break from playing his mind games? Evidently, he had already arranged everything, but had tried to fool her into believing that he was making last-minute plans for the video shoot. All along, he must have had the whole thing scheduled and booked.

Holding her Blackberry, she accessed her Twitter Page. "Hello Everyone… I'm on my way 2 the Caribbean 2 shoot a video. I will upd8 u when I get 2 the beach. B ez, Starr."

Cam smiled, and hit 'send'. "Well, Mr. Heywood. You might've got me on this one, but this'll be the last time you run your played out little games on me."

Cam stashed her phone and notebook into her Louis Vuitton messenger bag and lifted herself from her chair. Flicking her middle finger at the bedroom door, she announced to the empty room, "Play me close, will you? That's alright. I'm about to get my life, and you better bet that you won't be a part of it."

THE FOUR-HOUR flight from BWI to Antigua went smoothly, once the plane left the DC area's wintry mix of sleet, slush and snow. Cam, never a big fan of flying, chewed through two packs of gum before they even took off. She accepted flying as a necessary evil in her profession, but soon it wouldn't be necessary. Flying was at the top of her list of things she wasn't going to do during her break.

At least I don't have to be bothered with Heywood this morning, Cam thought happily to herself. He had booked her early morning flight as another one of his passive/aggressive moves. She had to leave at an ungodly hour, while he was flying to Miami on 'business'. Cam, however, knew better. He was going to hang out at South Beach and get his picture splashed on a few magazines before taking a private jet to Antigua. Knowing Heywood, he was also probably trying to make sure the paparazzi would trail him to the island.

Cam wasn't beat about his absence. In her mind, she was already separating from him, and the less time she spent with him, the better she felt. She squeezed her eyes shut, and comfortably positioned herself in the window seat in the third row of First Class.

Allison, next to her, knowing that Cam hated to fly, tried to divert her attention by reading passages from concert reviews. The *Washington Post* called it "an event beyond comparison," while *Rolling Stone* and *Variety* gave it rave reviews. The blogs were lit up too. There were numerous uploads on YouTube, most saying that Starr had "slayed" the crowd. Responses on her Twitter and Facebook pages were overwhelmingly positive. They made Cam feel much better. She had left her fans with something special.

Cam tried to relax, with Big Mac watching her back, and Allison next to her, humming away on her Blackberry. The sight of Allison's PDA jarred something in Cam, and she whipped out her own Blackberry and made a quick call to her Aunt Mary to let her know where she was going. Once she had spoken to her aunt and grandmother, Cam was able to relax for real. She shut off her phone, tucked it away in her messenger bag, and pulled out her iPod®.

Nestled in her comfortable first class seat with her soft travel blanket, Cam listened to the soft tones of Rachelle Farrell as they caressed her ears through her Bose headphones. Cam absolutely loved Rachelle's voice and her strict command of her vocals. Her voice was truly the "first instrument," and Cam aspired to be like her. In more ways than one. She admired Rachelle for not compromising her talent. Like Sade and Prince, she was not motivated by commercial success, but flourished by performing for adoring fans. She was true to herself. Cam had seen that. She had caught Rachelle a few years ago when she was performing at DC's Blues Alley.

Rachelle Ferrell was one of the few non-gospel singers Aunt Mary would listen to, so when Cam heard that Rachelle was going to be in town, she took Aunt Mary out for dinner at the Market Inn, and then surprised her with tickets to the show. With Big Mac's assistance, and camouflaged with a large floppy rain hat, Aunt Mary and Cam had slipped into the show unrecognized. Once the house lights went down, Cam removed her hat, and entered another world. When Rachelle's band fired up and she took the stage, even Aunt Mary grooved a little.

When her idol started on those ebony and ivory keys, Cam visualized the notes and inflections. Rachelle hit each one perfectly. Cam could only dream of having that range and control in her voice. She had been stunned, when, midway through Rachelle's repertoire, she heard the opening chords of one of her own hits. Aunt Mary's shriek nearly blew Cam's cover.

"This is one of my favorite songs, y'all. This young lady has what it takes to make it. This is called '*Starr Struck*,' and I must admit, I was floored when I first heard it."

With Aunt Mary squealing and elbowing Cam at the table, there was no greater rush than hearing such a revered artist perform her song, and then to compliment it like she did. Cam was star struck.

At the end of her show, Cam slipped the waiter a $100 bill, and a note to give to Ms. Ferrell that said, "From your biggest fan." Even when she met Rachelle later that year, Cam never told her about her experience at Blues Alley. Despite her fame, wealth and recognition, she was still as much a fan, as she was a star.

A heady, eclectic mix of Rachelle, Prince, Mary J. Blige, EPMD, and The Police helped elevate the wings of the plane and made for a smooth flight down to the island. The only problem was that Heywood had purposely booked them on an airline that allowed in-flight use of cellphones. So, he continuously interrupted nods, naps, and quick conversations with a semi-hung over Allison, with constant calls and demands to generally do everything except fly the aircraft.

While Cam kept her eyes closed and her mind fixated on the music, she could tell that Allison was getting more and more agitated with the phone calls. Yawning, Cam switched the iPod® off, and glanced at Allison.

"What's going on? Was that Heywood again?"

Allison nodded. "He's saying that all of the pictures Artist sent him don't fit what he had in mind for the video."

Cam removed her headphones. "Here we go with the bullshit. I haven't even gotten there yet, and he's not even there, and he's trying to get some drama started. How can he not like what he sees? Wasn't it his idea to go down there in the first place? I can see it already. The 'wrap by Wednesday' nonsense is out the door. He's gonna try to drag this out as long as possible."

Allison shook her head. "I don't know about that. Antigua is no joke. And they aren't making very many concessions, so I know this shoot is costin' a grip."

Cam gnashed her teeth and thought, *He'll find some way to charge me for it, I'm sure.*

"Whatever, just do me a favor. I really don't want to do any local publicity if I can help it."

"Don't worry, Cam. This came up so quick, I didn't have time to schedule anything. But, you know that once they find out you're there, the radio stations are gonna want to talk to you."

Rubbing her eyes, Cam thought about her fans and reconsidered. "Right. Just don't seek them out. And don't let Heywood line up anything either, Allison. For real. I'm serious. But, if they do contact you, then I'll do it. And if not, that's fine. I just want to make the most of the trip, if I can. Maybe we can go lay out on the beach and get our tan on."

Drumming a pen on her laptop, Allison continued shaking her head. "That's a nice thought, but it might not be that simple. It's raining like mad down there, and they really don't know when it's going to stop. I just checked the weather channel, and it's predicting rain for the next few days."

Allison continued, recounting Heywood's complaints. He was upset about the weather, and, even though Artist had basically scoped the whole island, he hadn't found anything that met Heywood's approval.

"How can he not find a spot that he likes? It's an island, for Christ's sake. Isn't it all going to look alike?" Cam closed her eyes.

Allison sighed, and motioned for the flight attendant to bring her another mimosa. "He's straight killin' my buzz this morning. He told me to just go ahead and check us into the hotel, and he's going to be in soon. I guess he sees his money flying out the window, and he wants to be there to help toss it."

"What hotel are we booked in?"

"The St. James Club & Villas."

"Let's find another spot. If he's coming there, I'd rather stay at the Holiday Inn."

"By the airport?"

"By the runway, if possible. Easy on and easy off."

Allison checked with the flight attendant, and by the time the jet landed on the short, rain-slicked runway at VC Bird International Airport, they were already booked at the Coco Bay Resort, and Cam's summer clothes had been redirected. Allison was competent. She always kept it together for Cam.

A makeshift group of paparazzi and fans greeted Cam at the airport, clearly a Heywood stunt. Cam was gracious and accommodating, but relieved when Allison whisked her away to their waiting tinted-window sedan.

Though the sun tried its best to beat the clouds and rain back, the rain overpowered its radiance and sent it retreating back into the atmosphere. Settling into their respective suites, Cam and Allison decided to enjoy the rain and the solitude that it brought.

With their cellphones switched off and stuffed in the pockets of their thick white terrycloth robes, they treated themselves to a lazy afternoon of massages and body wraps. While their bodies were getting much needed attention, they plotted their next cherished Heywood-free moments.

"Let's tour the island. I think I'd like to take a walk on the beach." Cam stretched as the nimble fingers of her masseuse worked out the kinks in her shoulders. Naked, except for the thin sheet that covered her unexposed areas, Cam relaxed. Faint sounds of island music played in the background, and she vibed with the mellow calypso tunes.

Allison, lying on an adjacent massage table, struggled to speak. "In the rain?" she asked, as she turned her towel-wrapped head toward Cam.

"I think so. It'll be okay. I just don't want to be cooped up in this hotel just because it's raining. And who knows when or if we'll get a chance to do anything once we get started."

"I hear you. But, you know your boy has probably put an APB out on you."

"Whatever. He knows I'm here, somewhere. I'm sure he'll figure it out."

Allison smiled. "I hear you, girl. And I like what I'm hearing. Miss Cam is feelin' her independence, and you wear it well. You go, girl."

Cam dozed off, and was awakened by a different grip and feel than had rocked her to sleep. There was also the faint scent of peppermint, which tickled her nostrils. Then she felt the masseuse lay something on her, which she knew instantly wasn't a hand or a finger.

Shocked, she jerked her head up. The masseuse's technique was too harsh, and she felt a foreign object on her thigh that made her uncomfortable. "Umm, excuse me. But you're—" Cam couldn't speak. Heywood, a self-satisfied smirk on his face, was next to her, naked under his open robe. His small peen was now resting on her leg.

"What are you doing here?" Cam shot up, gathering the sheet in the front. Heywood rubbed his hands together.

The background music was still on, but the whole aura had changed. Cam peered over Heywood's shoulder to see Allison sitting up on her massage table too, with a disgusted look on her face.

"Whassup, baby? I'm here to finish yo' massage." Heywood grabbed a bottle of massage oil and squirted a pool in the palm of his hand. "Ya want a little hot oil now?"

Cam shook her head. "I don't believe this."

"He sent your masseuse away, Cam," Allison said, as she hopped to her feet. She grabbed their robes and tossed Cam's to her. "I'm gonna go get dressed," Allison said as she slipped her robe on, and flipped Heywood the finger behind his back. "I'll see you in the waiting room."

Allison left the room, mumbling under her breath, while Heywood snapped, "Next time, ya betta answer ya phone, girl. Ya know I need to know where Cam is at all times." He threw the words over his shoulder, but never took his eyes away from Cam. "Ya know ya can't get away from me."

Cam held her robe, and let her feet dangle from the side of the massage table. She started to answer him, but decided against it. "I didn't want to stay at the other hotel. I wanted to stay here."

"An' stay here ya will. At least until tomorrow. I'm not feelin' this place. We goin' to Montserrat to shoot the vid. This place just ain't happenin' for me." Heywood went on to say that Art had already flown over to confirm the locales.

"Montserrat? Where is that? What is that?" She was done. Done with Heywood and his craziness. "What's this all about? First you drag me all the way down here to Antigua, and now you want to go somewhere else? I never even heard of Montserrat." She stood up. "What are you looking for that you can't find here? An island is an island, isn't it?"

"They're not the same. Look, I'll know what I'm lookin' for when I see it. Trust me. You'll probably like that spot a little better. It's less commercial an' congested than here, an' I know you'll like that. It's not my steel-o, though."

Cam slipped her robe over her sheet and started walking toward the door. "Whatever, Heywood. I just want this to be over. O-V-E-R."

When Cam found out that Heywood had switched his hotel to the Coco Bay, she really was ready to check in at the Holiday Inn by the airport. Really.

She managed to avoid him as she and Allison toured the island, Big Mac in tow. Hot and muggy, the rain was as warm as the air and anything but cooling. But Cam was undeterred. By this time, most of the locals were heading home, and the streets were relatively tourist-free, who were probably staying in to avoid the torrential downpours. Cam reveled in the peace and quiet, sporting her Morton Salt Girl hat and rain slicker, anonymous as she window-shopped and picked up trinkets for her family.

Antigua itself was lovely, even in the rain. It had rich history, much of it preserved in the cobblestone streets and stone towers that rose on the otherwise flat landscape. To have endured hundreds of years of harsh conditions and thick, salty sea air was a testament to their endurance.

They combed the countryside, visiting the empty beaches, exploring areas where islanders lived, and took crazy pictures in the rain. They went to Betty's Hope, the sugar mill, and even over to St. John's Harbour and Heritage Cay, where the massive cruise ships were docked. They were tempted to try to sneak aboard, but Cam didn't want anyone to recognize her. Instead, they just hung out, drenched and carefree, as time wiled away.

Along their journey, Cam took pictures of everything, from the landscape, to the buildings, to the people. Photography just felt so personal for her, another of the few connections she had to her mother.

As the day drew to a close, the showers finally subsided, and the sky broke open in a purplish-orange glow. It was under that kaleidoscope of colors that the trio happened upon a local restaurant, OJ's Bar & Grill, in the friendly neighborhood of Crabbe Hill.

With doors and windows that opened to the hills, OJ's enticing aromas beckoned them in. Having had only airplane food and spa nibbles all day, the promise of enjoying a real dinner with real people was a no-brainer. They were in the door and looking at a menu within seconds. Between them, Cam and Allison ordered almost everything on the small menu, enjoying the scenery inside and outside the café equally.

The other patrons were friendly and helpful, showing them the best ways to season and eat island specialties, from pepper pot and fungii to plaintains and macaroni pie. They pigged out, treasuring every minute of their "alone" time. Of the three, Cam was particularly in heaven. There hadn't been too many times lately that she'd been able to eat out with friends without being mobbed by fans or paparazzi.

Sipping an English Harbor Rum Swizzle, the headiness of the day made Cam giggle. That and the alcohol. She wasn't much of a drinker, and after a few sips, she was buzzed.

With Big Mac seated a short distance away at the bar, but ever watchful, Allison and Cam kicked back and ripped on Heywood and his actions. And about how lame his excuse was that he couldn't find a suitable location on Antigua.

While Cam reviewed the day's pictures on her digital camera, Allison accessed the Internet from her PDA, and gave Cam the low down on Montserrat. She confirmed that Heywood was right. Montserrat was a lot less congested than Antigua.

"How can that be?" Cam asked. It wasn't like Antigua was a bustling metropolis or urban hub.

"Well, it is. And if old boy is looking for something off the beaten path, then that's where it's at," Allison said, gulping down the last of her swizzle, but keeping her eyes glued to the screen of her handheld device.

"I don't know why Heywood is so hellbent on doing the shoot this way. I'd be fine to hit one of these three hundred and something beaches here, now that the weather's broken, and call it a day."

Allison looked up and surveyed Cam's face. "It might not be that bad. Look," Allison said, handing her PDA to Cam. "It's beautiful."

Cam placed her camera on the table and looked at the screen. "It's just like here."

Allison nodded. "You're right. But, you know what? Naw, never mind. I don't know if we need to go back down that road again."

Cam peered at the screen again, and asked her what she was talking about.

"We could always go and stay at a villa over there," Allison said. "According to the 'net, millionaires from the UK have these huge mansions that they rent out when they're not here. I'm sure I can find us a nice place that'll keep Mr. Kennard away. I know high-post Heywood wouldn't want to be anywhere near a villa. He'd think it was too low brow. Not enough going on for him and not as many chances to be caught on camera."

Suddenly the sun was shining again in Cam's world. "Hmmm. You're right about all that. You can read Hey like a book. A villa sounds perfect. That just might work. You think you can find someplace this late?"

"Allison can work it out," she said with a grin, and started clicking away on her PDA.

"I see why they call that thing a CrackBerry. It is the cure-all for everything. See, that's why I have you in my life, Alli. You always keep me sane."

"That's my job. Now, let's get us another swizzle."

Cam stared at her nearly full glass and shook her head. "I'd better switch to some hibiscus juice or something. You're not gonna have me looking all hung over tomorrow, fooling around with you. I don't want to be the reason for delaying this. No way."

"I'll drink to that," Allison said.

Against the backdrop of swaying palm trees and the sounds of sultry reggae music, the partners in crime lifted their glasses and clinked them together.

chapter ten

THE HALF-HOUR flight on the 19-seat private jet was the least white-knuckled ride Cam had ever taken. As the plane approached the island, dubbed the "Emerald Island of the Caribbean," its picturesque landscape mesmerized her.

The weather was perfect, and as the plane circled the runway, Cam could see the captivating crests and hills, and even ash-covered volcanic peaks. Dramatic rock-faced cliffs stretched like fingertips to heaven, and to her, it was simply breathtaking.

The flight was so brief that by the time they landed, Heywood hadn't had a chance to work Cam's nerves. Or orchestrate another publicity stunt at the airport. Even when she told him that she was staying in a villa, he just shrugged and went back to flirting with the flight attendant. She was a leggy, island lady named Daphne, who had flowing hair, and deep cleavage. Cam surprised herself. She felt nothing but revulsion at Heywood's antics.

Heywood had been busy during the 30-minute flight. In between the non-stop flirting and references to being a card carrying member of the "mile high club," he played "Guts and In-Between," a truncated, high-stakes poker game, where he was picking the pockets of Duck and several others in his entourage. The rest of the plane was filled with a few of his Kennetic Record staffers, and Heywood ruled the skies, alternating between fielding and placing numerous loud phone calls back to the States and running his "yes people."

The sounds of lively steel-drum bands greeted them as they exited the plane, and the calypso music, radiant heat, sapphire water, and craggy mountains made Cam euphoric. Exiting through customs, she felt like Montserrat was embracing her. It was simply gorgeous, and the people were beautiful and welcoming.

Green eyed, coco-colored little girls with beads and ribbons in their hair beckoned Cam, and she snapped numerous shots of the pretty little waifs. Shirtless little boys, some with curly ringlets and others with long dreadlocks, tried to sell her carved coconut hulls with cartoon faces. Speaking in melodic tones, with crisp British accents, Cam was enthralled by their energy and high spirits.

As the children twirled and danced in the beaming sunlight, Cam also saw young men and women sprinkled around the airport's exit, hawking jewelry, pottery, and other island wares. Leaving Heywood with his posse, she drifted off to a cluster of shady palm trees, where the older men were seated, carving thick coconut hulls and braiding the tree's leaves into decorative hats.

Big Mac wasn't far behind her, and Allison was still busy trying to locate their transportation. Cam was glad to be away from all that. Even the airport staffers were on the run, acting like royalty had arrived. They probably assumed Heywood was some kind of prince, with his imperial posturing and all of his fussing. *He's a prince all right,* Cam thought to herself. *A clown prince.*

Cam tuned it all out, and closely watched the calloused, yet nimble fingers of the old men as they worked their craft. Keeping up a light, familiar banter between each other, they were very respectful and polite to the tourists who approached them.

It was amazing to watch the craftsmen create something so beautiful out of a discard. Cam was so caught up in watching these artists of the earth that she didn't feel Heywood touch her shoulder.

"Art's here, an' I think we've found the spot. We're gonna check it out, an' get everything set up." He brushed his cheek across Cam's. "I'll call ya lata, but we should be good to go tomorrow."

Cam didn't acknowledge him as he spoke or as he left. Still too captivated with the crafting, she barely heard another voice as it broke through the music, general chatter, and airport noise.

"His heart is black and dark as the eye of barracuda."

Cam turned her head to see who was talking, and her eyes fell upon one of the old men, seated not too far from her.

His rich, dark skin had deep etchings in it, but was as smooth as tanned leather. His eyes, however, spoke louder than his voice. They were stark grey, and the contrast against his nearly ebony skin was spooky. Cam wasn't sure if he had cataracts or what, and she removed her dark shades to see if she could tell. He stared through her like she was a plate glass window, while his quick fingers kept braiding the leaves, forming it into a wide-brimmed hat.

"Excuse me?" All other noises faded as Cam cocked her head toward the man.

The old man kept braiding and staring. "His heart is black. He has the soul of the devil." Cam was stunned. She felt like he was speaking to her soul.

Knees shaking, she stepped back and nearly fell into Big Mac's arms. "Come on, Cam. Our ride is here," he said, taking her arm and leading her back towards the airport.

Cam started to ask Mac if he had heard the old man, but instead, she just gazed back at him over her shoulder as they walked to the waiting string of black Land Rovers.

She was shook. Disturbed. Was he one of those medicine men who practiced voodoo? Why had he spoken out when he did, and why did he say that about Heywood? How could he even see?

The old man's words bounced around in Cam's head like greased superballs. Even as Allison prattled on and nudged her as they passed every photo-worthy site, Cam was too preoccupied to react. Eventually, the old man disappeared from her mind when Cam reached the luxurious villa Allison had booked. It was absolutely stunning. Complete with an in-ground infinity pool, it overlooked the harbor and had sweeping views of the whole island. It was like a living postcard.

It was the perfect day for the beach, and Cam wanted to get out there as soon as possible. Allison, unfortunately, had to stay at the villa to help Heywood's staffers coordinate the arrival of Torrie, Necy, and the production crew for the next day, so Cam and Big Mac headed for Rendezvous Beach, the only white sand beach on the island.

The beach overflowed with a variety of patrons and visitors, partaking in a wide range of activities from sunbathing to parasailing. Native Montserratians, young and old; tourists, pale and overbaked, were all part of the kaleidoscope of people enjoying the extremely warm day at the beautiful place where clearly, God's lips had kissed the sand and caressed the sea.

Natives hawked their wares up and down the beach, and a conclave of artisans commandeered a corner of the concession area, while their salesmen tried to entice the tourists toward their direction. Other artists, barefoot and in paint-smeared clothing, huddled under sun-dried tarps, drawing island scenes on handmade canvases. Yet others used actual coal bits to sketch portraits on rough-edged paper.

Big Mac created a mini-oasis for Cam, with two long, white lounge chairs and a huge beach umbrella anchored in the center. Wearing huge Versace shades and a floppy hat, Cam, clad in a colorful red and yellow two-piece bathing suit and matching sarong, slathered on sunblock 55 and got her beach on. From under the brim of her hat, she watched and snapped pictures of the goings-on, or sunbathed, or swam in the warm, soothing, crystal blue water.

Near Cam's lounge chair, a group of children attempted to build a castle with the powdery white sand. Their creation was a flop, but she enjoyed watching and listening to them during their failed construction project. When they finally gave up, she sent them off to buy popsicles from the nearby concession stand, then moved her chair close enough to the water's edge so that the white foam licked the soles of her feet. It was so relaxing, so completely soothing, that she thanked Heywood, to herself, for forcing her to come there. She closed her eyes and exhaled, feeling some of the tension flow out of her body.

She felt so free. No ties to bind her. No Heywood in her ear, demanding this, that, and a third. It was just her and God and peace on that beach.

She let her mind drift. She thought about the creepy island man and his warning. Never one to be superstitious, she had to admit that his words had stuck with her. What did he mean? Why had he talked to her?

Nestling in her chair, she tried to get comfortable. She had been to the islands before, and knew that they worshipped differently than most Americans. However, most also had African roots, and there was a deep sense of spirituality coursing through all of their veins. People just applied it differently, Cam reasoned. She took it a step further. Even her bible-toting, God-fearing Aunt Mary was capable of being a bit superstitious. Besides believing in herbal remedies and other Southern traditions, Aunt Mary was steadfast in some of her less than saintly convictions. She believed in lifting her feet when she crossed a railroad track, and she had even insisted that Cam bury money in the ground when she moved into her new home. And it wasn't a little bit, either.

Prior to closing on her Woodmore home, Aunt Mary had told Cam to put some money aside, "just in case." On the evening after the movers delivered their furnishings, Aunt Mary asked for the money. Puzzled, Cam went to retrieve it, and returned to find Aunt Mary in the kitchen, emptying a can of coffee into a Ziploc bag.

"What are you doing, Auntie?" Cam had asked.

"I'll show you in a second. Is that the money?" Aunt Mary asked, and pointed to the envelope Cam was holding. Cam nodded, and Aunt Mary motioned for her to give it to her.

"Very good," Aunt Mary said. "How much is it?"

"Five thousand dollars."

"Five thousand. Is that all?"

"Yeah, I didn't know how much you wanted." Cam said, and then headed toward the Sub Zero refrigerator. She opened the door, reached in and pulled out a plum. "Have one?"

"No, thank you. Now, Camara," Aunt Mary said sternly. "I told you to get some money together, and I thought you would've gotten more than that." Aunt Mary reached in her pocket and pulled out a wad of bills secured by a large rubberband.

"I have ten thousand here. I've been saving this a long time," she said, and stuffed it into the plastic bag with Cam's funds.

"What are you doing, Auntie? You know I don't need your money."

"This isn't for you right now, Camara. It's for posterity. Now, close that refrigerator door."

Cam had been mindlessly propping the door open, and she shut it quickly. Aunt Mary peered out into the darkening sky. "It's almost dusk, honey. When the moon is right over your back yard, full up in the sky, I want you to take this," she took the plastic bag and stuffed it in the empty Maxwell House coffee can, then popped on the plastic lid. "And bury it in your yard."

Cam tried not to look at her aunt like she was a complete loon. What on earth made her think that she would take fifteen thousand dollars and bury it in her yard?

Mary caught Cam's expression, and carefully placed the coffee can on the marble island countertop. "Poor thing," she said, smiling at her niece. "You just don't understand, do you? See, doing this means that you'll never be poor. It means that your house will never be without money. It's there, just in case you ever fall on hard times and need it."

"We do it in the country all the time. Except, we normally don't have this much money to rest. You already have what you need and you won't miss this."

It took a few minutes for the whole idea to sink in. Cam realized that her aunt meant business, so she reluctantly did as she was told. Aunt Mary actually stood watch as Cam buried her treasure, making sure that no one saw the place in the yard Cam had chosen. It had been a strange evening, made even stranger because she and her aunt never spoke of it again. But now that Cam thought about it, it gave her reason to pause. Some people confuse their spirituality with superstition, and it was acceptable to them. She reasoned that as long as their intentions were good, superstitions were all right. Cam knew that her aunt's intentions were good, and somehow she felt that the old man's were too. Or so she hoped.

After she had rationalized her feelings, she no longer felt spooked. Finally able to let her mind and body relax, the lull of the ocean rocked her to sleep.

chapter eleven

"MA'AM, WOULD ya like a drink?"

Cam had dozed off, but the soft female voice awakened her. She blinked and opened her eyes. There stood an attractive young woman, her braided hair upswept into a florid head wrap. Dressed in cut-off jean shorts and a long-sleeved white tee shirt, her clothes were worn, but clean. The girl smiled shyly, revealing white, even teeth. She was about Cam's age, so Cam wondered why the girl was calling her ma'am.

"I'm sorry, ma'am, I didn't mean to disturb ya," she said in her halting island voice. "But, ya've been in the sun for a while now, and that can dry ya out. I thought that ya might want cool drink." She laughed nervously. "I meant, um, ya might want *a* cool drink."

Cam tried to speak, but her voice cracked. She yawned, and wiped the corners of her eyes. Her throat was truly dry, and she was parched and dehydrated. She hadn't intended to fall asleep in the sun, and now she was a little burned. Cam nodded to the island girl, retreating back under the umbrella.

The girl, with a collapsible cooler draped over her shoulder, followed Cam back to the shaded area and then stooped down. She laid her bag beside her, and looked into Cam's face. Her face was beautiful.

Exotic features and smooth, pecan brown skin.

"I have some of our island juices— soursop, mango, cashew, guava, tamarind, papaya and gooseberry." She peered at Cam cautiously. "But, I also have American soda, if ya'd like."

Cam smiled and rubbed her burning arms. "I think I'll be adventurous and try one of your island drinks. Which one would you recommend?"

The girl returned the smile, reached into her sack, and withdrew an unmarked red bottle. She passed the icy can to Cam, who tried not to let her skepticism show.

"Don't worry, ma'am. It's okay. The rum shop in my neighborhood makes it fresh everyday. They let me buy it, an' sell it here on the beach."

"Oh, I see," Cam said, as she allowed the cold water from the bottle to drip on her achy skin. "How much do I owe you?"

"That's two-dollars. American is fine, ma'am."

"What's your name?"

"Marisol."

"Marisol, I'm Cam. And you don't have to call me ma'am. I'm sure we're almost the same age."

The girl grinned as Cam reached for her bag and pulled out her wallet. The smallest bill she had was a twenty, so she asked Marisol if she had change.

Marisol squatted on her ankles, fished inside the zippered compartment of the cooler, and pulled out a handful of crinkled Eastern Caribbean and U.S. bills. While she counted the money, Cam took the bottle and rubbed it on her arms.

"Ya musta burned a bit," she said. She reached into another compartment and removed a tiny jar with no label. She unscrewed the top and handed the jar to Cam. "Try some of this."

"The rum shop makes this too?" Cam asked, and set her bottle of juice down beside her.

"No, it's aloe juice," Marisol laughed, and continued counting the bills. "I make that me self."

"You're pretty resourceful, aren't you?" Cam poured a little of the juice in her palms, and began rubbing her arms. The salve instantly cooled her burning extremities. "Oooh. That feels so good."

Marisol smiled and passed Cam her change. "Yes, I've learned to be. I've been pretty much on me own for a while now."

Cam was intrigued. It could've just been a line, a sad story that the girl had concocted, but somehow she felt that her words were truthful. And, as Cam was about to embark on a new path of being on her own, she was interested in hearing about how this young lady had managed it. "On your own? How can that be? You don't look much older than a teenager."

"I just turned 19, ma'am," she giggled. "I'm sorry. I meant Ca-Cam." She swallowed deeply. "But, I've been on me own since I was fort-teen."

"Wow," Cam said. She felt for this girl. This stranger. A child who had been forced, like herself, to grow up too soon.

Looking in Marisol's deep-set eyes and observing the manner in which she conducted her business, she reminded Cam of herself. Like Cam had been at fourteen, when she was thrust from the sheltered world of singing gospel to the hardscrabble universe of hip-hop and R&B. Cam sensed the parallels in their lives, even though Marisol hadn't even disclosed much about herself yet.

Cam managed to collect her thoughts, took out a ten-dollar bill, and gave it back to Marisol. "Thanks for the drink. And the aloe."

Marisol grinned at the tip, and quickly added it to her stash. "You're welcome. An' if ya need anything while ya're here, I'll be 'round. I can show ya the best tourist places, tell ya 'bout the rum bars, everythin'. Places where ya can just lime."

"Lime?"

"Hang out," she said. "Have fun." Marisol gathered up her belongings, but before she could pick up her cooler, Cam motioned for her to take a seat.

"Why don't you sit down for a few? I know you have to be tired, dragging that heavy bag in this hot sun. Plus, I really want to hear more about your island, and how you've done it on your own."

Marisol's eyes darted around, as if she was sizing up the situation. To see if this was a trick. To see if this pretty stranger really just wanted to talk to her. Or to see how her competition might fare if she took some time off. "Well, I don't know. I really need to sell my juices."

"What if I buy a drink for you and for Big Mac, that big, handsome brother back there?" Cam offered. "He might even drink more than one or two." Sales in hand, they were enough to persuade the hard-working girl to take an unexpected, yet well-deserved break.

Sipping her guava juice, Marisol was guarded at first, but eventually warmed up to Cam. In fact, the more she talked, the more she reminded Cam of herself. She was shy, but had innate survival skills. Although they had grown up in different cultures, they were really quite similar. Almost kindred spirits.

As the cooling tradewinds sliced through the suffocating island heat, Marisol told Cam all about her little island. She encouraged Cam to see the famous sites, and indulge on tasty dishes such as Goat Water and Mountain Chicken.

She relayed the history of the island, telling Cam the story of how the island had almost been wiped out by a volcano, and how the elders of the islands believed that they were spared because of their faith. Cam asked her about the elders, and Marisol said that they were the wisest and the most revered individuals on the isle. In fact her grandfather had been one of the most respected elders on the island before he died.

When Cam asked about her grandfather, Marisol's whole demeanor changed. Her eyes misted over, and she became even quieter. Her grandfather had been the one who had held her family together. Her mother had been wild, but her grandfather had been able to keep her in check. An only child, Marisol had been close to her Poppi, a relationship her mother had resented.

When her grandfather died, Marisol's mother fell victim to the worst of the island. She allowed strangers into their home, and never believed Marisol when she told her that her drunken male friends had tried to assault her.

One evening, after fighting two of them off while her mother lay passed out on the porch, Marisol, only 14 years old, left her home in Salem and never returned. The cobblestone streets and black sand beaches became Marisol's home, for her mother never tried to find her or bring her home. Since the island was so small, Marisol had learned that her mother had apparently left the island to go to Antigua with one of her boyfriends, and never returned. Despite their differences, Marisol said that she often found herself staring into the faces of strangers, looking for her mother.

The topic was sobering, and Cam felt Marisol's pain. It was the same pain she had experienced in her own life, but at least she had her Aunt Mary and her grandmother. Cam wondered where she would have been and what she would have become if her aunt hadn't been there for her. Her admiration for Marisol grew as she spoke. Cam admired the fact that Marisol learned how to support herself honestly, and that her only regrets were that she had never left the island, and had never finished her education. But, she was working to do both. They weren't huge goals, but they were what she wanted. Silently, Cam vowed to help her in any way that she could.

Cam lightened the mood by steering the conversation back to the Montserrat, and all of its wonderful offerings. Marisol said she was look-ing forward to the upcoming national holiday, the Festival, slated to start next week. Cam surprised herself; she actually gave a passing thought to sticking around for it, to enjoy the experience. And especially since she had such a wonderful feeling about the little sanctuary.

Marisol also said that she was excited at the rumor that a famous celebrity was coming to visit the island, and that she might get a chance to meet her. Cam just smiled.

Worried about not making her daily sales quota, Marisol went back to peddling her juices. Cam, with Big Mac not far behind, ventured over to the concession area to try some of the Goat Water that Marisol had enthused about.

Cam was enjoying herself in a way she hadn't in a long time. An island man came by the stand, strolling in the surf, strumming a worn guitar with stickers slapped across everything except the strings. Coming out of character, Cam coaxed him into letting her play his instrument.

Sitting on a picnic table, Cam started strumming the guitar, and before long, she had almost the whole beach joining in as she sang Bob Marley's anthem, "No Woman, No Cry."

★

Marisol ventured over to the concession area for change when she heard the singing. She stood there in awe of Cam's voice, clapping enthusiastically at every song. It seemed like the whole beach was drawn to the big voice of the little lady in the tiny tiki-bar with its colorful picnic tables scattered about.

Cam was in heaven until an open-shirted Heywood appeared. With his boisterous entourage surrounding him, he was grinning like a crack fiend on his latest binge. Ice dipped and swathed in white linen from head to toe, Cam igged him, and kept right on singing with the crowd until he stepped away from his posse and broke up the impromptu concert.

"Big Mac, get on your job, man," he admonished. "Now, now, everyone. Ya just got treated to a free concert by the one and only Starr Child, entertainer extraordinary." He pulled his shades off and grinned. "Now, y'all know who I am, right? I'm Heywood Kennard. Producer extraordinary."

The crowd oohed and ahhed at the fact that there were bona fide celebrities on their island, and scrambled for napkins and slips of paper for them to autograph. Heywood's chest poked out as he pulled her to the side.

"Did you just have to come and make a scene?" Cam asked.

"Ya know how I do." Heywood smiled crookedly. "Whassup, ma? Ya look like ya got a little sun, huh? The bronze looks good on ya. But, don't get no more. Ya know your fans like that light bright in ya.

"I hate to break up your little lovefest here, but we found the perfect spot. Just perfect. We're gonna film at a remote area down near Soufriere Hills. Ya don't know where that's at, but it's got just the right look. So, we're tryin' to get everyone down here tomorrow so that we can be ready to roll on Thursday." He continued on to say that everyone was being lined up, including one of the better choreographers and a body double stuntwoman for Cam, which made her question why that was needed.

"Let's just say that Imma take this video to anotha level. See, it's gonna look like yo' being kidnapped by some island thugs, who threaten to kill ya, but then ya get rescued. Don't worry, it's gonna be tight, you'll see.

"We're gonna have to get there by boat, though. So get your sea legs together, baby."

Cam didn't like boats, just like she didn't like planes. She preferred land under her feet. *Damn. That Heywood was working overtime to make this shoot as miserable for her as possible,* she thought to herself. Just the idea of being out on that huge ocean in a tiny boat almost made her as anxious as boarding an aircraft.

Cam's eyebrows rose. "By boat? You mean we can't drive there?"

"It's a remote locale, Cam. An' it'll be easier to transport all of the equipment that way. Trust me, you'll be aiight. We ain't goin' out on some little dinghy. Ya know how I do."

He pecked her on the cheek, and stepped toward some autograph seekers. Once again, it just seemed like Heywood was going out of his way to make her as uncomfortable as possible.

But, she put her best face forward as the crowd swarmed towards her, and she graciously signed t-shirts and napkins, refusing to let Heywood's flippant attitude affect her interaction with her fans. She motioned to Big Mac that she was ready to go, and she smiled and patiently signed autographs until he collected her belongings.

As Big Mac approached, he announced to the disappointed crowd that Starr was going to have to leave, but that she would return again soon. Cam signed her last autograph, and as she turned to depart, an eerie voice spoke to her.

"He is evil. He has no soul." It was the same old man, the vendor from the airport.

"He will bring nothin' but grief to ya. Nothin' but grief."

Cam stopped, but Big Mac grabbed her elbow and pulled her forward. "Come on, Cam."

"Did you hear what he said?"

"Who?"

"That man over there." Cam turned to point to the man, but he was gone.

Big Mac parted the crowd and as they were walking to their Land Rover, Cam spotted a crying Marisol being screamed at by an older woman. Rail thin and a shade or two darker than burnt orange, the woman had one hand on her hip and the other in Marisol's face. The drinks from Marisol's cooler were strewn across the grassy sand. Instinctively, Cam went to her new friend's side.

"Marisol, what's up?"

Through sobs, Marisol choked out the words. "Missus Scott tol' me that I shouldn't be workin' this beach today. That this is her beach. She says I owe her money. An' I need me money for me rent."

"Who is you?" the woman asked, and glared at Cam. "An' how is this your bidness, missy?"

"Never you mind, ma'am," Big Mac said, sliding his imposing figure between Cam and the irate woman.

"I'm a friend of hers," Cam said. "And I don't like to see her crying." Cam reached for her beach bag. "How much do you think she owes you?"

The old woman looked Cam up and down. "Twenty dollars. American."

Cam reached in her bag and handed the woman a twenty dollar bill. "Here you go. And if you ever see my friend again, look away, okay? You have no right to talk to her like that. No right at all."

Marisol sniffled, "Thank you," then she reached down to pick up her inventory.

"Don't worry about that. Let her get it. She just bought it, so it's all hers," Big Mac said, and shot the witch a menacing look.

"Come on, Marisol," Cam said and then grabbed Marisol's arm. "I want you to come with us."

chapter twelve

MARISOL LOOKED around the villa with an awestruck expression. "Wow," she said, and peeked at the crystal pieces and ornate plates positioned on the sofa table behind the oversized Remington sofa. "I've never seen such before in me life."

Cam flopped down on the sofa, and sprawled out, reaching for her gum. "Well, enjoy it, Marisol. Come," Cam said, and patted the pillow next to her. "Have a seat. Rest yourself."

When they arrived, Cam had introduced Allison to Marisol, and explained that she was going to be their tour guide/production assistant during their stay. Allison, a Philadelphia-born cynic, was clearly skeptical, and thought that picking up strays was out of Cam's character. However, she soon warmed to the idea of Marisol being there to assist her. That made the plan a lot more tolerable.

"Yeah, enjoy it tonight, Marisol. Because we have a lot of work to do tomorrow," Allison added.

"No problem, ma'am," Marisol said, still standing by the entrance.

"Good. But before you get started, I need some information from you. You want to get paid, right?" Allison asked, then turned to Cam. "Did you all discuss pay?"

Cam shook her head. "I figured we could work something out."

"You figured, huh? Well, tell me, Miss Marisol. How much do you normally make selling your drinks and what-not on a good day?"

"Oh, maybe about twenty American. On a good day."

Allison tried not to laugh. "I'm sure we can at least match that."

Cam threw a pillow at her assistant. "Get real, Allison. We can do much better than that. Stop playin'."

"Okay," Allison said. "But at least let me get some information so we can make sure you get paid. What's your last name?"

"It's Kent," Marisol giggled. "And thank you so much for lettin' me work wit' you while you're here. Wow, I just can't believe that I have the honor of working with someone as great as Starr. I absolutely love her music, an' they play it on the radio all the time. An' to think, I didn't even know who she was."

"You didn't?" Allison shot Cam an incredulous look, and Cam shook her head. "Let me find out."

"She really didn't," Cam said.

"Oh, come on, now. I don't believe that," Allison said. "Everybody knows who Starr is. She's like the hottest singer in hip-hop now."

Again Cam shook her head. "Well, no one on the beach knew who I was, and that was cool. Remember, I was up under this floppy hat and dark glasses. It wasn't until Heywood showed up and—"

"Say no more," Allison said, and plopped down on the loveseat. "I can only imagine that he came out there and took over. Boss talkin' and profilin' with all those loud assed clowns he carts around."

Marisol finally sat down, on the edge of the sofa, and Cam playfully pushed her back. "Look, relax. It's all good here. You'll help us out and we'll help you out. We promise."

"Now, tell me where I can get some of that delicious Mountain Chicken you were talking about. I'm starved," Cam said.

Marisol camped out at the villa, and took Cam and Allison around the island, giving them a native's perspective. They passed Runaway Ghaut, one of the many deep ravines that carried rainwater down from the mountains to the sea. Marisol encouraged them to drink from it because the island legend was that people who drank from there would be drawn to return to Montserrat again and again. It was encouragement enough to make both Cam and Allison gulp down several mouthfuls.

Over the course of the evening, they dined and partied, until the sun crested in the Western sky and an exhausted, but exhilarated Cam decided to save her adventures for the next day.

Rising early the next morning, and, per specific instructions from Heywood, they were driven to the pier in Little Bay, where Heywood had procured a huge yacht from Antigua, *The Proud Mary*, along with several smaller boats to transport the crew and equipment.

The 150' *Proud Mary* had a crew of five that included a portly captain and several taut and tanned European deckhands. The yacht itself was quite commanding, and dwarfed the other boats in the harbor. Its presence was just like Heywood. Ostentatious.

The local dancers, awestruck and intense, listened attentively to Katt, the choreographer. The extras milled about, while the Kennetic staffers signed them in and recorded their information, making sure that the proper waivers were signed, including N-Snips. Call Heywood what you wanted, but he always made sure to CYA.

Artist greeted Cam warmly, and commented on how much he was looking forward to creating a work of art with her. Heywood was busy playing Captain Stubing from "The Love Boat," wearing a faux white navy outfit and matching hat, and barking out orders. While Artist and Heywood sorted out the final details before departing, their respective entourages scurried about, securing the watercrafts and equipment. Allison hung back on the dock waiting for last-minute instructions from Heywood, while, Cam, Marisol, and Big Mac boarded *The Proud Mary*, entering the salon where Torrie and Necy were organizing their gear.

"Hey girl!" Torrie and Necy both screeched in unison. They dropped their tools and ran over to Cam.

"Girl, I missed you already," Torrie said, giving Cam a big hug.

"It's only been a couple of days," Necy said, and shook her head.

"Whateva. I missed my girl. Plus, you know how much I loves the island mens. Let's hurry up and get this thang over so we can go and find us some island meat," Torrie said, licking her lips.

Necy ran her fingers through Cam's hair. "Umph, umph, umph. What has this island done to your hair? We haven't seen the treatment, so I don't have any idea what I should do with this head of yours."

Cam crossed the room, and sat down on a bar stool. "You can wrap it up in a scarf for all I care. I just want this over with."

"Who's your friend?" Torrie asked, with a brow raised.

Cam pardoned her ill manners and introduced them to Marisol, who was quietly standing in the cabin's doorway with Cam's bag clutched to her chest. They greeted her warmly, and when Torrie and Necy learned that Marisol was from Montserrat, they figured she would fit in just fine.

"That's cool, girl," Torrie said, as she opened a trunk and pulled out several outfits. "When we get back, you can show us around. Take us to where the men hang out."

"Real talk," Necy said.

"Excuse me?" Marisol asked, and everyone laughed.

Cam motioned for Marisol to set her bag down and come to where she was sitting. Cam then placed a protective arm around her protégée. "She meant like, 'for real' or like 'really.'"

Marisol nodded and smiled. "Oh, I see. I would love to show ya our island. It would be me pleasure."

Allison finally joined them, with a stack of papers tucked under her arm. "Here's the treatment," she said, and handed a stapled set to Cam. "And you'll be happy to know that the stuntwoman Heywood hired was a no-show. Seems like she broke her toe getting on the flight to Antigua, so he'll have to scratch whatever he had in mind for her."

That news was not reassuring to Cam, particularly after she flipped through the pages of the script. It called for Cam to be lost on a deserted island, and then found by cannibals who try to cook her. She is rescued by a buff island man, and they swim off together into the sunset. She had no comment.

Allison, in her best professional manner, summarized the video to everyone, and Torrie and Necy fought to hold their laughter. Finally, Torrie spoke.

"You mean to tell me, this is what we came down here for? Hell, we coulda shot this at the Y. This is kinda corny, don't 'cha think?"

"It is what it is. I don't give a shit. Peep this. If Heywood wanted to spend his chedda on a vacay for us, then so be it. I ain't mad at him. Like Cam said. Let's get this thing wrapped with a quickness so we can get our fun on," Necy said. "All I have to do is stick a bone in Cam's head, an' you can put some rips in those clothes an' we'll be good to go."

"A bone in her head," Torrie snickered. "Maybe we can make her look like Pebbles Flintstone."

Allison shook her head. "Y'all got jokes, huh? Well, don't think for one minute it's gonna be that easy, y'all. This is just the original treatment. You know when Heywood's involved, anything can happen. Everything's subject to change."

"That's right, anythin' can happen," a lurking Heywood said as he leaned in the doorway. "An' as long as y'all are on my dime, it's about workin'. So, let's get it crackin.'"

In the background, the rumble of marine engines being started filled the air, and the smell of diesel fuel and smoked seeped into the cabin.

"That's Art an' his crew. They've gone ahead to do the set up, but we're about to shove off, too. Cam, you and I need to talk. Now."

Heywood guided Cam to the upper deck, and they watched the shore disappear from sight as the captain ably maneuvered the beautiful yacht away from the pier. As Cam leaned against the railing, and inhaled the moist, salty air, Heywood sidled up next to her.

"Ain't it beautiful, beautiful?"

"It's lovely, Heywood. But, you know I'm not crazy about all of this water."

"You'll be aiight. Ya know I'm gonna take care of ya, right?"

When Cam didn't respond, Heywood kept talking. "Ya know I'm doin' all this for you, right?"

Cam rolled her eyes behind her Gucci shades. "If you say so."

He grabbed Cam's arms and turned her toward him. "Why ya act like ya don't give a fuck about me? I don't understand. Ya haven't called me or tried to be wit' me since we been here. I don't get it."

"There's nothing to get, Heywood. I'm closing that chapter of my life.

I told you before, it's not about you. It's about me."

Heywood dropped his hands and folded his arms. "That's what ya say. But, yo' probably beat about that picture ya saw. I told ya, that ain't nothin' but business, ma."

Cam tried to turn away, but he grabbed her again, this time almost roughly. "Heywood, we've had this conversation before, and I'm done with it. Now, if you can't accept it, then I can't help you. It's not that I don't care for you, because I do. But right now, I have to care for me. For real."

"Ya sure it ain't no other nigga? I know how these niggas been checkin' for ya, 'specially since they think ya ain't wit' nobody."

Heywood knew that there wasn't anybody else in Cam's life. He made sure of that. Throughout their professional relationship, she had attended most industry events with him, and even when she recorded duets with hot male singers like Usher and Jamie, she was never romantically linked to them. Every now and then, when Jamie was between jump-offs or models, he and Cam would hook up and go to an event, but they were just childhood friends.

"There's no one else, Heywood. No one. Now, can we drop it? I'd really like to relax before we have to start shooting."

"Well, if it ain't no other nigga, is it some bitch? I'm just sayin', ya know if that's what yo' into, let a nigga know. I can get down wit' that."

Cam raised her shades and gritted on him. "Don't even go there. And if it was, that would be my business, too, now wouldn't it?"

"It might make sense. I mean, who's this gal ya picked up? One of yo' island pieces?" Heywood laughed. "Maybe that's what it is. Cause I know there ain't no other nigga gonna be able to fill my shoes."

Cam sighed and restrained herself from saying what she was thinking. Anyone could fill those baby shoes. She lowered her shades and said, "Don't flatter yourself, Heywood. Please don't."

"Aww, I was just fuckin' wit' ya. I just don't understand why ya want to give all this up." Heywood extended his arms, and stood back so that the fading island became his backdrop. "We could do this whenever ya wanted. This ain't no thing. You could have anythin'."

"The only thing I want is peace of mind."

Before Heywood could continue, they were interrupted by a timid

Marisol. "Umm, Cam. 'Scuse me, but they need ya. To do ya hair." Her voice quivered and her slight body trembled.

Heywood scowled and then turned his back to Marisol while she was speaking, but then turned to face her with a phony smile. "Well, excuse me, miss. I don't think that we've ever been properly introduced. I'm Heywood. An' you are?"

"She's Marisol," Cam said, and stood. "And she's my new assistant to Allison." Cam walked to the stairs where Marisol was standing.

"Pleased to meet ya, sir," Marisol said.

"That accent is hot, girl. An' so are you, Marisol. We're gonna have to keep ya around here. Good lookin' out, Cam." He winked at Marisol, and she scurried down the deck stairs.

chapter thirteen

AS THE ship continued towards Soufriere Hills, the girls worked on creating Starr. Necy decided to braid her hair and added a few extensions to give it length. Marisol helped Torrie by steaming Cam's outfits, and, because she and Cam were nearly the same skin tone, Torrie tested the makeup on her to see which would film best.

It didn't take long for Necy to finish Cam's hair and pin it up. Cam was about to start selecting her outfits when they heard the engines slow, and the ship drop anchor. The sound of the other boats could be heard in the background, and Heywood's voice rose above all of the racket.

Everyone but Marisol ventured out to the main deck, to find Artist and the other boats idling nearby. Heywood, surrounded by two of his minions and with a cell phone glued to his ear, was holding a heated debate with the Captain.

"I don't give a fuck what they say, Artist," he barked into the phone, and pointed to the shore. "I want to go there. This is my vision of what *Hallowed Ground* is about."

"But, sir. I can't allow you to go there. It's part of the exclusion zone and we are forbidden to be there," the captain said, beads of sweat popping out on his forehead.

"Nobody tells me where I can't go. Money talks, man, and if I tell ya that's where I want to go, then that's where I'm going." He motioned to the gofer who was holding his briefcase. Heywood grabbed it and opened it, revealing several rows of banded cash.

"Like I said, money talks. How much is it gonna take to get there?"

The captain scratched his chin, and wiped his brow. Eyeing the money, he spoke slowly, in his thick accent. "It's not really only a matter of money, sir. It is illegal to go there, and I can't get this boat any closer to the shore. From this point on, the water is too shallow."

"Whatcha afraid of, a little fine? I'll pay it." Heywood placed the receiver to his lips. "Artist, go on over and unload. An' then come back an' get us. We'll be ready."

Heywood reached into the case and pulled out two stacks of bills. "Well, then you get us as close to the shore as ya can, an' then ya anchor this tub, ya understand?" He handed the money to the ruddy-faced captain. "An' then, when that anchor's down, what I'll do is I'll take the keys wit' me, just so I know you'll be here when we get back, aiight? An' I think I'll leave one of my bodyguards here to keep ya company."

Cam witnessed the whole scene with disgust, and then turned and headed back into the salon with Allison, Torrie, and Necy on her heels. She nearly knocked Marisol over, who was straightening up, holding a set of curling irons.

"I'm sorry, Marisol. Please excuse me," Cam said, and then started to pace up and down in the small space.

"She's just a little stressed out," Allison said, and opened up her Blackberry.

"I just don't believe it," Torrie said, and reached for her purse. "I can't believe that he's throwin' a hissy fit in the middle of the damned ocean. I mean, come on. I need a damned cigarette after all that bullshit." She pulled out a pack and tapped it in her palm.

"I need a drink," Necy said.

Allison just shook her head. "I don't know why he's trippin' like this. Why would he have a conniption about trying to get us into a damned restricted area?"

"Because he's Heywood," Torrie and Necy said in unison.

Marisol cleared her throat, her eyes darting around at each of them. "Excuse me, did ya say 'restricted area'?"

Allison pointed the screen of her PDA toward her. "Yeah. Heywood wants to go here. Soufriere Hills."

Marisol dropped the curling irons and started stuttering. "Oh my. Uh, I, I, did not know," she said.

"Girl, what's wrong with you?" Necy snapped. "I know you workin' for Cam and what-not, but those things are expensive. I know you don't want to blow your whole check on a broken set of irons."

Cam stopped pacing. "Marisol? What's the matter?"

Marisol was shaking, as she begged Necy's pardon. She swept down to pick up the irons and said, "You'll think me silly, but no one can go there. They say it's cursed."

They all stopped and stared at Marisol.

"Get the fuck outta here. Fuck this cigarette. I need a damned blunt," Torrie said.

Cam sat down on the arm of the sofa. "Why do they say it's cursed?"

Marisol placed the curlers on Necy's table, and looked at all of them, terror written plainly on her face. "That's where the volcano erupted. Out of nowhere. Many people killed. Many families gone. Many peoples lost their minds afterwards. The Elders think it is an evil place. Kill so many people."

Cam immediately marched to the upper deck, where Heywood was peering through a pair of long lens binoculars, and one of his gofers/wannabe rappers, a young kid named Parsley, was two-finger typing on a laptop. Parsley was Duck's nephew, and almost like a son to him. His real name was Petey, but Heywood had named him Parsley, because he was always hanging around. He had nickname for everyone, usually not too complimentary.

"Heywood, I'm not playing with you. I am not going over there. I'm not."

He kept gazing through the lenses, and motioned for his staff to leave. They hurriedly gathered their things and left. When everyone was out of earshot, he nonchalantly asked, "Why not?"

Cam repeated Marisol's story, while Heywood puffed on a fat Cohiba. When she finished, he immediately dismissed it as nonsense.

"That's just some old island tale. Evil spirits an' shit. *Ooooohhh.*" Heywood wiggled his fingers like a ghoul. "I don't believe that shit for a minute. I'm from New York, baby. I've seen an' heard worse than that in the Bronx."

He frowned. "It takes a little more than some old-assed folk tale to scare me." He shook his head, and gave Cam a disgusted look. "I can't believe—" His words were cut off when his phone rang. He answered it, listened, and mumbled a few inaudible words into the receiver. He raised his voice and said, "Cool, we'll be there in a few."

He looked at Cam and shrugged. "Tough, Baby Girl. That was Artist an' everythin's set. So, I suggest ya go an' get yo' crew an' let's do this thing. Time is money an' money's time, ya feel me?"

A speechless Cam spun around, and he grabbed her arm, gripping it so tightly that his manicured nails dug into it. As he leaned into her ear, and his hot, minty breath repelled her.

"So, whatcha gonna do, leave? That's real pro-fessional of ya, Miss Lady. I know ya think yo' all high an' mighty, but I don't think ya can walk on water. At least not all the way back to port.

"So, I suggest that ya get yo' ass together an' make it hot an' make it happen over there. If ya know what's really good."

Heywood chuckled as Cam walked away. She was so heated that she barely grunted at a slick, sunscreen-drenched Duck as they passed each other on the narrow stairs.

"Whassup with Starr, man?" Duck asked as he joined Heywood on the upper deck. He was holding Heywood's case, as usual.

"Nuttin.' She's just tryna get her diva on." Heywood said, leaning against the railing. His Bvlgari sunglasses reflected the bright sun and the colorful water.

"Oh, word? That don't sound like her." Duck said, shrugging. "Oh, well. I guess she deserve it. It's hotter than a mutha fucka out here, an' I know she don't wanna be out here on this water. I'm fryin' my damn self."

"Whateva, Duck. It ain't for her to say. I run this shit, ya heard?"

Duck nodded, and Heywood asked, "Ya get all them N-Snips signed?" he asked, and Duck nodded again.

"Cool," Heywood said. "I don't want nobody runnin' they mouths 'bout this shoot, ya heard? I wanna make sure that it's on the DL until we blow it out the stations. It's gonna be an exclusive. Everybody's gonna be fightin' to run it first."

"Yeah, I'm sure, Heywood. It's gonna be tight. Just like the rest of her songs. But, for real, ya might have problem with the remix you're doin' on her other joint. I know ya was thinkin' about goin' wit' that new cat Casbar, but I don't think he's up to par yet. I'm just sayin'. I heard him lay a few verses on it an' it ain't the business. Not the empire business."

Heywood sometimes listened to Duck when it came to the rappers and their lyrics, but today, he didn't want to hear it. Still, he was curious as to where Duck was going with all of this unsolicited input.

"So, what ya sayin'? Casbar can't hang? Dude can't rhyme?"

Duck set the case down, and leaned against the railing near Heywood. "I'm just sayin', maybe you could give Parsley a shot. He's good peoples, 'naw mean? Plus, he's here, he's got some good shit, an' he could probably come up with somethin' that'll flow better than that shit Casbar got."

Casbar was an artist Heywood had stolen from one of his Dirty South Rivals, and he was determined to make him a star. Or, at least make some money off him and his reckless behavior.

"Yeah, I hear ya, Duck. An' I know Parsley is ya peeps, but give it a rest, will ya? But, ya know what? I'll give it some consideration." Heywood inhaled the steamy salty sea air and exhaled. "But right now, I need a drink. Ya think ya can handle that? Better yet, why don't ya get ya boy Parsley to get it. You're such a big fan of his, he can write, he can rhyme, he can vibe. I'm thinkin' he should be able to mix a helluva drink, too. At least the one I get better be the bomb."

Duck shook his head. "Aiight, Heywood. I hear ya. I'll get your drink."

"Good lookin' out, Duck. An' next time, I'll let ya know when I want your opinion, ya feel me?" Heywood lowered his expensive black shades and looked around the boat. "An' go find me one of the finest dancers we got on the set. There was a little honey down there that had a bangin' ass an' tight little waist. Her face wasn't all that, but I can bag her an' tag her," he said. "Just go find her an' tell her I can make her a star. I need a private dancer right about now."

Cam brooded for the rest of the afternoon. She could not believe that Heywood was on such a power trip. He had always been that way; he would never change.

The island they were looking at was totally choked with underbrush, and clearly uninhabitable. Iguanas and giant ditch frogs seemed shocked at their presence, and even the bright red hibiscus plants were straggly, apparently finding growing there a test of endurance.

White-tailed Tropicbirds and brown pelicans cried out in the sky, while the normally seafaring Grebes landed cautiously on the surf to check them out. The ominous greetings by the animal world unnerved Marisol even more, but she remained quiet, shadowing Cam's moves and jumping to every one of Allison's commands.

Heywood was relentless. Every time he got a new thought or a different idea about what he was trying to capture, he insisted that Artist and the crew pack up and relocate. It was blazing hot, and the humidity was overbearing, but he was Heywood. People obeyed him. Necy struggled to keep Cam's hair on point, while Torrie chainsmoked and Allison vigorously punched the keyboard of her PDA.

Heywood ventured deeper and deeper into hills, directing his gun-toting security detail closer and closer to the base of the volcano. The location finally seemed to satisfy him, and as the sun started its descent, Heywood insisted that they keep shooting.

The sky blackened, and rumblings of thunder were in the distance. Everyone was getting a little shook, so Artist hurriedly shot multiple scenes, each one more and more menacing as the sky turned blacker and blacker. Heywood could barely contain his delight.

The tradewinds picked up, and Marisol was shaking, but she stuck to Cam and Allison. Cam grew increasingly uncomfortable, and though she tried not to show it, her nerves were etched on her face. Finally, Artist called for a break.

"Heywood, we need to wrap this up," he said, pulling his headphones from his ears and dropping them around his neck. "I'm pickin' up all these noises in the background, and it sounds like a stor's coming up.

"We got enough footage in the can and I can edit what we have. The video's gonna be hot," Artist said.

Heywood sat in his director's chair, a vacant expression on his face. He held his hands up and formed a frame. "Aiight. But I want just one more scene. Torrie, ya got another outfit like Cam has on?"

Torrie responded positively, so Heywood continued. "Good. I want ya to put it on Cam's girl over there," he said and flicked his thumb toward Marisol. "Instead of the last scene being that she swims away wit' ol' boy, I want to use that girl to show that she saves herself. Ya feel me?

Artist grabbed his laptop, boarded Heywood's thoughts, and went about setting up the scene. Everyone on the set worked quickly, as the gathering storm threatened to shut down production at any moment. The rumblings that Artist mentioned earlier were getting louder and louder, too loud for anyone to ignore. People were tense and visibly anxious. As the scene was set up and the markers placed, Cam took her position.

The fake cannibals danced around Cam, who was standing in a replica of a fire pit. Then Heywood gave the signal to a cloaked Marisol, who approached the make-believe fire. The dancing cannibals parted and as Marisol approached Cam and reached out for her hand, a thunderous explosion shook the ground.

"OH SHIT!" somebody screamed and everyone started running for cover, trampling over camera equipment and their less fleet-footed associates. The earth had split open between Cam and Marisol and a flash of white-hot gas, water, and steam spewed out over them, engulfing both and obliterating them from sight.

THE SOUNDS in the cramped waiting room outside of the emergency room at Glendon Hospital constantly changed from eerie quiet to hysterical sobbing. Heywood, still wearing his dark shades, was inconsolable, refusing support from anyone. He just paced, his bare feet moving soundlessly across the sandy floor. He had lost his shoes somewhere, and hadn't even noticed. His clothes were stained and disheveled from holding Cam's head as she lay writhing on the speedboat as it sped back to the city.

Katt, the choreographer, and one of the ship's mates, were the only ones with medical training. She had immediately started spraying bottled water on both Cam and Marisol to try to manage their burns. The mate made sure that their extremities stayed elevated, and after the bottled water ran out, Katt tried to keep everyone else calm as the boat raced back to the mainland.

At the hospital, the staff had to almost pry Cam from Heywood's arms, and he had to be physically restrained from barging into the emergency room. Hospital staffers quickly learned to stay away from the waiting room, as Heywood roughly confronted each person walking by, demanding to know Cam's condition.

Marisol and Cam were being treated in the same room, which had been cordoned off, with Heywood's bodyguards posted at each entrance, denying access to any non-Heywood authorized person.

In the waiting room, Necy and Torrie sobbed without ceasing, their heads buried in each others arms. Every now and then, one would howl out in agony. Even Big Mac, hovering by the window and mindlessly fiddling with the drapes, looked despondent and near tears.

A nurse had tried to collect as much information as possible about the incident and about Cam and Marisol. Allison, totally unraveled, could barely recall Marisol's last name. Her frustration grew when she couldn't find Cam's personal belongings or provide any of her medical information. Allison knew Cam was a Red Cross blood donor, and that she kept the donor card in her wallet. Allison had sent Parsley back to the boat to check for Cam's bag, with specific instructions that she would cut him if he didn't bring everything back intact.

For the first and worst time since she had been working for Cam, Allison felt useless, but she tried to tell the nurse all that she knew about Cam's known allergies or other medical conditions.

Once the nurse left, Allison paced, tears streaming from her eyes, and shaking her head in disbelief. "I-I, I can't believe it," she repeated, over and over, and to no one in particular. "I can't believe it. I don't know what to do. Heywood? Heywood! What should I do?"

Heywood completely ignored her until she pulled out her cell phone. "What the fuck ya doin'?" He shot her a look that nearly lifted her off the floor.

"I, uh, I don't know. We need to call somebody. Cam's aunt. We need to call her. She needs to know. She's gotta know."

Heywood stopped in his tracks, and snatched his shades off. He growled under his breath. "Ya ain't gonna call nobody, ya hear me? Especially not Cam's aunt. No fuckin' way. We don't even know nothin' to call nobody about."

"It's not like you can keep this quiet, Heywood. You know that the folks on this island already know. They already know. This island ain't but this," she snapped her fingers, "big." She ran to the window and lifted the blinds and pointed outside. "See? There's a crowd outside already. People talk. What you gonna do? Make them sign your goddamned N-Snips? You can't control everything." Allison's voice and hands were trembling.

Everyone in the room stopped whatever they were doing and fell quiet, anxious to see Heywood's response. Uncharacteristically, he said nothing, just glared at Allison.

Allison's chest heaved, and her voice remained amplified. "It's not right. Cam's aunt needs to know. I'm sure she'd be on her way here if she knew.

"And we need to let her know before she hears it from anyone else. Hell, I'm sure somebody on this island has a computer and is spreading the story on the web right now. And you know that the local TV stations and newspapers are already looking into it. This is major. It's only a matter of time before everyone in the States has it. We need to get in front of it."

"I don't care," he replied. "No one's gonna make a mockery of Cam, not now an' not ever. Nothin' leaks out of this room, ya hear me?"

He turned to Duck and barked. "Don't let nobody make no phone calls. None. Not 'til I say so."

"Got it, dawg," Duck said.

Big Mac turned from the window and folded his arms across his chest. "No disrespect, Heywood, but I don't work for you. An' I believe what Allison said is what's up. Cam would want Aunt Mary here."

Duck eyed Heywood with a "You want me to handle this G.I. Joe mutha fucka?" look. He had been itching to bring Big Mac down, but Heywood shook his head.

"I hear ya Mac, an' I know ya upset. An' I'm not sayin' that we're not gonna call Cam's aunt. I just said we gonna wait until we know somethin'. Ya don't want her to have no heart attack, do ya?

"Nobody talks to no one, understand?" Heywood said, and whirled his index finger around the room. "No one. Not even your mommas. In fact, y'all are all under NDAs, ya heard?" He then shoved his shades back on, and scowled at everyone in the room as they mumbled in agreement. "Don't make me take your damned cellphones and throw them in the fuckin' ocean."

He nodded at Duck. "An' go find whoever's in charge of this Popsicle stand an' let 'em know that they've been forewarned. If I see one Tweet or anythin', Imma clock somebody. If one word about Cam leaks out, I mean one word, a verb, adverb, noun, or even a pronoun, I'll shut this motherfucka down. I swear, I'll own this bitch."

Duck nodded, and scrambled out of the waiting room, towards the hospital lobby and the administrator's office.

Necy lifted her tear-stained face, her makeup streaked beyond repair. "We need to pray, people. We gotta pray."

Big Mac stepped up first. "Y'all heard the lady. We need to pray. Now, close your goddamned eyes and get with it."

Everyone except Heywood created a prayer circle. As they wiped their tears and closed their eyes, Necy lead a choked-filled, up-lifting prayer while Heywood continued pacing and swearing out loud.

Outside, the collected crowd of onlookers began to pray, too. They had heard that the volcano had shaken the earth, and rumors spread rampantly about who had been injured. As rumors swirled that the American superstar had been the one gravely wounded, the locals had flocked to the tiny island hospital to pray for her recovery. In the middle of the islanders holding vigil stood the old grey-eyed medicine man. He stood, leaning on his knobby cane, and with his blank eyes fixed on the sky, he prayed toward heaven.

As both groups of prayer ended, the doors from the ER swung open, and a tall, thin, doctor clad in green scrubs emerged. Wearing a mask, surgical hat, and rimless glasses, only his eyes were visible, and they looked tired.

He slid his mask down until it hung under his chin and looked around the room. "Are you all 'ere with the burn victims?" he asked.

Heywood immediately stepped forward, while everyone fell in behind him. "Yeah, Doc. We're here with her. Can I see her? I need to see her. How, uh, how's she doin'?"

The doctor squinted from behind his glasses. "Are you the next of kin?"

The words 'next of kin' caused everyone to gasp.

"Next of kin?" Allison asked, and clutched her bag in her arms. "Your don't mean that she's—"

"No ma'am," the doctor said, cutting her off. "I just need to confirm that I am speaking with a family member."

"Yeah, well, uh, I'm her fiancé," Heywood said without missing a beat. Allison gulped, and Torrie and Necy elbowed each other.

"I'm Dr. Mangrum and I've been working with both of the burn patients. Before I can provide any information, I need consent from an actual family member or a legal representative. For both patients."

"You can't even tell us how she's, well, how they're doing, doctor?" Allison asked. "I work for Camara, and I'm a very close family friend. Her family is in the United States, and we haven't even contacted them about the accident, because we didn't know what to say."

"I understand, Miss, but I have to adhere to hospital protocol. Right now, because of the confusion while they were being brought in, we didn't correctly identify the patients. We're testing their blood to determine the type, but we need to be able to verify the results based on their medical history."

"What the fuck?" Heywood bellowed, and beat his chest with both fists. "What ya mean, ya don't know which one is which? *Shee-it*. We gotta get Cam outta this bootleg, backwoods clinic. Right now. They don't even know who the fuck she is."

"Don't worry, sir. Both patients are getting the best care possible," Dr. Mangrum said.

"I don't give a fuck about that other broad. I'm only concerned about Cam. An' I know who she is. She had on the, uh, shit! Torrie! What the hell did she have on?" Heywood spun around and glared at Torrie.

"Her clothes were gone, Heywood," Torrie said, her voice quivering. "Remember? We cut them off when we, when we—" She couldn't finish as she broke down, and Big Mac kept her from falling.

"They were both dressed alike anyway," Allison said, her voice shaking, but controlled. She steadied herself and said, "I know that Cam has a blood donor card, and we're trying to get it, but if you need me to, I can identify her now, doctor."

"No, you won't, Allison. I'll identify her. I will," Heywood said and faced the doctor. "Y'all had betta be sure Cam gets the best damned care ya got in this fuckin' joint."

Before Dr. Mangrum could respond, Duck reappeared, with a short, stout, leisure suit wearing man trailing beside him. He quickly identified himself as Maurice Davies, the hospital administrator.

Mr. Davies held his hand out as if to hush the doctor. "Dr. Mangrum, before you continue, Mr. Harter here has explained to me that we have a very important person in the ER. One of the burn patients is the singer, Starr, from the States. Due to the nature of the accident and Miss Starr's fame, we have to handle this very delicately."

"We're going to ensure that the crowds disperse outside, or at least remain a respectable distance from the building. All other patients and their families will be treated in another area of the hospital, to ensure Miss Starr's privacy. And no information will be given to the media."

Heywood nodded to Duck, and extended a hand to Mr. Davies. "Thank you, Mr. Davies. And I'm sure that Duck, I mean, my assistant Mr. Harter told ya who I am," Heywood said, grabbing his arm.

"Indeed," Mr. Davies said, and you could almost hear a cash register ringing. "I am very aware of who you are, Mr. Heywood. Who wouldn't know you, sir?"

"Good. Then ya know that I expect an' demand the best. Especially for Starr. An' I'm quite generous to those that prove worthy of my generosity."

Mr. Davies nodded, with an expression of concern on his face. "If you'll pardon us for one moment," he said, and led Dr. Mangrum to an isolated corner. Duck grabbed Heywood, and gripped his shoulder. "Don't worry, Hey. Ya know I took care of everything."

After a few long moments, Mr. Davies and Dr. Mangrum returned, with the good doctor looking like he was caught between a rock and a hard place. In the uncomfortable space between hospital bureaucracy and his Hippocratic Oath.

Dr. Mangrum began speaking. "Both of the patients have been burned fairly extensively. We're managing their pain to prevent them from going into deeper shock, which would further compromise their condition. They are both being given antibiotics, to combat infection. They're both unconscious, which is probably the best thing for them, at the moment. But, rest assured, we're watching them very, very closely. Every moment is critical to their recovery.

"Now, although I can't give you their specific prognosis, I do need to obtain the medical background of both patients."

"I, uh, don't mean to sound harsh, but, I don't give a—" Heywood started, but Allison cut him off.

"Um, Dr. Mangrum, we have only minimal medical history on Starr, uh, Ms. Addison, and we don't have any history or information on Marisol. She's from here, and I understand she's pretty much an orphan. She doesn't have any family here, and I've given the nurse all the information that I have."

"Thank you, but you do understand that it is imperative that we get a better understanding of their medical backgrounds. Knowing that information can be the difference between life and death."

"I just want to know how Cam is, doctor. That's all. And if she's going to be okay," Heywood said.

Dr. Mangrum glanced at Mr. Davies and proceeded slowly. "We really can't say. They have both suffered severe burns, and required blood transfusions. We're trying to restore their fluids intravenously, and to stabilize them. They are both in a pretty precarious situation. Normally, serious burn victims like your friends are air-lifted over to Antigua or to other better-equipped burn centers, but right now, their vitals are too unstable."

"What ya mean?" Heywood's voice rose.

"We don't have the facilities to properly treat them," Dr. Mangrum said, and looked around the room at the anxious eyes focused on him.

Heywood repeated his earlier question, and this time he got in the doctor's face. The doctor cautiously stepped backward.

"Let me be more clear. The burns these young ladies have experienced are life-threatening. This hospital does not have the facilities to care for burn victims of this magnitude. We've done all that we can, in terms of cleaning the affected regions, but they should be moved to a burn center that can better treat their condition. However, as I said, neither can be moved right now."

"Can't be moved?" Heywood scoffed. "If ya don't have what my girl needs, then I'll get it." He turned to Duck again. "Call the States. Find some doctor, some specialist somewhere that can fly a hospital down here. Hell, find a flying hospital, goddammit. Get somebody here! Now!"

Mr. Davies reached for Heywood's arm, but he snatched it away. "Now, Mr. Heywood. As Dr. Mangrum said, Ms. Addison can't be moved. No physician is going to move her in the condition she's in. She has to be stabilized first."

The doctor continued. "And once she's stable and able to be moved, she won't be able to go very far. She needs to get to the closest burn center. When she's stable, I will send her to the Luis Eduardo Aybar Hospital Burn Center, the main burn unit of the Dominican Republic."

Heywood shook his head. "No way. That's not going to happen. I don't want her going to some other third-world country. I want her back in the States. What about Miami?"

Dr. Mangrum shook his head, and sighed. "Mr. Davies, I'll leave this to you. I need to get back to the patients." He turned to Allison. "We really need to get in touch with their next of kin. Do you think you could help?"

Allison choked back tears. "I-I-I can help. Is it really that serious, doctor? I mean, she is going to live, isn't she?"

"Your friends have been critically injured. We're doing all that we can."

"Is there anything we can do to help?" Torrie asked.

Dr. Mangrum folded his arms, and his expression relaxed. "Well, we may need some more blood. So, if any of you would consider donating, it would help." Dropping his arms by his side, he sighed heavily. "Other than that, I would suggest that you pray." Dr. Mangrum composed himself. "Now, if you'll excuse me, I'd like to get back and check on their progress."

Heywood cut the doctor's path off. "That's not good enough. Duck, do what I said. Get me somebody down here now. Never mind, I'll make some calls myself. I'm not gonna take this bullshit as the final answer on Cam." He turned toward the doctor, with a buck in his posture. He set his jaw. "Hear this. I wanna see her. Now."

This time, a wary Dr. Mangrum didn't step back. "Really only next of kin are able to see them. They're isolated and prone to serious infection. Only immediate family is allowed."

Heywood glared at the doctor. "I told ya, I'm her family."

Mr. Davies gently reached for Heywood's arm. "I'm sure that we can work something out. If you're willing to sign the proper forms, shower and put on a protective suit. Then I think we can let you see her. But only you."

"I'm the only one who matters."

A winded, sweat-soaked Parsley reappeared in the ER while Heywood was preparing to see Cam, and handed Allison Cam's messenger bag. She rummaged through it, desperately pushing aside Cam's personal items such as her iPod® and songbook, until she found Cam's wallet. She quickly opened it and pulled out Cam's donor card. Triumphant, Allison and Big Mac scrambled to find Dr. Mangrum, but when they were unable to locate him, they reluctantly settled for one of the nurses. Allison relinquished the ID, but demanded that the nurse return it as soon as they had obtained positive confirmation.

A few moments later, Heywood, freshly showered and wearing scrubs, mesh hat, mask, and protective shoe coverings, stood outside the tiny intensive care unit, while a similarly dressed Mr. Davies blocked the door to Cam and Marisol's room.

"Okay, I'm ready, Davies," Heywood announced, and tried to brush past the administrator.

Mr. Davies shook his head and placed a stubby arm across the doorway. "Not yet, not so fast. I need to make sure you're prepared for what you're about to see."

"I'm prepared. Now, get out my face, an' step."

"Are you sure? It's nothing like anything you're ever witnessed before. It's pretty grim."

"Look, Davies. How do you know what I've seen? I'm a grown-assed man. I'll make sure you an' your little 'hospital' get yo' donation for allowin' me to see my girl, but right now, I want ya to get the fuck outta my way. Now."

Heywood shoved Davies aside and barged into the room. It was a small area, with a handful of nurses and Dr. Mangrum observing Cam and Marisol through a windowed wall, monitoring two machines that were connected to others in the ICU. Sheets tented around them, they lay on egg-crated beds, surrounded by clicking, beeping, and humming machines. Their bodies still and lifeless, the only thing moving in the room were the ventilators. Heywood stopped suddenly, and addressed the doctor.

"Have ya figured out which one is Cam, or do I have to do that for ya?" His voice was muffled behind the mask, but his words were clear.

"The results just came in, and as luck would have it, they both have similar blood types," Dr. Mangrum replied.

Before Heywood could blow a gasket, Dr. Mangrum proceeded. "But, thank God one was positive and one was negative, and the nurse just went in to place their charts."

Heywood was indignant. "I'll see about that. I know Cam, and I'll let ya know if ya coconuts have got it twisted or not," he said and swung open the door to the room, causing it to hit the wall.

The shrouded nurse dropped the charts as Heywood stormed into the room. "I'm sorry, sir. I was just placing their—"

"Get out!" Heywood yelled.

The nurse scrambled to pick up the boards, and quickly glanced at the covers. She then clumsily shoved them in the holders at the foot of each of the beds.

The room's temperature felt like the inside of a refrigerator, and the chilly air was choking with a pungent mix of burnt flesh and various medicines. Heywood manned up and swallowed, and started walking toward the beds.

Mr. Davies stuck his head in the room. "Please calm yourself, Mr. Heywood. You must be very quiet. These patients are critically ill."

Heywood swung around to see an angered Dr. Mangrum and an upset nursing staff staring at him. The doctor motioned for the nurse to leave and she scurried past him.

Heywood's eyes fell on both of the injured women. Both of their heads were wrapped and their greased eyes swollen shut. "Her, their, um, faces. How bad were they damaged?"

Mr. Davies shook his head. "Yes, but I don't know to what degree. The swelling is part of the trauma, more or less, and should come down over time. If they survive."

"So, you're tellin' me that she's gonna look like some kind of monster or somethin'?"

"No, I'm not saying that. There may be some scarring or disfigurement, but I don't know. Right now, it's about prayin' that they'll both live."

Lowering his voice, Heywood shifted his glance toward Mr. Davies. He scowled at the administrator. "Look, Mortimer. I want some privacy, ya got that? Tell all these folks to get the hell outta here."

Mr. Davies stammered. "Uh, my name is Maurice. And we can't do that. They need constant monitoring. Constant."

"An' I need some time alone wit' my girl, ya hear me? An' after all that I've laced ya wit', I'm sure ya can make that happen. In fact, I know ya will." He gave Mr. Davies a dirty look, and then he stepped toward the bed closest to the observation window.

As Mr. Davies slinked into the nursing area, Heywood looked at the two women, and his chest sunk. He couldn't see their faces, for they were draped with sheets. He peeked at both. They were almost identical. Size wise and in their mummified state, Heywood couldn't tell them apart. They were lightly covered with white burn pads and gauze, and their wounds were too much for him. Still unsure which one was which, Heywood checked the chart from the first bed and exhaled. It read: KENT, M.

Mr. Davies opened the door and stuck his head in. "You have three minutes. That's all I can allow."

Heywood placed his fist to his lip and turned toward the second bed. "I just wanna know if she's gonna make it. If she's gonna be aiight."

The corners of Mr. Davies mouth dropped and he shook his head, and shut the door behind him. His voice was a low whisper. "It doesn't look good for either one right now. They have respiratory problems. They're on respirators to help them breathe." Mr. Davies pointed to the tiny machine that had the blue balloon attached to it. It filled and expelled, like a plastic lung.

"They can both survive, though, mainly because they're young and in good shape. But, the damage has been done. It'll probably take months, maybe even years for them to recover."

"She's on a respirator. She needs help breathin'?" Heywood repeated Davies's words like a child. "Respiratory problems? Ya mean somethin' might've happened to her voice?"

"It's possible. We don't know."

"What about her looks? How she gonna look?"

Mr. Davies checked over his shoulder to see if the medical staff was still present, and they were. "Look, Mr. Kennard, we don't know. But you can see that both of their faces have been injured. Who knows? I can't really say anything more."

He opened the door, and motioned for the doctor and nurses to leave. "You have three minutes. We'll be right outside, and the staff will return promptly."

Heywood reached for Cam's arm, and then withdrew his hand. He knew he couldn't touch her. His once beautiful girl was now destroyed. He leaned toward her, and the acrid smell of the burns permeated through his mask, causing his stomach to bubble. It sickened him.

"Cam, baby, Cam," he whispered. "I can't believe this shit happened to you. Not you." He shook his head, and swallowed hard, his Adam's apple bobbing in his neck. Hot tears burned his lids, and he looked away and tried to focus. Biting his lower lip, he collected himself.

"What am I gonna do? I'm sorry this happened, ya gotta believe me. I just don't know what to do. I can't imagine you lookin' like some kinda monster or somethin'. Not you. An' not bein' able to sing. I know ya wouldn't wanna live like that." He sniffled, his voice was tinged with emotion. "I just know it."

He paused and looked toward the observation window, and realized that his private time was quickly ending. "I don't want ya to suffer, baby. I don't. An' I know ya don't want me to suffer either," he said and traced the clear plastic tube that was connected to the ventilator.

"I know you'd understand, Cam," he said, pinching the tubing so that the airway was cut off. The monitor light on the machine changed from green to yellow, and a low beep emanated. "Sometimes bad things happen to good people, an' I'm sorry that this shit happened to ya.

"Ya know we've been ridin' together for a while, an' we've been buildin'. You an' me have done some phenomenal things. Made some beautiful music together. But shit's changed, an' I gotta roll with the punches. Ya know how I do. I gotta do me. I gotta make the best of a fucked up situation. But I'll be aiight. Just like I know ya will, Baby Girl."

He tightened his grip on the tube and squeezed it until the sides met. The monitor light changed to red, and the sound of the alarm blared. "Good night, Sweet Princess."

Outside of the hospital, in the prayer vigil, the old medicine man fell to his knees and howled toward heaven.

THE SERVICE on that snowy Monday morning in December 2006 was worthy of the star she was. The world was mourning, and had come together to give Cam the home going service she deserved. Aunt Mary had insisted that the service remain private, at Cam's home church, First Baptist Church. Though distraught, Aunt Mary allowed Allison to plan the ceremony, but she severely limited the invitees. Only a small number of Cam's industry associates had been invited. The majority of invitations were reserved for Cam's extended church family, the officers of her fan clubs, and the children from the youth organization Cam supported.

There would be a closed casket, with no cameras, recording devices or cellphones allowed. Aunt Mary was determined to have a traditional, dignified homegoing, one befitting her darling niece Camara, not the superstar Starr.

The entertainment industry was in a state of shock and suspended animation. One of its most promising stars had ascended in a spectacular sense, and just as she was beginning to shine her brightest, she had been extinguished. Virtually no information had been released about the accident or its aftermath, dealing the media a sore blow. The Internet was afire with conspiracy theories and supposition, and speculation was rampant.

The mainstream and African American media were dogged in their pursuit of the truth, but there was a communications blackout. With everyone sworn to secrecy, under threat of being blackballed or catching a beat down, their lips were sealed ultimately by Heywood's No Snitchin' Papers. No one breathed a word.

It took days for the media to even confirm who was present at the time of the accident, and when Artist and Katt were finally identified, Art issued a standard "no comment" and Katt released a statement saying, "Ms. Jones is too distraught to discuss the death of her friend and entertainer," through her rep. It was only known that Cam had been fatally injured on the set of a video shoot in Montserrat.

The media stayed on the story, convinced there was more to it. Payoffs to the officials and administrators at the hospital in Montserrat did not uncover any titillating facts. It was if Cam's death was a bad dream that everyone wanted to wake up from.

Heywood had gone into seclusion; it was rumored that he would only surface for the funeral. His Twitter page was updated with a single line comment, "The World Shines a Little Less Bright Without Our Starr." Some of the blogs reported that Jamie had been hospitalized when he heard Cam had died, but he had checked himself out of Cedars Sinai in time to attend the service. It was rumored that he was going to sing at the funeral, but up to the last moment, was unsure if he had the strength or the ability to do it.

Media trucks from all over the world descended upon the red-brick edifice, with reporters, photographers and video cameramen providing live coverage of every sorrowful moment. BET, MTV, CNN, and a host of local, and syndicated radio and television personalities filed solemnly into the church. DC's finest, the Metropolitan Police Department, lined Sheriff Road in an attempt to maintain order among the legions of weepy-eyed, bundled-up fans and well-wishers with tear-stained cheeks who lined the snow-covered street to say goodbye to their beloved Camara.

Local radio stations, WKYS, WHUR, and WPGC, dedicated the day to Starr, playing all of her recordings and interviews, while cutting in testimonies from listeners and fans. The list of invitees was broad. Local dignitaries, including DC's mayor, slowly proceeded into the service alongside industry associates like Manny, Starr's road manager, and Billy, her lighting technician.

Leading the small contingency of Cam's fan club dignitaries was the wheelchair-bound Rashad. Allison made sure that he attended, and Big Mac had been dispatched to ensure that Starr's biggest fan would be present to pay his last respects. Big Mac assisted Rashad when he arrived in a black van with several other fan club members. As the motorized lift on the van lowered his black-shrouded chair in front of the church, a sobbing Rashad held a single white rose in his gloved hand.

A clearly distraught Jamie arrived in a somber black on black limo, carrying a single red rose. Accompanied by two beefy bodyguards and his close friend, the celebrated black action movie star Gary Edwards, Jamie could barely walk. He declined all interviews, didn't confirm if he was going to sing during the service, and then quickly ducked into the church.

Then came the moment the crowd had been waiting for, and didn't want to see. The confirmation that their beloved Starr was indeed gone. The bright white Rolls Royce hearse inching its way through the crowded street left no doubt. The processional caused the crowd to gasp and emote, and tussle to get a closer look at the flower-strewn white and gold casket it carried behind its oversized glass windows. As it stopped at the front of the church, piercing wails and loud sobs arose from the throngs, and the DCMPD struggled to maintain order and control.

Trailing directly behind the police-led hearse was a white Bentley limousine, with black privacy windows. The crowd hushed as the casket was removed from the hearse, and the passengers slowly exited from the limo. With a team of black-suited bodyguards and armed policemen surrounding them, an uncharacteristically subdued Heywood assisted Cam's Aunt Mary and her wheelchair-bound grandmother to the service. Deftly ignoring the paparazzi, reporters, and cameras, a soberly dressed Heywood played his part well. He was a stoic pillar of strength during the family's period of bereavement. In his conservative black cashmere coat, plain dark shades, and black fedora, he was quiet and commanding, seemingly a changed man after witnessing the tragic event. To watch him selflessly hold Aunt Mary's arm, and humbly push the wheelchair of her grandmother was almost surreal. Flashbulbs flashed and the shutters of countless cameras clicked, as if to capture the second most shocking and surreal events of the month.

Heywood's iconic photograph was carried in numerous mainstream magazines and newspapers the next day, and was etched into the memory of all who bore witness to it. And it was rumored, though never confirmed, that Jamie did join the choir in song, and nearly stretched out everyone in the pews with his touching rendition of *Precious Lord, Take My Hand.*

chapter sixteen

MASKED AIDES buzzed around her, adjusting her dressings and bedding. Each time they touched her, it sent ripples of pain through her body, but she didn't wince. She said nothing. She kept her eyes tightly closed while they were there, wishing they were gone.

They left after a few long moments, and the patient opened her eyes. Lying on the air chamber mattress, she stared hazily through ointment-filled eyes at the drawn blinds that closed out the clear blue Caribbean sky. Her breathing was shallow, and every breath she drew was painful, as the restrictive bindings of pressure garments were wrapped tightly around every part of her body.

Every five minutes, a machine would hum, and a gush of warm air would rush into the mattress, and she would groan. The slight movement of her body was uncomfortable, and tears would brim in her eyes. Sounds were muted by the throbbing in her head, and a kaleidoscope of thoughts ran rampant in her mind.

"What the hell happened to me?" she thought. She remembered being on the water, on a boat, a big luxurious boat, and then feeling like she had been run over by that same vessel. Then she was on a beautiful tropical island. She remembered laughing, and many different faces and

voices. Everyone was excited, and music was playing. Loud music. Bright lights were shining, and people were dancing. Then the memories stopped, and a piercing pain shot through her head.

Consumed with agony and fractured memories, she was unaware of the doctor and nurse observing her through a small window.

★

"'Ere's her chart, doctor," the nurse said, as she passed the loose-leaf binder to him. Nurse Ora was short, but thick and sturdy, and strong across her broad shoulders. Her years of experience had allowed her to work in many areas in the hospital, from intake to recovery. Ora had seen her share of smart alecky interns and residents, so she knew what to expect from this newbie. She placed her hands on her ample hips and waited for his response.

The doctor opened the book and frowned. There were only a few papers inside, and when he flipped through the pages, he found the information was quite generic.

"What's this? You all call this a chart? There's barely anything in here," he mumbled, and glanced at the RN.

Ora cleared her throat, and placed her index finger in the air. "As I told you, we've only had this patient for a few days. She was injured at one of the outer, smaller islands. Montserrat, it was, and she had to stay there until she was stable enough to be transferred. So, aside from keepin' her fluids up and monitorin' her vitals, there ain't been much for us to document. It's not like she's really talkin' that much or anythin' and we certainly ain't gonna make anythin' up."

Despite his deeply religious beliefs, Dr. Randolph Williams was growing a bit tired of the nurse's surly attitude. He knew that hazing the new guy was part of his indoctrination. Hell, it came with the territory, but everyone was in the same boat. If the goal is to help the patient, why try to make it more difficult for someone who was just trying to do his job well? He'd have to pray for her.

Randolph Williams was a recent graduate of Dartmouth Medical School, and after being sequestered in the bowels of New Hampshire, he was intent on getting out and getting his life. He was ecstatic about his graduation, but his full ride fellowship required that he perform charitable medical work for a period in a third world nation. Shortly after graduating, and a year or so after his grueling residency, Randolph headed to the Congo for a six-month stint working with the international Red Cross.

He actually enjoyed working in Africa, and when he returned to the States, he studied for his boards and took a residency position at Northwestern Memorial Hospital in Chicago. Before he accepted the position, he obtained the hospital's approval for his working in the USA Freedom Corps, a program where doctors volunteer their time in underserved countries. It was his way of giving back, and Randolph even donated some of his time to the city's free clinic whenever his schedule would permit.

A second generation college graduate, Randolph and his older sister Robin were raised in suburbs of Philly, by late in life parents who were both overprotective and deeply religious. As children, Randolph and Robin had been exposed to a number of so-called "white" activities, such as lacrosse, field hockey, and swimming. Because of this, they were always considered Oreos by their black peers and family members.

Eventually, Robin rebelled and chose to chart her own course in life. But, Randolph, hiding behind his thick glasses, acquiesced and abided by his parents strict doctrines. He moved from prep schools, with summers abroad, to the Ivy League, staying in New Hampshire for both undergrad and graduate school. Though his parents thought that they were doing the right thing by gearing his social activities towards all things wholesome, good, and White, they didn't realize the impact minimizing his interactions with other black folks would have.

It didn't help that most of his relatives were graduates of HBCUs, and that they were steering their children toward their alma maters, while he was off to the lily White region of the Upper Northeast. With his nose stuck in books for the last five years, he was an isolated prisoner of his own success.

Though separated from Robin for nearly all of his adult life, they were still close. Though polar opposites, she accepted who he was, and didn't try to convert him. While her conversations with him were peppered with the latest slang, she always translated for him. And on the rare occasions that he could get away, he visited her in Atlanta, where she had been working as a high school teacher since graduating from Spelman College. Robin was proud of her brother and his accomplishments, but she was always down to take him shopping for some trendier "gear," and urged him to see an optometrist to get fitted for contact lenses. Of course, Randolph had never had the time, although he promised to do so every time they spoke on the phone.

Living the life of a deeply religious, studious, and sheltered Black man had not been easy, but Randolph didn't want any sympathy. He had a plan, and was committed to working it. Though quiet and reserved on the outside, he knew inwardly that he had a lot of resolve. And that resolve would prove to be the greatest asset in obtaining his greatest accomplishment. And it was not what one would think. Besides obtaining a medical degree, his biggest achievement was not getting hooked up with a white girl. And that was almost harder than getting his degree.

"So, generally speaking, how has the patient, Miss, Miss," he glanced at the chart, "Miss Kent been doing?"

Nurse Ora adjusted her attitude and ran down the specifics of Marisol's case. Tests indicated that there was no apparent damage to the lungs or the airway, yet the patient seemed reluctant to speak. Her burns were severe, both second and third degree, but thankfully, they were primarily located on anterior section of her body. The majority were located on her upper thigh area and torso, and on a small section on the right side of her face. The preliminary care she had received had helped reduce the damage to her skin, but the patient was going to require extensive treatment in order to fully recover.

She hadn't been able to eat anything yet, she was being fed by IV, and she was on 24-hour intravenous pain medication. They had not determined if there had been any damage to Miss Kent's vision, and had made no determination yet on her mental state.

Dr. Williams listened intently to the nurse, and reviewed the miniscule notes in the chart. After aiding some of the victims from 9/11, he had developed a keen interest in working with people suffering from burn injuries. After his first nine months at Northwestern, an opportunity had opened in a burn center in the Dominican Republic. One of his fellow doctors had been scheduled to take the opening, but had to cancel due to health problems. Randolph had jumped at the opportunity, first to get out of the bone-chilling Chicago weather, and second, because he'd get a chance to work in one of the most innovative burn centers in the world, under Dr. Luis Salazar, an internationally-renowned burn specialist.

Dr. Salazar was a leader in the practice of promoting patient wellness through a combination of holistic and spiritual support and medicine. Randolph was very interested in this innovative new practice and wanted to see if this practice was a viable alternative, especially when patients were burn victims.

While all of the patients in the center suffered from injuries of various types and degrees, Miss Kent was one of the worst. Her survival alone had been a near miracle, based on inner strength, and not the usual familial support. Even though her medical history was sparse, the words "No Immediate Family" had been written clearly in her Montserrat medical records. That immediately triggered something in his mind. A good family support system was usually an integral part of the patient's healing process. He was concerned that this key element was lacking, and would have to compensate for this in her care plan.

Dr. Williams thanked the nurse and steeled himself to enter the patient's room. As he quietly closed the door behind him, the patient didn't move. She just kept staring at the blinds.

There was something about her. Even as she lay there, there was an aura about her that was warm and beckoning. He didn't know if it was sympathy or pity that he felt, but it wasn't a feeling that a doctor was supposed to have. He cleared his throat, and walked around to the side of the bed, stepping into her line of sight. She didn't blink or even acknowledge him.

"Miss Kent? I'm Dr. Williams. I'm going to be working with you. How are you feeling today?"

"*Miss Kent?*" she thought. "*Why is he calling me that?*" Still, she said nothing, just continued to gaze out the window as if she didn't see him.

"Can you speak?" No response. "Well, okay then. I'm going to perform a few simple examinations on you, and then check your dressings. Please respond if you can, okay?"

As he got closer to her, there was that sensation again. Fragile, covered in bandages, but still, there was something definitely alluring about her. Dr. Williams went through a series of questions and answers to check her mental capacity. She didn't respond. He shined a small light in her eyes, and she didn't blink. Dr. Williams scribbled a few notes on the chart, and looked for a box of latex gloves. Squeezing his large hands into a pair, he lifted an area of the dressing on her leg to see how it was progressing. It was still very raw, very raw.

Another nurse came in, and he spoke with her briefly about the patient's care, all the while observing the patient, who seemed patently detached. He ordered an ophthalmology assessment, to see if there had been any damage to her eyes that would account for her fixed gaze. After the nurse left, Dr. Williams announced his departure.

"Okay, Miss Kent. I'll see you later."

Her non–responsiveness continued for the next several visits. Even after conferring with Dr. Salazar and getting an okay from the ophthalmologist, her behavior remained unchanged. He decided to give her until the end of the week before calling for a psychiatric consult. On his next visit, Dr. Williams ventured to slightly open the blinds.

"Oww," she whispered, and it startled him.

"That hurts," she said, her voice small and faint.

Dr. Williams quickly closed the blinds and suppressed a smile. "Well, she speaks. How are you today, Miss Kent? Or do I have your permission to call you Marisol?"

"That burns my eyes. I'm sorry, but it's too bright."

He pulled up a chair, and sat down near her so that he could look in her face. "You need the sunlight. It's good for you and your healing. If you stay in here, in constant darkness, it will not help you get better. Mentally or physically."

"Get better? What's wrong with me?" Her eyes questioned him, and she grimaced as she tried to raise her head and move her arms. Searing pain jabbed at the inside of her diaphragm.

"Try to be still, okay?" He rested an arm against her railing, being careful not to move the bed. "I'm sorry to be the one to tell you, but you were burned over a large part of your body. You were treated at the hospital in Montserrat, but you were moved here to this burn treatment center in the Dominican Republic because we can take better care of you." He paused and let the words sink in. After a few moments, he continued. "I'm Dr. Willams, and if we have anything to do with it, with the grace of God, you'll get better."

She tried to move, but again, the searing pain stopped her. She looked down and saw the bandages, and her eyes immediately teared up. Dr. Williams grabbed a tissue from a box next to the bed, and dabbed her eyes.

"Now, now, Marisol. It's good to see that your tear ducts work," he said, forcing a smile. "But you'll have to take it easy. We have a plan to help you with your ROM, or range of motion skills, and it looks like we can get started on that soon." He smiled and she lowered her eyes.

"How bad am I?" her voice was still faint.

"I'm going to be honest with you. Your burns were pretty severe," he said, and then quickly added, "but nothing we can't help." Dr. Williams looked puzzled, and tilted his ear toward her, and asked her to repeat what she had just said. When she did, he checked her chart again. "You're from Montserrat, right? I thought you would've had more of an accent than you have."

"Maybe it got burned too," she said softly.

Dr. Williams tried not to laugh, but appreciated her self-deprecating humor. He admired the fact that despite the terrible pain she must be in, her disposition was still pleasant. There was really something special about this young lady.

Her throat was bone dry, and achy. "Can I have somethin' to drink?"

"That's a good sign," he said. "But, for right now, we can only give you ice chips. We need to see if you are able to tolerate fluids. And if you can, we can get you off the IV and onto some liquids. And then solids."

"Can I have some gum?" she asked.

Dr. Williams smiled. "Well, let's see. I don't want you to do any excessive movements like chewing at the moment. At least until we see if your facial muscles don't interfere with or make your neck muscles sore. The minute we're sure that your vascular system is okay, I'll bring you a pack of gum myself."

She looked down, and hoped that the nurse would come soon with her ice chips. She tried to be pleasant, but she really wanted to scream. "By the way, where am I?"

"You're in Santo Domingo in the Dominican Republic. At the Aybar Burn Center. You're going to get really good care here, I promise."

"But, you sound American. What are you doin' here?"

Dr. Williams explained how he had come to the center, and gave her a little information about himself. He wanted her to feel more comfortable with him, but he didn't want to become too familiar, or cross the line between patient and doctor. But she was easy to talk to.

"Now, I need to explain a couple of things to you. Because of the circumstances of your arrival, we didn't have a lot of history or detail to rely on in charting your recovery. However, we made a judgment call, and I hope you don't mind. But, due to your age, which we are estimating to be in your early twenties, we assumed that you would be a great candidate for a cutting edge procedure in treating burn victims.

"It's called a bio-bandage. We used human fetal cells that should speed up and dramatically improve your healing process."

"Bio-bandage?" she asked, her voice a faint whisper.

"Yes, I realize that if you are Catholic, it may go against your faith, but believe me, these cells were donated by caring individuals who wanted to assist patients like you who have suffered severe burns."

She didn't recall how she had gotten burned, or even when. She had a million questions, but her mind fixed on the *severe burns* statement he had just made. Since the details on her chart were so sketchy, even Dr. Williams couldn't fill in the blanks and tell her how she had been burned. All he could do was encourage her to focus on the future. And on getting well.

"Getting well is up to you, Marisol. No matter what these charts say, if you have faith and conviction, you can be healed. The mental and spiritual aspects of healing are just as important as the clinical."

He cleared his throat. "We have a holistic approach to here, and it's important that we try to help our patients in every aspect of their lives. And we've also found that having family or loved ones around is also very helpful to the healing process. So, is there anyone you'd like for us to contact or notify? There wasn't anyone indicated in your charts."

She panicked and nearly stared to cry. "No, there's no one to contact 'bout me, doctor," she said quietly.

"Well, don't worry. We'll take good care of you. And taking good care of you will start today," he said, his bedside manner warm and sincere.

She tried to appreciate his words, but the reality was crippling. He wanted her to get up and get moving to help the skin renew itself and to reduce her difficulty in walking. Even though it hadn't been a long time since the accident, every moment was critical. She didn't know why or what inside of her was compelling her, but she was determined to do whatever she could to get better. She just had to. So she nodded in agreement.

Dr. Williams smiled. "This is just the first step. We are prayerful, if you don't mind me saying so, that you will heal very well, and there are some other progressive treatments that you would be a candidate for if you still scar heavily. But, we can cross that bridge when we get there. Until then, we'll just keep the faith."

He seemed sincere and harmless, but she really didn't know if she could trust the good doctor or not. She had no way of knowing who he was or what he could do, but she had to admit that there was something in his demeanor and a compassion in his spirit that put her at ease. Then she did something she hadn't done in a while. She smiled. And even though it hurt, it was a good hurt.

The ice chips turned to water which eventually turned to clear juice and broth. As the days turned to weeks, Dr. Williams and Marisol forged a strong bond based on trust and a mutual sense of loneliness. On his days off, instead of frolicking on the beach or partying in the nightclubs, Dr. Williams spent them with Marisol. He was always pushing her around in her wheelchair, or observing her while she got her treatments. And, as he promised, he brought her a pack of gum as soon as she was able to chew without soreness.

★

Getting to know her came easily for Dr. Williams. They had a spiritual foundation, and he would often read scripture to her. They would venture down to the hospital chapel and spend moments in silence. Eventually they even shared prayers.

Following through with her plan of care, Marisol's psychiatric evaluation revealed that she had effectively blocked out the trauma of the fire, and refused to discuss her past. The psychiatrist noted that this was not unusual, but that her mental state would require ongoing analysis.

Her rigorous physical therapy sessions were getting results and the once vegetative patient was finally thriving. Her scars were healing, thanks to the aggressive approach they used to manage the damaged skin tissue, and she was able to walk with the assistance of a walker. She had regained the use of her arms, fingers, and hands, and with each success, a layer of the pressure dressing was removed. Although she was very sensitive about her appearance, especially her face, it didn't stop her from being an uplifting presence around the hospital.

While not neglecting his other patients, it was clear to everyone that Dr. Williams had a special attachment to Marisol. And it was pretty apparent that she had developed a special attachment to him also. It was a necessary connection for the shy doctor and the damaged goods. They both had finally found a place of acceptance without judgment or expectation, and it generated feelings that neither one had ever experienced, or imagined.

chapter seventeen

GRUNTING AND groaning, her head bobbing up and down, she tried giving him a blowjob that would blow his mind. She didn't have a lot to work with, and doing the "lemon squeeze" wasn't working with her whole hand, so she had to adjust, and twist his Vienna sausage-sized dick between her index finger and thumb. "Come on, daddy," she moaned. "Give it to me."

It was the day after Cam's funeral, and a voice crackled over the intercom on Heywood's desk. "Wendy Williams is on line one, Heywood." It was Mona his secretary beeping in.

With his pants and boxers bunched up around his ankles, a dark shaded Heywood grunted, and when Skye paused, he nudged her with his fist. "Who told ya to stop?" he snarled. "Just watch all that goddamned slobbering, will ya? Be neat with yours, ya feel me?"

He shook his head with disgust, then pressed the intercom button on his phone, and snapped. "I ain't talkin' to that drag queen. She gets no love from me. Nuttin'. Tell her I'm indisposed. Betta yet, send her ass to Rae, an' let her handle it."

Rae Daniels was Heywood's love-to-hate publicist. They had a longstanding relationship that was up one minute and down the next. He'd fire her at will, and rehire within a week's time because no one else could really deal with him.

He clicked off the button with a flourish and vigorously tapped the top of Skye's head. She was on her knees, under his desk, sucking him off, and it just wasn't happening. Heywood was no closer to coming than he was twenty minutes ago when she started. "Go on, get up. Ya just ain't doin' the job right."

Skye crawled from under the desk, and pulled her short mini-skirt down over her curvy hips as she stood. She wiped her mouth, and glared at him. She tried to ignore Duck, who was slouched down in a chair watching videos on one of the television screens less than ten feet from Heywood's desk.

"Aiight, Heywood. I'm out. So, whassup? You want me to go lay down some tracks today or what?"

"I want ya to lay down somethin', cause ya sho' wasn't layin' down shit a few minutes ago. Let's hope yo' singin' skills are a lot better than yo' head game, 'cause that shit was straight busted. He pointed to her Balenciaga bag that lay on his desk. "Now step. Get your grip an' go make me some scrilla."

Skye's voice was quiet, but had an edge of sullenness. "Am I going to the studio or what?"

"Go. An' don't leave 'til ya got somethin' worth listenin' to, ya feel me?"

Skye snatched her bag and started rummaging inside. She pulled out a compact, and started to open it.

"Ah, naw, hell no. Do that shit outside," he said. "This ain't no fuckin' dressing room."

Duck placed a large hand over his mouth and snickered from his chair, and Skye turned on her four-inch Christian Louboutin pumps and headed to the door, mumbling the whole way.

"Ya say somethin'?" Heywood said, standing up, his limp dick slipping back in the sleep position.

"I didn't say nothin', Heywood," she said.

He gathered up his shorts and slacks and fastened them around his waist. "I thought so. Ya betta recognize, Skye." He snapped his fingers.

"Ya 'bout this close to gettin' dropped, ya feel me? Ya betta get yo' shit together, girl. An' be ready fo' me lata."

She dropped her head and grunted. She headed out, closing the door behind her.

"Trick ass bitch," Heywood said, and fell back in his oversized Herman Miller chair.

"Who ya talkin' about, Wendy? Yeah, I was wonderin' why ya blew her ass off like that."

Heywood frowned. "Naw, nigga, I wasn't talkin' bout Wendy. I was talkin' about Skye.

"Wendy gets no love from me after she tried to clown me last year talkin' 'bout me usin' a ghostwriter on my songs. Fuck her. I write my own shit, she betta recognize. That bitch must have the shortest fuckin' memory on earth, or either she think I do. Whatever. My story's too big for her second rate, face for the radio ass. Before I say anythin' to anyone, I wanna be on the front page. Television maybe. Some Barbara Walters or Dianne Sawyer shit. Fuck Wendy Williams."

"I wouldn't," Duck said. "She look like a hungry bitch. Like she eat a nigga alive. She'd probably try to take my shit and fuck me with it."

They laughed for a few, and Heywood settled into his chair. "Duck, I swear, she's on some foul shit."

Duck nodded. "Speak on it. Wendy's been all in yo' ass about that."

Heywood gritted his teeth. "Stay wit' me, Duck. I was talkin' 'bout Skye."

"Oh," Duck said and pointed to the desk. "Ya mean *that* shit."

"Yeah. I swear, Cam wouldn't never do no common trick-assed shit like that. Wouldn't even think about no gully shit like that. Suckin' goddamned dick under a goddamned desk while another mutha fucka's in the room. What kinda shit is that? She ain't got no class at all. None."

Duck nodded from his position. "I hear ya, dawg. That was kinda foul. How she gonna represent wit some knee caps all ashy an' rubbed off an' shit? Skank hoe."

Heywood laughed and shook his head. "Now, now, that's my protégée yo' talkin' 'bout." They both burst into peals of laughter, and gave each other pounds. When Heywood finally composed himself, he exhaled heavily, and raised his hands, his palms close to his face. "She's just like all of the rest of them tricks. Except she's a little luckier. Every bitch wanna come up. Wanna be put on, an' they think they gotta do it on they knees. Oh well. Let 'em keep thinkin' that. I ain't gonna stop 'em. They can keep right on slobbin' the knob an' gettin' played."

"It's gonna be hard to find anotha one like Starr, man," Duck said. "She was the bomb. A real class act. A fuckin' lady. I just didn't know that y'all was dealin' like that. So, y'all was engaged, huh? Man, I ain't have a clue y'all was gettin' down like that."

Heywood stroked his chin. "Well, ya know, Cam was real private wit' hers. But, on the real, we thought it was best that nobody knew it was like that between us. It mighta messed up her image an' shit."

"Oh, I dig. But I'm ya boy. Ya coulda told me," Duck said. "Ya know I really dug me some Starr. She was the shit, man."

"Yeah, ya right. She was the real deal. That's why I gotta make sure don't nobody fuck up her name. Or her image."

"Word."

"I'm serious, Duck. Imma shut down any mutha fucka that tries to mess wit' her name like that. Like these fuckin' gossip websites an' shit. Folks gettin' on there tellin' all types of lies, an' shit." Heywood mocked the phantom bloggers. "Oooh, Starr was pregnant when she died. Or, 'I know Starr had several abortions, when she was in high school.' Or, 'Starr lied about graduating from high school.' Bullshit. She was an angel, man. She was the real thing, dawg. All that. She had somethin' that these other bitches can't even dream of," Heywood said.

"What's that? Talent?" Duck snorted.

"Yeah, that too. But I was thinkin' she was like really real. Like, she had standards an' shit. She had home trainin'. She knew how to conduct herself. She wouldn't let nobody treat her like a trick, even though she was fine as hell. I mean, she was a dime, but she was inwardly beautiful, ya feel me? She was like, innocent, but she wasn't no fool neither," Heywood said. "She listened to me, an' she understood what I was sayin'. Not like these other bitches who ya gotta keep tellin' shit over an' over. Not Cam. Naw, she understood how this fuckin' entertainment game is played. She knew how to work it. She knew what to give, how much to give, an' when to give it. To her fans an' to the goddamned press. She could really keep her shit on the low, but still do her thing. An' it was all good."

"Yeah," Duck said. "I could tell ya had mad respect for her an' her game, dawg."

"For real, Duck. She had mad skills. *Shee-it*, these other chicken heads ain't got nothin' on her. Nothin'. They couldn't even stand in the shadows an' sing backup for her," Heywood said.

"They couldn't even hold a damned mic stand for her, could they Wood?"

"Ya ain't never lied. Their asses didn't even deserve to be on the same stage wit' her."

Duck dropped his chin. "It's just a mutha fuckin' shame she went out like she did," he said. "It just don't seem real, ya know?"

Heywood sighed, and removed his shades rubbed his goatee for dramatic effect. He placed his elbow on the arm of the chair and held his chin. "Yeah, it don't seem real. I really miss that girl, man. Ya know she was my heart, right?"

"I knew ya was really feelin' her. Not like these otha knuckleheads. I could tell ya had mad love for Cam."

Heywood sighed again. "Yeah, an' I still do. But this is show biz, an' how they say, the show must go on. Ya know how I do. I can work miracles wit' these broads."

"Ya got the Midas touch, Heywood," Duck said, head-bobbing.

"Midas? *Shee-it*. I gots the platinum mutha fuckin' touch. An' Imma do what I gotta do to keep the lights on, ya feel me? We still gotta eat."

"Word," Duck said. "An' I'm a hungry mutha fucka."

Heywood laughed, and reached for his humidor. "Naw, you's a greedy ass mutha fucka."

When Heywood reached for the cigar holder, Duck quickly ambled to his feet, and trotted over to the desk. "Hold up, dawg. I'll get it for ya," Duck said, quickly opened the case. "What ya feelin'? What ya in the mood for?"

Heywood suddenly mellowed. "I dunno, man. Since Cam's been gone, I ain't been in the mood for much of nothin'. I can barely eat. I ain't even been sleepin' right. Things just don't feel the same without her bein' around."

There was a tinge of sincerity in Heywood's words. He had iced every media outlet since Cam's death. He and Rae were working on a masterful plan to pimp the public for all it was worth. He was back to updating his own personal blogs to his benefit, in an all out PR/pity blitz.

Heywood looked out of window of his 65th floor office on Fifth Avenue, and admired the New York skyline. Even without the World Trade Centers, it was still breathtaking.

"I dunno what I wanna smoke, Duck," he said, and waved a hand. "Surprise me. Just make it good."

Duck handed him a long, thick, aromatic Nicaraguan Churchill and his cutter. Heywood clipped the tips, removed the wrapper, and ran it under his nose. "Ahhhh," he said, and placed it between his lips while Duck lit it with Heywood's platinum desk lighter. "That's good."

"Man, that's some good shit." He pointed to the humidor. "Go on, Duck. Get ya one."

"I'm on it."

Heywood's office was 21st century at its finest. He had black and white pictures of his idols Frank Sinatra and Al Capone sprinkled in between the awards, framed news articles about himself and the magazine covers he had graced.

Two giant plasma TVs were affixed to his walls, one that constantly looped MTV and BET, and the other CNN and MSNBC. Everyone was reporting about Cam's death and funeral and showing clips of Heywood's dutiful attendance.

On his desk were three mid-sized monitors, one with a constant feed from his studio, the other looping the more popular blogs, and the third fixed on *USA Today*. He would never be uninformed or caught wrong about anything if he could help it.

Heywood's eyes scanned the screens, until his eyes landed on the monitor showing CNN, and a familiar face was displayed. "Turn that up, Duck," Heywood yelled, and Duck scrambled for the remote.

The newscaster, a round-faced blonde White woman, was speaking, with a mug shot over her left shoulder.

"Today, in New York Superior Court, indictments were handed down for convicted drug lord Tyrone "Typhoon" Moon. Moon, who is currently serving 15 years to life on RICO charges related to interstate gun trafficking violations, has been indicted on murder charges for the gangland style shooting of one of his alleged business rivals. Sylvester "Sly" Curtis was gunned down in March 2003 on a crowded street in Queens. Despite the lack of eyewitnesses and evidence, authorities were finally able to indict Moon after one of his former employees turned State's evidence against him. Moon could be facing a life sentence if convicted."

Heywood rested his hand on his chin, while Duck lamented. "Damn, that's fucked up. I heard that one of the guys that used to run for him, that nigga, Ronnie, Ronnie Sousa, dropped dime on Typhoon. Man, I hate a snitch," Duck said.

"I feel ya. The Feds musta made the deal awfully sweet for him if he's willing to go out like that on Typhoon."

"Word," Duck said. "They had to do some serious diggin' to get at Ty like that though. Ya know his shit was tighter than tight. That nigga was caked up. His ass was sittin' on top o' the world."

"*Shee-it*, he was the world," Heywood said quietly.

Duck sighed. "They goin' back to 0-3 to pull up some shit on Typhoon, an' try to pin it on 'em. They ain't neva gonna let 'em see the light of day no more, is they?"

Heywood shook his head. "It don't seem like it. Seems like they are out for blood on good ol' Ty. An' that's fucked up."

"I'm sayin', dawg. That's your boy, Heywood. Ya ain't know nothin' 'bout this? Ain't there nuttin' ya can do to help Ty out, man?"

Heywood shrugged. Typhoon was his boy, and when Heywood was starting out, Typhoon gave him work moving some weight for him. And Typhoon was the one who trusted Heywood to diversify and legalize some of his drug profits by getting into the music business. With Typhoon's backing and Heywood's musical Midas touch, they took Kutthroat Records, home of hardcore rap and hip-hop, and evolved it into the signature Kennetic label. From the onset, Typhoon was the quintessential silent partner who had allowed Heywood to run the music business separate and apart from any of Typhoon's shady dealings. So, by all accounts, Heywood was clean.

Of all of the folks that were around at the beginning, only Duck was still alive who even remotely knew of Heywood and Typhoon's association. And even Heywood was careful not to let Duck know how truly extensive their binds were. But, the bigger Heywood got, the more he tried to distance himself from Typhoon. Yeah, he knew he owed him for his start, but the blood and sweat and tears were all Heywood's, not Typhoon's. And as time went on, Heywood found himself resenting the owing part of their relationship.

"Naw, I didn't know nothin' 'bout this, Duck. All I know is that it's a damned shame. That nigga Ronnie betta grow eyes in the back of his head. Cause Typhoon still got juice on the streets, ya know?

"But, for real, ya know I still got love for Typhoon, an' I'm gonna keep lookin' out for him. Ya know how I do."

Duck punched his fist in his wide palm. "Yeah, I know ya cool like that, Heywood. An' that's one of the things I straight up dig about ya. Ya ain't never forget where ya came from. Ya always lookin' out. Parsley even told me that ya said he was gonna get his shot on the mic soon, and I think that's mad cool of ya."

Heywood kept a poker face. "Yeah, uh, right Duck. Imma put Parsley out there as soon as the time is right."

"Word, Heywood. Word. That's how it should be, man. Brothas lookin' out for brothas. So, I'm wit' ya on that snitch nigga. Son's gonna get got. Ya know Typhoon don't hardly play that."

Motioning for Duck to turn the volume down, Heywood shook his head. "I hear ya, Duck, but ya know what? He might get got, but that still won't get Typhoon out. That's how the game's changed from how it used to be. Before it was all about gettin' yours an' protectin' what's yours. Now it's about gettin' yours, protectin' yours, an' keepin' the fuckin' feds outta yo' shit. That's what I think about. How to keep my shit," he said, and pointed around his office. "That's whassup."

And Heywood meant every word he said. He knew that his existence was more than that of a ghetto superstar, drug man, or shooter. He was meant to be on TV, but not on the news in a mugshot. He wasn't about to be convicted for anything. He was about the red carpets and Fashion Week, and traveling to Milan and Dubai and being featured in magazine articles. It was about his life, his lifestyle, his persona, his brand.

It was about his office and everything he had worked for that was in it. The décor was ultra modern, with his numerous magazine covers and photos with other celebrities. Sleek marble wall cabinets held replicas of every award he or his artists had ever won. He wanted them all. Heywood figured if any of his peoples won anything, then he was partially responsible for their success. Shit, he owned them so he owned their awards too. Real talk. And that was a part of the business no one, not even Duck or Typhoon would know about. One of the rules of the street was never, ever let the right hand know what the left was doing, and Heywood embraced that. He might be indebted to Typhoon, it was true, but Heywood had a greater indebtedness to himself and what he deserved.

It had been a busy morning, the day after Cam's funeral. He and his publicist Rae had worked overtime to find some value to Heywood during his moment of grief. And it was working.

During the ten days it took to ship Cam's body back to the States, and to hold the public viewing and private funeral, Heywood had orchestrated every public and personal move associated with Cam's death. Everything was staged to come off without a hitch.

The first thing he did was strategically leak to the top gossip blogs that he and Cam were engaged, and they ran with it. Even though they had played that "we're not together" bullshit when Cam was alive, Heywood now had to make a move that would endear him to the public, and make them sympathetic to his loss. Not just professional loss, but to a greater degree, now his personal loss.

When the press contacted Rae, she uttered the standard, "No comment. We wish to provide Starr's family with every opportunity to mourn privately during their time of bereavement." It was sensational. It garnered sympathy for Heywood, and upped his respect game.

Now that it had been revealed that he and Cam were involved, every picture they ever took and every event they ever attended together was scrutinized and talked about. Cam's name was number one in hits on the search engines like Yahoo! and Google, while Heywood's was second. A distant second, but he topped other more relevant newsmakers. His stock, as high as it was, had risen too. In addition to Cam's CD sales.

Since Cam's death, her national and international sales had skyrocketed. Fans were downloading all of her songs at a record pace, and ringtone sales were in the top five across all musical genres. Her previous releases were sold out, and Heywood had the label cranking out hundreds of thousands more. The surge in her popularity was surreal. But he had to play it just right. He didn't want to flood the market and have her stuff get old and stale too quick. He had to leave the public wanting more, but drive up the desire at the same time. To turn tragedy into triumph. Death into re-birth. And he had to get his hands on Cam's masters to make sure that he controlled her legacy, and her earnings.

A slew of websites had popped up, all commemorating and memorializing Cam. Replete with photos, music clips, and videos, Heywood was happy that folks were boosting Cam's sales, but he didn't want anyone stepping into his territory. So, he sicced his team of pit-bull lawyers on it, to ensure that no one executed any copyright infringements. But, the legal wrangling had to come from Cam's estate, and Heywood had to play his cards right. Now everyone would have to deal with him because he had positioned himself as Cam's estate.

By leaking his and Cam's relationship and lying about it, Heywood was also able to get in with Cam's Aunt Mary. Devastated by Cam's death, Heywood handily infiltrated Cam's family circle, which now only consisted of her aunt and grandmother. After all, he had been there for Cam when her mother died, and he wanted Aunt Mary to believe that he would be there for her too. He was sensitive to her needs, but his goal was to work his plan. And Aunt Mary, the backbone of the family, was nearly inconsolable over losing Cam, and deferred a lot of Cam's business for Heywood to consult with Cam's attorneys. It was working just like he had planned.

But, he had to play it just right. He had to appear to the media that he was working to help Cam's family, so any inkling of involvement in Cam's estate had to be kept quiet. He would pay top dollar to ensure that no information ever leaked out regarding that.

At that moment, one of Heywood's disposable cellphones chirped in

Duck's briefcase. Automatically, Duck removed the phone from the case, and handed it to Heywood without looking at the screen.

Heywood quickly hit the read button and scanned the screen. It read:

THE WEATHER'S GETTING BAD AT THE FARM. REQUIRES ATTN.

Heywood grabbed a heavy crystal decanter from the corner of his desk and smashed the cellphone into pieces, banging the beverage holder onto the desk until it nearly broke.

"What the fuck?" Duck jumped in his chair. "Whassup, Heywood?"

Heywood took his arm and swept the bits of the phone onto the floor. "Nuthin'. I don't ever want to see another one of those things again, ya heard?"

A puzzled expression crossed Duck's face. "But, Hey. What? All I did was hold the phone. Ya gave 'em to me, remember? Ya tryna to say ya don't want me to—"

"I don't want ya to worry 'bout holdin' that phone for me anymore. Not until I say otherwise." Heywood rolled himself back from his desk, stood up, and proceeded to grind the remaining parts of the phone into the carpeted floor. "Now, I'm outta here for a few. Get this shit cleaned up, an' I'll catch up wit' ya later," he said, leaving a confused Duck to do his bidding.

The air in the private steam room was thick, damp and heavy. The Mortal Man Spa in Midtown was known for catering to celebrity clientele. With its secret entrances and CIA type concierge service, it was one of the few places Heywood felt comfortable conducting business.

Heywood's eyes were closed as he leaned against the slick travertine wall. Alone and naked except for a towel wrapped around his thick waist and the eucalyptus body wrap that engulfed his less than toned neck and chest, he breathed the dense air into his lungs, and exhaled deeply. In between breaths, he sipped on a sweaty bottle of Pellegrino water.

The door cracked open, allowing some of the steam to escape, and another man with a towel wrapped aound his waist, entered and sat down on an adjacent bench.

"Mr. Jones?" the man asked, sniffling loudly. Heywood didn't respond.

The man asked again, and finally Heywood opened his eyes. "Mr. Smith?"

The man nodded, and sniffled. "Man, it's hot in here. Was this the only place we could meet? It's messing my sinuses up to no end."

Heywood stared at the man, and inhaled again. "It's good for ya. Helps to cleanse an' detox ya body. Gets all those toxins an' shit out ya pores. Naw mean? Get all them impurifications an' drugs out ya system." Heywood snorted. "But, hey, I didn't ask to meet ya here for no free health consultation." He leaned forward and gazed at the man intensely. "Now, did I?"

The man cleared his throat, and sniffled again. "Seriously, Heywood, I need some tissue or something. I think I'm about to catch a nose bleed."

Heywood motioned towards a rack of thick white towels on the wall behind the man's head. "Use one of those," he said, and sipped from his bottle. "An' get ya some water. It'll keep ya hydrated."

The man followed Heywood's instructions, and quickly resumed his position catty-cornered from Heywood. "First off, please let me extend my condolences to you on the devastating loss of Camara. I read in the *New York Times* that you two were engaged. Who knew?" He sighed and sniffled. "She was truly a lovely, special young lady."

Heywood grunted, and the man kept talking. "But I must say, I was really surprised to hear from you. Especially, given the circumstances."

"Let's cut through the bullshit, Kevin. I'm sure ya know why you're here. An' it's not for the steam."

Kevin wiped his nose. "I really don't Heywood. I was truly surprised to receive your phone call from Montserrat to set up this meeting with me, and to hear that you wanted to hire me as your attorney. And then, wow, to hear about Cam's passing. It's a bit surreal."

"Actually, it's pretty tragic."

"Hmmm," Kevin said, and sniffled again. "Tragic. Poor Camara. Seems like she could never escape tragedy in her life. First she loses her mother at an early age, and then she perishes in a freak accident at a young age herself. It is truly—"

"Tragic," Heywood interjected.

"Yes, tragic. And unfortunately, a little coincidental."

Heywood folded his arms across his chest, rustling his leafy wrap. "Come again?"

"Coincidental. You call me, out of the clear blue, making question-able inquiries at what then happens to be under questionable circum-stances. The questionable circumstances being that the next thing I hear is that Camara has died."

"Questionable circumstances? Hell, I was there when Cam was in the hospital. I saw how fucked up she was. Now, don't get it twisted, I was concerned 'bout her health, but give me a fuckin' break. I'm a business-man too. Ya can't expect me not to act like one, even under 'questionable circumstances.'"

Kevin shook his head. "Heywood, you are something else. I guess it broke your heart to see your protégée, or should I say your fiancée, hurt like that."

"Real talk. Broke my heart." Heywood tapped his bare chest.

"Well, I guess better to break your heart than your wallet, huh?" Kevin asked. "Because I'm not sensing a great deal of pain from you."

Again Heywood tapped near his heart. "I'm suffering on the inside. Deep inside."

"Well, I guess everyone that was there is suffering deep inside too, or experiencing paralysis of the tongue because no one's saying a word. Not even Cam's assistant Allison. My uncle's been trying to find out what happened for the family's sake. All we know is that you all were down there for a video shoot, and she got injured on the set. That one page bullshit coroner's report that we got from the island only said that Cam died from complications from extensive burns. Now, we ordered but haven't even gotten our private M.E.'s report back yet, but we all know Cam was badly burned. I guess that's why you wanted to cremate her body, huh? Too much to bear?"

"Exactly."

"Right. But of course, you should've known that her Aunt Mary was-n't going to go for that. I also understand that you identified the body. That was to spare Aunt Mary, I guess?"

"I thought I was doin' what was best."

"I'm sure. Unfortunately, the question is, who was it best for?"

"I was just tryin' to minimize everyone's pain. It was tragic enough."

"There's that word again. I still say that it's all a bit too coincidental," Kevin rebuffed.

The two men glared at each other, both jockeying for the upper hand. Finally, Kevin spoke.

"Let's dispense with the formalities, Heywood, okay? Don't try the okey doke on me. You call me, requesting that I become your lawyer, then you want to invoke some kind of attorney client privilege, and then you ask me about Cam's will. Well, I didn't handle any of Cam's affairs, so I can't help you. Nor legally, could I disclose any of her information to you. So, I don't know why you'd want me as your attorney when you can afford any attorney of your choosing."

"I know I can. But I don't need just any kind of lawyer. I need one that's smart, bookwise, an' street smart, an' has some connects. An' maybe I do want somethin' ya have. But, understand, I'm only speakin' to ya as a client."

"Is that why you have me in this oven, because you're afraid of speaking to me in public? What am I going to do, tape you? Well, if it was all that, I might have a damned microphone under my balls or in the crack of my ass or something. You want to check?" Kevin stood up and dropped his towel, and Heywood chuckled.

"Sit your ass down, man. An' cover that shit up. Now, don't try to play me. Lawyer or not, I'm not impressed. I do my homework too, so guess what? I know all about ya. All I need to know, anyway."

Kevin replaced his towel and stared at Heywood. "What are you saying?"

"I'm sayin' that we're more alike than we are different. So, even though ya got a piece of paper that says 'Juris Doctorate,' it don't mean nothin' to me." Heywood pulled a huge stack of $100 dollar bills from under his towel. "This," he said, pointing to the money, "talks. Bullshit walks."

Kevin eyed the damp stack and licked his lips. "This is a little unorthodox, Heywood."

"A little unorthodox? Give me a fuckin' break. Nigga, I told ya, I know all about ya. Don't tell me ya got a hearin' problem to go along wit' that nose problem ya got."

Kevin stammered, and tried to defend his position, but Heywood was unyielding. "Yeah, I told ya I did my homework. I hear ya like to gamble, too. I don't consider myself to be a high roller like that. I take calculated risks, ya feel me? But, I guess a risk is a risk is a risk, huh? So, I guess we got a little in common. Like, I know that we have, or should I say, we've had the same employer."

"I don't know who you're talking about. And if I did know, I don't know what that has to do with this conversation at this moment."

"Yeah, I'm sure ya do. But I'll get to that in a minute. What's really good right now is that we have a mutual interest in how Cam's estate is gonna be settled. It could be very beneficial to us both."

"Go on," Kevin said. "That has a nice ring to it."

"I just need for ya to find out if yo' uncle did a will for Cam, an' if so, I need a copy of it."

Kevin stammered again. "I don't know, Heywood. My uncle doesn't play around with things like that. If there is one, it has already been filed in DC and probably Maryland too. But, you already knew that, so why are you trying to act like you didn't? It'll all be part of public records, once her estate is settled. Until then, you best believe her stuff will be on lock."

Heywood was testing Kevin, and thus far he was passing. "I need ya to confirm that. And if ya can't get me a copy, then I need some specifics. Like, when it was signed. I don't want to have any problems with the one Cam completed right after we became engaged. Naw mean?"

Kevin slitted his eyes at Heywood. "Engaged? Oh yeah, that's right. Engaged. Sure, I know exactly what you mean. I'm sure your engagement is going to be the topic of many conversations. Well, I'll give you a free piece of advice. You better know that if a will turns up that my uncle didn't sign, then it's going to get contested."

"No doubt," Heywood said. "I expect nothin' less."

"As long as you know. He'll hang you up in Probate Court for years."

"As long as you know that this is just a means to an end for right now. A formality. It's what Cam would have wanted, an' I'm prepared to do what I gotta do to make that happen."

Kevin eyed Heywood's stack again, and sniffled. "Okay, so help me to understand something. You bring me here to tell you something that you already knew, to tell you that I couldn't do what you already knew I couldn't do anyway. So, why are you still dangling a stack in front of my face? I know that what I told you isn't going to get me that," he said, and pointed to the bills.

Heywood inched the money toward Kevin, and it dragged along the watery seat. "Consider it a small retainer. Plus, if I feel like I'm able to trust ya on this, we can possibly do business that's a little more lucrative. In fact a lot more lucrative."

"Business like what?"

"Business as in Tyrone "Typhoon" Moon.""

chapter eighteen

HEYWOOD HAD done his homework on Kevin. He didn't believe in luck, but he did believe in capitalizing on any opportunity that availed itself to him. And though Cam's accident and subsequent death were flukes, Heywood's spur of the moment decision to relieve Cam from her world of suffering was by chance, and had set off a series of events that Heywood would masterfully control. And implement.

But, Heywood had street smarts and the cojones to make just about anything work in his favor. He had to act, and act quickly, to make sure that Cam's untimely death was worth it. And unfortunately, Cam was worth more to Heywood dead than she ever would've been alive. Especially if she was trying to make her own decisions, and remained determined not to renew their contract.

So, faced with the split-second gamble to euthanize her, Heywood had to hedge his bets. He knew that her Aunt Mary was country dumb, slow talking and walking, but really pretty sharp. She was smart enough to have some impenetrable forces around, especially that damned attorney Deacon Owens. Or, so she thought.

Owens was strong, but he had a weak link with his nephew Kevin. And the old man was smart enough to know that, so he never knowingly involved Kevin in any of Cam's dealings. Or so he thought. The mere fact that Cam was his client wasn't happenstance. Kevin had a great deal to do with that.

Although not directly involved with Typhoon and Kevin's business relationship, Heywood knew that Typhoon didn't have Kevin around for show. Heywood, using his uncanny knack, did some digging and found out that Kevin was pretty corrupt. He was always frontin', pretending like he was so sophisticated and educated, but had a few dangerous habits. He was a gambler. And while he was always looking for the come up, he always ended up on the short end. Heywood, watching from the wings, knew that was how Typhoon controlled him. Despite Kevin being quite the dealmaker, he was as lucky as he was unlucky.

Kevin was lucky enough to have been Cam's mother Faith's attorney, yet unlucky enough to owe big money to Typhoon, who made him pay off his markers by doing his light work. The kind of grimy stuff that Typhoon couldn't involve his Fifth Avenue suits with. The street stuff. It was also the kind of dirty dealings that got Kevin caught up in the drug game, like so many of his clients.

Kevin, despite his frailties, always delivered on his promises and commitments to Typhoon. He talked a good game, but he knew that he needed Typhoon to keep him in the game. So, he had willingly represented many of Typhoon's low level dealers, especially those in the DC area. Kevin worked diligently hard to keep Typhoon's illegal gambling houses open, and bargained with DA's and judges to lower or drop charges against his girls on the streets. In other words, Kevin handled a lot of the dirty work, and unfortunately, he got a little dirt on himself, as well.

He reaped the benefits of being in Typhoon's good graces, but hanging with the dope boys and other elements of the street game led Kevin down a path of no return. He began partying too much, and ran up steep debts at Typhoon's gambling houses. Debts he couldn't repay with his legal work, especially not under his uncle's hawkish eye. So, owing more than he could repay, Typhoon bought his markers, and the only way Kevin figured he could repay him was to serve up Cam.

Recording stars were notorious for signing bad contracts, and Keving would have to ensure that any contract made with Cam to Typhoon's record label would be greatly beneficial to him. And knowing his uncle, he would have to slip the clause in after he had reviewed it. If Cam was a success, Typhoon could make millions off of her. All Kevin had to do was to convince Faith.

Kevin, knowing Faith's desire to get Cam put on, was an easy sell. The only obstacle would be Aunt Mary. Kevin presented the proposal to Typhoon, who deferred it to Heywood. Heywood, upon hearing Cam sing, sanctioned the deal, and satisfied Typhoon. Heywood was cool with getting Cam in his fold because she would clean up his Kutthroat image, and be the crown jewel of the new Kennetic Records showcase. She would legitimize his game, and Heywood's instincts knew that she would be instrumental in taking him to the next level in the industry.

After his uncle reviewed and okayed the contract, Kevin buried a management clause in it that ensured that Typhoon would profit from Cam's career as her silent investor. Kevin had done a lot of underhanded dealings for Typhoon. He was also instrumental in signing Vic as Cam's manager, and Vic was nothing but a straw man for Typhoon.

But, even though Typhoon was making a grip on the back end of Cam's contract, it still wasn't enough to keep Kevin out of his debt. Kevin kept gambling, and his liabilities kept mounting. Even when Typhoon landed in prison himself, he kept Kevin in his indebtedness. Kevin helped Typhoon maneuver while incarcerated, but tried to find a way to terminate the association. It was almost over when Faith somehow found out that Kevin and Typhoon had run a game on her, and that they were taking advantage of Cam.

Kevin panicked when she threatened to tell his uncle, so he ran to Typhoon. When Heywood found out that Faith was threatening to blow up their spot, he concocted a plan to get her out of the way. He told Kevin that he would offer Faith a music deal if she'd just shut up and let Cam's contract ride. It was the perfect plan, and Kevin convinced Faith that it was the right thing to do. But it didn't work out. In a matter of days, Faith had OD'd, and Kevin asked no questions. Kevin knew he was lucky; he just didn't want to know how lucky he really was. Or who was really behind his luck.

So, while Typhoon never told Heywood about the extent of his association with Kevin, it didn't take much for Heywood to figure it out. Heywood just didn't know how he was going to make it work to his advantage. Not until Typhoon got hit with charges that he probably wouldn't get out from under, and definitely not until after Cam died.

Heywood, like Kevin, owed Typhoon too. And his indebtedness never seemed to diminish either. As much as Heywood owed Typhoon for staking him in the game, it was his hard work and sweat that made Kutthroat, now revamped as Kinnetic Records, what it was. But, despite him making major bank for Typhoon for almost ten years, and having repaid the initial debt ten times over, Heywood was still expected to send thirty percent of his profits to one of Typhoon's off-shore holding companies. It was a payment Heywood was constantly finding ways to reduce, and eventualy, eliminate.

So, with Typhoon facing major charges and his funds drying up, it was the perfect time for Heywood to sever ties with him. Typhoon had been locked up for over eight years, and during that time, he had lost most of his rep and a lot of his street cred. He was legendary, but people spoke of him in the past tense now. He was an urban legend. His name no longer instilled fear in anyone.

And now, with the Feds seizing and freezing all of his cash and assets, Typhoon's only source of income was from his covert alliance with Heywood, filtered back through dummy corporations. And his legal fees for his defense team quickly absorbed what little money he got. So, even from the McCreary Federal Penitentiary in West Bumfuck, Kentucky, or code name "The Farm," Typhoon kept the pressure on Heywood to keep the money coming in. And he relied on Kevin to continue toeing the line between the legal and illegal, and to ensure that his phantom interests and investments were protected. Typhoon lived by the street code of never allowing the right hand to know what the left was doing, and his duties for Kevin were always separate and distinct from anything he ever had Heywood associated with or involved in. So through a skeletal, yet intricate channel and network of messengers and couriers, Typhoon was able to maintain a semblance of order and control over his waning domain.

But, Heywood didn't like being beholden to anyone, let alone a captive man. Yes, there was something to be said about a caged or chained up dog being more vicious than a free one, but Heywood didn't care. Though he once highly respected Typhoon, he now realized that he was an apparition; more to be pitied than feared.

Because of the charges that were constantly being levied against him, and any minor infraction that they could charge him with while imprisoned, the U.S. Attorney had more than enough motivation and authorization to relocate Typhoon at will. Since he had been locked up, he had been moved to at least three Federal pens, each with graduated reputations and security. At the moment, Typhoon was being housed at a supposedly undisclosed location. The undisclosed location meant that he was only allowed visits from his legal team, clergy, and immediate family. And if he was found communicating with anyone off the approved list, it was cause for immediate relocation. For those reasons, Typhoon had to rely on his prison guard connections and the jailhouse network to ensure that he kept in contact with Heywood.

Typhoon didn't have the muscle anymore to inject fear. Heywood could more than afford to protect himself from any threat Typhoon could produce. Most of the members of Typhoon's organization were either locked up, dead, or had changed loyalty to the newer cats in the game. There were only a few loyalists who still checked on him or stayed on his payroll. They were mainly family members, but they didn't provide the type of intimidation factor needed to fully maintain Typhoon's position on the streets. All that was left of his once formidable empire was his legal and financial holdings. And the main ones were his cut in Kennetic Records and Cam's contract. And the more Heywood made from either, the less inclined he was to share it with Typhoon.

In Heywood's mind, what he did for Typhoon was just out of courtesy, and he was not feeling so courteous anymore. Heywood figured if he could falsify Kennetic's earnings and make the value of Cam's contract disappear, so would his debt to Typhoon. But it wouldn't be easy. Typhoon was anything but a fool. And he was unyielding. In fact, it was the person who had called Heywood on one of his untraceable phones earlier that day.

Heywood and Typhoon had created an elaborate system of communicating, paying off guards to slip Typhoon untraceable phones and encrypted laptops. Heywood would never show his face at the farm. Only when Typhoon demanded a face-to-face, would Heywood have Duck send one of the peons on fourth level of the food chain to run the message. It was set up for the errand boy to sign in to see a guard-approved innocuous inmate, and then the guards would give Heywood's representative some face time with Typhoon. It stayed off the books and prison records. To date, this system had worked pretty well for both of them, and kept Heywood fully insulated and disconnected from anything Typhoon-related.

On a more regular basis, Typhoon and Heywood worked the system by getting messages channeled through the paid-off guards. It was fourth and fifth-party deep, and Heywood made certain that his name was never associated with anything. But, today when Typhoon texted him, he wanted an immediate teleconference. All of that was getting old, and the only thing Typhoon ever wanted from Heywood was money, money, and more money. The more Typhoon demanded, the less inclined Heywood was to part with his ends. So, he had to devise a foolproof way to get Typhoon's hand out of his pocket.

It wasn't going to be easy. Typhoon hadn't gotten where he was without being smart. Heywood knew that he needed to put together a flawless plan to extract himself from Typhoon. It had to be as untraceable as those phones they used. He had been plotting it in his mind for months, but now that he was positioning himself to rule Cam's estate, he really didn't want Typhoon in on that. Heywood needed Kevin to make his plan work. And Heywood was shrewd enough to know that Kevin probably wouldn't willingly comply. Kevin needed just the right leverage to motivate him. So, acquiring the knowledge of Kevin's gambling and narcotics issues was just the solution. He was betting that their shared desire to free themselves from Typhoon's shackles would be compelling enough for both men.

"Tyrone Moon?" Kevin started sweating through the steam.

"Don't play me stupid, Kevin. I know ya work for Typhoon. I know you've been workin' for him. Since back in the day."

"Excuse me? He's my client. I'm one of his attorneys."

"He owns yo' ass. Ya just his errand boy. Always have been an' always will be."

Kevin glared at Heywood. "I don't know what ya talking about. I have no idea."

"Yeah, well get an idea. I know that Typhoon had ya doin' his dirty work down there in DC. I know ya was reppin' Cam's mama, that's how Cam got put on. I know all that. An' ya know I do."

"I'm sure you do. But that's not illegal. And moreover, what does that have to do with anything?"

"Oh, it might not be illegal, but I think it might be a little 'unethical,' son. Anyways, I'm sure yo' good old uncle didn't know nothin' 'bout it. It mighta caused old dude to stroke out."

Heywood's words were met with silence. "Yeah, ya try to play Mister High and Mighty, but I know the real deal. Ya been shady for a long time. But, dig this. Typhoon used ya then, like he's usin' ya now, clown. I know he uses ya to invoke that 'client-attorney' privilege so he can talk to ya about doin' all types of shit an' not be monitored."

"Kudos to you, Heywood. Did you pick that up from an episode of *Law & Order* or did you figure that out for yourself?"

"Yeah, I know ya been workin' for Typhoon long before that show ever came on TV."

"Okay, Heywood. Let me make this easy for you. There is no way in hell I'm going to betray Tyrone. No way. Whatever you have is just hearsay, and could never be substantiated. Never."

"An' to think you're so fuckin' smart. Too fuckin' smart to even listen to what I have to say."

"I'm loyal. That's what my clients pay me for."

"An' what if they can't pay ya?"

"Pardon me?"

"You're smart. You're an opportunist. You can read. Don't ya see the handwritin' on the wall? Typhoon's reign is over. His money's gettin' real funny."

"I don't know how true that is, Heywood. Tyrone has a lot of resources, and I'm sure that he'll eat as long as you eat."

"Yeah, but my diet's changin', an' I don't think he can get down wit' what I grub on anymore."

Kevin grunted. "*Hmmph.* I'm sure there's some kind of ghetto meaning to all of that, so please, go on."

Heywood wiped his moustache and smirked. "I'm just sayin'. I'm tryna offer ya an opportunity. Now, ya can be over wit' him, or ya can get over, unlike him."

chapter nineteen

MARISOL'S HEALTH drastically improved during the weeks and months after being admitted to the burn center, and she credited her improvement to the constant care of the attentive Dr. Williams. Her mobility and strength had increased, and layers upon layers of bandages had come off. Her medical team was very pleased with her progress, and confident that with continued proper treatment, she would have an almost complete recovery.

One of the nurses had styled her hair in dreadlocks, and they were now long and flowing. She had regained most of the dexterity in her fingers and limbs, through arduous sessions with her physical and occupational therapists.

She spent most of her moments away from therapy with Dr. Williams or Randolph as he now insisted that she call him. He was kind and supportive, and as he helped to guide her back to health, she felt strangely connected to him. Even on his days off, he would spend time with her, often surreptitiously watching her during her therapy sessions, with a hint of pride in his eyes as she slowly regained her skills.

She trusted and relied on him, feelings she could not recall having experienced before. But there were many things that she couldn't recall, including most of her past. Her psychiatrist assured her that her memory would come back, as sure as her scars would one day heal.

She tried to focus on things that felt familiar, and found that being around children was one of those things. She spent hours in the children's ward, where she found that being around them, most of whom were burned like herself, made her feel a lot less self-conscious about her own appearance.

They played games, like marbles or dominoes, in the hospital's courtyard, where she would often catch Randolph gazing at her from a window of one of the upper floors. As she met his glance, they would both look away like shy children.

Marisol also felt especially at ease when listening to music. When the kids were singing island ditties or folk songs, she never joined in, but her soul moved as she heard the staccato steel drums and the rhythm of the Caribbean music. The songs made her feel like she was missing something; something deep in her spirit.

And it wasn't just her past that she found herself missing. She missed Randolph when he wasn't around. For the past week or so, he had been tied up, prepping for his presentation to a group of patrons and benefactors scheduled to arrive the following week for their annual two-day horse and pony show.

In his absence, Marisol worked twice as hard to get better. She was ecstatic that her sense of helplessness was dissipating and being replaced with aptitude and ability. Even her therapists encouraged her to take it easy, but she continued her punishing workout. There was nothing to see by looking backward. She had to keep looking forward. And rewarding her small steps. And looking forward to relaxing later in the whirlpool tub in the rehab center. Her skin was taut, and the mineral-enriched whirlpool helped to increase its pliability.

The bio-bandage process had really helped to minimize the freezing of her skin, and Randolph had assured her that it was also to reduce the amount of scarring. The more she took the therapeutic baths, the better she was able to tolerate them. They became even easier to endure when she saw how well her body was responding to them.

Her body was healing well, and with the aloe she was using, and the island herbs she was ingesting, she was well on her way to restorative health. But, despite how well her body was improving, she was still morbidly ashamed of her face. So ashamed that she refused to look in a mirror, and had the one in her room covered with an island tapestry.

With the island sounds playing in the background, she relaxed in the whirlpool and touched her lightly bandaged face. Today, her nurse was a visiting American named Terry, who was lively and funny, and familiar to Marisol in an odd way.

"How you doing in there, Marisol?" Terry asked as she leaned against the steel edge of the spa. Her face was warm and round, and she had bright, full eyes, and a thick New York accent. Her ornately decorated nails tapped the faucet and controls, and immediately caught Marisol's eye.

"I know, right? My nails are seriously trippin' everybody out down here." Terry held her hand in the air and looked at them approvingly. "The staff is trying to say that my tips are 'inappropriate,' so I might have to cut these bad boys." She frowned. "But, I could keep 'em gloved up. Shoot. As much as these girls cost me, I need to keep 'em on as long as possible. I might not be able to get 'em filled in until I get back to New York."

Terry smiled and tapped the faucet again. "So, how's the temperature feel today? We increased it by a few degrees, and it's great if your body can tolerate it. But, if not, let me know, okay?"

Marisol nodded, as Terry continued chattering. "Girl, you're doing really well. From what I've read on your chart, your progress has been amazing. You gotta hurry up and get well so we can hang out. I mean, I like the staff down here, but there really aren't a lot of young folks around, 'naw mean?" She winked at Marisol, and Marisol smiled.

It was comforting to be around someone close to her own age for a change. And Marisol was enjoying listening to Terry carry on about hanging out with her when she got better. That was until Terry brought up a subject that made her strangely uncomfortable.

"And girl, we gotta hang out. There are no happenings around here. I mean, some of the brothers on the staff are kinda cute, but they got me pullin' so many hours that the only one I see on the regular is that fine ass Dr. Williams. He's your doctor, right? He's cute, but a little corny. But shoot, when the pickins is slim, you get with the pickins, 'naw mean?" She smiled. "I'm just kidding. He's kinda handsome and mad cool, too. I could see a sista gettin' with him."

Marisol swirled her fingers around in the tepid water, and forced a smile. Why did Terry's words make her feel funny, deep in the pit of her stomach? She and Randolph spent a lot of time together, and perhaps it was a little more than just a doctor/patient relationship. But, she never thought about what it was that they shared. Until now.

Suddenly, Marisol's chest tightened and she felt anxious. Was she jealous? She and Randolph weren't involved or anything, but they were spending a lot of time together. He did ask her to call him Randolph, but maybe that was part of her treatment. Had she caught feelings for him? She quickly dismissed that thought. Of course he couldn't feel anything for her except pity. He probably felt like Terry. He just gravitated to her because she was young like him, and he would probably be attracted to Terry for the same reason. At least Terry was healthy and not disfigured. And she would no doubt be very aggressive in letting him know that she was interested.

Terry rattled on, while Marisol ruminated. In her mind, Terry would swoop in and take Randolph away, while she continued skulking around the burn ward like a modern day Bride of Frankenstein. Marisol was so consumed by her thoughts that she hadn't even noticed that Terry had sidled over to the stereo, and was fumbling with the stations.

"Marisol, I know you're from the islands and what not, but I've been down here a few weeks, and this calypso music is driving me straight crazy." She pulled a CD from the pocket of her smock, opened the drawer, and slipped it in.

"Listen to this," she said as she hit the 'on' button on the system. "This shit, I'm sorry, this CD is slammin'. I know you probably don't know a lot about American music, but you have to have heard of this singer before. She's the, excuse me, but she's the shit. This album is off the chain."

As Terry pressed 'play' and the first note of the song filled the room, Marisol's throat and lungs tightened like a vise, and it became difficult to breathe.

Terry popped her fingers and gyrated, completely oblivious to Marisol's distress. "Yeah, this is the, well, it's the shit. This song is called *Hallowed Ground*. It's a damned shame what happened to the chick who sang it," she said, and turned up the volume. "She was mad cool. One of the best artists in a long time. And she seemed real down to earth, too."

Marisol's head pounded, and she started gasping. As the music filled the room, Marisol's body stiffened, paralysis gripped her extremities, and she began sliding, powerless, into the bubbling water. She tried to talk, she tried to scream, but her voice was mute.

"Yeah, buddy. Starr was the shi—," Terry's words cut off as she turned around and saw Marisol sinking into the water. "Oh my God! Help!" she screamed, and ran over to the tub.

★

The oxygen burned her nostrils, but when she awakened, she didn't want to open her eyes. The voices in the room spoke in hushed tones, speaking about her condition.

"BP's normal."

"I wonder what could've caused her to collapse."

Then she heard a familiar voice. "She was doing so well. I need to know what happened to her." It was Randolph.

The sound of his voice almost made her open her eyes, but she fought the impulse and commanded them to stay closed. She lay still, hoping that they would leave soon. Her prayers were answered when a few moments later, everyone but Randolph quietly left the room. He lingered for a little while longer, gently rubbing her hand.

"Get well, Marisol," he whispered softly. "I don't know what set you back the other day, but I want you to know that you're going to be fine." He said a short prayer, soothingly touched her forehead, and sighed heavily before walking slowly out of the room

Lying in bed, a thousand thoughts ran through her mind. She was scared and confused. She had wanted to reach out to him, but didn't know if she should. Now she was alone and afraid, left to deal with the memories that had come crashing down on her when she heard that song.

It was if her life was being replayed backwards, from the moment that she was in Montserrat, filming that video. And that song was playing in the background. That same song that Terry had played. The same song that had shattered her life.

She remembered being dressed like an island girl, wearing a colorful outfit. She remembered that there was another girl, who looked a lot like her. She remembered smiling and laughing, and joking around with the others, the crew. And the lights, and the dancers. She remembered the music, the lyrics, and the melody. Then she remembered that the weather was threatening. And then she remembered. She clutched her head and cringed. She remembered the most frightening thought of the day. She remembered that she was Starr. She remembered that she was Cam.

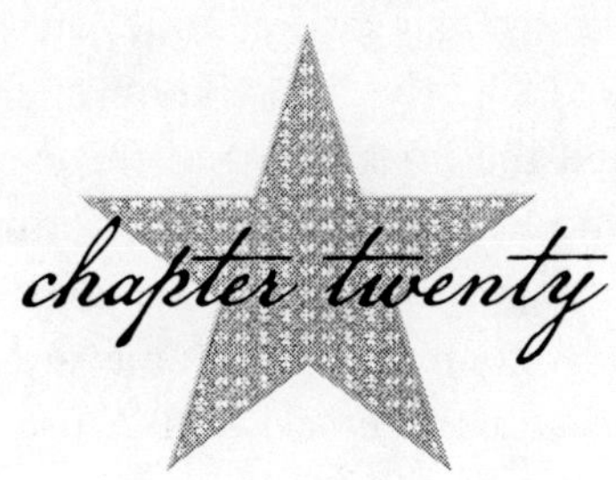

chapter twenty

SMILING SLIGHTLY, a dark-shaded Heywood approached the stage to a rousing standing ovation. He was at the star-studded Grammy Awards, at Los Angeles Staples Center, and the crowd stood on their feet, whistling and clapping as he made his way to the stage. Singers, East and West Coast rappers, producers, and other music moguls gave him the utmost respect. Everyone, that is, but one major star. As the camera panned the crowd, it rested on the solemn gaze of Jamie Tee, seated next to Noah Parker. While Noah appeared to be genuinely happy for Heywood, Jamie's contemptuous expression was evident even behind his shaded eyes. While Noah and everyone surrounding Jamie clapped enthusiastically, Jamie's arms were folded across his Armani suited chest, his lips pressed firmly together in a look of total disgust.

But, Heywood didn't notice. As the slim, statuesque models guided him over to the microphone, he paused to give the presenters, Snoop Dogg a pound and Sheryl Crow a lingering hug. He stood before the podium, waiting for the roar of the crowd to die down.

Nearly blinded by camera flashes, and unable to speak above the roar, Heywood waited for a moment.

"On-on-on behalf of my girl Starr, God rest her soul— I accept this award. She was such an amazing talent. I just wish she could be standing here to receive all these awards herself. Thank you for recognizing her as the best female R&B singer for 2007, an' for the Album of the Year." His voice cracked slightly. "I just know she's lookin' down on us an' smilin'." He hoisted the final award of the evening for Song of the Year toward the sky and kissed it. "I miss ya, Starr. An' I love ya."

Heywood sauntered off the stage, followed by the thunderous applause. Cam had been nominated for four awards, including Album of the Year, Song of the Year, Best Female R&B Artist, and Best Female Pop Artist. And she had swept them all.

It had been nearly six months since Cam's death, and he was still playing his position as the mournful fiance. With his dour expression and low-key manner, he was pulling it off well. He had peeped Jamie and Noah in the crowd, and he wanted to rub their noses in his accomplishment.

Many artists and celebrities offered both their congratulations and condolences, while the female singers vied for his attention. Between hugs and sympathetic gestures, they told him to "call me, when you're feeling up to it," or something similar. Heywood was the golden boy with the Midas touch, and everyone, especially those females, wanted to be touched.

Heywood slyly played them off, and gave his bodyguards the signal to get him out of there. Parsley, Duck, and three of his bodyguards were waiting for him in the wings of the grand arena.

Heywood, clutching the award, leaned over and whispered in Duck's ear. "Ya see that nigga Noah? His ass was heated that I, I mean Starr, won this. His jive ass artists ain't get shit worth havin'." Heywood smirked, and then stepped back. "Come on, let's bounce." His voice was low and slow. He had to keep it cute. He knew all eyes were on him.

"What, we not stayin'?" Parsley asked, as he held Cam's other three awards. "We gonna miss Skye. Ain't she supposed to be performin' in the closing act? That tribute to *We Are the World*?"

Duck shot him a dirty look. "Shut up, nigga. Ya heard the man. Why ya askin' him somethin' like that, fool? Skye works for him, not the other way 'round."

Heywood sighed and stepped. "Look, I'm not feelin' this crowd tonight," Heywood said, and motioned for his bodyguards to clear the path for him. Kennetic Records was hosting a post-Grammy party at the Wilshire Grand Hotel, and Heywood had to at least make an appearance. But, not before he got his X on.

"Duck, just make sure Skye's where she needs to be when she needs to be there. Got it?"

"Got it," Duck said, and immediately turned to Parsley, and grabbed the awards from his hands. "Find one of Skye's peeps and let 'em know whassup."

"Then we gonna roll?" Parsley asked.

"Naw," Heywood said, his eyes darting around behind his black shades. "*We* gonna roll. *You* gonna stay here an' do what you do, ya heard? Be my eyes an' ears up in this muthafucka. I want to know everything that goes down while I'm out. Who says what an' when. Word for fuckin' word."

Duck patiently waited in the limousine for Heywood as he made his way through the fans, paparazzi, and media. As soon as Heywood slid into the limousine, his dour demeanor changed when Duck gave him the good word.

"Hey, ya phone's been blowin' up all night, man. Lotsa folks tryna holla, sendin' their regards. Ya boy Fitz called. He said he had a little set for ya to attend tonight. Said everybody's gonna be there, an' for ya to make sure ya made it. After ya party, of course."

Heywood grunted. Fitz had given him a job as at intern at his label, and he had proven to be a relatively decent mentor to him. Fitz had schooled him on the ways of the industry, and had helped him out. But, Fitz got down in ways that were only recreational to Heywood, but a lifestyle to Fitz and his other old cronies in the music game. Heywood learned a long time ago that you had to do certain things that you didn't necessarily want to, just to get ahead. And wielding that kind of power over others could be intoxicating, even if it wasn't that stimulating.

Getting ahead in the music industry required that you put out to get put on, bottom line. It was like an initiation of sorts. Just like in prison, and unfortunately, a lot of recent movers and shakers in the industry had that lockup background. The strong took advantage of the weak. It was a known secret and yes, Heywood did get down like that, just to keep his folks in check sometimes. And yes, he did get bent for Fitz and his boys, but damn. Every time Fitz had a set, that was the standard operating procedure. Get drunk, get high, get bent. Replete with porn stars, paid escorts, high class trade, and rent boys, anything and everything was bound to happen. Assured that your actions were protected under the careful provisions of the required NDAs, after you partook, you could watch your career flourish. And be expected to continue the cycle.

That was one reason why Heywood didn't like Noah. It was his understanding that Noah hadn't bent over for no one, and wasn't trying to either. Yet, he was still managing to make moves and no one seemed to be beat about stopping him. He would attend the functions, and as soon as things got a little heavy, he'd dip out. Maybe it was his little Bachelor's degree, or his movie star good looks and athletic all-American straight male persona that got him put on, but even Fitz hadn't tried him. And that really bugged Heywood. He had to pay his dues just like everybody else.

He figured that if Noah was going to be at Fitz's party, tonight was going to be his night to pay up. He methodically plotted his actions, making sure that Duck had everything that he needed to make his operation "Hit Back" run flawlessly. Duck confirmed that he had what was needed, and assured him that everything was arranged.

"Okay Wood, you're set for Fitz's party. Now, for real, ya got anotha issue that needs to handled. That cat Owens, has been tryna get at ya."

"Owens? What that nigga want? I ain't got no dealings wit' him."

"He wants those awards. He says they're Starr's. An' part of her estate."

"Fuck him."

Duck scratched his head. "I dunno 'bout that, Heywood. He's talkin' injunctions an' shit."

"Fuck him an' his injunctions," Heywood said, and snatched the Versace shades from his face. "I don't take orders from him or nobody else. That old bitch." Heywood glared at Duck. "Give me a phone. One of them untraceable ones. Now!"

Duck rummaged through his ever present briefcase, past the tiny micro camcorder, several other untraceable cellphones, and pulled out a phone. Heywood snatched it from his hands, and promptly dialed a number.

"Ya betta put that old man in check, nigga," Heywood barked into the earpiece.

"Huh? Do you know what time it is?" Kevin asked, his voice groggy and thick. Either he was completely in la-la land, or sleeping something off.

"I could give a fuck."

"Um, what are you talkin' about?"

"I'm talkin' about ya goddamned uncle, mutha fucka. Now either ya handle him, or I will. I don't discriminate against the old, ya feel me? Fossil or not, I'll get at his old ass just like I do the youngsters."

Kevin grunted while Heywood railing. "Don't have that old mutha fucka callin' me demandin' nothin', ya heard?"

Kevin yawned and held the phone for a few moments. "Come again?"

"These awards. Your uncle called me sellin' some wolf tickets about Cam's Grammies. Ain't it past his bedtime? Give that ol' fool a glass of warm milk, rub him down in some liniment, an' put his old ass to bed."

"They're not yours, Heywood. You accepted property on national television that didn't belong to you. What you should've done is had her Aunt there with you. That would've been the classy and the right thing to do."

"What ya tryna say?"

"I just said it. You did it, so now deal with it. You don't even have an argument for accepting those awards. There is absolutely nothing you or I can do about that one."

Heywood fumed, and banged his fist on the back seat. "Pull this bitch over. Now."

Duck cocked his head. "Hey, say what? We can't do that, man. We on the freeway."

"I don't care if we're on a launch pad, in a mutha fuckin' spaceship an' the count is down to five. Pull this bitch over."

Duck glumly complied and managed to get the limo driver to bob and weave until he was able to safely pull over on the busy highway, and then Heywood told him to get out.

"Listen, Kevin. You're beginnin' to make me wonder about ya. See, if ya can't even keep yo' nobody uncle off my nuts, what the fuck I need ya for?"

"You tell me, Heywood. You're the one ringing my phone, not vice versa."

"That's what I like about ya, Kevin. Ya a true mouthpiece, aren't ya? Ya always got a comeback. That shit's cute for a minute or two, but don't get it twisted. It's gettin' old fast. 'Bout as old as yo' uncle, son.

"Now, I thought we had a deal," Heywood said.

"You proposed a deal, Heywood. I don't recall accepting it. Moreover, I got you the specifics of Cam's will, didn't I?"

"True dat," Heywood said. "An' it served the initial purpose. An' don't forget, I paid off yo' markers wit' Typhoon."

"So you said. But, I never said that I was going to be your bitch, either. I'm not your puppet on a string, and I'm not going to be forever tethered to you."

"The way I see, ya really don't have much of a choice. It's either be my puppet on a string, or be a fish on a hook."

"Heywood, I told you before. I'm not trying to get out of Typhoon's debt just to be in yours. That wouldn't be very bright of me, now would it? I might as well stay with him. At least he's locked up and I don't have to talk to him every day. Plus, you make it sound like working with Typhoon is so bad."

"I never said it was bad. I just said that his time was up. Through. An' if ya wanna be with a winner, I was gonna give ya a chance to be one. An' not be a lackey."

Their cat and mouse exchange continued for a few more moments, becoming more heated with each man trying to make his point. Finally, the gauntlet was down and entrenched to the point where it couldn't be removed.

"I'm a professional, Heywood. And you're going to treat me as such," Kevin said.

"I hear ya. An' yo' not gonna treat me like some sucker from the 'hood who don't know shit. Ya do what I need for ya to do, then I'm gonna be cool with ya, ya heard? Cross me, an' it's ya ass."

Then Heywood proceeded to pelt Kevin with questions, who coolly responded like a seasoned litigator.

"Did ya peep them masters yet?"

"Excuse me?"

Heywood cleared his throat, and began speaking like the Damon Wayan's handi-man character from *In Living Color*. "Did you find out where the masters are?"

"No, not yet."

"What about her notebooks? The music books? Them an' the masters are worth a whole lotta money."

"No, but I should have some info on their whereabouts soon. See, I don't want my uncle to get suspicious, and I've never been that close to Cam's Aunt Mary, so I have to work this just right. It's taking a little time, but with Cam's will being tied up, it's not like there's any rush. It could be in probate for quite a while."

"Maybe there's no rush to you, but time is money, and money is time. So, ya know what? Imma handle this my goddamned self. All ya gotta do is arrange for your uncle to be outta his office next Thursday. Simple as that. Send his ass to the golf course or to the altar, I don't give a shit. Then, I'll find out what I need to know my mutha fuckin' self."

"I didn't hear that, Heywood. And please don't repeat whatever you just said that I didn't hear, okay?"

"See, ya just don't get it, do ya? How many times I gotta tell ya, I give the orders, not the other way around," Heywood snapped. "Now, either ya do what I need ya to do, or ya do what I need ya to do. It's just that simple, ya feel me?"

Heywood clicked the phone off, pressed the window button on the door handle, and hurled the encrypted phone out the window. It narrowly missed Duck as he stood by the canyon, taking a leak.

"What the fuck?" he yelled, and quickly shook himself off and headed for the limo.

"Get your triflin' ass in here," Heywood said, and pointed Cam's award at Duck. "Pissin' on the side of the road. Ain't ya got no fuckin' class?"

Before Duck could sit down and close the door, Heywood told the driver to pull off, and Duck hurriedly slammed the door. "Hey, you trippin'. What the fuck's goin' on?"

Heywood shook the award and glared at Duck. "If he thinks I'm givin' him these, he's out his fuckin' mind. Duck, ya find out where I can get some copies of these shits made. Damned good ones. Yeah, that's what his ass'll get. A copy. His old ass won't know the fuckin' difference."

chapter twenty-one

"I KNOW I shouldn't say this, but I have to. Marisol, you really scared me. I, uh, I was so afraid that I, uh, I mean that we were going to lose you." Randolph's words were heartfelt and sincere. She felt badly that she couldn't be as truthful with him.

After her collapse in the whirlpool a few weeks before, Cam had done a lot of praying and soul searching. Part of her ached to know how she had gotten where she was, and how everyone had abandoned her. But, another part of her didn't want to know.

When she had been able to get out of bed, she had taken the tapestry off the mirror, and examined herself closely. She was indeed Camara, and though her dreadlocks were now flowing, and part of her face had been severely burned and was terribly scarred, she could still see who she was. The meds and steroids had swollen her cheeks, and the island food had filled out her figure. She could still see Cam, and even a little of Starr, in herself, but, thankfully, no one else could. Especially Randolph.

Cam spent countless hours trying to remember details of the accident, and more trying to piece together what happened afterwards. Evidently, somehow she had been mis-identified as Marisol. How had that happened? What had happened to Marisol? Had she died at the video shoot? What had happened to everyone else? The frustration of not knowing gnawed at her. And she was saddened that because of her, that innocent young lady had lost her life. If she had never befriended Marisol, the lovely girl would still be alive and peddling her drinks on the beach. How could she have known? How could she ever have guess that trying to help someone would result in their death?

The "what if's" swirled constantly in her thoughts, totally consuming her. The unanswered questions, the remorse, the abandonment. How could anyone, especially her girls, her crew, even Heywood, not know who she was? All she could do was think. And try to avoid Randolph. But today, as he had cornered her in a shaded section of the hospital garden, she had no choice but to face him.

The fact that he didn't know who Starr was gave Cam some degree of comfort. His strict religious upbringing, followed by the years he had spent in med school, and then the long hours of his residency, hadn't left him much time to be drawn into an affair with hip-hop music. He was young, but had an old soul, and really didn't get caught up in a lot of worldly things. As Cam reflected on some of their past conversations, he seemed to really care about the world and its' people. And how he could contribute to, not gain, from both.

During the past six months, Cam had grown to admire Randolph, not just as a doctor, but as a man. She knew she felt grateful to him for engineering her recovery, but her feelings for him went way beyond gratitude. They had innocently created a personal bond, had shared many things, and discovered that they had much in common. Even before she knew who she was, Cam knew that. And that was what really mattered. She was no longer recognizable to Randolph or the world as Camara or Starr.

And that was both a blessing and a curse. Recalling her identity was truly a blessing, but now she was cursed by the memories. And by the lack of memories. She wanted to know what had happened in Montserrat; she needed to fill in the blanks. She remembered being on the video shoot, and some of the circumstances that led up to her being there, but the details of that day were still pretty hazy for her. She was a superstar. That was her song on the radio. And she remembered that she had been planning to leave it all behind. That the video shoot was supposed to have been her last act for awhile. As things turned out, it really had been her last act. Did she want it to be? How had this happened? Why had it happened? How was her aunt holding up? Her grandmother?

Questions. There were so many questions that remained unanswered. Questions that aggravated her soul. She needed to know the truth and felt that Marisol and whatever family she had deserved to know the truth, as well. Surely, her own grandmother and aunt must be grief-stricken. It wasn't right, and Cam knew it. She just didn't know what to do about it.

She felt wounded and alone, even more now than when she had nearly died from the burns. Despite the misgivings she had about her present circumstances, somehow she felt better when Randolph reached out to her, and forced her to listen to him. Hearing his words ignited feelings in her that were hauntingly absent from her memories or being, and caused her to temporarily delay trying to find a reason, purpose, or cause for everything she had endured. His caring and concerned heart and words had touched a part of her soul that she never knew existed.

The wrought iron chair became uncomfortable, and she shifted in her seat. He pulled another chair beside her, and surveyed her face. She tried to turn her head, but he gently raised her chin, careful not to touch her healing skin, and looked into her eyes. "I know it's not right, Marisol, but I have developed feelings for you," he said. His voice was halting, while his expression was honest and sincere.

She grabbed his wrist and shook her head. "No, no, you don't, Randolph. You just feel sorry for me, that's all. An' I don't want your pity. Yours or anyone else's." She was now speaking with an authentic Caribbean accent, one that flowed naturally, given the number of months she had been surrounded by the island dialect.

He sighed, but didn't release her chin. "I'm going to be honest with you, Marisol. I asked myself that. I had to. I really wanted to understand what I was feeling. I haven't been a doctor that long, so I needed to be sure. I really had to examine my attachment to you. And I didn't want to jeopardize my career by doing anything inappropriate or unethical, but I can't lie to myself. I care for you. I honestly do."

"But, you can't. I'm practically a monster."

"No, no you aren't. You are beautiful to me and always will be. But I understand how you must feel. You have to feel vulnerable, and I don't want you to feel like I'm taking advantage of you or this situation. And you don't have to respond to anything that I'm saying. I just wanted you to know how I felt. Especially, since you may be released soon."

Her heart thumped in her chest, and then leaped to her throat. She had forgotten that Terry, the physical therapist, had mentioned that they were considering a release date for her. She didn't want to panic, but now she felt it coming on.

She would have to continue her rehab, and she had thought about getting a job at the hospital. Still unsure of who she really was going to be, she figured that where she would be or what she'd be doing wouldn't really matter. But then, she never thought that Randolph would profess any feelings for her. That thought had never crossed her mind.

"I appreciate you sharing your thoughts. An' I'm glad that you understand that I'm really kind of confused by what you're sayin'.

I just don't see how you can possibly care for me. I'm absolutely hideous."

"You're beautiful. Scars can heal, they're only temporary. And you're beautiful with them. Inside and out."

Even as the birds of paradise chirped in the background, Cam wondered if she was hearing bullshit, even if it was playing against a Caribbean backdrop. But there was nothing insincere about his words, or about the way he was looking at her. To him, she was just an island girl, nearly burned to a crisp, with no address and no worldly possessions. She was wearing donated clothes from the hospital's Catholic mission. She literally had nothing. But he made her feel like she had everything. And, right then, she did. For at that moment, he was giving her himself.

She didn't know how to respond. Randolph was a tall, handsome, talented, and compassionate man. He was accomplished and intelligent. She could not imagine what he could possibly see in her. But, she felt his pure acceptance, And, deep in her soul, she knew it was the real deal. Just as real as what she felt for him.

Cam felt badly that he was pouring out his heart and soul to her, yet he didn't know who she was and she couldn't tell him. At least not yet.

Not necessarily because she didn't trust him, but because she was too unsure of herself.

She didn't know what she was going to do. Her first priority was to continue getting better, and to reconcile within herself that she would never look the same. Her appearance had drastically changed. She prayed and prayed, and asked the Lord to give her strength not to dwell on what she had lost, but on what she had found.

She hadn't even thought about whether she'd ever be Cam again or would remain who everyone thought she was; Marisol Kent. She had wondered, however, if there would ever be a time she could hear the name Marisol and not experience waves of guilt and a terrible tightening of her chest.

Cam just wanted to be healthy, happy, and free. And, she had to admit, she had wanted a change, and now she had one. A big one. But, it wasn't the one she thought it would be.

She had wanted a break from her career, and now she had that too. She remembered hearing her Aunt Mary say, "Be careful what you wish or pray for. You just might get it, and it won't be what you wanted or what you thought it would be. Be grateful for what you have and thank God you're alive." Her aunt was a wise soul. Cam's heart ached at the thought of the pain she must be in, the pain her supposed death had caused. She couldn't think about it now.

"Look, Randolph. You really don't know me," she said, and tried to pull away from him.

Reluctantly releasing her chin, he lightly placed his large hand on her arm. "I know enough. You're a good, kind, wonderful woman. You have suffered through unimaginable pain, yet you never complained. And I know it had to be hard. And the minute you could get around, you thought about others. You went down to the children's ward and offered them your love and comfort."

"I admire your strength, Marisol. And that strength clearly comes from your soul and from your faith in God. What else do I need to know about you? That's enough for me."

She smiled, and for once, the tightness in her facial muscles didn't bother her. "No one's ever said anythin' like that to me before. Not that I can recall." She placed her hand over his and allowed herself to look at him like she had never looked at him prior to that moment.

His hands were strong, yet gentle. He had wonderful traits, so warm and kind. And he was extremely handsome. The kind of handsome that one could really appreciate. He was the kind of virile, manly man who didn't know how attractive he really was. Who didn't need designer clothes and blinding jewelry to define who he was. But, she saw how good looking he was. Even behind those horn-rimmed glasses.

Randolph had smooth, rich cocoa-brown skin, a strong jaw and deep, shimmering eyes. With eyelashes that were long enough to brush against his lenses, his face was sculpted and chiseled, and his hair was neatly cropped. Even with a five o'clock shadow, his facial hair was silky and lush; even his thick eyebrows lay down as if he had combed them. And when he smiled, and parted those full, perfectly shaped lips, he revealed teeth that were even and pearly white. Her body tingled at the authenticity of his being. The quiet resolve of his presence and masculinity.

"I, uh, I never thought about you like that, Randolph."

"You're all I've thought about, Marisol. But I had to tell you how I felt. But, I don't want to overwhelm you. I know you have a lot on your mind. And a lot to figure out."

"Well, maybe you can help me do that," she said, the words slipping out of her mouth before she could stop herself.

"I'll do everything I can," he said.

They talked for hours in that quiet garden, ignoring the lingering looks and curious glances of those passing by, and the comings and goings of those venturing into their little haven.

Despite the vast differences in their backgrounds, they shared a lot of commonalities. Besides their religious upbringings, they both had a strong commitment to core values and being considerate of others.

Eventually, their conversations led to the topic of relationships. And while she struggled sharing her thoughts, vascillating between what was real in her world and what wasn't, he opened up about his lack of experience in the dating world.

She was both touched and endeared by his words. Like celebrities, doctors also had groupies. Patients always wanted to introduce him to their daughters. Sometimes, they wanted him for themselves. He seemed flattered, yet appalled by the female attention. It was so atypical. He clearly wasn't out for show or to mack as many women as possible, even though all he had to do was play his 'I'm a doctor' card. He actually seemed a little leery about meeting women, and told her that he had really only been seriously involved with one woman. Apparently the relationship hadn't worked out, partly because of his work, and partly because it hadn't met his lofty expectations.

He had grown up with parents who loved each other and stayed together, and he was looking for the same kind of committed relationship for himself. Knowing that he was so inexperienced at love made her feel sad for him, but oddly grateful. Especially when she thought of what she had with Heywood. She really didn't know what to call it. Relationship wasn't quite the right word, but it had been something. Was it a situation? Whatever it was, it was truly warped and unhealthy. And it occurred to her that she really never had any guidance on how to be in a healthy relationship.

She found employment at the hospital, and the staff was delighted she decided to stay. Her recovery had been exceptional, and was being documented and used in numerous research papers and presentations around the world. In fact, because she was so valuable to the program, they asked her if she would mind allowing them to continue to document her progress. In return, they would pay her a stipend that would allow her to rent her own flat and cover other personal expenses. The stipend would be in addition to her salary.

Cam was ecstatic. Pieces of her new life were falling into place, and she would now have the time to think about what she should do next, who she should be. A new life, whatever it was, was waiting for her. However, one thing was not waiting. Randolph's training at the hospital would be ending in January, a few months away, and he would be leaving for Chicago.

Randolph talked to Cam about this often. He tried to convince her that his intentions were honorable, and that he wanted her to know that he wanted to be a part of her life.

The depth of Randolph's feelings really touched her. She couldn't believe what her ears were hearing, or what her heart was feeling. But, was he just feeling sorry for her? Swept away with pity, mistaking it for love? "Never," he answered, and vowed to show her how much he really loved her. "By word and by deed," he had said. And now she had to make sure that she wasn't being swept away by words that had never been spoken to her before.

For the moment, she didn't have to think about whether she would be Cam or Marisol. It didn't matter. So many of the questions that ravaged her mind were quietly put aside, allowing her time for their resolution. Aunt Mary and her grandmother would be okay. She would eventually come to terms and be able to do the right thing by them and by Marisol and her family. Right now, it was time for her to heal. To heal her heart, her body, and her spirit. It was time for her to get well and stay well, and the authorization and permission was being dictated to her by the Man upstairs, and by the angel in hospital scrubs God had sent to watch over her.

chapter twenty-two

HE WASN'T going to do an O.J. Simpson. Heywood made sure he was in a highly visible locale the night of the break-in, not that he thought he would need an alibi. Duck had arranged it, through Parsley and some fourth and fifth parties, so that the trail would never lead back to him.

"She wasn't on her period, was she?"

"Naw. I'da worked through that if need be."

"Cool. Was the sheets fucked up when ya finished?"

"Word. That bitch got bust wide open. Her ass was slayed."

"That's my nigga. I know ya wrapped ya shit up tight, didn't ya?"

"Ya know it. Ran through plenty rubbers."

"Yeah, that's the shit I'm talkin' bout. But, for real tho', did ya get that nut?"

"Nutted all over that bitch. But most def, there ain't gonna be no oops babies happenin'."

"That's what I likes to hear, playa. No oops. No slip-ups."

"Right, right. Ya ain't fall asleep in that bitch afterwards, did ya?"

"Naw, ya know betta than that, Wood. I gets mine, then I bounce."

"Word. I knew ya'd get the goods, son."

Duck was leaned over, whispering in Heywood's ear. Speaking in code, he had confirmed everything that Heywood needed to know. As he sipped on a snifter of Remy XO and puffed on a super thick Camacho Legend cigar, the covert conversation with Duck was about the ransacking and theft at Deacon Owens's office. Translated, 'her being on her period' was code for 'problems'. The 'sheets fucked up' was code for 'toss up the joint'.

The bitch being 'slayed' was the affirmative. They messed the office up really well. 'Wrapping up tight' meant that they left no fingerprints. 'Gettin' the nut,' meant that they got Cam's files, and some random files, just to make sure that their tracks were covered. And, according to Duck, the job looked real. Like a genuine burglary.

Heywood gave Duck a pound, and then motioned for him to step. Heywood had cordoned most of the VIP section, and the liquor was flowing, the pills were poppin', the honeys were dippin', and the music was bangin'.

It was his first major outing on the social scene since Cam's death, and Heywood was really feeling himself. Things were really going his way. The post-Grammy at Fitz's proved to be pretty rewarding, and he had definitely set himself up to make sure no one, especially Noah, challenged his spot again. He just had to wait for the right time to play that card. He smiled smugly behind his shades, and sipped on his drink.

Tonight was a good night. Prior to Duck dropping the good news, Heywood had already gotten a lap dance from one of his favorite video vixens, head from a blazed-out former teen screen queen now new pop sensation in one of the private rooms, and plenty of invites for post-club sexcapades at various locales.

The groupies were thirsty, and out in full effect. Trays of condoms were being passed around like bottles of Dom, Ace of Spades, and Cristal. Pro athletes were in the house. Actors and actresses, hip-hop stars, rappers, music producers, and any other celebrity you could name. Everybody that was anybody, and everybody that wanted to be somebody. The paparazzi was staked out in the front and in the rear of the club, with their high impact lenses focused in to see who was coming, going, and cattin' around. And everyone's bodyguards were working overtime to stop cellphone cameras from snapping or recording the hedonistic events of the evening.

It was a hotbed for celebrities, the SET nightclub in South Beach. Heywood was truly feeling the love, with the ballers posting him up and giving him the handshake and the hug like the brothers do. His musical counterparts and adversaries were sending bottles of Patron and Remy XO to his table as a sign of respect. The gestures were both welcomed and expected.

Nestled between his protégée Skye and Cam's former background singer wannabe headliner Shaye, he was enjoying them vie for his attention, rubbing his chest and crotch and pursing their shiny lips. With his arms draped around their shoulders, Heywood, with a long toothpick dangling out of his mouth, was completely oblivious to other guests in the lounge. He was perched on his throne like King of the World. The only things missing were his velvet robe, jeweled crown, and golden staff.

Everyone was paying homage to Heywood, and he was loving it. With the exception of a few haters who didn't recognize the rules of engagement, Heywood was returning kisses to the ladies, and giving pounds and hugs to everyone else. He only gave Noah his back.

Dante' Vance, an actor/wannabe rapper, was one of the first ones to corner Heywood and welcome him back on the scene.

"Whassup, son?" Vance hollered out to Heywood. Two fine model types were draped over his shoulders.

"What up, uh, Vince, right?" Heywood was known for checking folk. Especially those brothers that looked better than him and were on something different than him. Especially if that something different was something that he wanted.

"Naw, it's Vance, man. Dante' Vance. But that's cool," he said, and then hugged Heywood, shook his hand, and gave him a pound.

Heywood nodded his head, then leaned in on Vance so he could speak directly in his ear. "That's what I said, playa. So, how's the flow?"

"It's aiight," Vance said, leaning back in Heywood's ear. "A little dark up in this joint, 'naw mean?"

Heywood glanced around, getting the gist of what Vance said. "Dark? Oh, ya mean ya don't like the dark chocolate, son? What, ya into the swirl or somethin'? Ya like the Beckys, huh?"

Vance flashed a smile, and when Heywood didn't reciprocate, he quickly frowned, and then shrugged. "They aiight. But, you know, I dig the sistas. In small doses. 'Naw mean? You know what the word is. 'Too much brown, too much sound.'"

Heywood pursed his lips and made a mental note about Vance. Heywood himself had many, many faults, but he never downed the sistas. Never. At least not exclusively. He was an equal opportunity dog. Light, dark, it didn't matter to him. Heywood gave him an icy laugh, and igged him the rest of the evening.

After downing several bottles of Ace of Spades, chuckling with his boys, and flirting with the other lovelies, Heywood motioned for his bodyguards, and one came running.

"I gotta go drain the snake, man," Heywood said.

"You want me to come?" Skye and Shaye said in unison, and then gave each other dirty looks.

"Yeah, y'all gonna come, but not right now." He grinned that slick grin. "For real, just chill. Keep it hot 'til I get back," Heywood said. He then stood up, and waited for his bodyguard to guide him to the restroom.

Once inside the plush VIP men's room, with its bamboo-covered walls, Heywood hurried past the small Latino attendant, and headed straight for the urinal. Unzipping his sagging signature jeans, he was oblivious to anyone else. He was so busy trying not to piss on himself, that he didn't notice Jamie Tee exiting the center stall.

"Well, well, well. Look who we got here," Jamie said. "Mister Magic Touch."

Heywood immediately bristled, but refused to acknowledge his presence or statement. He just kept right on doing his business.

Jamie's eyes were red, and his linen shirt clung to his skin, damp with perspiration. "Oh, I'm sorry, Heywood. Did I not address you properly? No disrespect. Well, I do apologize. Hello, Mister Heywood."

Heywood's eyes slitted, and he shook himself off, and flushed. He extended his dirty hand to Jamie. "Whassup, man. What ya doin' up here in the VIP? Shouldn't ya be in the H-B-P? The room for 'Has Been Peoples?'"

Jamie recoiled at his gesture. "You disgust me, Heywood." He looked down at Heywood's hand. "In more ways than one."

Heywood laughed. "How can I disgust you, ya fuckin' faggot? I know you've handled worst than my runoff. Ya ought to consider it a compliment." He sneered, spit in the urinal, and brushed past Jamie as he walked to the sink. "Especially after having to handle that punk ass Noah "know-it-all" Parker's shit." Heywood shuddered with exaggeration. "*Illll*. I'm sure he got ya givin' good brain everyday keepin' that contract ya got good."

Jamie flexed. "You fuckin' joke. You wanna call me a faggot? What do you call yourself? An equal opportunity fucker?"

Again Heywood laughed, and turned on the faucet to wash his hands. "Hey, whateva, gal. Shouldn't ya be in the little girl's room?"

"I got your little girl, you closet case. You're just mad that I wouldn't let you screw me. Literally or figuratively," Jamie said. "Unlike those other pitiful little boys trapped on your label."

Scrubbing his hands and preening in the mirror, Heywood rolled his eyes. "Screw you? Why would I wanna do that?"

"Because you screw everybody. Figa, figer, figuratively and literally." Jamie's eyelids stretched as he struggled to speak.

"Don't flatter yourself, queen. Nobody wants ya. Ya a used up piece of ass that couldn't get screwed if ya got butt-assed naked an' vogued across that dance floor out there. Noah just put ya on 'cause he's probably a queen too, an' y'all look out for each other."

"Fuck you, Heywood. You can talk that slick shit to your other little lackeys, but you won't come at me like that." Jamie's words were slurred, but his intent was clear.

"I know the deal. I been knowin' the deal. I know how fucked up you are. I know how dirty you tried to do Cam, God rest her soul. I'm just glad that she didn't fall for your bullshit."

"Goes to show how much ya know. Nothin'," Heywood said.

"I know enough to know that my girl wasn't engaged to your ass. I do know that. And I also know that she wasn't into you like that, if at all."

Heywood continued washing his hands and profiling in the mirror. "Aww, ya ass is just mad that she wasn't feelin' yo' ass. She didn't return ya unrequited love an' what not. Poor Jamie. Always the bridesmaid, neva the bride," he said with a chuckle.

Jamie scowled. "Is that the best you can do, Heywood? I mean, really.

I thought that you would've improved your name calling game by now. And for the record, yeah, I had mad love for Camara. She was my fam. She was my little sister. I would've never tried to take advantage of her, unlike you, you pervert. But, I also know that she wouldn't have given you and your, um, shortcomings, the time of day. So, you can spin your tall tales all you want, but I don't believe it."

Heywood shut off the faucet and extended his hands for the attendant to place a linen towel in it. "I don't give a shit 'bout what ya believe. An' I don't give a shit 'bout what yo' sayin' eitha, nigga. An' if ya keep speakin' on shit ya don't know about, ya gonna speak yo' ass into some issues an' complications. Ya feel me?"

"I ain't scared of you, you clown. You'll never get me to hop, skip, and jump like those other wind-up toys and blow-up dolls you got on your roster. Not me, not Jamie T. Don't nobody own me.

"And I know that Cam didn't want you tryna to own her either. And you know what? It makes me wonder, though. Why was it that when she decided she was gonna break away from your triflin' ass, that she suddenly up and dies? And nobody's sayin' nothin'. Hmmm. It really makes me wonder."

Heywood snatched the towel from the attendant, who shrank into the bathroom corner. He brusquely wiped his hands, then threw the towel down to the floor. Clinching his fists, he then stepped toward Jamie, his face shrouded with anger.

"Say again, mutha fucka? I don't think I heard ya."

"You heard me. Somethin' ain't right. It just ain't right. And I'm gonna find out what happened to my girl. Believe that."

"Keep it up, an' folks gonna be askin' what happened to yo' ass."

Just as Heywood squared his shoulders and nosed up to Jamie, Gary Edwards, the hulking action star, emerged from the same center stall that Jamie had exited from a short while ago.

"Whassup, Jamie? You got a problem here?" Gary asked, as he stepped behind Jamie and placed a large hand on his shoulder.

Jamie turned his head and leaned his cheek on Gary's hand, but continued glaring at Heywood. He remained silent.

Heywood unclenched his fist, smiled and head nodded at Gary.

"Naw, we cool. Whassup, Gary? Long time no see."

Gary returned the nod. "I'm glad to hear that y'all are cool, Heywood." He steered Jamie toward the sink. "Come on, Jay. Let's get outta here."

Heywood sneered, and marched towards the door, not even attempting to tip the bewildered attendant.

"This ain't over, Heywood," Jamie said.

"It's as over as your career is, son," Heywood said, as he opened the bathroom door, plastered a million dollar smile on his grill, and left, descending into the crowded hallway.

chapter twenty-three

IT WAS bliss. Pure bliss. She and Randolph's relationship had greatly intensified over the past few months, and although the last day of his internship was approaching, their connection was stronger than ever.

Though all they had ever shared was a gentle kiss, she knew that there was a fire burning just below the surface of their touch. She was working as a floating receptionist at the hospital, continuing her recovery protocol, and spending her free time either with Randolph or visiting the children in the burn unit. Her new life was gelling, and she was easily transforming into Marisol. The hospital staff and nuns had been wonderful; they had contributed funds and household items to outfit her nearby cozy flat.

And no one was more wonderful than Randolph. He was her rock. Safe and steady, he was her knight in shining armor, a sayer and a doer. Without any bravado and boss talk. He was a compassionate, thinking man; one who cared enough to think before he spoke.

In all the time they had spent together, he never raised his voice or demonstrated any behavior she didn't like. She cherished him and their relationship, and for the longest time, she was content in the cocoon she had created.

It was difficult, but she tried not to think of her grandmother or her Aunt Mary, or even Jamie Tee or her girls, too often. With the exception of her disfigurement, her not being in contact with them was her greatest source of pain. But, to survive, she had to close off that part of her life, and find solace in the fact that if she was presumed to be dead, then at least her estate would take care of her family.

During her quiet moments, when she wasn't working and Randolph was at the hospital, she did think about her loved ones and her former life. But, then she'd pass a mirror, and gasp at the scarred skin so evident on her face. It was a continual, painful reminder that she could never return to her former self or life as she looked now.

And although Randolph accepted her as she was, she couldn't help but question what would happen once he left the little island. It was the elephant in the room whenever they were together. She tried to downplay how she felt, because she just assumed that when he left, that would be it. Then she would have to face her face, and her life as Marisol. Or would she?

Her life had been turned inside out. Outside in. She had prayed for a chance to walk away from her life as a megastar, but not like this. Clearly it was God's will, and she had to accept it. She had to come to terms with a lot of things, and Randolph had made it easier for her. But now, as she faced his pending departure, she felt like reality was settling in. And she really didn't know what to do about it.

The topic of Randolph's return to the States came up again after an intimate dinner in her new second floor apartment. Yes, she had even learned to cook a few dishes, and her meal of broiled grouper, fried plantains, rice, and peas, had been a big hit with him.

As they cleared the small table the nuns had given her, she took a handful of dishes to the sink, and Randolph approached her from behind, wrapping his arms around her waist.

There was a bay window above the sink, and it provided a decent view of the DR's downtown. Gazing through the window panes, she leaned her head back, and he gently kissed her cheek.

"I'm really going to miss this place," he said.

"Is that the only thing you're goin' ta' miss?" she asked, her voice teasing. She tried to mask her true thoughts.

He turned her around to face him, and he smiled softly. "Of course not, Marisol. But, I don't want to miss you."

Her brows furrowed. "What do you mean, Randy?"

He stepped back, and lowered his head, so that he could meet her at eye level. "I don't want to leave you. I want you to come with me."

She was stunned. She hadn't expected that. Not that she didn't want it, but how could she? She was comfortable here. Everyone knew her and took care of her. They were kind and compassionate, and she knew that it would not be like that back in the States. They'd treat her like a leper. She knew how they would be. The only good thing was that she would never be recognized as Cam. She'd just be known as the Bride of Frankenstein. Her mind was racing, and she asked him to repeat what he had just said.

"I said that I want you to come with me."

She stuttered and stammered. The reality of his leaving was crashing around her, and she suddenly realized that she didn't want a new life if it didn't include him.

Her mind raced. It would be so much easier if they just stayed on the island. But, she knew Randolph had obligations and commitments. She had been trying to get away from hers when this catastrophe struck in the first place. Even so, she had to grasp at the straws in front of her.

"Randy, why, um, why don't you just stay here? Wouldn't that be wonderful? I'm sure the hospital would love for you to stay."

He led her over to her donated loveseat, and forced her to sit down. He sat beside her, and held her hand. Looking her in the eyes, he spoke slowly, but firmly. "You know I can't do that. As much as I'd like to stay and help, I can't. That's not what I signed up for.

"And I want you to see more than what you've seen in your life. The mountains, snow, big old oak trees and big, crowded cities with great, tall buildings. I mean, you've never been to the States, have you?"

She didn't want to answer, so she turned away. But he refused to let her run.

"There's so much for you do there. And be. Whatever you want, you know I'll support you. If you want to go to school. If you don't.

Whatever. I'll just be happy if you're there with me."

"I, uh, can't Randy. I just can't. I'm not fit to be seen in public. 'Specially in a place as big as the U.S. Wit' all their big crowded cities an' big oak trees."

He laughed, and tried to ease her concerns. "I know you're probably scared. And I don't blame you. I don't want you to feel like I'm pushing you or trying to take advantage of you. I don't expect you to live with me. I'd help you get your own place, near me of course, and help you get your bearings. You know that, right?"

She remained still, trying to process what he was saying. He continued. "Most important, I want you to know that I don't care about your scars, Marisol. And I'm sure that most people won't either. They really aren't that noticeable."

"But I care about them. I know what I used to look like and it bothers me that I look like I do now. I know I'm self-conscious, but I don't want people starin' at me like I'm a creature."

He sighed, as if he was reluctant to continue. "You're not a monster, baby. But, I knew that was what you were going to say. And I do understand, even though it bothers me to hear you speak of yourself like that.

"Listen, all I want you to do is be happy. I don't want you to come to the States and hide away in some darkened room. I want you to thrive. And be free. And not have any worries or doubts. At least none that I can't help you with."

"I'm not sure what that means, Randy."

"It means that I want you to feel comfortable with yourself, wherever you are. And if your scars hinder you from feeling that way, then I want to help you do something about them."

"What do you mean?"

"It means that when you're ready, there are other options you can consider. There are advanced surgical procedures available now in Europe, and who knows? Dr. Salazar may be able to get them here on a trial basis. There are procedures like dermal regeneration that really helps eliminate the scarring on burn victims, but I'm not trying to rush you or push you. It's totally your decision. Only yours. And I want you to know that I'm here for you, no matter what you decide to do."

"I 'ere you, Randolph. But, I, uh, I don't know what to say."

"Know this. Know that I love you, Marisol."

His words rendered her speechless. "You, you, love me? How can you. I can't believe that."

"If you don't believe what I say, let me show you." He slipped his arms under her legs, and swept her up into his arms.

He carried her to her bedroom, and laid her down on the bed. With delicate deliberation, he knelt down and kissed her, and she inhaled the warm fragrance of his Bijan cologne. She tried to protest, but her body yielded to his seductive touch.

He slowly removed his scrubs, and held his hands out to his sides. His body was long, but not very taut. He wasn't flabby, but he didn't have washboard, six-packed abs either. It was the body of a scholar. Too much time in the hospital, and not enough time in the gym.

"See, I'm not perfect either." His self-effacing humor lightened the moment. "Nobody is."

She stood up in front of him, trembling and shivering. He removed her head wrap, and her locks fell freely down her back. Using both of his hands, he lifted her hair and placed it over her shoulders, and gently started taking off her clothes. She wanted to stop him. Her body was shaking. She was overcome with the reality that he was about to see her. Not in a clinical way, but in a carnal manner. She was ashamed of how she would look. But, the shame she felt for her scarred body melted as she felt his eyes and saw his underwear bulge at the sight of her curvaceous body. Overwhelmed by emotions and senses, that night was the first time they made love.

Sweetly, tenderly. Sitting on the edge of the bed, he spread his legs and pulled her close to him. He caressed every inch of her blemished body with trembling fingers, hands, and lips. Hesitant at first, his actions were unsure and anxious. She encouraged him to touch her, feel her, and make her feel like he really wanted her. She was afraid too; afraid that being held in such a way might be painful for her, and she tried not to tense up when he wrapped his arms around her. She held her breath. It was a little uncomfortable, but it was mind over matter, she convinced herself. Her heart was beating fast, and her nerves and muscles tightened.

She responded. Hungrily. Her body ached for his touch, and the closeness of his body on hers.

Tears sprang to her eyes. She breathed deeply as he kissed and licked her scarred stomach, and then she relaxed. And then she felt her skin relax. The slight pain evolved into distinct and decisive pleasure, a tingling sensation, and she knew that she would be able to enjoy being intimate with him.

"You okay?" he asked.

"I'm, I'm okay," she smiled.

"I don't want you to think that I'm some sort of player, Marisol. Because I'm not."

"I believe you," she said, the words escaping her mouth before she even thought.

Holding her waist, he lay down on the bed, and gently pulled her on top of him. Kissing her neck, he spoke softly. "You sure?"

"I'm sure."

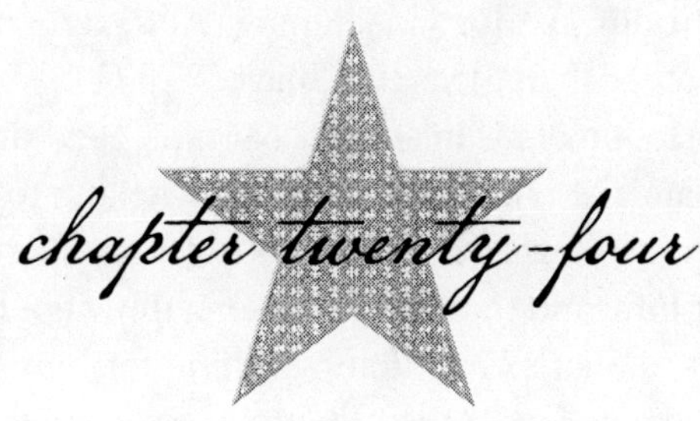

chapter twenty-four

FULL LIPS traced the curves of her breasts, and her nipples hardened at the touch. Slowly, the tongue dragged down her navel, to her wet punany. She moaned in ecstasy.

"Cut!" Heywood yelled, and clicked the pause button on his expensive digital videocamera. Wearing only black silk boxer shorts and an open matching robe, he turned away from the viewfinder, and shook his head. "That shit don't even look real. It don't even sound real. What da fuck."

Shaye removed her flushed face from Skye's crotch, and fell backwards on her knees with a repressed expression of exasperation on her face. "What, Heywood? I'm doin' it like you said. No disrespect, Skye. But, I ain't really into chicks like that, for real."

"Fuck that," he said, and pulled a vial out of his pocket. He opened it, popped two blue pills in his mouth, and washed them down with the remains of the Grey Goose Vodka and cranberry juice he had been drinking since the trio had gathered after a party at the 40/40 Club in Manhattan. "Then ya must not really be into makin' music. At least not wit' me, ya ain't."

Heywood had always secretly videotaped his liaisons in his penthouse and safeguarded his films in his hidden vault until he felt like showing them to his boys. Lately, though, he had ended the secrecy. Now he openly filmed his sexual encounters with willing participants and had even outfitted a room just for videotaping. And, tonight's pseudo-porn stars were none other than Skye and Shaye.

With the protection of his infamous "N-Snips," and the right drugs, he found that his wannabe talent was more than willing to do whatever he wanted them to do in terms of making a hot porn flick. Usually it was entertainment for him, and translated into something hot for his boys later. Tonight, however, the girls were doing nothing for him. He saw nothing hot through the camera lens. At least nothing hot enough for him.

It was the wee hours of the morning, and while waiting for the effects of his X to kick in, Haywood marched over to the bed and shoved the two women apart. Uninhibited by drugs, they both lay with their legs open. They displayed fresh Brazilians as they rested on their elbows.

"This shit is wack," he said, and plunked his beverage down on the nightstand. "Whitney said 'crack is wack,' but y'all cracks is wack. Ya cracks an' ya asses. Damn. Y'all shit ain't even hot enough to get me excited now, an' it sho' nuff ain't gonna be hot enough to get me off later. I ain't wastin' my good film on this shit, ya heard?"

Skye reached for his flaccid crotch and he shoved her hand away. "Get off me, trick!" he snapped. "I told ya that shit didn't make me hot. Now look," he said and grabbed Shaye's hand. "I want ya to make it look real, bitch. Like this shit is really happenin'. Lick your fingers, shove it in her ass, do somethin'." He leaned over and hocked up a jawful of spit, and blew it onto Skye's clit. "Like that. Wet it up. Damn. No wonder your music ain't got no passion. Y'all ain't got no passion. Y'all need some sexy back real bad, ya heard?"

As Skye tried wiping his spit off of her, Haywood continued barking out orders and directions. In the adjoining room, one of his cellphones rang. There was a rap on the door, and Duck called out. "Yo, Wood. Ya got a call."

"Get this shit poppin' while I take this call," he said and slid off the bed, his robe flailing open. He grabbed his drink from the stand, and took another swig. "When I come back, I want to see some fiyah. Some asses shakin' an' some titties jigglin'. Make it hawt!" He snapped his fingers.

Storming out of the room, Heywood slammed the door behind him, and it shook the walls as it hit the frame. Duck was slumped down on an Eames style chaise lounge, his arm extended, holding one of Heywood's untraceable phones.

"Speak!" Heywood barked into the receiver.

"Is that how you greet your homey, partner?"

Heywood's bravado dropped, and he mouthed the words, "Get the fuck out," to Duck. As Duck ambled off the chair and headed toward the kitchen, Heywood absently scratched his neck, and leveled his voice. He cleared his throat and downed the remains of his drink. "Yo, yo, whassup, my brotha? How ya doin'?"

"How am I'm doin'? I'm livin' large, haven't you heard?" The voice paused and then nearly shouted into the receiver. "How the fuck you think I'm doin' up in this fuckin' joint?"

Heywood held the phone away from his ear, and when Duck was out of earshot, he placed it back to his face and continued talking. "I know, Bo. I know it ain't easy on a bruh." Bo was Typhoon's code name. It was a play off on bow-tie, dropping the tie for Ty. Heywood's code name was Nat, which was an anagram for Wood, and shortened from Natalie Wood.

Typhoon grunted, and Heywood closed his robe like Typhoon could see him, and walked toward the floor to ceiling window. City lights dotted the skyline, and there was a whirl of cars trailing through down the streets and across the blocks, streaming colorful lights in the pre-dawn darkness.

"Man, I gotta give it to you straight, son. I'm not diggin' the vibes I'm gettin' from you these days," Typhoon's baritone voice crackled in Heywood's earpiece, and he shook his head.

Heywood absently toyed with the empty glass in his hand. "I, uh, what ya mean, Bo? I'm still ridin' wit' ya."

"Ridin' with me? *Shee-it.* Yo' ass is ridin' off me, nigga. You'd still be catchin' the bus if it wasn't for me, Nat. Hell, you'd probably still be walkin' on those goddamned turned over shoes yo' broke ass used to wear. *Hmmph.* How quick we forget shit. But you know I ain't about to let you forget about me, son. An' that's why I'm trippin' over the fact that you tryna avoid me an' shit."

"I'm, I'm not tryna avoid ya, Bo. But, ya know the deal. I got yo' message, an', an' I was gonna get wit' ya. Ya know we gotta be careful, man. Everybody an' they momma's checkin' for me, watchin' my moves an' shit, so I'm just tryna be cool wit' ours. I'm watchin' out for me an' you."

"*Hmmph.* I don't feel so watched out for, son."

"For real. I got ya message the other day, an' I was gonna get wit' ya. Somethin' just rolled up on me that I had to deal wit' an' it kinda side-tracked me, that's all."

"Somethin' just came up? What the fuck? You know ain't nothin' never more important than me, son. At least that's how it used to be. Now, I'm gettin' the feelin' like you gettin' all brand new on me an' shit."

"Naw, Bo. It ain't like that. I'm still lookin' out. I just gotta be care-ful, ya heard? Like this. We gotta keep it cute. Ya know all eyes are watchin'. Ya know we ain't supposed to be havin' no late night chats like this. Not unless we're sure it's culpa static."

Again Typhoon grunted. "Culpa static? Listen at you. You done real-ly got big time, ain't you? Insteada callin' you Heywood, I might as well call you Hollywood."

Heywood cringed when Typhoon called him by his government name. He got the message that Typhoon was growing wary of him. By dropping his name like that, he was letting Heywood know that he was putting him out there. And that even behind bars, Typhoon still had power to rule him. Heywood's eyes fell upon his city, while his mind processed the subliminal messages Typhoon was sending, and tried to keep his temper in check. He was tempted to call Typhoon's name, but rethought it.

"Money ain't right, Heywood. I need to know why my money's gettin' so short from you, 'specially when I see you out here glossin' an' flossin' an' jet settin' all over the fuckin' planet. I can't turn on the fuckin' idiot box or open up a goddamned magazine unless I see yo' ass either grinnin' an' skinnin' or tryna look hard. Scowlin' like you constipated or somethin'.'"

Heywood sighed. "It's business, Bo. Ya know, it takes a lot to keep the company runnin'. An' since I'm the face of the business, I gotta get out an' promote an' shit. People expect me to be here an' there. That builds the brand. Frames the image. Image is everythang, an' that's who I am. That's what I do."

"I don't give a fuck about what you do. I just don't want my ends gettin' short. An' if they do, then I need to see yo' shit gettin' short, too, money."

Heywood shook his head and clenched his jaw. Typhoon didn't know shit about the music business, never did, and now he wanted to tell him what to do. But, he had to bring it down a thousand.

He lowered his voice and spoke through gnashed teeth. "I'm tellin' ya, it's just business. It costs to be the boss. An' on the real tip, I gotta be extra careful, ya know? All eyes are on the financials, an' I gotta make sure that what's meant to be in the background stays in the background. From what I understand, Big Brother's checkin' an' recheckin' the overseas accounts, an' even tryna push paper through the normal channels is tight."

"Um, hum. I just know my shit is gettin' real short, and it's affecting my business. My attorneys don't work for free, ya know."

Heywood took a deep breath. This conversation was grating on his nerves. He was trying to get Typhoon off his back, but this cat was digging in. "I feel ya, Bo. But, ya know I just lost my cash cow. That was a major loss, an' it's really put a hurtin' on things. Big time."

Typhoon swore under his breath. "Tell that shit to someone who don't know no fuckin' better. You gotta contract. If anything, she's probably worth more now than she was alive. At least to you."

"It's not that simple. Everything's all tied up. I ain't seein' no paper."

"Right, right. An' in the interim, until the shit gets untied, I'm sure you're workin' that shit to your advantage. If you ain't gettin' now, you greasin' the skids so it'll come later. I know how the game's played, son. Whateva you doin', I wants mines. You need to make sure I don't come up short no more. An' you also need to make sure you don't develop a sudden case of amnesia when it comes to who I am. For real."

Their conversation continued for a few more tense moments, with Typhoon repeating Heywood's name over and over. Fortunately for Heywood, he was able to maintain his composure, but it wasn't easy. When he had reached his boiling point, the conversation abruptly ended. Typhoon's guard had told him the call was a wrap; it was time for a shift change. Typhoon, however, had made it clear that he expected Heywood to do exactly as he had been told. To live up to their agreement and pay up. Heywood had said all the right things, but meant none of them. The phone call just renewed his determination to sever all ties with Typhoon, who Heywood now saw as useless and powerless. He was a relic and had become a liability. And liabilities were meant to be eliminated.

After he clicked off his phone, Heywood hurled his empty glass against the wall, and it shattered as it hit one of his original Keith Haring paintings. The noise caused Duck to yell out from the other room.

"Yo, Wood. You aiight in there?" Duck cracked the door open, and stuck his head in. He peered around, and spotted the broken glass on the carpeted floor.

"I'm okay, nigga," Heywood snapped, and flicked his thumb at the mess. "Make sure—"

"That shit gets cleaned up," Duck interrupted.

Heywood overlooked Duck's impertinence and turned back toward the window and started muttering to himself. "Yeah, I'm aiight. But, that's more than I can say about that fuckin' Typhoon, that washed up mutha fucka. He got more balls than a little if he thinks he's still gonna try to run me. Fuck him. He betta recognize. I'm gonna show him who's runnin' things. Me, mutha fucka. Me. But, he'll find out. 'Cause his ass is done. Finished. Through. He ain't gonna know what hit him. I'm cancellin' his ass. This contract is terminated. It's a wrap. An' there ain't gonna be a god-damned thing he can do about it. Except bend over, an' unzip that orange jumpsuit of his. He'll be grabbin' his ashy-assed ankles an' takin' it."

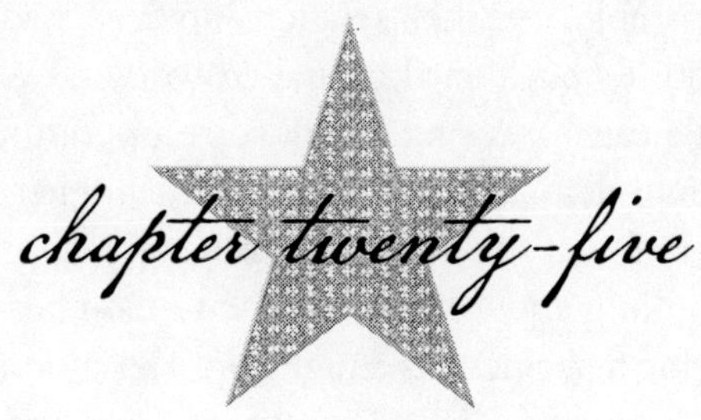

chapter twenty-five

AS SHE opened the door of her hospital locker, she stared at the picture of her and Randolph that was taped to the inside of the door. Like a love-struck teenager, she gazed at the picture of him hugging her, her face buried in his chest. Randolph had set the self-timer on his digital camera so that he could take the picture. This was the first photograph of them together.

Prior to this one, she had shied away from pictures, but Randolph had been insistent. He wanted a photo of her to take with him, and he had a copy made for her. She stared at it, and reluctantly acknowledged that it was a conscious depiction of her subconscious reaction. She had purposely turned her face away from the camera at the last minute, so that it would not capture her scarred image.

It had been a couple of weeks since Randolph returned to the States, where he had accepted a residency at the prestigious Hahnemann University Hospital in Philadelphia. Although he had pleaded with her to join him, and she hadn't wanted him to leave, she just wasn't ready to go. For the moment, she was living a lie, but didn't want to be a liar. Or so she reasoned. She had too many unresolved issues, and the calm and anonymity of the little island was best for her. At least until she was able to sort out her life.

After he professed and expressed his love for her, she and Randolph had become inseparable, and their relationship deepened to the point that they no longer hid it from their hospital co-workers. While some of the nurses were a little catty at losing a handsome opportunity like the good doctor, no one could deny that he was honestly into her. With him in her life, she was able to forget the haunting thoughts that tormented her.

Instead of thinking about them, she focused on her new-found love. He made it easy for her. She was caught up. Her emotions were almost as raw as her wounds had been. They spent every moment they could together, walking the beach, playing with the pediatric patients, or just holding each other and watching the sun rise through the sliding glass doors of her tiny flat.

Randolph made her feel loved and secure. He was open and honest with her, and they talked about just about everything. He was magnificent, yet humble. He was smart and worldly, yet innocent. A lot like her.

His departure hadn't been easy, but before he left, he kissed her tear-streaked cheek and promised that he would always be faithful to her, and always love her. She wanted to believe him, but she had her doubts. With everything else in her life so crazy, he would probably end up being crazy too.

But, he was firm about wanting her to join him, but only when she was ready. And until she was ready, he promised to wait. And visit as often as he could. And before he headed home, he presented her with a laptop and cellphone, so that they could keep in close contact. The computer came equipped with a videocam, so they could even see each other over the miles.

It sounded like a great plan, but once Randolph started at the hospital in Philly, he was working crazy hours and odd shifts. He was normally exhausted, but always found time to either text a message or send her a quick email. She, in turn, kept her cellphone by her side, hoping he would call. She also texted him often, just to let him know that she missed him and was thinking of him.

Cam was still hesitant about saying that she loved him, although she would end her emails with a *"Love, Me,"* closing. Part of her wanted to say that she loved him, a large part of her really did, but she just wasn't ready to go there. She had never uttered those words before, and given her present state, she didn't want to say them now. He didn't press her about it, and she was relieved, but still bothered that she could not return his sentiments.

She felt awful that she wasn't being completely truthful with him, as Randolph deserved the truth. She recalled their earlier conversations about his love life, and vowed never to hurt him, either purposely or by accident.

So, for now, she kept the words "I Love You" bottled up inside, and decided to deal with her issues. With Randolph around, she was able to avoid and hide, but now she had a lot of free time on her hands. She also had a new computer, although she felt guilty about surfing the net if she wasn't conversing with him. Also, she didn't know what was out there on the Internet, and didn't know if she wanted to find out. Cam wasn't sure she was ready to see what information, fact or fiction, gossip, or downright lies, were out there on the late Starr. She simply didn't want to tempt fate, so she purposefully kept the computer off.

Cam gently rubbed the picture, and slowly closed the locker door. She had just finished her shift, and was contemplating what she was going to do that evening. With her boyfriend gone, she spent most of her free time at the hospital, in the pediatric burn unit and rehab center. But, today, she decided to do something different. It was still gorgeous outside, so she decided to venture over to her favorite fruit stand, grab some fresh mangoes, and go relax on the beach.

It would be a good time to clear her head. Normally, the beaches would be crowded with tourists, but with the onset of hurricane season, there weren't as many people vying for the lounge chairs and best spots. So, she sent Randolph a quick text message, threw on her favorite linen hoodie, and headed out of the hospital.

After securing two ripe mangoes and an ice cold Ting, she wandered around the beach, searching for the perfect spot. Not too secluded, but not too close to anyone else. She tucked her dangling locks under her hoodie, and carefully slid on an oversized pair of shades. She wasn't covering up, like Starr used to. Cam was just trying to deter strangers from gawking at her injured face.

The Boca Chica Beach was still a little crowded, and most of the lounge chairs were occupied. Scanning the area, she spotted a middle-aged European couple packing away their belongings. She darted over to where they were, and waited while they stuffed everything into their giant straw bags. She glanced up at the clear sky and smiled. There were a few good hours of daylight remaining, and she wanted to make the most of it.

The couple smiled as they left, and she swooped down on their now-vacant area. She found a folded newspaper on one of their chairs, and called out to the couple. However, her voice was apparently drowned out by the surf, and they continued on. Cam shrugged, and just as she was about to toss it into a nearby trash receptacle, she saw the cover. It was the *Sun*, a UK tabloid that documented the triumphs and trials of the world's celebrities. Cam's eyes scanned the pictures of the stars, most in protective poses, as if they were seeking to avoid the stalkarazzi. Oh how well she recalled those moments. Her eyes swept to the lower left corner of the rag, and she gasped. There was an older picture of her, one of the last promo shots that she had taken. The caption under the photo read:

FALLEN STARR. THE TRAGEDY CONTINUES.

Her legs gave way, and she fell onto the white plastic chaise lounge. Everything fell from her hand to the ground except the tabloid. As soon as she got her bearings, she flipped through the pages until she located the one-page article on her demise.

She pored over every word, reading and rereading every sentence. The article brushed over the details of her death, but focused on current events happening with her estate. According to the author, Heywood was mourning her passing, was struggling with their secret engagement, and was totally broken up about their approaching wedding date. The lies sickened her.

Apparently, a battle was brewing over Starr's estate, with Heywood fighting Aunt Mary for control. Heywood said he was trying to control the estate the way Starr wanted it. An unnamed source accused Heywood of using fixers to shut down the U.S. media whenever they reported anything negative about him or Starr. This highly-financed, systematic blackout even reached the websites and blogs. The unnamed source had chosen to go to the *Sun* because he "would not be silenced." The statement immediately made her think of Rashad.

The article was filled with Heywood's lies and falsehoods. The idea that he was fighting with her Aunt Mary and grandmother over her estate made her see red. Suddenly, she couldn't bear not knowing what strings Heywood was pulling now, or what strings he had pulled prior to her reported death. The lid had been blown off of her contained curiosity, and now there was nothing she could do except try to piece together the fragments of her life. She quickly shoved the paper under her arm and ran home, oblivious to anyone or anything in her path, determined to find out the complete truth.

She spent the evening poring over the Internet. She checked her and Heywood's Twitter and Facebook pages. Hers were frozen in time, shut down because of the number of entries submitted by her fans. She nearly gagged when she read Heywood's pages, where he professed his undying love for her. She grew even more ill after reading the condolence messages addressed to him. She felt for the bloggers who expressed genuine concern, but was unsettled by Heywood's public, and totally untrue, confessions.

She continued searching. She Googled every aspect of her life, probing every article, word, and intent. Her eyes were bleary, but remained fixed on the screen. They were bloodshot and achy, but remained glued to her new MacBook Pro.

She didn't sleep, barely taking a break to go to the bathroom or gulp down a hot cup of espresso. She was driven, incensed. Hurt. The more she read, the angrier she became. Even though, until today, she had been ready to deny her very existence, that was before she discovered that Heywood was tampering with her family's well being and with her estate. After repeated searches, Cam discovered that most of her fan websites had been taken down. The main one left standing was Rashad's. She had been right to believe that he was the unnamed source in the *Sun* article because his website was now devoted to his concerns about Cam's death and her music. It was titled, "I will not be silenced." Rashad's website mentioned rumors of a new will, with Heywood the beneficiary. It also stated that her last book of music was missing. Cam's gloves were coming off.

★

She had resigned herself to the fact that as long as her family was okay, and had her fortune to maintain themselves, she would be content being Marisol. However, now that they were being threatened by Heywood, she knew she couldn't sit idly by and let them be hurt or taken advantage of. Her will had ensured her family's financial security; she could not believe Heywood was trying to steal it from them.

She was vexed. How had this happened? How had the accident happened? Had it even been an accident? How could everyone think she was dead? True, she and Marisol had resembled each other, but her girls knew who she was. Had they been in on it? Had the whole thing been planned so Heywood could gain control of everything she had?

"STARR SUCCOMBS TO INJURIES SUFFERED DURING VIDEO SHOOT," the headline screamed. Cam read further. There had been a freak accident at the remote site of the video shoot, and the volcano had a small, but powerful eruption. She remembered Heywood's insistence that they shoot at the restricted site. Granted, he was evil, but even he couldn't make a volcano erupt. And why would he, especially since he was right there with them?

There was no rhyme or reason. It had been a freak accident, but how had their identities been confused? She had to know, but how could she know for certain? Who could she trust? And, if there was more to the story than an innocent mistake, she wouldn't be safe just popping back on the scene.

In her heart, she felt that Heywood was somehow involved, since he was lying about their relationship and contesting her will, forcing her estate into probate. Yes, he was the one who stood to gain the most from her death, and though he hadn't wanted her to take any time off, her permanent leave of absence obviously was working wonders for him and his checkbook.

She didn't want to think that he was capable of this and had thought so little of her, that she was so expendable, but it was painfully clear now. Why hadn't he known she wasn't the one who died? Either he didn't want to know or he did know, and wanted it like that.

Cam continued to scour and comb the Internet for more answers. When she read that Heywood had wanted to have her body cremated before it was returned to the States, it was another red flag. Why would he want to cremate her unless he was trying to hide something? Why would he do something that would be so totally against the wishes of her family?

She had to find out what had really happened, and how she had ended up at the burn center. The nuns at the hospital told her that initially, her hospital bills had been paid by Cam's assistant until the payments suddenly ceased. Cam realized that this had happened because Heywood had filed an injunction to freeze her assets. Every piece of new information made her more incensed.

Her Internet searches hit dead end after dead end. "How can I find out what happened in Montserrat when I don't have any money?" she asked herself aloud. "I've got to get back there."

Using her new cellphone from Randolph, she called the hospital in Montserrat, but was told the hospital administrator was the only person she could speak with, and he was on a leave of absence. Looking for Marisol's relatives was another dead end; only after hours searching the 'net did she recall Randolph mentioning that her medical records had stated that there was no immediate family available for consult. "That may have been the only thing correct on either of their charts," Cam mused to herself. Then, she recalled Marisol telling her the same thing.

Completely overwhelmed by her thoughts and troubled by the reality that she was suddenly faced with, Cam reached out to the place she has always found comfort. Her faith. She prayed for strength and direction, but teetered between being hell-bent on finding the truth and being too numb and afraid to do anything.

"I need to know," she thought to herself. "I can't start a new life with Randolph until my old one is straightened out. I worked too hard to have everything taken away, especially by Heywood." It had been different when she had decided to walk away, but to be pushed away? Not acceptable.

She had to know what was happening to her family. What was going on with Jamie and Rashad? What had happened to her girls? Allison? What about her charities? Everything that was important to her. And as long as she didn't have to drag Randolph into this uncertainty, she would deal with it on her own.

And it hit her that she really was on her own. With Randolph thousands of miles away, there was no one she could rely on. No one but herself. So she dug deep within, and in the following weeks, she spent countless days trying to piece together what was reported about her death, and what really occurred. She then realized that she would never be able to find the answers to all of her questions where she was and as she was, so she made the crucial decision to go back to the States. But not like this.

First, she would accept Randolph's offer to have the facial reconstruction surgery, and then she would figure out exactly what she would have to do when she returned to the States. She contemplated telling him the truth, but she thought better of it. Could she trust him? Was she afraid to trust him? Afraid to tell him? The only thing that she knew for sure at the moment was that she was moving forward, and plotting to return home. Probably still as Marisol, but with the hopes and goal of somehow also reclaiming her life as Camara "Starr" Addison.

chapter twenty-six

HE WAS slouched down in the rear corner booth of one of his favorite haunts in Brooklyn, feeling quite Rat Packish. Dressed like one of his idols, Frank Sinatra, Heywood was outfitted in a form-fitted black suit with thin lapels, stark white shirt, and loosened black and white striped tie.

With his extra dark glasses on, he had tucked a big white napkin in his collar, and was enjoying a piece of savory garlic bread. Every now and then he liked to get his 'classic gangsta' on, and nothing made him feel in character more than being at Bamonte's, tucked away on Withers Street. It was similar to the other local celebrity favorite, Lucali's, over on Henry Street, but that place had gotten a little too popular lately.

Bamonte's was a place where no one saw you and no one heard you; a place that held many secrets. With its red and white checked table-cloths, faded pictures, and cracked black vinyl booths, no one would ever mistake it for a place for the chic people. Customers even had to bring their own wine, but Heywood didn't mind. With his bodyguards strategically placed around the bustling restaurant, he felt like Al Capone in the movie *The Untouchables*. Completely untouchable.

He was sitting on top of the Big Apple, and loving every minute of it. *My Way* was playing on the jukebox, sung by none other than his idol, Frank Sinatra. He wanted to sing along. Things were definitely going his way.

The staged break-in at Deacon Owen's office had gone off without a hitch, and could never be traced back to him. It had two key benefits. First, it had rattled Kevin and old man Owens. Second, it made Cam's attorney look pretty incompetent when he reported to the court that some of Cam's and other clients' documents had been stolen. Heywood congratulated himself silently. That coup could only shore up his case for removing the good deacon as Cam's attorney. The theft had yielded everything that he wanted, except Cam's priceless music books.

At present, Heywood's high-priced legal team was making the case for the updated will, he was making stacks of money off Cam's music, and he was controlling every aspect of her image. He had even decided to let a little dirt get on that image, just because he was getting a little bored with all of the oohing and aahhing about what an angel she had been. It played out. And he was getting tired of paying fixers to shut down misinformation like that. In his mind's eye, anything he did or didn't do was okay. There was no one to question or stop him.

Even though he couldn't locate the music books, he did have a court order requiring them to be produced, but Owens was contesting it. Heywood's legal team had forced Aunt Mary to sign an affidavit swearing that she didn't know where they were, and he had to believe that she didn't know. Aunt Mary was many things, but she wasn't a liar.

Heywood's lawyers had also wrangled a complete list of Cam's accounts, including her safe deposit boxes. When they were accessed and inventoried, the books weren't there either. It bothered him that he couldn't put his hands on them, but at least he had the one Cam had with her during the videoshoot, but that wasn't enough. He knew she had at least four others somewhere, and he wasn't about to let them go. They were gold mines, and he was determined to find them, no matter what. No one but him was going to benefit from anything of Cam's.

The elderly waitress, long past her prime, but still wearing the make-up from her stunna' days, came over and brought him the bottle of chilled Chianti he had brought from his private stock. She poured him a glass with her liver-spotted hands, was polite but not intrusive, and asked if he needed anything else.

"No ma'am," he replied. He never looked at her, just continued eating his bread. To his right was the kitchen, with full swinging doors, and twin portal windows. One door swung open, Kevin emerged, and slipped into the booth next to Heywood.

"Drink?" Heywood asked, and motioned toward the wine bottle.

Kevin shook his head, but quickly changed his mind. He raised his hands and looked as his palms, and then smoothed down his suit. "Yeah, I need something. What the hell, Heywood? Why do you have me walking through some greasy kitchen?"

"That's how I do things 'round here."

Kevin sighed and again shook his head. "I don't appreciate you calling me down here like some little flunky. We've had this discussion before, and I don't like that. Now, if I'm supposed to be working with you, I'd appreciate a little more respect."

Heywood motioned for the waitress to bring another wine glass. The old woman immediately stopped what she had been doing, brought a glass over, and filled it. She tried to hand Kevin a menu, but he declined, waving her away as if she were an insect. She asked him if she could get him anything else, and again he declined. She walked away, muttering under her breath.

Heywood chuckled, and looked Kevin up and down. "Boy, you really got no love for workin' class folks, do ya Kev?"

"I didn't realize that I was here to demonstrate love to the masses. I thought you wanted to talk to me about something important."

"I feel ya. Yo, yo' right. That's what I wanted to talk to ya about. Our working relationship."

Kevin peered at the glass and sipped carefully. "What? What do you want now? Didn't you already get everything that you need? From where I sit, you've set yourself up pretty well. Let's see," he said and held up his hand. Flicking through his fingers, he counted off his charges. "Number one, you figured out a way to try to invalidate Cam's will. You've got her estate all tied up. Two, you got so many gag orders and NDAs out here that no one's talking about what you're doing. Three, you were able to get an injunction to get access to her masters, and you've got a list of all of her accounts and safe deposit boxes. Four, you've finagled control over her music so you're getting paid on both the front and back end. And five, well, hell, you're having your cake and eating it too. I've run out of fingers, so how is that not doing well?"

Heywood polished off his bread and sipped his wine. "Well, the term 'well' is relative. I'm okay, at least for the moment. But, I've got to be concerned about the next steps, ya feel me? I gotta stay ahead of the pack. So, I need to know what yo' uncle's got up his sleeve."

Kevin rolled his eyes. "Look Heywood. I told you from the jump I had concerns about doing business with you. I know you're considered to be a pretty smart guy, but why wouldn't you, if in fact you did create another will for Cam, why wouldn't you include any of her charities? Hello? That was a pretty selfish move, if I say so myself. And I think that's something that might draw a little suspicion."

Heywood shifted in his seat and said, "If, by chance, I did create said will, then perhaps it was an oversight. Perhaps. But, anyway, I'm not beat about that shit. What's done is done. An' if all I need to do is worry 'bout a few of her raggedy assed charities for some busted-assed kids, then trust me, son. I ain't got nothin' to worry about."

Kevin shook his head. "My, my. Let's just say, those little raggedy charities might be your downfall. Anyone that knew Cam knew those were really important to her. But, I guess in your eyes, you are more important, so—"

"So, yeah, yo' right. I am more important. Shame she's not here to consign that."

"Be that as it may, some people don't share the same sentiments. Namely, my dear uncle for one, and Cam's aunt for the other. Believe me, they aren't going to take that lying down. And frankly, I don't blame them. They know enough to be concerned, and that's my free advice to you today.

"And that's about all I can share for free. But for my little issues, I wouldn't even be here right now. However, I realize that you still have some of my markers, and I'd like to see them paid off."

"I'm sure ya would."

"So, what do I stand to gain by continuing this little liaison? What's in it for me other than continued indentured servitude?"

Heywood laughed and placed his arm on the back of the booth, above Kevin's shoulders. "Kevin, Kevin, Kevin. Didn't I say that I'd take care of ya? Damn, ya act like ya question my integrity or somethin'."

Kevin smirked. "Okay, Heywood. It's not your integrity that I question. I just don't like all the drama. You asked for something, I got it for you. From where I sit, we should be even. Our business should be concluded. Isn't that what you said last time we met?"

The waitress brought over Heywood's bowl of linguine and clams, and he shoved his fork in with gusto. "Naw, son. Our business is far from done."

"Well, it is if you expect me to tell you what my uncle's doing. You know just as much as I do. He's determined to figure out where you got that updated copy of Cam's will, and how it can be authenticated. And you already know that all your suits are doing is tying him up on it. What else is there to tell?"

Heywood, never a stickler for manners, leaned his head back as he shoveled a large forkful of noodles into his open mouth. Still chewing, he said, "Yeah, I guess yo' right. I have everything I need, an' my lawyers'll make sure it takes forever for yo' uncle to get anythin' through." Wiping his mouth with the napkin, said, "So, regarding Cam's stuff, we're straight."

Heywood then removed an envelope from his coat pocket and placed it on the table. Kevin grabbed for the envelope and peeked inside. It contained most of his markers, almost $60k of the $100k Heywood had bought. "Good," Kevin said, tucking the envelope into his breast pocket. He emptied his glass of wine, and started to rise from the table. "So, I guess that's it. Good doing business with you, Heywood."

Heywood picked up his knife and stabbed the table. "Not so fast, Mr. Lawyer." he said. "We ain't done yet."

Kevin squinted and sat down again heavily. "What, Heywood? What is it now?" He placed his hand over his breast pocket. "Isn't this all of the markers you had? What? You have some laundry you need picked up? Have one of your boys do it. Not me."

"Very funny, Kevin. This ain't no joke, son. An' those ain't all yo' markers. Ya still gotta pay the balance, boy, an' I know how yo' gonna do that. Tyrone Moon, remember him?"

Kevin's mouth dropped open. "I told you, Heywood, I'm not down for that. I am not messing with Tyrone. Under any circumstances."

"Too late, son. At least the way I see it. See, I don't know if ya know, but I have business dealings with Mr. Moon, an' I know ya do, too. Let's say that I got some very lucrative business dealings wit' him. Yours may be of a different nature, but I don't think that he values yours as much as he values mine."

"What are you saying?"

"I'm sayin' that I make him money, ya cost him money. So, who do ya think he values more?" Heywood burped loudly.

Kevin leaned back in the booth and folded his hands on the table. "I can't double-cross Typhoon. I might as well go ahead and take a dive off the Brooklyn Bridge."

"True dat. But, ya really don't have a choice. See, my man over there?" Heywood jiggled the knife handle until it was freed from the table, and then he pointed it at one of his bodyguards. "He's got some-body right outside the gates at Typhoon's prison, just waitin' to go in an' let him know that you've been caught up in some shit, your gam-blin' an' what not, an' the only way to get from under yo' shit is to give him up. Yeah, they gonna tell him how ya talkin' to the Feds about his businesses an' shit. Sellin' his ass out. All I gots to do is give him the sign an' it's a wrap for ya."

Kevin squirmed in his chair. "Why would you want to do that? What on earth have I done to you? Why do you want to set me up?"

"I'm not settin' ya up, man. This is business. My business. Survival of the fittest, ya heard? Now, if I have to choose between me an' ya sur-vivin', guess what? Imma choose me. No doubt. Hey, I gotta eat. I gotta lotta mouths to feed, ya feel me? See, look at it like this. I'm not askin' ya to double-cross Typhoon. I'm just askin' ya to do what's in yo' best interest for a change. Look out for yourself. Ya always poppin' off about how ya don't wanna be my flunky. *Shee-it*, that's all ya was to Typhoon. He never treated ya no betta. Had ya out doin' his dirty work for him."

Kevin folded his arms, feeling like Heywood was just trying to call his bluff. "*Hmmph.* If you know so much, tell me."

"Tell ya? Ya already know. I know Typhoon had ya doin' that grimy stuff he couldn't get his Fifth Avenue suits to touch. I know he had ya put a clause in Cam's contract that got him gettin' ten percent off the top. I know that was somethin' illegal, after the fact bullshit that could get yo' ass disbarred, mutha fucka."

Heywood went on, clearly enjoying himself. "I know ya schemed on Cam a long time ago. Ya had dealings wit' her moms, that's how Cam got the deal in the first place. Ya sold her ass out to Typhoon to get rid o' some otha gamblin' debts ya owed him. I bet yo' uncle didn't know that either."

"None of that is true. "I just helped get Camara signed to your label, which is what her mother wanted. Where did you get all of this misinformation?" Kevin demanded.

"Give me a break. Face it, Cam was yo' ticket to ride. If her moms hadn't been no addict, an' Cam didn't have such mad skills, I'm thinkin' that Typhoon might've cancelled yo' ass a long time ago. An' if I hadn't agreed to take Cam on, then ya wouldna had no deal for Typhoon to take. So, of course I knew that ya had gamed Cam to pay back Typhoon. You was in the right place at the right time. Ya been lucky, but yo' luck's about to run out."

Kevin sat back in the booth, a defeated expression on his face. "If you knew all this before, why didn't you just say something instead of playing these games, Heywood?"

"I had to see what ya was made of. Hell, ya sold out Cam's moms, ya sold out yo' uncle. I just wanted to see why ya was givin' me such a hard time."

"Nobody really got hurt. Cam got a deal, and Typhoon got a good investment. So, I don't consider what I did to be selling out anyone. I had to do what I had to do."

"Word. That's all I'm sayin' now, Kev. Do what ya have to do now. We both know that nigga Typhoon is facin' more years than he got breaths to breathe. An' this time, he ain't gettin' off."

"*Hmmph*. You act like you know something no one else seems to know."

"I know enough. I know enough to get off the ship before it sinks. I'm just offerin' ya the same opportunity."

★

Kevin mulled over Heywood's words. Typhoon, for all of his faults, was ruthless and cruel. But he operated by the code of the streets. As he looked at Heywood, smug and ghetto-fabulous, Kevin sensed a different breed. Someone who had no code of ethics. Someone who would sell his soul to the devil to get ahead of the man who was responsible for all of his success. The one who put him on. Heywood had no respect. No regard. But he had money. And lots of it. And nowadays, that's what really mattered.

"What do you want me to do, Heywood?"

"Exactly what you've been doin'. You his eyes an' ears on the ground, right? He relies on ya to keep his shit legit, right? Cool. Ya keep doin' that, feedin' him info, parleyin' shit. Except, from time to time, I'll be givin' ya some information especially for him. An' I might need ya to cosign some things too."

"That sounds illegal. Sounds like you want me to break the law, and I'm not down for that," Kevin said.

Heywood chuckled. "Break the law? Ya got that twisted, son. I don't fuck around with the law. Now, I ain't sayin' that I don't get my nut off on her, now. Believe that. I'll go down on that bitch Lady Justice, I'll eat her pussy real good. But I ain't gonna fuck her. Naw, never that."

Heywood smirked as Kevin left the table to go to the restroom. Heywood was on top of his game. So what if some of his detractors said he had a pact with the devil or others said he was the devil's spawn. To him, he was just gifted and knew how to put things together. Connect the dots. Take advantage of and exploit any situation. Capitalize on matters. Kevin, while he was a little challenging, was no different than anyone or anything else.

Heywood knew that there was a way to exploit everybody. Find their weak spot. While some haters called it manipulation, he called it good business skills. He had it all worked out. He wasn't about to tell Kevin anything other than what he wanted him to know. And all Kevin needed to know was that he was to continue with Typhoon, business as usual, while Heywood worked his magic on his side.

He was going to crush Typhoon, and Typhoon would never know what hit him. Heywood was tired of Typhoon demanding money, and although Heywood had started reducing Typhoon's cut exponentially, using two sets of books and reporting less and less to Typhoon's CPAs, he was still giving up too much. So, in order to get Typhoon out of his pocket faster, Heywood had to dry up his resources. It was risky, but he knew it could be done without it ever being traced back to him.

First, he had to plug up Typhoon's cash flow. By severely limiting his income, Typhoon would be unable to conduct business as usual. Heywood had to find a way to anonymously tip the Feds off so that they would find and freeze Typhoon's off-shore bank accounts, especially the one that Heywood was funneling cash through.

With no money, Typhoon wouldn't be able to pay his high-priced legal team, and he would be left with an overworked public defender. There would be no protection money for the prison guards. The money to pay off the cops to stay away from his gambling houses would end. Using his street connects, Heywood would make sure that Typhoon's competitors were tipped off to any moves he had planned. They would intercept his deliveries, which would further decrease his paper. Typhoon would be seen as weak and useless, something worse to him than being killed. Once the word was out that he was strapped for cash, it would lend credibility to the rumor that he was turning State's evidence and snitching to the Feds to save his ass.

Then Typhoon's crew would abandon him. He wouldn't know who to trust. Alone and powerless, he'd have no one willing to run messages to him. Without money to protect him, Typhoon would be nothing. Nothing but a low-life has-been, a straight-up convict.

Heywood had it all mapped out. All he had to do was get Kevin on board to put a legitimate seal on it. Heywood knew that throwing a few nickles would buy him what he wanted on the streets, but getting Kevin on board would be a little more costly. And dangerous. But it would be worth it.

Everyone had a price, and he knew Kevin's would be high. Yes, he had a gambling problem and a recreational drug problem, but even

Heywood knew that wouldn't be enough for Kevin to betray Typhoon. He was too scared for that. Heywood had to go deep and go hard to find the right motivator for Kevin, but he knew that one existed. And he found it.

It was a beautiful plan, a wonderful plan, and all Heywood had to do was put on his director's hat and get the actors to play their parts. Like it or not, Kevin had a starring role.

"That sounds too simple, Heywood. Give me a little credit. I want to know what the real deal is before I agree to anything," Kevin said, when he returned from the bathroom.

Heywood raised his bowl and shoveled the remaining pasta into his mouth, then chased it with a swig of the wine. "I think that's it, Kevin. As long as ya play ya position, we'll be cool. I'll cover the rest of ya markers, an' ya should have Typhoon off ya back for the rest of yo' life. However long that may be."

Kevin bit his lip. "Umm, I don't know. It sounds way too easy. Way too easy."

Heywood raised his linen napkin and wiped his mouth, smearing dark red marinara sauce on it. Snapping his fingers at the elderly waitress, he said nonchalantly, "Oh yeah, well, I forgot to mention the most important thing. If ya don't do it, then I might have to let the cops know that ya killed Cam's mother. *Shee-it*, how could I forget that?"

chapter twenty-seven

*Money and intimidation are great equalizers. By planting the right seeds
at the right time, the right tree will come forth and bear fruit.*

~ Fitz Bassford, Record Industry Exec

IT HAD been a whirlwind month. As soon as she indicated that she was
ready to undergo the dermal regeneration treatment, Randolph and Dr.
Salazar contacted the specialist who had developed the procedure and
invited him to the Dominican Republic. Only too happy to combine a
vacation with work, the specialist readily agreed and had his calendar
cleared within two weeks.

The reconstructive surgical procedure required that the scarred tissue be removed, and a dermal treatment placed over it to repair the tissue. The final step would be to replace or graft the skin.

It was a relatively new procedure, but one with a lot of promise. It
might not make her 100%, but, barring complications, she would look
far better than she did now. It was a risk she was willing to take. There
was no way she could ever return to the U.S. looking like a cross between
Freddy Kruger and Leatherface from the *Texas Chainsaw Massacre*.

Although he had helped arrange for the specialist, Randolph hadn't
been able to be there because of his schedule. However, he did observe,

using a specially installed sterilized webcam in the operating room. And he remained in constant Internet and telephone contact with the specialist, Dr. Salazar, and the hospital staff during her recovery.

Randolph was busy in Philly, working and looking for an apartment for his Marisol. Any arrangements he made would be temporary, but he wanted to be able to present her with a new life the next time they saw each other.

During her recovery, Cam had plenty of time to plot how she was going to reclaim her life. Though torn about her future, she knew that she could not sit idly by and watch Heywood ruin her memories, disrespect and take advantage of her family, and illegally benefit from all of her hard work. No, she was not going to do that.

So, she continued her web sleuthing, carefully documenting every event that had occurred since her supposed demise. And there was an enormous amount of information available. As she Googled her name, Heywood's name almost always popped up too. Then she saw the report about how her attorney's office had been robbed, and that some of her files had been stolen. She was certain that Heywood had been behind that.

She also stayed up to date on the legal wrangling surrounding her estate, but couldn't find much through her regular Internet channels. She gained most of her information from Rashad's website and from the PanacheReport.com. Other news outlets had either been shut down or bought off.

Repairing her face was the first step in her plans. As soon as she was looking all right, she was going to have to further develop her plans. She couldn't just walk back on the scene as Starr and announce that she wasn't dead. That would never work. So, she was going to have to stick to her Marisol cover, at least until she was able to figure out how she could safely unveil the truth. Cam silently offered a prayer to Marisol, telling her she was going to do right by her when this was all over, and apologizing for having to continue using her name.

It was a delicate balance, existing between the true and the false. And during those lonely nights while she was recovering, she sometimes questioned her own motives. Her heart ached to tell Randolph the truth, but she fought the urge. He loved someone named Marisol, and for the time being, that was what she had to consider. Plus, she had made a promise never to hurt him, and she didn't want to do anything that might cause him any pain.

She was also afraid. Would he, could he, love the real her? While he seemed so strong, Randolph had a fragile component to him that made her pause. It was probably his heart. And although she was anxious to be with him in the States, she had to stay grounded in her reality. It was a good thing that he realized that she needed her own place, because the distance and space would enable her to get her life in order while she acclimated to his. She wanted to be the loving, honest person he truly deserved, not the fragmented woman that she was. Marisol. Cam. Starr. Dead. Near death. Alive.

In addition to her Internet searches, Cam had a number of things to do or get to prepare for a new life in Philadelphia. She needed a visa, passport, and identification papers. Not knowing Marisol's birth date, she had to request her own medical records. Thankfully, someone at the Montserrat Hospital had been thorough, at least with her transfer papers. Her full name was Marisol Kent, born December 7, 1989, in Salem. She felt sad that Marisol had missed her birthday, and silently apologized to the real Marisol again. Then, it reminded her that she had also missed her own birthday back in February.

But she had to keep it moving. Using her hospital-issued work ID, she was able to obtain an identification card issued by the Dominican Republic. She applied for a duplicate copy of Marisol's birth certificate from Montserrat, which she needed to secure her visa. Everything hinged on the birth certificate, and she anxiously awaited its arrival.

Another arrival she was anxiously awaiting was Randolph's. Though they had been in constant contact, and he had charted her progress and recovery, his schedule had not allowed him to get back to the island to be with her. And she missed him terribly.

Randolph apparently missed her, too, and he expressed his regret for being absent on numerous occasions, and in many ways. He Fedexed colorful calla lilies and soft teddy bears, often dressed in surgical scrubs. And his text messages were constant and endearing. He asked her to keep her webcam on just so he could pop in and say hello. And to tell her how much he loved her and was praying for her. By word and by deed, he had really entrenched himself in her mind, heart, and soul.

She ached for him, but part of her was glad that he wasn't there. These were crucial moments, and the feelings and love she had for him could only cloud her judgment, vision and focus.

He had tried to be there the day her bandages were removed. He did all that he could, worked extra shifts and swapped schedules, but in the end, he just couldn't make it. He was clearly down when he called her to tell her the disappointing news. But, as he had been during the actual procedure, he was with her in spirit and via webcam.

With the lens pointed directly in her face, Dr. Salazar prepared her to remove the bandages.

"You'll be fine," Randolph said, his voice choppy and his image spotty on her laptop screen. "I'm right here with you."

She shifted nervously on the edge of the examining table. "Umm, I know, Randolph. I know."

"Sure she will," Dr. Salazar said as he gloved up and selected a pair of scissors from the surgical tray. "She's in good hands."

She forced a smile as the doctor approached her. He instructed her to lean her head back, and he started snipping the bandages. He started with the bandages that covered her chest, legs and torso, and finally got to the bandages on her neck and face. The ointment-soaked gauze fell to the floor, and after a few moments, Randolph gasped.

"What is it?" she cried, and reached for her face. Dr. Salazar swiftly intercepted her hand.

"No, no. Please, don't touch," he said. "You're fine." He turned and picked up a mirror from the rolling cart where the rest of his tools were.

"I'm sorry, Marisol," Randolph said. "I, I didn't mean anything. You're, you are, well, show her, Dr. Salazar."

The doctor held the mirror up to her face, and she gasped also. "It's amazing!" she nearly screamed.

"You're beautiful," Randolph said, tears in his eyes, and Dr. Salazar nodded. "You always were," Randolph said, grinning a toothy smile.

"Here, here," Dr. Salazar said, handing her the mirror. "As I knew you would be." He surveyed her body, gingerly touching her skin, and tilting her head back and forward, and to the side, as he inspected her face.

"Yes, you are truly blessed, young lady. For you to look like this after what happened, the Lord has really been working in you." He winked. "You have healed remarkably well. Even better than I imagined." He turned toward the webcam. "Do you concur, Dr. Williams?" All Randolph could do was nod.

"You are well on your way, Miss Marisol. The wounds on your body have also healed very well. They should clear up nicely. You just need to make sure to wear loose fitting garments for at least a month or so, and stay out of the sun. But, I'm sure that's not your primary concern. I'm sure that you're much more interested in what is planned for your face. Now, regarding the skin grafting, we're going to take care of that."

She drew a deep breath, never removing her eyes from her reflection. "When? An' will it be painful?"

"Well, we'll try to make it as painless as possible. But, that leads me to another topic I'd like to discuss," the doctor said.

"What's that?" Randolph asked.

"Well, I'm holding off doing your grafting at the moment, mainly because we need to give the area time to breathe. In the interim, I'll prescribe a mild painkiller, in case you experience any discomfort, and give you a little topical steroid to apply with a sterile glove. It will also promote healing. The main thing is to keep this beautiful face of yours out of direct sunlight. But, if everything works out, that shouldn't be too hard, since you'll be leaving our fine island soon."

She was enthralled with her image, and barely heard what the doctor said. With most of the scarring removed, she looked like her old self, only slightly different. There was still evidence of pinkish discoloration and a minor webbed area with faint scarring, but those could be hidden with makeup, once she could use it. Her face was fuller, more worldly, and even her eyes were a lot less innocent.

She had been tried by fire, and she had survived. But who was she? She was so absorbed with her thoughts that she hadn't really been listening to Dr. Salazar or Randolph, but something Dr. Salazar said caught her attention.

"Excuse me? What did you say, Dr. Salazar?"

He repeated himself, and she wondered what he was talking about. She couldn't surpress the surprised look on her face.

Dr. Salazar laughed. "Marisol, I guess I shouldn't have said it quite like that. I didn't mean to be presumptuous, but I have some good news for you."

He stepped back and stood between his patient and the camera. "I was speaking to one of my old college buddies, Dr. Gruber, about your case, and he offered to put the finishing touches on our dear patient 'ere. He can refine your skin, remove any discoloration. If you had a picture of yourself before the injury, he can make you look exactly like that."

"Dr. Gruber? Are you talking about Dr. Hans Guber, the internationally renowned plastic surgeon?" Randolph asked.

"One and the same. We went to med school together," Dr. Salazar said. "He has time next week to do it, which is perfect. There is only one condition. She'll have to go to Switzerland. He is head of the cosmetic surgery and facial reconstruction department at the University of Lausanne and has agreed to do this, but only in his own hospital."

"Switzerland?" She and Randolph said in unison.

"Well, uh, how am I goin' to do that? I can't go there, Dr. Salazar." She fell over her words. "I mean, I can't afford to go there. I appreciate you tryin' to help me, but I don't see how I can."

What she was really thinking was that Europe was not in her plans. She had to get prepared to go to the States, and there was no way that she could incorporate Europe in her plans.

"Dr. Salazar, that's a great offer, and I'll be happy to pay for her," Randolph offered.

"No need, Randolph. Miss Marisol doesn't have to worry about anything. The University Hospital at Lausanne is a teaching facility, and they're willing to pay for her travel, accommodations, living stipend, and everythin'. She'll be part of a research project. Based on my recommendation, of course."

"But, I haven't even gotten my visa yet," she said, her mind racing.

Again, Dr. Salazar allayed her concerns. "We here at Aybar will handle all of that. We'll get you a medical visa, and send you yours when it arrives. Until then, all you have to do is recover. And Dr. Williams, I would ask that you make sure that Miss Kent has some warm clothes. Fall in the Alps can be a little chilly. But, I'm sure you'll be able to find her warm clothing in Philadelphia."

"Not a problem," Randolph replied.

Dr. Salazar continued. "And by the way, Randolph, Dr. Gruber is going to personally contact your Chief of Staff and request that you be available as a consult to Miss Kent. Especially since you are so familiar with her medical history. I hope you don't mind."

Randolph could barely contain himself. "Dr. Salazar, you're kidding, right? You did that? For us, um, I mean for me? Thank you so much."

Cam was speechless. She didn't want to seem ungrateful, but this change was really putting a hitch in her plans. But, it might be for the best. If Dr. Gruber could remove all traces of the scarring and improve her looks, how could she not go? And how could she ever thank Dr. Salazar for making this all possible? Cam reached up, took his face in her hands, and kissed him on both cheeks. Dr. Salazar blushed, and lowered his head in embarrassment.

"Thank you so much, Dr. Salazar. You've given me a new life. You've given me a future. I owe you so very much, and I'll never forget it." And, he had also given her Randolph, live and in person.

chapter twenty-eight

ALMOST EVERYTHING happened exactly as Dr. Salazar said. The procedure was pushed out a few weeks and it appeared she might be spending the holidays in Switzerland. When the procedure was finally scheduled, the hospital staff helped pack her meager belongings, obtained her medical visa, granted her an extended leave of absence, and threw her a big going-away party. They even tucked a few hundred Euros in her pocket so she would have spending money. Cam had forgotten that such nice people actually existed, and felt blessed to have known them.

Randolph flew over to Lausanne, just in time to scrub in for what she hoped would be her final surgery. As their latest research subject, Dr. Gruber and his team treated her exceptionally well, and her surgical procedure was a profound success. Randolph never left her side throughout the whole ordeal, sleeping in her room, helping her to the bathroom, changing her dressings. The time together, though painful for Cam, cemented her feelings for this incredibly exceptional man.

She and Randolph had just left the hospital, enraptured and oblivious to practically everyone. Her visa had arrived, and she had met with Dr. Gruber for a final evaluation, where he signed her release papers and cleared her to leave. She was free to start her new life, healed and happy.

Free from the confines of hospitals and sterile recovery rooms, she was walking on clouds, absorbing the sights, smells, and sounds of the quaint city, as they headed toward their charming hotel. For the first time in a long time, she was able to enjoy the beauty of her surroundings. And Switzerland was lovely.

They snuggled close together, briskly trotting past the steel grey Gothic styled buildings, museums, monuments and lightly bundled up villagers. It was chilly in the bustling city of Lausanne, it nestled between the shores of Lake Geneva and the snow capped Jura Mountains.

Arriving at the small hotel, they giggled like school kids, and playfully rubbed each others shoulders when they realized just how chilly it was outside. It had been so long since she had experienced less than tropical temperatures that it really affected her body. But, Randolph had dutifully kept her close and warm, even as they rode the tiny elevator up to their third floor room.

"Is it everything you imagined, Marisol?" Randolph asked, as he peered over her shoulder. He placed a loving hand on her waist and pulled her close to him.

They were standing in front of the oblong dresser mirror in their cozy room at the hotel City Lausanne, where they had been staying since she had been released from the hospital. It was a comfortably appointed efficiency, complete with Ikea style furnishings, and floor to ceiling windows that overlooked the hotel's courtyard. The exterior chill had etched the windows with a thin, frosty coating. As they stood together in front of the mirror, she stared at their reflection in the mirror and smiled. She was Cam again, with just a fuller face and wiser eyes. *No worse for the wear,* she thought, and smiled. She lovingly placed a hand over his. She was finally feeling whole again.

"Yes, Randy. It's everythin' I imagined," she said, still using her island lilt. Watching them both in the mirror, Cam was thankful the knot in her stomach was not evident. This handsome man, with love, not lust, in his eyes, absorbed her with his warmth. He was caring and sensitive, and completely selfless. And she felt guilty as hell about deceiving him.

But what else could she do? She still couldn't tell him the truth. Things were much too complicated. It wasn't that she didn't trust him;

she didn't trust the world. And she didn't know how he would react, and didn't want to find out.

She reasoned away some of her guilt by deciding that Randolph had enough on his plate without adding her trials and tribulations to it. He needed to focus on what he needed to do to complete his residency, and she needed to focus on what she needed to do to reclaim her life and legacy. She might not be telling him the whole truth about herself, but she knew one thing was true. Her love for him.

She lifted her long dreads above head. "What do you think, Randy? Should I cut them off?"

He turned her around, so that she faced him. Gently placing a kiss on her lips, he said, "Do whatever you like. You're gorgeous anyway you are. Short hair, long hair, bald. It doesn't matter."

She dropped her locks and kissed him, long and deep. She felt immersed in him, in his sincerity and in his unspoken commitment. She loved that he loved her. As their tongues swirled and bodies melted together, a melody began playing in her head. It was a sensation that she hadn't felt in months. It was lyrical emotion. It was a rhapsody. It was the desire to sing again. His unconditional love had helped her survive and come back alive. His love had given her music back. Tears sprang to her eyes, and she forced herself apart from him. She held his face within her hands. "Thank you, baby. I needed to hear that."

"I needed to say that," he said, turning his head and kissing her palms. He clasped her hands in his. "You know, you give me a sense of purpose, right? You give my life meaning."

"Oh, Randy. You say the sweetest things. But, you already have a purpose. Much greater than me. You're a healer. You help people. What do I do?"

"You help me," he said. "And you help others. Look at what you've been through. You did it all by yourself. No help, no family, just God and you. Yet, you've always smiled. You were never mean or nasty to anyone. And look at what you did for all the kids at Aybar. You heal people too, and you don't even know it."

She was speechless. Not that she wanted or needed his validation, and not that he was trying to validate her, but she felt warmed by his words. In her prior life, to hear Heywood talk, for as much as she was and for as much as she did, she had never done enough, and never been enough.

Heywood was always warning her that someone was nipping at her heels, ready to take her spot should she ever slip. He would amp her up, then slyly talk about her deficiencies. She thought it was his desire for perfection, but now, she realized it was manipulation and his way of controlling her. Despite her skills and commitment, she always had to be on her grind. And even then, she was subject to his veiled persecution and criticism.

Any comparison between the two men, if you could call Heywood a man, was impossible. What had she ever seen in him? Why had she even given him a moment of her time? Or her body? Here, standing right in front of her, was a real man. A man who was able to communicate and share with her. A man who really didn't even know her, yet saw so much value in her. Value for talents and skills she had never really acknowledged herself.

Perhaps it was time to really step back and embrace what Randolph was saying. For so long, her life had been defined by how she sang or how she performed, not really for who she was. While these thoughts ran through her mind, Randolph kept talking. "Now, I just have to go back to the hospital to finish up some paperwork, and then we can get ready to go."

He laid her hands by her side, and turned away. The thought of his leaving made her stomach drop. They really hadn't discussed what she was going to do, but she knew he wanted her to go back to the States with him. Now that the time was finally here, she was panicky. She took a deep breath, and tried to calm herself. Could she go through with this?

"You okay?" he asked, as he searched for his jacket.

"I think so." She didn't want to sound whiney or needy, but that's how she felt.

He found his jacket, and slipped it on. "Aww, don't worry. Everything'll be okay." He smiled, reached into his inner jacket pocket, and pulled out a white envelope. "Plus, I thought since we have a few days before I have to be back at work, it might be nice to take a quick trip down to the South of France. We can't stay too long, but I thought it would be fun. How does that sound?" He waved the envelope around, teasing her with it.

"The South of France?" she said incredulously.

"Yes. Dr. Gruber told me about a great little bed and breakfast that we can stay in. And these—," he said, holding the envelope up, "are train tickets to St. Raphael. The B&B is near the water, so I figured you might like that. You'll get a chance to see a nice beach one more time before I whisk you away to dreary old Philadelphia."

Cam was astounded yet again by his love and generosity. She couldn't believe her ears. Even after Randolph confirmed and reconfirmed that he had everything arranged, she could hardly digest the news. *What an amazing man*, she thought to herself, and prayed to God that she would always be worthy of his love, now and forever. That was a rather foreign feeling for her, but even in its' unfamiliarity, his love eased her mind and her heart.

After he left for the hospital, she quickly gathered up their belongings, and decided to take a long, mildly warm shower. She planned on surprising him with room service and a special treat. Caviar, authentic French champagne, and her full-bodied self.

She carefully stepped into the mosaic tiled shower and let the cool water hit her rejuvenated body. It was exhilarating. No pain at all, just a tingly feeling where the water hit her new skin. She owed so much to everyone for getting to this point. Who would ever have believed it was possible?

She thought of Randolph, and a song filled her heart. It flowed from her heart to her lungs, and finally to her throat. She opened her mouth and the words to Whitney Houston's *You Give Good Love*, rang out. The sound she emitted shocked her.

Her voice was deeper, more mature. It had grown. Her lows were lower and her highs higher. She ran through a chorus, effortlessly releasing her diaphragm, and the words bounced off the tiles with flawless pitch and control. She was amazed at the depth. And her range.

She sang and sang, running her voice through exercises and songs and verses. She lost track of time, having stepped back into the zone, into her world. When the water started getting cold, she realized how long she had been in there and turned the faucets off. But she couldn't turn off her happiness. Her music had returned, and she was happier and more confident than she had been since the accident.

Now, it would be hard, but she had to get her mind right and back to the present. Get ready for her man's return.

After a deeply satisfying night of long-awaited passion and intense love-making, she and Randolph acted like two love-sick teenagers on the train to St. Raphael. The ride itself was lovely, postcard-perfect outside every window. The happy couple took countless pictures with disposable cameras, and reveled in their togetherness. They sipped light and effervescent Ruinart Brut Champagne, fed each other oven warm bread and full bodied Roquefort and Comte' cheeses, and nibbled on licorice edged blackberries as the train sped them to their destination. A tiny rented Peugeot carried them from St. Raphael to the B&B, which just happened to be in St. Tropez.

She couldn't believe it. St. Tropez? She had always associated the place with globetrotting, jet-setting Jamie, and it made her smile. She had never been there herself, but remembered that Jamie had been on his way the last time they had spoken. Was it a sign? A good omen? When she had been a celebrity, she had never had a desire to go to the playground of the rich and famous. It certainly had never crossed her mind that she would be going now.

But, being with Randolph as a non-celebrity made it even more special. No matter where they were, everything with him was more enjoyable, but she couldn't figure out if it was because she wasn't under the microscopic glare of her fame, or just the way he made her feel.

St. Tropez was warm, soothing, and delightful, picturesque and bustling. Since they were only there for two nights, they decided to try to cram everything in, to see and do as much as they could. After dropping their suitcases off at the charming B&B, they headed out to see the city, armed with tourist maps, books, and advice from the inn owner.

The narrow streets were jammed with tourists from all over the world, local salesmen selling their wares, and natives going about their daily routines. Tiny taxicabs and flatbed trucks jockeyed for position between the pedestrians and the peddler's carts and the bicyclists.

It was warm and sunny, and Cam had slathered on sunscreen. She was also wearing a wide-brimmed hat and dark shades to protect her skin. Randolph carried a small backpack, making certain they had everything they needed before venturing out into the city.

Arms linked, they walked along the marina and harbor in the center of the town. Luxurious yachts filled the waterways and animated fishermen hawked their fresh catches. Colorful pushcarts filled the narrow cobblestone streets, and the lovebirds noticed very little except their own contentment.

Suddenly, a pack of tourists raced past them towards the edge of the harbor, joining a crowd that was roaring and cheering. Photographers were everywhere, some climbing poles or standing on truck beds, while others were hanging out of nearby windows, all pointing their telescopic lenses towards the water.

The actions and noises of the crowd were familiar, but uncomfortable, and she held tight to Randolph's arm. "I wonder what's goin' on," she said, trying to see above the crowd, but failing miserably.

"I don't know, but I'll find out," he said. Randolph, who spoke a little textbook French, asked a nearby fruit vendor what the fuss was about. "*Que continue-t-il?*"

"*Il y a des célébrités en ville pour les récompenses. La Musique Mondiale Attribue. Grande affaire,*" the lean, stain smocked middle-aged woman with grayish teeth replied.

"Merci," he said, nodding to the woman. He then turned toward Cam and shook his head.

"Well, what did she say?" she asked him, as he plucked the melons. The word "musique," the woman muttered, had instantly pierced her ears.

"No big deal. Just some famous people, celebrities, in town for an awards show or something."

Her heart sank. She had completely lost track of space and time. It was November. "Um, dear, what awards is it?" She asked, trying not to sound too interested.

Randolph shrugged. "I think the woman said the World Music Awards," he said, and held the melon up to her nose. "She said that there were tons of celebrities here, and everyone, well mainly the other tourists, just go nuts. The locals don't pay much attention."

Instinctively, she pushed the dark sunglasses up higher on her nose, cradled her long hair around her face, and pulled her hat down further. "Oh, I see. Celebrities from where?"

He picked up another melon and held it near his nose and then hers. "All over, I guess. I didn't ask."

Another crowd of tourists rushed past them, this time towards a group of people slicing through the packed sidewalk, walking to one of the private piers. *No wonder everyone was looking,* she thought. Each one of the women walking by was more beautiful than the next. Long flowing hair, pouty lips and dressed in the latest in colorful "St. Tropez" beach and swimwear, they were, indeed, crowd-stopping. She assumed they were supermodels, as they wore their expensive clothes with ease, and had the model look, presence, and packaging.

Surrounded by several bodyguards, the women were being led through the crowd by a huge mountain of a man. Bald, deep chocolate, and sweating bullets, he was able to easily separate the crowd. "'Scuse us. Comin' through," his voice boomed, as he held out his massive arms for the crowd to part.

The sea of paparazzi and hangers-on pushed forward, nearly knocking her and Randolph into the rickety jewelry cart. She lost her balance, and started to fall. He grabbed her arm, his body instinctively leaning forward to catch her. As she fell backwards, she glanced over and caught the profile of the man in the middle of the parade of women. Her knees gave away when she recognized Heywood's smug face.

chapter twenty-nine

"MAN, THAT shit's too weird," Heywood said, pulling on a thick brown blunt of Copenhagen's finest. "Somethin' felt real fucked up out there." He puffed like a madman, occasionally leaning toward the guardrail and peering out onto the crowded streets below like he was looking for something. Or someone.

Duck side-eyed him. They were lounging on the balcony of the penthouse suite of the Hotel Byblos in the heart of St. Tropez. Despite having leased a yacht, Heywood still booked a suite, so he could be seen coming and going, making his grand entrances and exits. He had heard that Noah Parker was planning to stay there; he wanted to make sure that he one-upped him. Maybe get an opportunity to taunt him a little more.

In the living room area, several supermodel types were getting warmed up. The rail-thin, angularly beautiful Asian, African–American, and European clotheshorses were working on their runway and stripper moves, snorting up a grip full of coke and downing several bottles of Krug Rose'.

"Man, you trippin'. That good-good got ya flipped the fuck out," Duck said, as he sipped on a glass of Remy straight.

Heywood was in town for the World Music Awards being held in nearby Monaco. Starr had been nominated for several awards, and he was going to take this opportunity to shine on the international stage. And even though the show was a few days away, he was looking to get as much face time in the international press as he could.

For some reason, though, he was feeling a little shook, and the weed wasn't making him feel any better. As hot as it was outside, he had felt a chill when they were walking to his chartered yacht, and he didn't like it. Not one bit. He needed this blunt to stunt whatever was trying to give him the shakes.

"Naw, I'm serious, Duck," Heywood said, finally taking his eyes off the crowded streets. "Somethin' just ain't right." He gripped the belt of his oversized snow white terry cloth robe and pulled it tight around his expanding waist.

Duck, decked out in a navy blue Rocawear warm-up suit with matching blue Converse sneakers, sipped on his drink. "It's all good, Wood. You ain't trippin' about Noah bein' here, is ya? I heard him an' his crew had checked in already."

"Who? That clown? Get the fuck outta here, Duck. I ain't trippin' off that know nothin' silver-spooned nigga. I don't even know why he's even over here. It ain't like his artists are gonna win nothin'."

"Well, I heard one of them cats on his label got nominated for somethin' big, but I don't know, man," Duck said.

"An' I don't care," Heywood said. "He's a stuntin' ass mutha fucka. I just hope I don't run into his frontin' ass, 'cause Imma hit him an' quit him. Lights out. Click."

Duck laughed. "Well, I don't know 'bout that. I heard he ain't scared to throw his hands up an' shit. Plus, he's got that otha suite ya wanted, an' I thought that mighta plucked a nerve."

"Ya oughta know better than that, Duck. Noah can't pluck nothin' of mine, not even the shit that gets stuck in my ass. *Hmmph*, he'll never steal my shine. Shit, I was runnin' thangs before he even got outta his little prep school. Ain't nothin' changed.

"An', if I run into him, an' he comes out the box sideways at me, he's gonna get got, ya feel me?"

"I feel ya. Ya know I got your back. He an' his crew betta be on the look out," Duck said.

"He knows the deal. I already told him he betta grow some eyes in the back of his fuckin' head," Heywood said. "Always somewhere tryna talk slick about me an' my shit. Fuck him. If he thinks he's next in line for that head spot at APB Records, he got anotha thought comin'. I'll get it an' turn it down before his name ever comes up."

"Word, son." Duck said. "He just ain't put in enough work yet. He gotta pay his dues." He sipped more of his drink, and fixed his lips for some more butt kissing on Heywood. "But on the real, don't get bent out the frame. Go on, get ya chill on. You know you the man. All ya gotta do is floss for the cameras, pick up some more of Baby Girl's recognitions, an' get yo' freak on," he said, and then nodded toward the model show-case going on inside. "Before ya know it, we'll be back to the States."

Heywood shook his head, puffing on the joint. Its' embers burned brightly, and as he inhaled, the smoke swirled around in his nostrils. "Ya know, it's kinda like I can almost feel her, ya know? Like I feel her spirit or some shit like that." He inhaled deeply, and held the smoke before slowly releasing it.

Duck shrugged and kept drinking. "Well, it'll be a year soon, since she's been gone. Man, maybe you just finally grievin' for her."

"Maybe. Ya know, I been tryna do her memory right, makin' sure her image is protected, an' that she's not forgotten by her fans. Ya know, I got that tribute song I'm workin' on an' shit, but, maybe I need to do more." Heywood offered the joint to Duck, who quickly grabbed it and held it to his lips. Duck shot him a, "you trippin'," look, but puffed instead of saying anything.

Heywood snapped his fingers, a flash of inspiration creasing his face. "I gotta come up with somethin' off the chain. I need to do it right for Baby Girl, an' I mean it's gotta be somethin' way off the hook."

Heywood stood and started pacing. "Maybe I'll do a movie about her life or a concert. Yeah, somethin' big ballin' like that."

Clearing his throat, Duck said, "Man, that's mad cool, an' I feel you about wantin' to make sure Starr's light don't ever stop shinin' an' shit. But—"

Heywood stopped pacing, and reached for the stubby joint, and took a deep drag. "But what, Duck? What ya tryna say?"

"Heywood, I know Starr was your girl an' all, but damn, bro. You got other cats an' talent on your label too, who could use a shot, 'naw mean?"

Heywood stopped puffing. "Yo, whassup with that, Duck? Now ya think ya know how to run my shit?"

"Naw, Wood. You know it ain't like that. It's just that, well, you be puttin' a lotta time an' energy in Starr an' you got folks dyin' on the vine. You got Trigga, that nigga's been puttin' in work for a minute. An' Casbar. He's really been workin' it out. An' don't forget about Parsley, ya know that cat's rhymes is tight. But, it's like you don't even see 'em."

Heywood snatched off his shades and leaned down into Duck's face. He was so close their noses almost touched.

"Look at me, Duck. Look at me in the mutha fuckin' eyes. Let me tell you what I see. " Heywood pointed at his lids, and glared at Duck.

"Yo, Heywood, all this ain't even necessary," Duck said, as he tried to turn his face away, but Heywood wouldn't let him.

"I said look at me, nigga!" Heywood shouted, spit spraying. "Ya see? Look," he said, staring into Duck's eyes.

"Yeah, I see, Heywood. I see."

"That's right, ya big stupid ass son of a bitch. Ya wanna know what I see? Cha-ching. Dolla signs, nigga. Dolla signs wit' a whole bunch o' zeros behind 'em." Heywood took his sunglasses and shoved them into Duck's drink, nearly forcing the glass from his big hands. "An', until those niggas start makin' me paper like Starr does, then they'll keep doin' exactly what they doin'. What the fuck I tell 'em to do."

Heywood threw his head backwards, but Duck didn't flinch. "What? Runnin' errands fo' ya, Heywood? That shit ain't right." Duck mumbled. He knew he was treading on dangerous ground, but even he couldn't let Heywood chump him but so much.

"What ya come out ya mouth an' say?" Heywood took a defensive stance, like he was getting ready to swing on Duck.

"You know what I'm sayin' is correct, man. Damn, bruh. Whassup? I mean, we go back, Heywood. Way back. Before any of this glitz an' glamour shit popped off. I remember then an' I remember when. So, ya know I ain't tryna front on you, an' you know I'm ya nigga. I rides wit' you. But shit, if you won't even listen to me, ya boy, then damn, who am I?"

Heywood looked Duck up and down. "Who are you?" He repeated the phrase twice more. "You are what I pay ya to be. Whateva I want ya to be when I want ya to be it. Fuck that 'I'm ya boy' shit. You ain't on my level, nigga. Face it, if I wasn't payin' ya ass and flyin' you around to places an' things ya ain't neva seen, ya ass wouldn't be here, real talk. Ya think since ya been hangin' 'round, seein' my flow, ya think ya know a little somethin' somethin'?" Heywood's nostrils flaired.

"An' what I know is that ya don't know shit. At least not enough for me to listen to a goddamned thing ya got to say. But if you're so concerned about Parsley's ass, I tell ya what. Why don't ya sign 'em to your label, huh? Oh, snap. That's right. Ya can't 'cause ya ain't got no mutha fuckin' label, nigga."

Heywood snatched his $1500 Gucci sunglasses from Duck's drink, shook them off in Duck's face, and then tossed them in his lap. "Now, before ya run off, startin' ya own label an' shit, why don't ya do the job ya ass is gettin' paid lovely for. Clean these bitches. I want 'em spotless, Duck."

"Aiight, Heywood," Duck said, wiping his face. "But, on the real, Wood, you didn't even have to go there. You know me. You tryna ride me like I'm some new nigga hangin' on ya jock. Shit, I wasn't tryna—"

Heywood cut him off. "Ya wasn't tryna what? Tell me how to run my shit?" He took the burning joint and shoved it into Duck's drink.

"Whateva, nigga. Now, drink that shit, every drop. Don't ya let my good liquor or my good collards go to waste, ya heard?

"Now," Heywood said, flipping the collar up on his robe, and walking toward the models. "Imma go in here an' handle my business. An' I expect ya to handle yours. Clean up my glasses an' stay the fuck outta my goddamned business."

chapter thirty: side a

HE HELD her hair and placed a cool cloth to the back of her neck as she vomited into the toilet. Her ribs were hurting from the heaves. She had been sick to her stomach since she had seen Heywood's wicked face. She felt like passing out, but held herself together, telling Randolph that she wasn't feeling well, and they made a beeline back to their room, and to the toilet.

"Are you feeling better yet, Marisol? I hope you didn't get too much sun today."

"Umm, I don't know Randy. I think everythin' might just have been too much for me, ya know?"

He nodded in agreement. "You may be right. I should've been more careful. You probably overdid it. I'm sorry. Do you want me to get you a ginger ale?" He gently brushed the side of her cheek and handed her a clean cloth to wipe her mouth.

"If you wouldn't mind."

When he left, she had to think quickly. Too many thoughts were racing through her mind. Rising from the bathroom floor, she checked her reflection in the mirror.

"Did he see me?" she asked aloud. She knew that under that hat and behind those sunglasses, she should've been completely unrecognizable. But she felt paranoid.

Maybe it was a sign. She grabbed her toothbrush and started brushing away the remnants of her ill feelings. Travelling around the world after all this time and nearly running into Heywood. Heywood of all people. The man she knew had something to do with her being injured and believed dead. And now he was singlehandedly taking over her legacy and stealing her money. She knew it, but didn't have a shred of evidence to prove anything.

After months and months of pain and recovery, prayer, questions, research, and planning, she wanted to repossess her life, but didn't know how to do it. Again, she thought about telling Randolph the whole truth, and once again talked herself out of it. She couldn't risk hurting him. But she would tell him that she needed some time to get herself together before saddling him with her troubles. She hoped that he would understand.

Quickly mapping out her plans, she practiced what she was going to say to Randolph when he returned. She couldn't go to the States, not just yet. First, she had to go back to Montserrat and find out what she could about the accident. Then, when she went to the States, she would make sure that she had her own place and could use her own resources to resolve her own mess. Telling him was not going to be easy.

Within ten minutes or so, Randolph returned with a ginger ale and a small box of saltine crisps.

"Thank you so much, Randolph," she said, kissing him gently on the cheek. "You always take such good care of me."

He smiled and opened the can as she held it. "I like taking care of you. And I like the way you take care of me too."

"I don't feel like I do enough for you, Randy."

"You do great. Especially after everything you've been through." He opened the crackers. She took a few out and placed them in her mouth.

He grabbed her hand, and led her to their balcony, which overlooked the city.

"I'm sorry that you're not feeling well. And that we can't stay here longer."

She nibbled on her crackers, trying to think of how she was actually going to say the words she had rehearsed while he was gone. "It's okay, Randolph. It really is. I'm sorry that I don't feel good, but it's probably for the best. Because I—"

He interrupted her, something that he rarely did. He reached one arm around her waist while he slipped his other hand in his pocket. "I'm sorry, but I can't wait. I wanted us to come here because I wanted to ask you something, Marisol."

He pulled a small box out of his pocket and held it toward her. "Although we weren't able to be here long this time, I was hoping that we could come back later, on our honeymoon." He pulled her close to him, and smiled, his lips nervously parting. His words were slow and deliberate.

"Marisol Kent, will you marry me?"

chapter thirty: side b

"YES, RANDY. I will. I will get some rest," she said, her voice sounding tired but happy. "I can't wait to see you, too."

"I love you," he said.

"I love you too," she said, as she kissed the phone and then hung it up. It was the second time she had said it to him since he had asked her to marry him. It was also six-thirty in the morning, and it was the third time Randolph had called to make sure she had arrived okay.

Wiggling her fingers, she stopped and held out her left hand. An exquisite, two-carat Princess Cut diamond in a platinum setting glinted back at her, and she smiled. "I can't believe I'm engaged," she said aloud, a gentle smile playing around her lips. How could she have said no? She loved him and wanted to be at his side for the rest of her life. However, Randolph still didn't know who she really was and what their new life would be like. Her smile faded as she considered everything she had to do before she was able to tell him the truth.

Randolph had shocked her with his proposal in St. Tropez, and had completely thrown her off her game. Married? Engaged? She was ecstatic when he asked, so much that she had forgotten all about reclaiming her life as Cam.

She was so happy and swept up in emotion that she had blurted out "Yes!" and "Oh, I love you so much, Randy," before she could even think straight. But, later that evening, when her feet were back on the ground, she knew that she could never marry him as Marisol. But when and how would she ever be Cam again?

She sighed and sipped her peppermint tea, and gazed at the screen on her laptop. Sitting on the sofa and chewing on a piece of wintergreen gum, she rubbed her tired, sore eyes. The last few weeks had been an absolute whirlwind. She was currently sitting in the living room of Randolph's Center City Apartment in downtown Philadelphia. The historic building was complete with a doorman, and the original windup elevator, and she had been surprised at its existence when she arrived at the building late last night.

Randolph's proposal had put a real kink in her plans. Now that they were engaged, it made sense that they live together. That had not been part of her original plan, but she would adjust. She had to.

It'll all work out, she thought. Randolph was ecstatic, and wasn't pressing her to set a date yet. She told him that she wasn't quite ready for marriage; that she needed to take some time to get adjusted to living in the States. He just didn't know the half of it.

From St. Tropez, Randolph had gone straight to Philadelphia. Using the engagement as an excuse, she took a side trip to Montserrat to finalize some personal business. She had most of her Euros left, and when she converted them, she actually had almost two hundred American dollars. Randolph had told her to keep her money. He wanted her to do whatever she needed to in Montserrat, to tie up all her loose ends, so that when she came to him in the States she wouldn't have to worry about anything back on the island. So, he had made and paid for her airline ticket to and hotel accommodations in Montserrat, along with a return ticket to Philadelphia.

As luck would have it, Randolph had to work the night she arrived, so she took a solo cab ride to his small apartment. It was truly different being back in the States, and she was glad to be there, but still torn under the circumstances. She felt duplicitous pretending to be Marisol, pretending never to have been in the United States before, but she loved

Randolph and wanted to share a life with him. She felt loved and safe with him, and right now, her primary concern was that she needed to feel safe. At least until she confirmed that she was not in danger from anyone in Montserrat or from her former life.

She sipped the warm tea and stared at the screen. She had so much to do. So much to process. She was happy that Randolph wanted to marry her, but overwhelmed and worried. He wanted her to meet his family, to attend social functions, and to plan the wedding. How could she pull all that off, or put all that off, without making him suspicious? And without getting in the way of the plans she had made regarding her past life, all of which she had to resolve before she could ever begin a new one.

As much as she wanted to, she just couldn't morph into another person. It wasn't fair to Randolph, the real Marisol, or even herself. Somehow, she had to find a way to make it right for all three of them. But in what order?

She had started another notebook. This one, titled "Wedding Plans," was a cover. With that name, she was certain Randolph would not be tempted to peek inside. Actually, she had devoted several pages to wedding plans, but most of the notebook was filling up with information she had gained about the accident along with plans for recovering her life and finances as Starr. Documenting her plans as she worked them out helped her to focus; every detail was becoming more and more critical.

Overall, her trip to Montserrat had been very productive. She had detailed every interaction in her notebook right after they occurred, but hadn't really had a chance to go over of her notes. Even so, she was troubled at her own memories of her time on Marisol's home turf.

She had tried to keep her arrival and appearance low-key. She went back to the villa where she, Marisol and Allison had stayed, hoping to jog her memory about that time, praying that she might remember something important or an elusive clue. It was occupied by other guests, and the cleaning and household staff had changed. There was nothing.

She went to the beach. She went to the marina and looked for *The Proud Mary*, the boat Heywood had chartered, but couldn't find it. After asking around, she found out that it had been chartered by someone in Antigua for an extended excursion. She tried not to be discouraged, but nothing was coming together. She had one last stop. The hospital where Starr had died and Marisol had survived.

Haunted by emotion, she braced herself and entered. Wrapped in dark shades, a linen pantsuit, and a wide brimmed straw hat, she was armed with nothing but determination and her newly-acquired accent. She hoped that it would pass muster. Once inside, she introduced herself and asked the receptionist who she might talk with that might have been working in the ER on the day of the accident. The receptionist referred her to the nurse's station in the emergency department, where the staff, while glad to see that she had recuperated so well, were reluctant to speak to her. They suggested that she speak to her attending physician, Dr. Mangrum, as he would know the details of her care.

Unfortunately, Dr. Mangrum was in surgery that morning, so she left a message for him and waited, sitting patiently in the very waiting room Heywood and her crew must have been in after the accident. Dr. Mangrum rushed in as soon as he was able, remembering her and her grave injuries well.

When she removed her hat and glasses, it was an understatement to say that he was stunned. The last time he had seen her, she had been terribly disfigured and near death. He asked her the details of her surgeries, treatment, and recovery, and thanked her profusely for coming back so he could see how well she had done. They spoke only briefly about the accident, and while he was gracious and sincere, didn't really offer any new insight that hadn't been in her transferred medical records, all of which she had in her possession.

Dr. Mangrum did say, however, that he had often wondered about her. He also said that the hospital had been in utter chaos when she was being treated, and when Starr died before they could get her stabilized.

Her heart sank at that information. When she told Dr. Mangrum that she'd like to thank the staff who had taken care of her, he gave her their names. Only one of the three nurses was working that day, and after checking around, she found Claudette, who was updating medical charts. Claudette greeted her warmly, pleasantly surprised by her visit and by her superb recovery.

"I can't believe it's you! Girl, when you came in, we cried. You were at death's door. An' now, look at you!"

"Thank you for takin' such good care o' me."

Two other nurses walked by and glanced over, curious expressions on their faces.

"You're so welcome, dear. I'm so happy to see you lookin' so good—like nothin' ever happened to you."

"Thank God," Cam said. "But, I wanted to thank you an' everyone else that helped me durin' the first hours. I understan' that the care I received 'ere was critical to my healing later."

"Indeed," Claudette said, glancing over her shoulder. She was acting a little skittish, and Cam sensed that she was uneasy talking to her.

"Is there somethin' wrong?" Cam asked. "You seem a little nervous."

Claudette forced a half smile. "Well, seeing you kind of reminds me of that day. It was pretty traumatic, ya know. Lotsa stuff happenin'. We were all nervous because of the young lady, that singer girl who got hurt wit' you. Poor thing. God rest her soul. So much goin' on, like we'd never seen before 'ere. An' then that big time manager of hers, he was actin' real crazy."

"Uhh, really? Who?"

"That Heywood guy. I know you've heard of him, he's real famous. Heywood. Kennard Heywood," Claudette said, and leaned forward. She lowered her voice. "He had everythin' and everybody crazy. Nobody knew what to do. He insisted on goin' in an' seein' her, even though the doctor said no an' she was in no condition to be seen by anyone."

"My goodness," Cam said, "I can't imagine how that musta been."

"I'll say. He pushed his way right on in. Went all the way to the top to get in, wit' you an' her layin' there with burns an' tubes all over, tryin' to stay alive."

"Oh, Jesus. I had no idea." Her mind raced. *That grimy bastard. Why would he force himself into a restricted area, just to see me? Especially if my diagnosis was so grim?*

"Well, you wouldn't. You both were hangin' by a thread, an' we had you in the same room in the ICU. See, we'd never seen injuries like yours, especially not two people at the same time. Every second was critical. I'm just glad to see you're doin' so well. An' I'm still hurt that poor girl died like she did. It was just awful. We didn't know what to do."

Cam sniffed and tried to imagine the emotionally charged scene. Tears sprang to her eyes, and she wasn't sure if it was because she was overwhelmed by sadness or anger. She felt something, a gnawing, eerie feeling.

"Wow," she said, struggling to keep the emotions in check. "Well, was that Heywood person able to see her before she died?"

Claudette was about to respond, when a heavy hand landed on Cam's shoulder. Cam looked down to see pinky rings and another large gold ring, and her heart stopped. Moving up the hand, she saw the glimmer of a bright gold Rolex Presidential watch. As she turned to see who was touching her, she noticed the worried expression on Claudette's face. A short, stout dark-skinned man stood behind her, the sweat glistening on his unfriendly face.

"Umm, Nurse Murray, I'll speak to Miss Kent now," he said. He half-smiled at Cam, while Claudette resumed her work, but not before calling out, "take good care," to her.

"Miss Kent," the man said, "I'm Maurice Davies. I'm the hospital administrator, an' I understand you have some questions about your stay here."

Cam bristled, but tried not to flinch when he firmly took her arm and directed her to a quiet corner of an adjoining waiting room. His suit was tight and ill-fitting, but had an expensive look and cut. The sunlight in the room allowed her to get a closer look at him, and the glare from his watch nearly blinded her. *How can he afford that?* she thought. Granted, some imported jewelry was cheaper in the islands, but even a bargain Rolex would cost thousands of dollars.

"Mr. Davies. A pleasure to meet you," she said. She studied his wooly gray afro and beady eyes, which looked everywhere but directly into hers. "I wished to thank everyone who had a hand in tendin' to me whilest I was 'ere."

"You're welcome, dear, an' congratulations on your recovery. You look remarkable," he said, almost leering at her. He stepped closer, a little too close, his cologne overwhelming.

"Considerin' how injured you were."

She forced a smile and took a step backward. "Considerin'," she repeated. "But, I was concerned that I would owe you all somethin' for my care. Considerin'."

"Well, don't worry your pretty little head about that. Your bills were taken care of." He paused dramatically, clearing his throat, "by the late Miss Starr's assistant."

Her eyes flickered. Her girl Allison had really come through for her.

"I can't believe it. That was so nice. How can I thank 'er? Do you know her name or address?"

Mr. Davies' leer dropped, and his expression became stone-like. "Her? Who said it was a her?"

Cam's maintained her composure. "Well, I met 'er before the accident. Just like I met Miss Starr."

Mr. Davies folded his arms. "Umm, I see. Anyway, it's my understandin' that your care was provided under the agreement that you would not contact any of the parties involved. It was also my understandin' that you had signed a non-disclosure form that stated such. I'm sure you remember that. Considerin'."

Heywood and those damned N-Snips, she thought. She was even more convinced that his hands were dirtier than she had originally thought. She forced herself to remain calm, keeping her expression kind and sincere. "Oh, I see. Well, I appreciate it just the same." She flashed a wary smile.

"So, while we welcome you back home, I must say I wonder why you're 'ere. Are you 'ere to stay?"

There was something off in his question and in his voice. If Cam had learned anything throughout this ordeal, she had learned to trust her instincts. And instinctively, she knew that Mr. Davies was a slimy as he appeared. She would never tell him anything near the truth.

"Uh, yes, I'll be 'ere a while before I return to Trinidad. I've decided to make it me home."

She chewed her gum and tried to recall every word of their conversation, along with his body language and facial expressions. Something had been going on with him. He just seemed shady. What was he hiding? How had he known she had signed an N-Snip? Where had he gotten that information? And that jewelry? Apparently, Mr. Davies was the top dog at the hospital. He must have been the person Heywood bullied into letting him into her room.

The rest of the trip, though pleasant, had been without incident. She had visited Salem, Marisol's birthplace, but hadn't been able to locate any of her relatives. Another dead-end. She had exhausted all sources of information, so she decided to catch an earlier flight to Philly.

Trying not to be depressed about the fact that there wasn't a single soul who missed Marisol, she sat alone in the back of the taxi, consumed with thoughts of Marisol and her sad and lonely life on the tiny island. Struggling to make a living, she had been a poor island girl whose fateful meeting with a celebrity ended up costing her life. She had been afforded no justice in her life, and now she had apparently been cheated again in death.

She paid the driver, and stepped out into the searing heat of the island, pulling her rolling suitcase behind her. As the porters jockeyed for her attention, she was careful to keep her hat pulled down and her sunglasses on, as she reached into her wallet to tip them.

Fishing around for some singles, she heard a hauntingly familiar voice. Rising above the noise and confusion of the airport departure area, it stopped her in her tracks.

"The dirty spirit is tryin' to destroy you."

Cam's heart skipped a beat. It was the old, blind village elder. The same one she had seen twice before, and he had warned her then, too. This time he was seated behind a pushcart next to the sliding glass entrance. He ignored the other tourists who were milling about, looking at his goods. His grey eyes were riveted on her.

She almost dropped her wallet. "Excuse me?" she asked, and cautiously stepped toward him. *Who was this man, and why did he keep appearing in her life? And how did he even know who she was, let alone that she would be here?*

"What did you say?" she asked him, struggling with her accent.

He picked up a small bracelet, and held it toward her. "The one with the black heart. He has the soul of the devil."

"He who?" she asked, her voice trembling, afraid to hear his response and afraid to take the bracelet. She wanted to run, but her feet were glued to the ground.

"The one who brought you 'ere. The evil one who wanted your soul." His lifeless eyes still bore holes into her.

She couldn't believe her ears. "I don't understand. What are you saying?"

The old man stared right through her. "Chile, keep this bracelet wit' you. An' never forget. He thinks he holds your fate. You must prove he don't. He took one of ours for his ill purpose. He must not get away wit' it."

She accepted the bracelet, then jumped when a sudden loud noise startled her. She turned her head, and realized it was the sound of a taxi horn directly behind her. She turned back to finish talking to the old man, but both he and his cart had disappeared into the crowd. She looked in every direction, but he was nowhere to be found.

She entered the airport, hoping to find him inside, but no luck. Cam looked down at the bracelet in her hand. It was woven leather, with brown stones that looked like eyes. She remembered Allison buying one of these. They were "evil eye" stones, meant to protect the wearer against evil. Cam carefully snapped the loop around her wrist. *This is too strange, but I guess it can't hurt,* she thought. *He's been right so far.* The bracelet and his words gave her the confirmation she had been seeking, even though she still had no evidence.

She opened her notebook, and jotted down a couple of random thoughts, including the words of the old man. Somehow she had to pull this all together, but her feelings and intuition and the rantings of an old island man were not enough. Heywood was definitely involved, but she couldn't prove anything. What had he done? Had he switched their identities? Why?

She couldn't shake the feeling that something had happened while he was in their hospital room. Why had he pushed so hard to get in there? And that creepy, shady, pimped out Mr. Davies. She made a note to herself. "Get a copy of the death certificate," she scribbled. But how?

It should be a matter of public record, but knowing Heywood, he had probably sealed that off too. She had to find out if the cause of death was burn injuries. Then she thought again. It probably didn't matter what it said on the piece of paper, however, because it may have been changed to suit Heywood, too. She hated to admit it, but if Heywood was involved, anything was possible. She scratched that idea.

Her tea was now cold, but she kept sipping anyway, staring at the laptop screen. She kept thinking, making entries in her notebook, and surfing the net.

She needed to find out more about the theft at her attorney's office. It had to be connected to Heywood. How could she find out what had been taken? She couldn't just call Deacon Owens and announce that she was alive. Or could she? She didn't know what to do, and was beginning to feel nervous. She didn't know if she could trust her own attorney.

Another thing. Heywood had claimed they were engaged, a complete setup. And clearly, it was a brilliant tactic for him to worm his way into her business and her estate. Then there was her will. The *New York Post* website cited there was a new will that named Heywood sole beneficiary.

So, at least she had proof that he was trying to steal her fortune, but even that didn't do her much good. She couldn't just reappear and challenge him. For if he really did think that she was dead or that he had killed her, he wouldn't let her live long enough to bring him down. She had to play it smart. Real smart.

She needed help. And she needed money. Randolph was generous, but she couldn't ask him for the kind of money she needed. She could use the wedding as an excuse for some of her expenses, but even that had a limit. She did have money, Cam remembered, the fifteen thousand her aunt had her bury in the backyard. But, how could she get to it?

Confused as to what her next steps should be, Cam, lost in thought, started untwisting one of her dreadlocks. Surprised that it unlocked so easily, she continued, untwisting until her hair was loose and flowing. Her last thought before falling asleep was a wish that she could untwist her life as easily as she had untwisted her hair.

HEYWOOD SLAMMED his Krog headphones down on the multi-colored Yamaha Recording Board, snatched the shotgun microphone from its stand, and screamed into it. "What the fuck was that, kid? That ain't got no feelin', son. Nothin'. I couldn't sell that shit to ya moms." He wrinkled his nose with disgust, and cut the mic off.

Casbar was on the mic boom in the recording studio Kennetic Records had leased for him. One of the artists Heywood had liberated from the Dirty South, he was trying to prove that he could hang. Outfitted in his camel colored Louis Vuitton shirt, baggy Acme jeans and wide open Timberlands, he was head bobbing and grabbing his stuff, trying to lay it down for his upcoming solo effort.

"Yo, Heywood, man. Ya know, it just ain't flowin'," he said, with his slow, dragged out Southern drawl.

Duck was in the corner of the booth. He scratched his head and rubbed his eyes. It was two-thirty in the morning and this was how Heywood got down. He would stay in the studio from midnight until the sun came up, days on end, until he got the product from his artists that he felt he deserved. And he wasn't feeling what he was hearing out of the swaybacked Casbar and his cast of clowns. Heywood had designated the month of

January to work with his artists in the studio. Time was scheduled and money had been spent. Now, was the time to make it happen. Time to earn.

The studio was crowded, and blazed over, thick with the smoke of joints being passed between hypemen, hangers on, wannabes, cognac swilling chicken heads, dope boys, and sprinkles of actual artists. Heywood was seated in front of the control board, surrounded by half-eaten containers of food, used napkins, and empty beer bottles. The tell-tale signs of the ravages of time and the munchies. His sound and mix engineers were drinking bottomless cups of black Starbucks coffee to keep up.

Heywood stood and stretched. Switching the mic back on, he reached for a blunt smoldering in a nearby ashtray. "Look, tell some of them broads over there to come give you an' them otha niggas some head so y'all can get ya other head right, okay?" He glanced at Duck and snarled back into the mic. "Imma take ten, an' when I come back, I wanna hear some balls slappin' up against somebody's cheeks, an' some decent sound comin' out ya mouths, ya heard? Otherwise, all of y'all is gonna get the fuck up outta here."

Still holding the blunt, he motioned for Duck to follow as he stormed out of the sound booth and into a private office down the hall from the recording room.

Duck wasn't about to say anything. Ever since he and Heywood had gotten into it in St. Tropez, he was walking soft. But, Casbar's antics tonight only proved his point. He wasn't shit. Duck just couldn't figure out why Heywood was so hyped about him.

Duck unlocked the office door and flicked on the light switch. Heywood shoved past him and flopped down on the red Natuzzi leather sofa, still puffing on his joint.

"Man, where's that little nigga Parsley?" Heywood yawned, his eyes rolling back in his head.

"Didn't you tell him to go get you a new *People* Magazine or somethin'?" Duck asked as he quietly shut the door behind them.

"Yeah, that's right. Ya know I'm 'bout to be on the cover of that joint, right? I hope that nigga don't forget to get me some more smoke. I'll send his ass back out in that hawk if he does." Heywood drew a deep breath. "It shouldn't take this goddamned long."

As if by magic, as soon as Heywood stopped speaking, there was a knock on the door.

"Who dis?" asked Duck.

"Who ya think?" Parsley answered. "Open up."

He had a stack of magazines in his hands, including *The Star*, *National Enquirer*, *NY Times*, *Variety*, *Rolling Stone*, *Vibe* and *Billboard*. In his skully and oversize leather bomber jacket, Parsley looked menacing, until he pulled his hoodie back and revealed a full, boyish face.

"Whassup, Duck?" He said as he head bobbed past the big guy, and handed the stack of rags to Heywood. He reached in his coat pocket and pulled out some Phillie Blunts and gallon size Ziplock bag of weed. "Where ya want this, Wood?"

Heywood frowned as he rifled through the magazines. He didn't even bother answering.

Duck intervened. "He don't want it, Parsley. Do what you do. Roll up some trees. I need a forest right about now."

"Enough to get me through this bullshit," Heywood said, never lifting his eyes from the magazine.

Parsley retreated to a corner of the office, and started to remove his coat.

"Not in here, nigga," barked Heywood. "Does this look like yo' office? Get the fuck outta here. An' be back in ten with a good one."

Parsley scurried out, and Duck swallowed hard. It was hard keeping his mouth shut, but he did. Duck closed the door and turned back to see Heywood still shuffling through the magazines, throwing them on the floor after going through them. He stopped, however, when he came to *Billboard*.

"I don't believe this shit," Heywood rumbled.

When Duck asked him what he was talking about, Heywood kicked over the ottoman in front of the sofa. "They got an article in here saying how Noah Parker's gonna be named the next head of APB Records. Over my dead body!"

Duck rubbed his eyes, and reached for the joint Heywood had been smoking. Heywood pushed his hand away.

"You ain't gettin' this. Wait for Parsley's ass to bring in the other ones. Pass me a fuckin' ashtray. An' get me a beer. Ain't this some shit?"

Heywood muttered. It was time for him to put his plan into motion. He had to shut Noah down in grand style, and shut up those industry insiders, too. It would be just the kick Heywood needed to send Noah running screaming into the night, never to be seen or heard from again.

Duck obliged, grabbing an onyx ashtray from the desk, and lumbered over to the wetbar on the adjacent wall. He pulled out two Becks from the refrigerator, and handed one to Heywood.

"Open it, nigga," snarled Heywood. "Damn."

Duck opened the bottle, and handed it to Heywood. "Man, it's on now. I'm 'bout sick of everybody singin' this mutha fucka's tune. Blah, blah, blah. I'm gonna change that shit. Right now." Heywood threw the *Billboard* to the floor, and went back to searching for his *People.* "I got a package I need delivered to Mr. Know-it-All. Personally delivered. Find out where he's at, an' let's get it crackin'. First thing this mornin'."

Duck nodded, while Heywood dug through the remaining magazines. When he found the People, he pulled it from the stack and stared at the cover like a gold-digger looking at the Neiman Marcus Christmas Catalog. Heywood salivated. He was on the cover, but not the cover shot. His photo was relegated to the lower right corner. But, he was happy, nonetheless.

"See, Duck? A nigga's arrived," he said, holding the magazine out in front of him. "Fuckin' Noah can't say that. *Shee-it*, he ain't gonna be sayin' much soon."

He flipped open the magazine and thumbed through the pages until he reached the article. He was mesmerized, trying to absorb every word.

Duck glanced over, saw the cover, and grunted. *Big deal,* he thought. He was about to sit down in one of the chairs beside the sofa when his eyes trailed down to the cover of the *Star Magazine.* One of the captions read:

STARR SEX TAPE. DOES IT REALLY EXIST?

"What the fuck?" Duck snapped, and scooped up the periodical. "Heywood, did you see that shit?" Duck held it like he could have ripped it apart.

"What?" Heywood said, still reading about himself. Duck took the paper and shoved it in Heywood's face.

"This."

"Oh that. What? What about it?"

"What about it?" Duck repeated himself. "Whatchu gonna do 'bout it, Heywood? I know you ain't gonna let this shit slide."

Heywood rolled his eyes. "What? Get real, Duck. Who ya think leaked that shit to the *Enquirer* an' the rest of 'em."

Duck couldn't believe his ears. "Why, Wood? I thought you was all about keepin' Starr's shine. Come on, dawg. That shit ain't true, is it? Why you do that, man? That's foul."

"That's business, Duck. I thought ya knew. Ya betta act like ya know. I'm tryna sell some records an' make some real money. That good girl shit is aiight, but folks is more interested in the dirt. Ya heard."

Duck shook his head. "That's foul, man. No disrespect."

Heywood glared at him. "None taken. It just goes to show ya that ya really don't know nothin'. I ain't sayin' it's true, but face it. It's interestin', ya heard? An' it keeps her name in the ink. It's newsworthy."

"Yo, but at what price, Heywood?"

"It's called the price of fame, son. An' everyone's gotta pay it. Even Starr."

"Well damn, didn't she pay the ultimate price? *Shee-it*." Duck's voice cracked.

"Damned shame, but true. She paid it, rest her soul, but just 'cause she died don't mean that I gotta die too. Shit, I still gotta eat."

"You look pretty well fed to me, bruh. But, I guess eatin's eatin', but real talk, ya ain't supposed to be eatin' off somebody else's plate," Duck said, his voice icy.

"Food's food, nigga. An' I see you ain't missed no meals either, Big Boy. An' it's my plate, my food, an' my kitchen ya been eatin' out of for real. So, real talk. Starr's image ain't gonna get tarnished by a little chit chatter. I'm tellin' ya, I know what I'm doin'. I'm buildin'. Showin' her flaws makes her seem more real. Chicks'll dig her more 'cause they'll be able to relate to her betta, an' niggas'll dig her more 'cause they can fantasize about her bein' a freak. It all works out.

"Plus, if I'm tryna sell the idea of making a movie about her life, I damn sure ain't gonna make no money makin' no G-rated Disney flick. Fuck that. An' I ain't interested in embarrassing myself by makin' no box office flop either." He finally finished his joint and extinguished it in the ashtray.

"Speakin' of movies," Heywood said, his eyes gleaming. "Did ya bring that camcorder like I told ya?"

Duck nodded toward the corner of the office where he had stored Heywood's briefcase and videocam earlier that evening.

"Good," Heywood said. "Now, go get Parsley an' Casbar. I wanna see how much work these niggas really want to put in to get put on. An' don't forget to get on that otha thing ya supposed to do. I want that shit done pronto."

"Yeah, Fitz. It's all good. You know a brotha's got ya back," Heywood said. "You ain't got nuttin' to worry about. I'll holla at ya lata."

Heywood put the Bang & Olufsen cordless phone down on his nightstand and smiled as he sat on the edge of his California King four-post bed. "Two down, one to go," he said aloud, as a sly smile creased his face. His fingers rested on a stack of DVDs. The top one had a cover with the words "NP-Post Grammy Production 2007" neatly typed across it. His plans were working like a fine Swiss timepiece. Tick tock.

He had just finished talking to his mentor, Fitz, who confirmed information Heywood had received earlier from Rae, his publicist. Noah issued a statement that he would not like to be considered for the head job at APB Records. Fitz, who was also mentoring Noah, called Heywood to see if he knew why Noah wasn't interested in what would clearly be a good move for him. And more pointedly, Fitz wanted to know if it had anything to do with the events of his post-Grammy gathering. Of course, Heywood pretended that he had no idea what Fitz was talking about, and tried to seem vaguely insulted that he was being accused of something.

Like any decent parent, Fitz wanted his children to get along. And if he ever thought that Heywood had broken the code and used pictures or information from one of his soirees to do harm to one of their brethren, there would be hell to pay. In their crazy code of conduct, it was fine to denigrate and control subordinates like that, but never a peer. It was simply unheard of. Heywood gloated. "If he only knew," he said aloud.

Heywood was getting comfortable pushing the limits and restructuring the boundaries. Yeah, he respected Fitz to a certain degree, but felt that he was now bigger than Fitz. Heywood had outgrown him, and no longer needed Fitz for counsel or advice. He also believed that he, Heywood, should have been offered that position at APB. When he found out he hadn't even been mentioned for that spot, whatever rules he was playing by had changed. And he had changed them.

He was alone that afternoon, having just finished a grueling week finishing Casbar's CD. He didn't want any company, and didn't want any sex. He was content. He was King of the World, or at least controller of the hip-hop universe.

Noah's package had been delivered to him personally two days ago, and the results were exactly as he had planned. Noah was out. Check and checkmate.

With his sagging boxers gathering around his paunchy midsection, he picked up the stack of DVDs, walked over to his vault, and pressed his thumbprint against the access pad. The wall opened, and he walked in to the neatly arranged chamber.

The vault was his heartbeat. Command central. In addition to his main security system, it also stored his most valuable jewels, the masters of some of his artists, and several shelves of mixed media and other treasures. He took the DVDs he held and placed them on the shelf in alphabetical order.

He washed his hands in the vault's small marble sink, and leered at himself in the mirror. "You's a sexy mutha fucka," he said, watching himself as he dried his hands on a supple Egyptian handtowel from the rack beside the sink.

He selected a watch from one of his synchronized watch cases, square faced Breitling Bentley, and slipped it on his wrist. He glanced at the security camera monitors and shrugged at the lack of activity.

Taking a seat at the arch-shaped mahogany desk in the rear of the vault, Heywood pulled out three ledgers that were neatly standing between two crystal bookends. Two, labeled "AI/AE" and "Expenses," he left closed. He opened the one labeled "TM" and smirked, recalling his earlier conversation with Kevin.

Frantic and afraid, Kevin had called that morning. He said that Typhoon didn't believe what he was telling him about the decline in Heywood's income. Heywood had cut off all communications with Typhoon, saying that they needed to chill out until things cooled off. And as Heywood predicted, without any money, Typhoon's high-priced legal team had all but deserted him. Kevin became his link to the outside world. And now that Kevin was on Heywood's team, that link was going to be his downfall.

Kevin was more manic than usual, and Heywood thought it might be the drugs he had been supplying him. In any event, he was keeping the pressure on him. The second he became more of a liability than an asset, Heywood would take care of him. Until then, he was going to ride Kevin until he crumbled. He just had to be certain that Kevin didn't crack before Typhoon did.

Heywood found the entries in the "TM" ledger or "Tyrone Moon" ledger pure comical fiction, because while he was documenting little or no income to share with Typhoon or his CPA, the other books were documenting a windfall. He had crippled that fucking Typhoon, and he had no clue.

As Kevin stammered and sweated, Heywood played him off. "Just keep tellin' him that the Feds are crawlin' all over me, tryna make a connection between us. Tell Typhoon to be easy, that I got him. Tell him I ain't makin' no money, but I ain't forgot about him. I got him."

Kevin continued hemming and hawing, pissing off Heywood. "Man up, nigga an' grow some balls," he barked, before dismissing him a click. Heywood was bored and tired of hearing him snivel, bitch, and moan, but he knew that Kevin would do what needed to be done. He was in too deep. He had too much on him. Or, at least that's what Kevin thought. And Heywood learned a long time ago that having power, real or imagined, was all that really mattered.

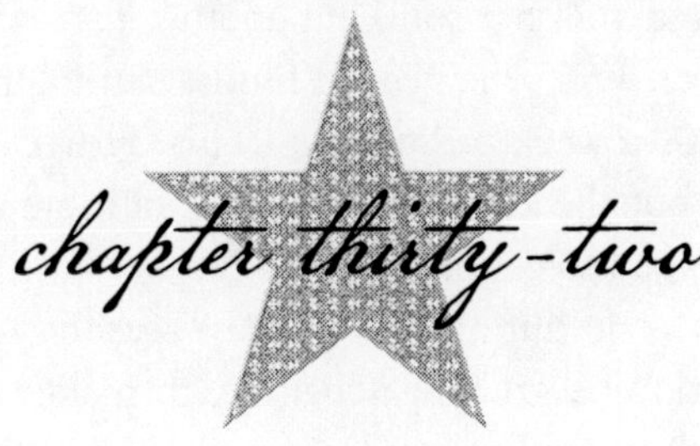

HER REUNION with Randolph was both touching and torrid. Uncomplicated and tender, he was thrilled that she was finally there, in his apartment, in the flesh. When she cooked dinner for him that first night, he even raved about her Caribbean spiced rice and lemon broiled salmon. He had to love her, she reassured herself, because cooking was certainly not her specialty.

She had surprised him with her new hairstyle. With her locks gone, her tresses fell luxuriously on her shoulders, and he clearly liked that he could run his fingers through her mane.

After an intimate night of lovemaking, they held each other and talked. They discussed their future together, and Randolph told her to take her time figuring out what she wanted to do with her life, besides marrying him, of course. Cam pretended to weigh her options. She tossed out the idea of possibly taking some classes, as soon as she figured out what she wanted to study. They agreed that they would not rush the wedding, to give her time to establish her own life and reach some of her own goals before becoming Mrs. Dr. Williams. And just as important was the fact that since they were engaged, their living together in sin wouldn't reflect too badly in the eyes of his parents. He drifted off to sleep with her snuggled in the crook of his arm, dreaming about their promising future.

She stayed awake, gazing at him as he slept. Part of her wanted to shake him back awake, and spill her soul, but another part knew she needed to come up with a plan. First, she needed funds. Randolph had insisted that she take at least $700 a week and use one of his credit cards until she landed a part time job, but she knew she needed a lot more than that to jump-start her plans. She had to get the money from her backyard, but how?

She mulled over it during the holiday season. It was quiet since Randolph was working a grueling schedule, to make up for the time he had spent away with her in Europe. He was apologetic for making her first Christmas in the States so lackluster, but it worked out well for her. It gave her an opportunity to plan, and by the time the New Year began, she had it all worked out. She was going to Maryland to retrieve her money.

Her Aunt Mary and grandmother were still living in the family house, even though, according to one of the blogs, Heywood had tried to bar them from the property. Fortunately, the courts overruled him, and ordered that they could remain there until Cam's estate was properly probated.

Without a driver's license, she knew she could easily get to Maryland by train, and knew exactly when she needed to get there. On a weekday between one and three, when her Aunt Mary and grandmother will be watching *The Bobby Jones Gospel Show* on BET.

While Randolph slept, she trolled the web, searching for bus service between New Carrollton and Mitchellville, but came up short. She would have to arrange for a cab to drop her off and pick her up near the back gate of her community. It was winter, it was cold, and the ground was going to be like concrete. She needed a smally, but sturdy shovel.

Her opportunity to make her move happened quickly. Randolph had a symposium the next week in Chicago, and wanted her to accompany him. She feigned being road weary, and said that she would rather stay in Philly and get better acquainted with her new home. Randolph, agreeable and appreciating her independent nature, told her to enjoy her "me" time.

For the next few days, every time Randolph left for the hospital, she left the apartment and went shopping. She purchased a small folding shovel, a little Black Diamond ice axe and sheath, round-trip train ticket, and winter clothing, including boots, thermals, waterproof backpack, scarf, knit cap, gloves, and a thick, hooded down jacket. She was all set.

But, she was anxious. This was the first and most critical part of her plan. Without the money, nothing else could happen. Evidently, she gave off some nervous energy when she helped Randolph prepare for his trip.

★

"What's up, baby? Are you scared to stay here alone? Have you changed your mind? Do you want to come with me? I can get you on a plane right now," Randolph offered as she handed him a neatly folded shirt.

"No, no. I'm fine. I'll be fine. I think I'm just tired. Maybe I'll get some sleep with you gone," she joked.

Willing herself to act as normal as possible, whatever that was now; she helped him pack, kissed him goodbye, and watched him catch his taxi to the airport. Certain that he was gone, she quickly dressed in her new outfit, pushed her hair into her new knit hat, grabbed her gear, and hustled to the 30th Street Station to catch the Amtrak train.

It was midday by the time she arrived in Mitchellville, having successfully arranged for a taxi to drop her off at a professional building down the street from the rear entrance of her subdivision.

Home. The thought made her palms clammy. How long had it been since she was home? Or seen her aunt and grandmother? She ached to see them, but she couldn't take a chance. It might endanger all of them. Besides, she was doing this for them, too, so she had to stay on point and focused.

The sky was grey and cloudy, and provided sufficient cover for her disguise. Bundled up, her knapsack strapped to her back, she could easily be one of the children attending Woodmore Elementary she trekked past. Maneuvering down the sidewalk-less, small shouldered, tree lined road, she safely made it to the unguarded rear gate. She consciously shielded her face from the posted security camera as she darted by it.

Checking her watch, she smiled. It was 1:18. Right on time. Feeling like Tom Cruise in *Mission Impossible,* she stepped up her pace, moving quickly until she reached the circular driveway of her next door neighbor's mini-mansion. She stopped abruptly. Seeing her home again was painful-ly bittersweet, and it took her breath away. Suddenly, she felt totally violat-ed. This home belonged to her and her family. She had worked hard for it. And Heywood was trying to take it all away. And it infuriated her that she had become an intruder at her own home.

The house looked the same. Her aunt had been maintaining it well, holding it down as Cam knew she would. The lawn was manicured, and the Leyland cypress trees surrounding the property seemed to have grown in her absence. They were one of the reasons she had fallen in love with the house in the first place. That and the fact that from the street, the house appeared much smaller than most of the other homes in the community, but the fenced-in, tree-lined backyard masked the large enclosed pool and pool house, the indoor/outdoor living area, and a fully-equipped recording studio. She paused to collect herself.

"You can do this," she whispered to herself, her breath forming fog and tiny crystals in the air. She glanced down at her lucky bracelet. "You have to do this. Get in there, and get outta there."

Walking purposefully through her neighbor's backyard, she reached the rear of her own property, which, thankfully, backed up to a wooded empty lot. She quickly scaled the wrought-iron fence, sticking close to the trees as she moved closer to the grape arbor.

Once she reached the grape arbor, she opened her backpack, removed her shovel and ice axe, and started to dig into the solid ground. Progress was slow and extremely difficult. Intent on her work, she was completely unaware that a person holding a gnarled walking stick was standing directly behind her.

"In the name of Jesus," the person cried and swung the stick toward her head. "I rebuke thee!"

They sat, nestled beside each other on the sofa in the pool house, and Aunt Mary held Cam's hand. Dressed in her long navy blue dress coat with a plaid wool scarf thrown loosely around her neck, Aunt Mary removed her black wool hat and revealed a shock of salt and pepper hair.

She smiled at Cam, the tears flowing down her cheeks.

"Praise the Lord," she repeated over and over. She clutched her heart. "He answered my prayers. I didn't ever believe that He had taken you from us. I never did." She removed Cam's hat and looked at her face. "And you. You look a little different, like you been through something, but so good. A sight for sore eyes, I tell you." She marveled at Cam's face.

Cam breathed a sigh of relief. She had been so busy trying not to be seen, she hadn't thought about herself or how she looked. She had gone through a complete transformation, but her aunt didn't seem to notice any major change in her appearance.

"I, uh, I guess hadn't thought that you would recognize me so easily."

Aunt Mary shook her head, "Not know you, child? My Camara? Please. I'd as soon not know myself. You're just as pretty as a picture. Now, you look a little more filled out, a little more like a grown woman, but oh, sweet Jesus. Thank you, Lord. Thank you, Father. My baby is back." She rocked back and forth. "I'm so sorry I took a swing at you earlier."

Cam silently thanked God that her aunt never had to see her after the accident. She knew that she probably would not have withstood the shock. She looked at her aunt's hair and face, and immediately felt guilty. Her aunt had aged so much since she had last seen her. Her grief and troubles with the house and estate had worn her down.

She rubbed her aunt's hands, feeling the veins on their backs. "Aunt Mary, you don't have to apologize. I'm glad you missed, though, but I need to apologize to you. I'm sorry I didn't contact you before. I'm so sorry. But, it just wasn't best. So much has gone on, that I just didn't know how to tell you. And then I didn't want to scare you to death."

Aunt Mary clucked and kissed Cam's hands. "I could never be afraid of you. I told you, I never lost faith. I believed that the Lord was going to bring you through. I know that whatever happened, you couldn't tell me that you were okay. But, I just knew it wasn't your time to leave this earth." She squeezed their hands together. "Oh Lord. We need to call Deacon Owens, don't we?"

"No, Aunt Mary. We can't right now. Not right now."

Cam tried to explain to her aunt why it wasn't a good idea to contact her attorney, but Aunt Mary believed she could trust him.

"Trust me, Aunt Mary, only me. I've been watching what's been going on with you and with this house, and with my music and my estate, and with my charities. Believe me, I'd like to call Deacon Owens, but, the only one in this whole mess I can trust is you. So please, don't say anything to anybody. Please. No one. Nobody can find out that I'm alive or that I've been here. Our lives might depend on you not saying anything to anyone."

Aunt Mary raised her eyebrows. "Lord, child! It's not as bad as all that, is it? Our lives? Really?"

"Auntie, look at what's happened already. Money does strange things to people. It makes them do stuff you'd never in a million years think they'd be capable of. I might be reaching a little when I said our lives might be in jeopardy, but you never know. I know what I've been through, and it wasn't pretty. And I know that Heywood is somehow involved, just by the way he's been acting. And I've come to realize that when he's involved, anything's possible."

"You don't have to say no more, child. I understand. I know that ol' Heywood is behind this. I never trusted him. Not one bit. He has a dark, dirty spirit. His soul is black. Nothing but pure evil. First, he tried to have you, I mean that poor child cremated, and I refused. I flat out refused. Then, he wanted to bury you, I mean her, with that cross you always wore. But, Allison had it, and she gave it to me. They wouldn't let me see your, Lord forgive me, let me see the body, but somethin' told me not to lay that cross in the casket. And when he said that y'all were engaged, I knew he was a liar. That devil is a liar. I knew then that my baby would never get engaged and not tell me. No sir."

Cam cringed. She could tell her aunt was getting more and more upset, so she changed the topic of conversation, telling her everything that had happened to her, from meeting Marisol to the video shoot to the accident, to finding out her identity had been switched. She purposely glossed over the number of surgical procedures she endured and her agonizing recovery, sparing her poor aunt most of the painful details.

As Cam talked, Aunt Mary prepared a pot of hot tea and chicken noodle soup. Cam was in heaven. She was at home, with her favorite person, having what had to have been the best meal of her life. Cam hadn't been this happy or comfortable in months. For a fleeting moment, she thought about telling Aunt Mary about Randolph, but immediately talked herself out of it. Her aunt would never approve of the fact that she had not been honest with him, that he didn't even know her true identity. It didn't matter what the reason was.

So, Cam was also glad that she had removed her engagement ring for safekeeping. She didn't ever want to risk losing it, and then it also helped her keep her dual lives separate. The ring belonged to Marisol, not her. And until she rectified that duality, she had to keep the two separated.

Cam's diversion plan worked, but only for a few minutes. Her aunt was back on Heywood again, and Cam smiled. Aunt Mary was no fool. She more than had Heywood's number.

"And then he comes up with this will. Now, I know good and well that ain't nothing you wrote. No sir. I didn't believe that either, but Deacon Owens said now we gotta wait. Just because it's a matter for the courts, and they have to consider everything that's presented." Aunt Mary shook her head.

"I tell you, baby, you've been in a pit of snakes. Serpents. That manager of yours, Victor. Worthless. Not worth a plug nickel. All of them people makin' money off of you, an' when you was gone, they was gone too. I think the only one who really cared about you was that assistant of yours. That girl Allison seems like she means well, but I guess you never really know. I can say that she's been keeping up with your foundation, but she never said nothin' to me either about what happened down there. Nothing. I understand that Heywood had them under some kind of agreement where they couldn't talk about it. An' I hear he was threatening to sue anyone who did. But, I still say she could've said somethin' to me."

Cam's eyes flashed, and she interrupted her aunt. "Aunt Mary, I'm sorry, but I need to know something. Do you have the notebook I had with me down there? Allison should've given it to you, too."

Aunt Mary shook her head. "No, sweetie. I don't have it. And I'm sorry, but I never even thought to ask about it."

"Maybe it got lost in all the confusion," Cam said, sounding more hopeful than she felt.

"Maybe. That notebook might be lost, but at least you're found. All praises to God, He has delivered you. Now, you just have to do as He directs you to do. You can't give up. He's brought you too far. Whatever happened, you got to make it right. You got to find out what happened, so that other child's soul can rest in peace. What about her poor family? What do they think happened to her?"

Cam met her aunt's questions with silence. Aunt Mary didn't notice, for she kept talking. "Whatever, baby. I'll help you anyway I can."

As the pool house warmed up, the windows steamed over, casting a hazy glaze and further ensuring their privacy from the outside world. Cam relaxed and then spent the next few hours talking about life in the Dominican Republic, her doctors, and Switzerland. She missed her cab, but didn't worry about it. She would have one pick her up from the house.

She was even able to peep in to see her grandmother, who was sleeping soundly in front of the television set. And, at the house, Aunt Mary gave her something precious. The necklace her mother had given her for her christening, the small diamond cross. Cam welled up when she saw it, not realizing how much she had missed seeing it every day. It must have been in her messenger bag, she realized, because she remembered taking it off on the day of the photo shoot. *I'm never taking this off again,* Cam vowed to herself. *Even if it means another lie to Randolph, I'll just have to eat that one. Maybe I'll tell him I found it. That would at least be partially true.*

Cam hadn't checked her phone all day, and when she saw that Randolph had called and texted her a number of times, she knew she had to get back to reality. She recovered her money from the yard, leaving a couple thousand for luck, and Aunt Mary gave her an additional grand she had stashed in the house.

Before Cam left her home, she prayed with her aunt. Together, they prayed that God would help Cam reclaim and restore her life. Aunt Mary then thanked God for bringing Cam home safely to her. "Amen," Cam said, and left for Philadelphia, armed with her aunt's faith and love and the money she needed to make her move to the second phase of her plan.

THE NEXT month passed quickly, with Cam getting used to cohabitating with Randolph, living in Philadelphia, celebrating the holidays as his fiancé, and additionally, making her other plans. Her conscience was troubled daily, as she balanced being Marisol against the covert activities she was required to do to one day be Camara again.

She could not shake the guilt she experienced every time she had to lie to Randolph, but she just couldn't deviate from her path. She was walking a thin line; a fragile tightrope threatened to snap under the weight of her duplicity.

Randolph wanted to get married, and was anxious to have her meet his family and introduce her to his friends. All things any happily engaged woman would be glad to do. But not her. Everything was so complicated. She loved Randolph and had never known such happiness before, but her desire to prove what a monster Heywood was outweighed everything else.

She acknowledged that taking on Heywood might jeopardize her future with Randolph, so she prayed nightly that when the time came and she explained everything, he would forgive her. She absolutely hated living a lie, but knew it was a necessary evil until she was able to be herself again. And she had no idea how much time or how many more lies that was going to take.

On Randolph's advice, she joined a nearby 24-hour gym on Walnut Street. Her membership turned out to be one of the best things she had done. Now she was able to hide anything she didn't want Randolph to see in her gym locker, and was able to use the gym as an excuse, a place to pretend to be if she wasn't home.

Actually, she spent a fair amount of time there, as the workouts helped keep her stress level down and she could work on her laptop in the Wi-Fi lounge. She would also freely use her cellphone, and made frequent calls to Aunt Mary to check on her and her grandmother, and to get an update on the ongoing battle with her estate.

Every day, as luck would have it, she passed an old recording studio on her way to the gym, and was drawn to it. One morning, she found the courage and ventured inside to ask the owner about off-hour recording time. He was only too pleased to book a new customer.

Since she hadn't sung since she was in Switzerland, the thought of singing again energized her. It filled yet another deep void that had been carved out of her life. Using some of the money from her backyard treasure to pay for the recording time, Cam felt guilty. She would have loved to share this huge part of her life with Randolph. Music was her passion. It fed her soul. It was who she was, and she felt she was concealing too much of herself from him. But she just couldn't tell him. Not now. Not yet.

Using some of the lyrics she had been writing in her new notebook, Cam decided to lay down a few tracks, but needed a producer. She asked around at the studio, and several artists recommended local producer B. Real, who sold beats and tracks on the Internet.

After listening to his samples, Cam purchased two tracks, one up tempo and the other a slow ballad. To keep her identity secret, she paid him through PayPal, using another new identity, "Tru Talent," and requested that the tracks be sent to Tru at the recording studio.

With a daily routine in place, Cam settled into a comfortable life with Randolph, time at the gym, time at the recording studio, and time plotting her future. It was hard switching into different identities, but she had a plan, and was beginning to formulate the second step.

She wanted to nail Heywood to the wall, but knew that if she was ever going to find anything that connected him to her misfortunes, if there were any clues to be found, they would be found in that mini-Fort Knox in his New York penthouse. Heywood, a control freak, wouldn't spread his hold cards around. He would keep them close to his vest.

Using her laptop at the gym, she was able to monitor Heywood's Twitter updates, where he, Mr. King of the World, always posted his comings and goings for the week. She tracked his social life, figuring that if he had booked appearances, he would stick to his schedule.

While she would have preferred it if he was out of the city, she didn't have time to wait. She decided it was now or never. She had to know if Heywood had anything to do with the accident, and she had to find the fake will. Now, she was ready for phase two. She was on a mission. She was going straight into the lion's den, straight to Heywood's lair.

Several weeks after her trip to Maryland, Cam expressed an interest to Randolph to go to New York, using bridal shopping as her cover. She told him she would like to visit a few of the bridal shops she had been reading about.

"I'm sorry, Marisol. You haven't really done anything fun since you've been here. Why don't we make a weekend of it? We could go to a Broadway show, or visit the museums."

She tried not to panic. "Randolph, I'm havin' fun. Aren't I 'ere with you every day, havin' fun? You can show me New York when you 'ave more time. I just want to go look around. I want to be a pretty bride for you, an' in the magazines, it says you have to order some dresses a year before the weddin'."

"Marisol, you could wear a bath towel and be more beautiful than any bride in those magazines you've been reading. But if you want to go shopping, go. Just try to find a dress that won't take a year to get. I don't mind waiting, but I don't want to wait that long."

Charting Randolph's schedule, she picked a day he had a double-shift, and confirmed it with him before purchasing a train ticket to New York. On the morning of her trip, she did a last minute check of Heywood's daily post on Twitter. He tweeted that on that night, he was scheduled to be at the premier of Artist's first feature film in Manhattan. It was the perfect opportunity for Cam to slip into Heywood's penthouse and penetrate his vault.

She knew she was working within very limited time constraints, so she planned her every move down to the most finite detail. She couldn't risk running into Heywood. She knew she wouldn't receive the same warm reception she had gotten from Aunt Mary.

So, she planned and replanned, covering every 'what if' scenario she could imagine. To Cam, the possibility of being arrested for breaking and entering was at the top of her list of 'what ifs'. She had never even gotten as much as a speeding ticket, and had certainly never committed a crime. And if that wasn't enough to worry about, she had a constant stomach ache, and hoped she wasn't developing an ulcer from the secrets she was harboring. It was so hard for her to live a lie, particularly with that wonderful man. But her real life was at stake, and she had to press on.

And press on she did. The late afternoon train ride from Philly to New York was a mere hour, and she arrived, blending in and gaining confidence from the Empire State energy. She grabbed a taxi to the Papaya King restaurant a few blocks from Heywood's apartment, and headed right to the bathroom. She emerged in a dark maintenance uniform and matching baseball cap, her braided hair tucked inside a black fitted baseball cap. *Thank goodness for the Internet*, Cam thought. It had been easy to purchase the work clothes online and have them shipped to her at the recording studio. She repacked her backpack with her traveling clothes, and was ready to go.

She briskly walked the two blocks to Heywood's Fifth Avenue digs. She took a quick trek past the building and down the alley near the underground garage entrance. With her cap pulled low over her face, she noted the location of the security cameras. Once she was certain that she could avoid making any face time with the hidden and stationary cameras, she planted herself in a window booth of the Dean & Deluca's across from his building, and watched and waited, until day turned to dusk.

Several cups of coffee later, Cam spotted what she had been waiting for. The paparazzi were arriving, stationing themselves around the entrance. A crowd had gathered in front of the building, drawn by the bright lights of one of the gaudy entertainment network vans. On cue, Heywood's huge, blacked out Hummer pulled up, and he strolled out the ornate entry doors of the building. Of course, he could have easily avoided all this hoopla and frenzy by leaving from the underground garage, but Heywood never rolled that way.

Cheesing for the photographers on his way to the Hummer, the chinchilla-draped Heywood disappeared behind the blacked-out windows of his whip, and lead a trail of paparazzi down the avenue like the Pied Piper of Manhattan. She checked her watch. It was almost 8 o'clock. She took a deep breath. Now was the time to get into action.

She rounded the block, avoiding the doorman at the front entrance, and quickly accessed the underground garage using the keypad. Careful to keep her head down and face covered, she slipped into the service elevator on the lower lobby, and rode up to the 12th floor, where Heywood's cleaning crew was located. It was the only floor, other than the lobby or lower lobby, that anyone could access Heywood's private service elevator using the keypad or keycard.

She grabbed one of the maintenance carts, and stashed her backpack on its lower shelf. In addition to her traveling clothes, the backpack held two disposable cameras, a pair of latex gloves, and her ice axe. It was her only weapon.

In her uniform, she looked like one of the nondescript maintenance workers she had seen working the overnight shift, polishing the chrome and brass in the common areas of the building. But she needed to make sure all of her bases were covered. She decided to take the cart as a prop or additional cover, just in case.

Nervous, she removed the latex gloves from her bag and braced herself yet again. Determined to see this through, she pressed the button for the private elevator and waited, nervously glancing over her shoulder. At the last minute, she dashed back into a nearby hallway, just in case the arriving elevator was occupied. Luckily, the coast was clear, and she pushed her cart through the open doors.

The next time the elevator doors opened, she was on the penthouse floor. Using the keypad, she gained access to the service entrance. Removing her backpack, she pushed the cart over to the corner, listening all the while for any sounds. Pulling a pencil-thin xenon flashlight from her backpack, she stuck it in her shirt pocket, just in case. The penthouse was eerily quiet as she slowly crept through the service door.

Catlike in her movements, she crossed the fully illuminated kitchen and galley, and ducked into the hidden door that led into Heywood's bedroom. Every second felt like an hour. She checked her watch. It was 9:45 p.m. Her heart was beating so fast she was afraid it was going to pop out of her chest. Being so close to Heywood, even though he wasn't physically there, made her legs weak, and not in a good way. In her mind, she smelled his signature cologne and felt his warm, minty breath. It shook her, but she forced herself to concentrate. She had come too far to fail, and she had far too much to lose.

Before opening the bedroom door, she stopped and listened. Hearing silence, she slowly pushed the door open, finding the room dark except for the small slivers of moonlight gleaming through the floor to ceiling windows. She sliced the light of her flashlight across the room, again making certain that she was alone, and moved swiftly to the door of the vault.

"I can do this," she whispered, saying a prayer as she removed the glove from her right hand, and pressed her thumb to the access pad.

He hadn't removed her access to the crypt. Why would he? She was supposed to be dead. She easily slipped into his inner sanctum. This was only the second time she had been in there, and though she had mapped out its layout in her mind, being inside was mind-boggling. It was like the hub of a top secret security agency. Except there was a large portrait of Heywood centered squarely on the rear wall. "What an ego maniac," Cam said, and shook her head.

She drew a deep breath, and put her glove back on. She knew she had to work quickly. There was so much to do, and so little time.

She checked the security camera monitors, and timed their intervals. The screens changed every 10 seconds, so she would be able to see if anyone was in the penthouse or on their way in.

Quickly scanning the equipment in the room, she realized, to her dismay, that Heywood had cameras everywhere and was recording everyone's movements. Talk about paranoid. There was even a live stream to Kinnetic Studios feeding directly into his monitors. *Oh my God,* she thought. *His poor artists. They don't know he's recording everything they say or do down there. What a freakin' nightmare.*

Checking the two-way mirror to ensure no one had entered the bedroom, she tried to shake off her angst. She had to figure out what she was looking for. She didn't know what it was, but knew that she would know it when she saw it.

It didn't take long. She noticed a DVD case lying open next to a keyboard. She turned it over, and the cover read, "Shaye & Skye 06.20.08. Track 2." The CD tray was open, and the DVD with the same title was staring at her. Curious, she pushed the drawer shut, and watched the screen as the DVD began to load.

"Oh my God," she gasped, as the blank screen came alive with images of Shaye and Skye, getting it on, girl-on-girl style. In the background, she could hear Heywood woofing out orders, while the girls obliged his every demand. Partway into the 'movie', Heywood made his appearance onscreen, just long enough for him to nearly asphyxiate Skye and give Shaye a golden shower. "Good Lord," Cam said, shutting off the computer and clutching her stomach. "He really is the devil."

She looked above the monitor, and saw racks and racks filled with DVDs. Each one was labeled like Skye and Shaye's, but the names and tracks are different. After scanning the racks for her own name, she thanked God again for never laying with him in the penthouse. However, her heart sank as her eyes read the names of nearly all of her labelmates, old and new, and other industry figures.

There were DVDs of Casbar and Parsley; even one of Noah Parker. She inserted the Casbar video, and almost retched. Poor Casbar was bent over, obviously in terrible pain. Heywood was sodomizing him, and forcing him to beg to stay on his label. It was completely dehumanizing and demoralizing.

She was repulsed and appalled. She couldn't imagine going to this extreme to keep a gig. She switched DVDs again, this time to Parsley's. Gross. Here, Heywood had flipped the script, forcing Parsley to give him head while he called him every name in the book.

It was too much. The rumors Heywood had looked her in the eye and denied for so long were true. There was no denying it now. The proof was in front of her eyes. Heywood was ruthless and soulless, and he was a monster. These DVDs were the reason his artists were so 'loyal' to him. They were also the reason so many disappeared from the music scene when they left Kinnetic. Some preferred to pump gas or go back to hustling, rather than to deal with Heywood or the music industry.

Though she didn't want to see any more of this, she felt, out of loyalty to Jamie, she needed to see the DVD of his manager. She could only bear to watch a few minutes of the 'Noah. Track 1' tape. While Casbar and Parsley appeared to be unwilling, humiliated participants in Heywood's sick domination videos, there was an even more sinister element to Noah's tape. He had a strange, drugged expression on his face, as if he had been slipped a roofie or another date-rape drug. Whatever it was, he was zoned out, his face completely devoid of human emotion. *Was he even coherent?* Cam wondered, slipping the DVD back into the case. It had clearly been a set-up. A groggy Noah had been lead into a room by someone she didn't recognize, stretched out on a bed, and summarily violated by a man who was videotaped from his torso down. It looked like Heywood, but Cam couldn't be sure. "Ooooh," she moaned, noticing the blood on the sheets. She was mortified. Poor Noah.

"How could I have gotten myself involved with such a horrible person?" she whispered aloud, and stifling her gag reflex. "I let him touch me. Oh my God. *Ugh.*" She shook her head, the memories piercing her like stab wounds. She clamped her eyes shut, and tried to pray the memories away, asking God to help her in what had become a crusade against this demon. Her face twisted with disgust, and to a certain degree, fear. She knew that if Heywood was capable of doing these things to others, he was definitely capable of trying to kill her. But, still, she had no proof.

She had almost forgotten what she was there for. She stood and walked past the DVDs, to the racks of reel-to-reel canisters and tapes. They were the masters of his artists, and once again, she was grateful to find that hers weren't there.

On his desk, she found three book-keeping ledgers. The first was titled "Expenses," the second, "AI/AE," and the third "TM." She opened the first one, and noted the entries and dates. She didn't know what she was looking at, and was not too good in math, but it seemed that the same entries were being recorded with different values in each book. Cam reasoned that whatever those books were for, they couldn't be legal. She decided to copy the same pages in each book. She could figure out what was going on when she had more time.

"Shoot," she said. "Why did I drink so much coffee?" Walking over to the small lavatory in the vault, she glanced in the mirror and was startled to see her picture hanging on the back of the bathroom door. "What the hell?" she said, her urge to urinate receding. "I don't believe this. What kind of sick, twisted pervert hangs someone's picture in a bathroom? He really is sick with his."

As she collected herself, a reflection in the vault's two-way caught her eye. A light had flicked on in the bedroom. *Oh no,* she thought, *I'm going to wet my pants before I die.*

She backed back into the bathroom, legs crossed, holding the door partially open so she could see through the mirror. Heywood, shouting back at someone, was the first to enter, his shirt open and a heavy diamond necklace bouncing across his kinky-haired chest. A curly-haired young woman was on his heels.

Cam held her hand against her mouth to contain her gasp, and she nearly choked. The woman with Heywood was her former assistant, Allison.

chapter thirty-four

"BITCH, I oughta fuck you up!" Heywood was almost frothing at the mouth as he pulled his shirttails out of his pants. He dragged Allison across the room and shoved her onto the bed.

Allison, her lipstick smeared, and hair a frightful mess, fell back with a dramatic flair, her slinky dress rising to show her crotch. Her eyes glistened with fear and tears.

He stopped and glared at her, holding his shirt out, revealing bright red stains across the bottom and the front of his white pants. "Ya see this shit? Damn! Bitch, what is ya, a fuckin' lush or what?"

Allison slinked off the bed and tried to approach Heywood, but he threw the shirt in her face. "Goddamn. This is a fifteen-hunnert dollar Marc Jacobs shirt, an' ya fucked it up. Wit' tomato juice of all things. Mutha-fuck," he snarled, his eyes glowering at her as she uttered her apologies. He took his hand and grabbed her chin, and shoved her down to the floor.

"I'm sorry, Heywood. I didn't know that the driver was gonna hit the brakes like that," she said, trying to stand up and stay away from him. "It spilled on me, too."

Heywood ignored her, and ranted about his soiled slacks. "An' look at this shit," he said, and held his pants legs out. "These shits is ruined too. An' ya betta hope this shit comes out my chinchilla." He whipped off his belt, and unbuttoned his trousers. He shoved them down to his ankles, stepped one foot out, and with the other one, kicked them in her face with gusto.

"I'll take care of them, Heywood. I promise," she whimpered. Her lips quivered as she looked at him, still ranting and raving.

"Ya damn right, ya will, bitch." He looked down and held up his necklace. "I don't believe it. Ya even got that shit on my ice," he snapped. He whipped the chain off his neck and flung it against the wall. Stripped down to his boxers, wifebeater, bronze Ferragamo hard bottoms, dress socks and garters, he stepped over her. As he walked toward one of his huge walk-in closets, she grabbed his leg.

"Come on, baby, don't be angry. It was an accident, and I can take care of it."

"Get off me, girl. This ain't no way to try to be one of my assistants. Not a good look."

She held onto his leg, and he tried to drag her. When he was unable to, he stopped and stomped his foot. "I'm warnin' ya, get the fuck off."

"Come on, Heywood. Don't be like that," she said, and her hand crept up his leg. "Let me fix it."

He suddenly raised his hand, and smacked her across the face. "Didn't I tell ya to stop?"

"Please, Heywood, don't do this," Allison pleaded, still clinging to him.

He lifted her off the floor, threw her on the bed, scattering his stained clothes on the floor. He started viciously smacking her about the head, taunting her as she tried to climb away from him. "Didn't-I-tell-ya-to-fuckin'-leave-me-alone!" he yelled, his words in syncopation with his blows.

Cam watched the scene, her hand still pressed against her mouth, her heart pounding. She was both sickened and angry. She could not believe that Allison was dealing with Heywood, and that she was allowing him to treat her like this. Aunt Mary's words echoed in her ears. "You've been in a pit of snakes." And she had been. If there had been one person in her old world she trusted, it was Allison. Thank God she hadn't contacted her. Cam had no idea how long they had been dealing, but even if it happened after the accident, Allison was lost to her.

Was it my fault? she thought. *Maybe it was the accident that's pushed her over the edge. Allison never drank like that before. Allison never drank like that when she was with me. That's not who she is.* This wasn't the Allison that Cam knew and loved almost like a sister. Could whatever have happened in Montserrat been the cause of Allison's visibly deep decline?

Nothing made sense. Allison had always been so together, so confident, so not into the whole industry thing. To see her groveling, and allowing herself to be degraded and demeaned by Heywood was too much of a contradiction. Cam felt sorry for her and angry with her at the same time. How could she be so stupid?

Although she couldn't hear what they were saying, and was too afraid to turn on the intercom, she could tell what was going on. Heywood continued pummeling Allison, with more slaps, hits and a few body shots.

"Now, get the fuck off me, so I can get dressed an' get to the premiere," he shouted, as he jumped off the bed, reaching back to give her a final slap on the backside, the force of which Cam could feel in the next room. Cam saw Allison shreik in pain, but Heywood didn't even turn around or break stride, and continued to march over to the dresser, and then stand like a peacock in front of the mirror.

Cam nearly dove to the floor. Then she recalled that he couldn't see her. Being separated by only the two-way mirror made her shudder. He was beyond evil. She was afraid to move, and afraid to breathe, still finding it hard to believe that he couldn't see her through the glass.

Allison had no shame. From the bed, she slithered onto the floor and crawled on all fours over to where Heywood stood. "I'm sorry, Daddy. I didn't mean it," her voice quivering. She stayed on her knees, looking like a dog begging for a bone.

"Ya neva do," he said, opening the cabinet and removing a white handkerchief. He wiped his face with it, and continued staring in the mirror. "See what ya make me do? Gettin' me all heated an' shit. Ya know I got shit to do."

Despite all of the thrashing, Allison wasn't bleeding, and her face was reddened in some areas. She slipped her hands in his boxers, and started rubbing his jewels. "Why waste all this, Daddy? Why don't you to give it to me right here," she said, licking her lips.

Heywood sighed deeply. Cam wanted to break through the mirror and punch him in his smug face and slap some sense into Allison's pathetic one.

"Well, then get on yo' job, bitch," he said. "That's if ya want one. I expect ya to put in work, ya heard? An' if ya do what ya need to do, then Daddy'll give it to ya. An' if not, Daddy's gonna give ya some more of this," he said, holding up his fist. "An' make sure ya stay unemployed."

Allison nodded, then went to work, giving Heywood a spit-filled blowjob as she talked dirty and he gripped the top of her head. Suddenly, he yanked her by the hair and shoved her into the dresser. With her face pressed up against the mirror, he mounted her from the back, like a dog in heat, and thrusted at her from behind.

"Ride me, Daddy. Ride me hard."

Heywood's face was contorted as he furiously humped her, digging his fingers into her back as he cursed and moaned. Soon, he howled like a wolf, and shoved her aside. "Now, get the fuck outta my way. I need to take a shower, an' get myself cleaned up."

"What about me?" Allison asked. "I need to change, and don't have anything else to wear."

Heywood grunted. "Ain't nobody checkin' fo' ya ass. Ya ain't front page, baby. *Shee-it*, you ain't even the back page of the local section."

Heywood brushed past her and walked toward his bathroom. "You can stay here, fo' all I care. This shit is yo' fault, so whateva."

"Yo, get ya some mouthwash an' take a whore's bath. Ya ain't gotta wash. Plus, I wanna smell me on ya all night, ya heard?" He held his hands up, like he was going to wash them.

Allison brushed down her wrinkled clothing, and trailed him into the bathroom, silently gathering up his discarded clothing along the way.

★

When they entered the master bath, Cam shook the fog from her head, trying not to dwell on the disturbing events she had just witnessed. She quickly weighed her options. What could she do? She was trapped, with no way out. She could only hope and pray that they would both get the hell out of there soon.

Now she was stuck. She'd have to wait until they left. But, she also had to know if there was anyone else in there, so she clicked on the intercom, and tuned into the other rooms. Convinced that it was only Allison and Heywood present, she switched the intercom to the master bedroom, so she could hear their conversation when they returned.

Heywood soon emerged, with a white towel draped around his shoulders. Cam, back behind the bathroom door, watched their every move.

"Hurry the fuck up, girl," Heywood snapped, and then walked into his winter closet.

Allison scurried out of the bathroom, holding Heywood's shoes and a stained polishing cloth. "These are done, Heywood. They look good. And I put some club soda on your clothes to get the juice out."

He said something indecipherable, and Allison glanced around. She set his shoes down, and walked over to where Heywood's chain lay on the floor.

"I'll clean it real quick," she said, picking up the necklace. Again, his response was garbled.

"Okay, then," she said, and laid the chain on the other dresser where Heywood stored his jewelry. "So, what you gonna wear instead?"

Heywood reappeared from his dressing room, wearing a pair of hot True Religion jeans and a black turtleneck, holding a black fitted New York Yankees cap.

"I dunno," he said, staring at himself again in the mirror. He walked over to his mini-jewelry counter, and frowned. "None of these shits," he said, flicking his finger over his sizeable collection. "I oughta wear that clef note joint I just got."

Cam's eyes trailed over to the jewelry display inside the vault, and again almost lost her bladder. There was the chain he was talking about.

"Now," he said, rubbing his cheek, and turning toward Allison. "Ya make yo'self scarce. I gotta moisturize, an' I need some privacy. In the meantime, go fix me a drink. An' try not to spill it. An' don't you get one neither. You've had enough."

Cam panicked. She frantically searched for a weapon, anything that she could use to knock him out. She didn't want to kill him, but what could she do? She grabbed the ice axe from her backpack, holding it in her trembling hands, as she waited for him to enter.

After ushering Allison out of the bedroom, Heywood locked the door behind her. Looking over his shoulder, he walked over to the vault's access pad. As he lifted his thumb to place it on the unit, there was a loud bang on the door.

"Yo, Heywood. Artist just called. They holdin' up the premiere waitin' on you. I know you wanna be fashionably late, an' shit, but they ain't gonna wait forever," Duck yelled.

"Fuck," Heywood said, and dropped his hand. He marched over to the door and flung it open. "Whateva, man. Go get the car, I'm comin' now." He scooped up the stained chain he had worn earlier and held it up. "An' tell Allison I want her ass to suck every drop o' juice off this chain. Right now," Heywood said, and slipped on his cap.

"Come on, yo. Let's get the fuck outta here."

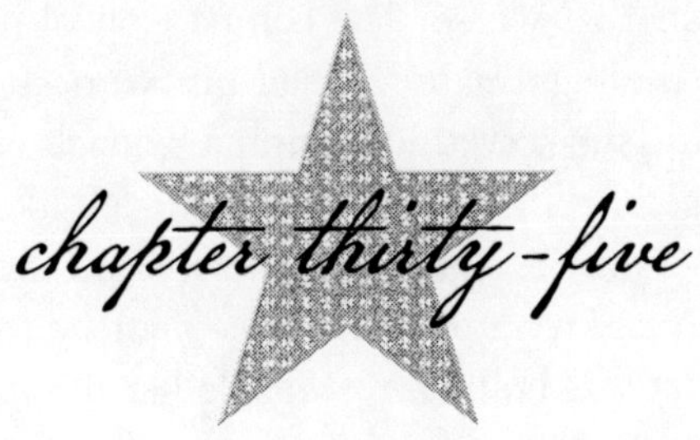

SHE FELT so dirty. Just plain filthy. Funky, filthy and nasty. On the way back to Philly, she dreamed of a hot bath. A scalding hot bath that would wash away anything to do with what she had seen or been near. She wished there was a way she could wash away what she had seen out of her mind, but knew those scenes would be burned forever in her memory.

Cam had to think and rethink her every thought, action, and word. Keeping so many different stories straight was beginning to wear her down, but she had to stay the course. And maintain appearances and priorities. Randolph was number one, though her quest for truth and justice was vying hard for the top spot.

Though her mind was a thousand light years away from the wedding, she made sure to pick up several magazines, including *Bride* and *Vogue's Wedding Guide*, from the train station.

No matter what, she had to put Randolph first, and think about him and his feelings. She was glad he wasn't calling and texting her as much as before, but she still felt awful sneaking around and lying about her whereabouts. The more secure he was in their relationship, the more deceptive she had become. Keeping secrets from him was becoming too easy, but she rationalized that she would tell him everything as soon as she could, just not now. Heywood was too dangerous. She had to keep all the balls she was juggling in the air as long as she could.

Once home, she felt worse. The comparison of her life with sweet Randolph against the nightmare she had just witnessed almost brought her to her knees. As she served Randolph a spinach omelet and salmon croquets and hugged him around his neck, she felt like one of those pod people from a sci-fi movie. A shell of a person in human form. A robot programmed to act and react on cue. She was forced to contain the cauldron of feelings that was boiling over inside her mind.

On the outside, she was calm and caring, with a perfect smile and sensibility. She pretended to have just awakened from a restful night's slumber, and threw in a few well-placed yawns for effect. False. All of it false. In actual fact, she had barely returned home, slipped on her engagement ring and an old t-shirt of Randolph's, and jumped into bed before he came in, dead tired, and kissed her on the forehead. She was so glad that he wanted her to rest with him, and to hold her until he dozed off.

Her soul was erupting from lies and deception. Erupting like Soufriere Hills, the volcano that had set off the unfortunate chain of events and set her squarely into the mess she was in. Tormented by the depravity she had witnessed and discovered at Heywood's, she was disgusted that she had to pile her own toxic lies to Randolph atop this heap of steaming waste.

After a few hours of wrestling with her thoughts, she slipped away from the comfort of Randolph's arms and stationed herself behind her laptop. She positioned herself so that she could see and hear him when he arose. She popped a piece of gum in her mouth, and then rubbed her eyes, trying to erase the images of what she had seen at Heywood's. Resting her head on her hands, she tried to quell her rising anger. As the encrypted document where she detailed her findings opened, she thought about what had happened after Heywood and Allison finally left the penthouse.

As she copied the pages from the ledgers, the copier had run out of paper, and she searched for more. After opening a few cabinet doors, she nearly keeled over when she opened the one that was directly underneath Heywood's oversized portrait. Inside was a mini-shrine. A mini-shrine dedicated to her.

On the top cabinet shelf, there was a large color picture of her, in an understated Tiffany silver frame. It was a candid shot, where her face was beat out and she was dressed in an off-the-shoulder, semi-formal dress, wearing glittery diamonds and sapphires on loan from Van Cleef & Arpels. She remembered that she had worn that to her first Grammy Awards.

Sick. In addition to the photo, there was a small battery-operated candle that flickered next to her picture, a thick leather bound photo album, and a stack of expandable legal folders. The album was filled with pictures and press clippings, all detailing the life and times of Starr.

She flipped through the album, astonished at its contents and the meticulous manner in which Heywood had documented her life. It was both eerie and surreal.

After stomaching as much of her photo album book as she could, she set it aside, and reached for the file folders. A quick look at the file labels told her all she needed to know. They were obviously the files that had been taken from Deacon Owens's office.

Someone had been very thorough. The stolen files included her will, her contract with Kennetic Records, other documents detailing the establishment of her charitable foundation, and records of her other business holdings.

Now she had proof that he was criminally involved with the theft, but she still had nothing concrete regarding his involvement in her supposed death.

Moving past her legal files, she found another folder, this one labeled KO. It contained photos, receipts, and payments to Kevin Owens and Victor Burton, clearly indicating that they were both on Heywood's payroll. Then she saw a folder labeled "MONTS. M. DAVIES." Inside that folder were several receipts, most notably a copy of a cashier's check in the amount of $10,000 to one Maurice Davies, the hospital administrator from Montserrat.

She sat on the floor and gulped air, trying not to hyperventilate. It was almost 11 pm, and she was running out of time. She needed to catch a train back to Philly that would arrive before Randolph got home.

She glanced over to the double-sided mirror to make sure the coast was still clear. Satisfied that she was still very much alone, she continued pulling files from the cabinet.

There was even more. The most devastating file was the last one. It contained information about her mother's death. Several obscure *Washington Post* articles, and a copy of her obituary. There were also several photos of her mother. Closeups. She was onstage somewhere, smiling. Cam shook her head, trying to clear it. Where had the pictures come from? Her mother had never been onstage. Where did he get them? And then there was a copy of a record contract in her mother's name. A record contract signed by her mother. Signed the day she died. Her mother didn't know Heywood like that. None of this made sense. The DVD in the folder was titled FA - 2001. The initials made her hands shake, and it took several tries for her trembling fingers to insert it into the PC.

Dropping to her knees, Cam looked up to see her mother, Faith, all decked out and singing alone in a spotlight. Tears filled her eyes as she checked the case again. It was also dated the day her mother died. Cam crawled over to the bathroom to splash cold water on her face, the sound of her mother's voice ringing in her ears. Her mother had been good. Very good. She sounded eerily like her, and when she wiped her face dry, she caught her reflection in the bathroom mirror and saw her mother looking back at her.

Her fingertips reached for the mirror, and her mother's image slowly melded into hers.

Nauseous as she was, she realized that none of this was a coincidence. Heywood had to know what happened to her mother. Either he or someone was there the night she died. The date on the tape was irrefutable evidence. The blood of her own mother was somehow on this man's hands. He had pretended to console her, had guided her career, and had pretended to protect her. Now she knew the bitter truth. All of it, every ounce, had been a lie.

She heard something on the tape that caused her to run back to the computer and hit the replay button. Her mother had stopped singing and had spoken to someone she called "Boo." That person had responded, but

Cam didn't recognize his voice. Then, just before the video ended, a good looking, fair-skinned man had joined her on the stage. Who was that? Her murderer?

The final nail in the coffin was her discovery that Heywood had her last music book. The one Allison had when they were in Montserrat. Maybe that was their connection. Who knew? But, there it was, on the lower shelf in the shrine, enclosed in a dust bag. It was a rash move that she would live to regret, but she had to take it. It was a part of herself that she couldn't allow him to have. It was risky, but having it back in her possession empowered her. She was slowly getting herself back. With Aunt Mary's words about being surrounded by serpents, echoing in her mind, Cam squeezed her eyes closed. "I'm gonna get that bastard," she said, her voice guttural and raw.

"What's the matter, baby? Marisol? Are you okay?"

She gasped and nearly swallowed her gum at being jarred so suddenly back into the present. She had no idea that a pajama-clad Randolph had awakened and was standing in the doorway.

"I'm okay, Randy," she said, snapping the laptop shut quickly. She took her "Wedding Book" notebook and placed it face-down on top of the computer. "I, uh, was just playin' an online game, an' it was cheatin,'" she lied, yet again.

He walked over to where she was sitting, and sat down beside her. He kissed her on the lips, his breath toothpaste-fresh. "I see," he said, with a yawn. "As long as it wasn't you cheating, I don't care." His bright eyes sparkled, and she felt ashamed by her lies. She wanted to blurt out everything to him, but stopped herself.

He glanced down at her notebook and smiled. "I know you're probably planning some top secret, hush-hush wedding stuff, but that's okay. I don't want you to feel stressed out about the wedding or think you have to do everything yourself. I'm here if you need me. And you know, my mother is good at planning things. Maybe she could help you too."

A genuine, yet strained smile crossed her face. "Thank you, luv. I appreciate the offer. I know you're a might busy, an' I can try to do what I can. An' it's good to know that yer mom can help out if need be. But, I have to be honest wit' you, Randy."

Concern cast over his face. "What's wrong?"

She sighed. "I guess I'm just a little torn about the wedding. Maybe we don't really need a big one, ya know. After all, I really don't have any family. None to speak of. An', it kind of makes me sad that I won't have anyone there to share it wit' me or even give me away."

He reached over to rub her shoulders. "I'm sorry, baby. That never occurred to me. Wow, how could I not think about that? I'm so sorry."

"Don't be. I'm enjoyin' workin' on it, I really am." *Lord, forgive me,* she thought. "I just want to let ya know that I may not want a big to-do."

"Whatever you want is okay with me," he said.

She kissed him gently on his lips. "Thank you for understandin'," she said. *I just hope that one day you'll really be able to understand.*

"Good, so now that we're okay with that, I've got good news, baby," he said, as he looked into her eyes. "I have the next few days off, and I have a few things planned." He smiled, gauging her reaction.

She brushed his cheek with her fingertips. "Oh, uh, that's wonderful, sweetie," she said, silently watching her own plans go up in smoke. "How'd that happen?" *And why did it have to happen now?*

"One of the other residents asked me to change schedules. Of course I said yes. Particularly because it meant I'd get a chance to spend some quality time with you. It seems like I hardly ever see you."

"I know," she said, forcing a smile. She stood and kissed his forehead, "It'll be wonderful to spend some time together. Now, let me fix you somethin' to eat." She wiped her eyes, and took the few short steps to their kitchen, where she began washing her hands.

He turned to face her. "Thanks, baby. But you know what? Let's do something different. Let's go out and grab a bite. I've got time, and it would be nice to give you a break for a change."

He smiled. "You know, these days off together will be great. It'll give us a chance to drive up and finally see my family, well, at least my parents. Robin's all over the place, but she promised to get here soon. But my folks are dying to meet you. They said they'd even come here if we don't have time to drive there."

Uh-oh, Cam thought. *How am I going to get out of this?* His parents, now living in the Poconos, called often, leaving dozens of messages since she had moved in. She'd made a point of never answering the phone when it rang, because she didn't want to meet them as Marisol. She didn't want to lie to anyone else, particularly not to Randolph's parents. It was bad enough lying to their son.

Cam knew she had to buy some time, and quickly. Scrubbing her hands, she rinsed them and shut the water off. She turned toward him and smiled. "Oh, that sounds lovely, Randy. But, they don't have to come here. Really, I'd rather take the drive an' see your folks. It would be nice to take a ride outta the city for a change."

He beamed at her response. "Wonderful," he said with a grin. "I'll give them a call and let them know we'll be there this week." He nearly bounded over to her, and grabbed her around the waist, pulling her close to him. "I love you so much, Marisol. And I know they're going to love you too."

She had no choice. She had to ruin Randolph's plans. After a mimosa-filled brunch at a nearby restaurant, she feigned food poisoning. Forcing herself to regurgitate was the only way she could think of to get out of a trip to the Poconos. However, it didn't free her from Randolph. She tried to encourage him to go alone, but he wouldn't think of it, again taking on the role of her doctor.

He barely left the apartment during his whole mini-vacation, until, miraculously, she recovered the evening before he was scheduled to go back to work. Consumed with remorse, she finally told him that her nerves must have caused her upset stomach. That she hadn't realized she was so nervous to meet his parents. She promised that the next time he had any time off, she would go there or ask them to come to Philadelphia. Silently, she hoped and prayed that he had a full schedule for the foreseeable future.

Feigning illness had been more exhausting and time-consuming than if she had just gone to see Randolph's parents. But, that precious time had come and gone, and after ushering Randolph out the door for his first day back to work, she left right behind him. She was intent on retrieving the bounty from her gym locker, and to go over every item, piece by piece.

And she did just that. Arming herself with a fresh pack of gum, her laptop, and headphones, she picked up her stash from the gym, and set herself up in a secluded corner of the public library that was down the street from the gym.

With her documents neatly stacked in front of her, she sat down at the desk, popped in a piece of gum and reviewed her stock. Her 'break-in' created as many questions as answers. A chill ran down her spine when she thought about the shrine Heywood had created. She had to pray to release those demons he had clearly summoned to captivate and manipulate her. It had taken every ounce of restraint not to destroy it, but she couldn't. However, she had taken a photo of it with her cell-phone, along with several photos of the files stolen from her attorney's office and of the three ledgers.

She had made copies of everything she could, including the ledger pages, the check stub to Mr. Davies, her mother's recording contract, and receipts of payments to Kevin Owens. Looking at the pictures of the ledgers, she tried to decipher what the initials "AI/AE" and "TM" designat-ed. Placing the pages from each book side by side, she compared some of the entries by date, and drew a startling conclusion. Trying to think like Heywood was easier than she thought. She quickly determined that "AI/AE" was for actual income/actual expenses. The ledgers chronicled dates and money going and coming from radio stations, deejays, and even veejays. This activity was called Payola, and was as old as the music industry itself. Unscrupulous record producers and owners paid other unscrupulous deejays and radio stations to play their artist's records, to generate interest and income. Sometimes, they were paid not to spin their competitor's records. Heywood had an entry for everyone and everything, even who he tipped and how much. *The cheap bastard,* she thought.

For the same dates in the other ledgers, many entries were either inflated or omitted. Both the "TM" and "Expenses" ledgers depicted minor income and heavy losses. If the "Expenses" file was for the IRS, they were being severely shorted. But, whoever or whatever the bene-factor of the "TM" ledger was, the profits reported in those tables had gone from a pretty substantial amount to next to nothing over the past two years.

She had to find out what "TM" stood for. It had to be someone Heywood was paying. Someone he owed money to. Someone who was collecting ends from him. And this someone, whoever it was, could not be happy seeing his residual income dwindle down from millions to less than $200K in 24 months. If she could only figure out who that person was, perhaps she could enlist him or her to strengthen her case against Heywood. Or at least reveal his criminal intentions.

She went to the Internet to search for any associates of Heywood's with those initials. She found no one. It wasn't until she did a cross-search of Heywood's first record label, Kutthroat Records, that she found the name of Tyrone Moon. She remembered that name. This was the man Heywood said had been like a father to him.

A few more searches revealed that Tyrone was known as "Typhoon" Moon, and that he had a widely varied and deeply criminal background. He had done extensive time in Federal prisons, charged with everything from drug trafficking to weapons charges. He was currently locked up, but murder charges had recently been filed against him.

She Googled his images and only a few pictures came up. Most were grainy, newsprint quality shots. Some pictures were of him seated in court, or being transported to and from court. From the images, he had a menacing appearance. He was a brown skinned man with thick corn-rows. According to the 'net, Typhoon's illicit activities also included gam-bling and prostitution up and down the East coast. He had a huge and profitable 'business' going at one point. And the dates of his alleged reign coincided with the dates that Heywood started Kutthroat Records. It all made sense to her now. Typhoon had started Heywood in the business. He had backed him. And all these years, Heywood hadn't been free and independent. He was merely the front man for Typhoon.

She jotted down Typhoon's name in her book, along with other pertinent bits and pieces of information she found. Apparently, he was incarcerated at an undisclosed location because of the number of Federal charges levied against him. How could she find out where he was? And how could she let him know that Heywood was short shrifting him?

And then there were the DVDs.

With no real plan and no real time, the only thing she could do back in the vault was remove the labels from the DVDs, quickly denote the originals with a Sharpie marker, and replace them in their cases with blanks. She hadn't taken all of them, just some of the people she knew who were probably suffering from their existence, like Parsley, Noah, and Casbar. She was torn about taking Allison's, but did so anyway. Even after what she had witnessed, Cam still felt protective of Allison, and couldn't turn her back on her. She couldn't allow a video like that to exist and not do something about it. She did have a heart.

Cam did take other videos that she didn't have time to review, but sensed that that they might be detrimental to someone somewhere. She took as many as she could, praying that by the time Heywood discovered that his precious videos were blanks, he would either believe that they had been stored on defective media or erased by a virus. Either way, if he figured out that they had been stolen, her name would never be considered. After all, she was supposed to be dead.

She sifted through the videos, slipping each in an individual plastic sleeve for their protection, until she found the one of her mother. Placing her headphones on her ears, she watched and re-watched it, hoping to find some sort of clue or hidden message.

Cam finally recognized the stage. Though she had never played it before, it looked like the Carter Barron. That was where her mother's body had been found. But, she wasn't sure. Wherever her mother was, it was dark and appeared to be outdoors. It had to be the Carter Barron. Her mother obviously had been lured there, and somehow Heywood was connected.

She watched the video again. Again, she was moved by her mother's voice. She had talent. True talent. She studied the video over and over, finally realizing that the young man her mother had called "Boo" had to be her father, Carlos.

She felt as though she had been punched in the stomach. It was her first glimpse of her father, and it happened on the night her mother died. Now she knows he was with her. Did he give her the drugs? Did he kill her? If he did, why? A thousand questions crossed her mind. She rifled through her papers until she found the copy of the recording contract signed by her mother. She pulled it from the stack, and looked for the signature of the witness. It was none other than Kevin Owens. It was apparent that all of these years, Kevin had been on Heywood's payroll. And he had knowledge of her mother's death. There was no other explanation. Had everyone lied to her about everything?

The only person who could answer any of these questions was her father. And she didn't know if he was even alive. She immediately connected to the Internet and Googled his name. She typed in "Carlos Bonds, Washington, D.C." Nothing came back that helped. Nothing remotely close. Dismayed, but not deterred, she sighed when she thought of the only person who could help her find her father. Her Aunt Mary.

And that was not a call she was looking forward to making. But she had to. She reached in her backpack for her disposable cellphone and was about to dial her aunt's number, when the phone started ringing. The incoming call was a local 215 number and she didn't recognize it.

Certain that it was the wrong number, she didn't answer. But, when the caller left a voicemail message, she listened to it. It was from the local producer she had purchased her tracks from, B. Real. He said that he had gotten her number from the studio owner, and needed to talk to her as soon as possible. He left his number.

B. Real would have to wait. She had to talk to her aunt. Again, as she was about to dial her aunt's number, the same 215 number called. This time she picked up.

Laying on her thick Caribbean accent she said, "Hello?"

"Hey, uh, is this Tru?"

"Who?" she asked, and then she caught herself. She had forgotten that she had given him a fake name. "Uh, yeah, naw, this ain't 'er. Hol' on a minute." She pressed the mute button, and tried to think quickly. She didn't want to sound like she was from the Islands, but Philly didn't have a real distinct dialect. She decided to give him a straight chick from the hood, a Baltimore or B-More sound.

"Hello? This is Tru. Who's this?" Baltimoreans had a distinct way of saying words that had the "ewe" sound in it.

"This is B. B. Real. I'm the cat ya bought those tracks from."

"Aiight," she said, slipping deeper into the vernacular. "Whassup? The check ain't clear?" She knew full well she had paid with PayPal, but being flip was part of the game.

B. chuckled. "Naw, ma. We good. I, uh, somethin' just went down here at the studio, an' I needed to holla at ya about it.

"See, I guess ya wasn't workin' wit' no real producers, 'cause some of your flows got left in the recording queue. Me and my mans came through, an' we was really diggin' 'em, so um, to make a long story short, we cleared the queue, an' they ended up on my laptop."

She frowned. "Say what? You lifted my shit?" She didn't like cussing, but it was appropriate for this character.

"Naw, naw. Nothin' like that. One of my otha peoples heard it, an' thought it was mine, so he put it on YouTube, MySpace an' Facebook. Check it out. It's under my name, B dash Real Deal Music. It's been gettin' crazy hits. Ya got mad talent, ma. No wonder ya called Tru Talent."

Cam nearly dropped the phone. How the hell did that happen? She remembered rushing to get back home the last time she was in the studio, but she had no idea she had left her recordings in the system. Was the world playing a cruel trick on her? She had to get her music off of there. Just as she was about to light into B., he stopped her with his next statements.

"I'm sayin', don't be mad with a brotha for recognizin' some sick skills. Real talk, I ain't heard vocals this tight since, well, probably since Starr an' shit. But for real, I think ya might even got her beat. Ya got a depth an' fullness to yo' shit, 'scuse me, I mean to yo' voice that she didn't have. I just want ya to know that I ain't no busta. I'm about business, ma, an' I got a few connects in the business. I ain't gonna lie, I really wanna work with ya."

Enter yet another hitch in her plans. Her initial reaction was to dismiss B.'s offer, but then she had second thoughts. YouTube was viral, and there was going to be no way to take back what was already out there. All she could do was try to figure out how to spin it to her best advantage. She had to give it some more thought, but she couldn't think about it now. She still had to contact her aunt, and finish figuring out how to get her life back without adding yet another one to her portfolio of identities.

She was Marisol. She was Cam. She was Starr, and now she was expected to be Tru. She told B. that she would get back with him, but she also told him that if he wanted to work with her, he'd have to keep their dealings on the low. He could never give out her name or telephone number to anyone, or tell anyone which recording studio she was using, even which city the recording studio was in. She didn't want anyone knowing anything about her at all. For real. Nothing about her at all. And he needed to tell the recording studio owner and anyone else working with them the same thing. If *Miss En You* was already out on his website, he'd be getting the calls and the emails, and Cam made it clear that she expected total silence from them or they'd never hear from her again. B. seemed puzzled by the request, but he agreed before he hung up.

Then she went to YouTube, and searched for the audio. She gasped when she heard the track to *Miss En You*. Though the production was raw, her vocals were on point. And B. was right. She sounded much better than Starr ever did, if said so herself.

As she listened to the track, she realized this was only going to further complicate her already convoluted life. Instead of solving problems, she was creating more. The puzzle of her life was expanding, not becoming any clearer. But, one thing was crystal clear. In all of the bad pieces of the puzzle, there was one common denominator. And that was Heywood.

chapter thirty-six

"YEAH, YEAH, it's gonna be a moneymaker, Fitz. I'm tellin' you," Heywood bellowed into his Bluetooth, as he huffed and puffed on the treadmill in his personal gym at his corporate offices. With sweat pouring down his face, he tried to get his mentor to think he had big things poppin'.

Really, he had nothing. His talks with movie producers on the possibility of making a movie about Starr's life had gone nowhere. All because he wanted to cast himself in the production. And unless he was willing to sign on as the executive producer and ante up some real scrilla, that wasn't going to happen. And he wasn't about to do that.

He wasn't willing to take that big of a risk with his own funds. Truth was, he enjoyed spending money; just not his own.

Heywood had always been good at making moves, getting what he wanted, how he wanted it. Whether it was getting others to front their money or working it so he made money off his artists, he was used to coming out on top. He had mad respect in the music game. But, it just didn't feel the same.

Lately, he was feeling *that* way about a lot of things. He was still making moves, putting work in, and making things happen. He still sidelined his competition. Since Noah removed himself from the running for the APB job, the powers at APB were scrambling to find a replacement. Heywood figured that they would be knocking on his front door any day now. And then he would open it, spit in their faces, and slam it back.

But, he still wasn't satisfied. While his artists were selling and making him stacks, he wasn't feeling the love or the limelight like he did when Starr was around. Hell, she was still outselling her peers in death. He needed her. He had no superstar. Without her, he had lost his mega starpower. No one on his current roster could generate a fraction of the shine Starr did.

"Aiight, Fitz. I'll get at ya in a few. Peace," he said, clicking off his cell and then shutting off the treadmill. As the belt wound down to a complete stop, he jumped off and grabbed a liter of designer water, downing it in one long gulp. As he headed for the stationary bike, he pressed the call button on his Bluetooth® and checked the messages on his disposable phone.

Kevin had called and left several messages. He was trying to speak in code, but Heywood could tell he was becoming more and more frazzled and unraveled. Heywood tossed the phone on a nearby chair, just as Duck barged into the gym, holding another one of Heywood's disposable phones and his iPod®.

"Yo, Wood. You know I wouldn't be botherin' you for nothing. You got a problem. That cat Kevin is downstairs buggin'. He's at the front door, tryna get in. He says he ain't leavin' until he sees you. Security is 'bout to call, 5-0, ya heard?"

Heywood grabbed another water bottle, and took a long drink. "Kevin, eh? Go down there an' slow walk him up. An' wait by the door, 'cause when I finish wit' him, I want ya to take him down the service area. Where the rest of the garbage is," Heywood said, flinging the half-empty bottle into an open trash can.

"Word," Duck said, and handed him his iPod®. "I updated your playlist, Wood. Check this, too," he said, pointing to the phone. "Somebody's been tryna get at you for a minute, aiight?"

As Duck walked out of the room, Heywood fumed, and slipped the electronics into his pocket. How dare Kevin show his face here. He knew better than to come out of pocket like that. And if he didn't know,

Heywood was about to show him.

Heywood quickly checked the messages on the phones. There were eight calls from Typhoon. Typhoon was mad as hell, and he let Heywood know it. Evidently, Kevin wasn't living up to his end of the bargain if Typhoon was still trying to contact him. He was about to shut him down for real.

Placing his iPod® earbuds in his ears, he hoisted himself onto the stationary bike. Once settled, he pressed the 'on' button and started pedaling as a disheveled Kevin was thrown through the door by Duck.

"Heywood," Kevin began, and Heywood ignored him. "Heywood," he said again, this time reaching for Heywood's shoulder. Heywood, immediately swuing on Kevin and connected with his jaw, causing his glasses to hit the floor.

Jumping off the bike, Heywood kicked the fallen attorney in the abdomen. "Mutha fucka, don't ya eva put ya hands on me," he spat. Nostrils flaring, he snatched his earbuds from his ears. He went nose to nose with Kevin, who was holding his jaw, perspiring and eyes fluttering.

"Heywood, I," Kevin tried to speak, but apparently found that speaking was too painful. He moved a bit to grab at his glasses, but Heywood beat him to them. Heywood stepped firmly on the lenses, crushing them into the rubber floor with his Nike Blazers.

Kevin coughed and scratched his head. Picking up his broken glasses, he said with obvious effort, "Look, Tyrone's not listening to me anymore. I, uh, told him not to contact you, and he said he was going to anyway. He doesn't trust me, and we all know what happens when Tyrone doesn't trust anyone." Kevin stopped to catch his breath. "They cease to exist."

Heywood looked him up and down. If Kevin was this much of a sweaty mess in front of Typhoon, no wonder Typhoon wasn't believing anything he said.

Kevin continued rambling, and Heywood stared at him, his face blank and disinterested. Kevin was clearly using, and suddenly he had lost any useful purpose for Heywood.

"He's, he's, falling apart, Heywood. Now that he has no money, he can't even get the guards to run for him. He's getting desperate. You need to call him, because, I think he knows something. Somebody's telling him something, and it's not me. I swear."

"Sounds like ya in a lotta of trouble, Kevin my man," Heywood said with a shrug. "Sounds like Ty done found ya ass out."

Kevin's arms fell slack by his side, the twisted glasses tilted on the bridge of his nose. "Whoa, wait a minute, Heywood. What are you saying? You and I, we had a deal. I was only doing what you wanted."

"Doin' what who wanted?" Heywood asked, brushing past him and cutting his eyes. "I don't know whatchu talkin' 'bout. Sounds to me like you was doin' what you wanted to do. Now, if I gotta make a call to Typhoon, that's what I gots to tell 'em, yo."

"I don't believe it. You would actually do that to me?"

Heywood snorted as he walked over to his mini-fridge, opened the door, and removed another bottle of water. He cracked open the top, and started sloshing water on Kevin as he gestured with his hands. "Who are you? Ya ain't nobody to me. I shoulda had security toss yo' ass on the curb. Fuck what ya heard. Ya come strollin' up here on my turf, wildin' out an' tryna put me on blast. I thought ya knew. Ya rolled the dice, an' ya crapped out."

Kevin held his arms out, in a hapless posture. "I crapped out? I bet on you, Heywood. I didn't have a choice, remember? I was doing your dirty work. All because you threatened to get me disbarred. Or to pin Faith's murder on me. Whatever, you're the one that's double-crossing Typhoon, not me."

Heywood yawned, stretching his mouth wide. He threw his head back, opened his mouth, and holding the water bottle high, poured some of the cold water down his throat. "Ya know what, Kevin? I'm done wit' ya. Done. Me an' Ty ain't got no squabbles. This sounds like it's between you an' him. Duck!" he yelled over his shoulder, and Duck instantly opened the door. "Come take this garbage out, man," Heywood said, and nodded toward Kevin.

Duck quickly crossed the room, and grabbed Kevin by the arm. "Heywood, are you serious? You're just going to throw me out? You're going to put me out there like this? What about our deal? What about me? What do you think's going to happen to me?" Kevin struggled futilely against Duck's powerful grip as he practically dragged him across the floor.

Heywood mounted the stationary bike and placed his earbuds back in his ears. Switching on his iPod®, he hit 'random' on the playlist, and got his pedal and groove on. He was rolling along fine, upping his resistance and mphs, until the playlist hit a new song called *Miss En You*, and he almost tumbled off the machine.

chapter thirty-seven

EXHAUSTED FROM an extra-long gym workout and the early ebbing Philly summer heat, Cam decided to go home and do a little research before Randolph's shift ended. She wanted to run through the DVDs she liberated from Heywood before she called her aunt. Something was gnawing at her. Had she missed something important? Moving past the DVDs she had already viewed, she looked closely at the names and initials on those she hadn't played yet.

After skimming through a few, just long enough to either identify the victim or capture more dates, she found one video that stopped her heart. In it, she was revolted to see that Heywood was about to have sex with a very young girl. He was clearly cajoling her, and the girl appeared to be confused and frightened. Cam couldn't bear to watch all of it, but was especially troubled because the little girl seemed familiar. She noted the date of the video, removed it from her laptop, and then tucked it away for safekeeping.

It was almost 1:30 in the afternoon, and she knew where her aunt would be. She dialed the pay-as-you-go phone, and wasted no time asking her aunt about her father. As she feared, Aunt Mary was obstinant. "I just don't understand why you need to know about that man. I don't even recall his name."

"Aunt Mary, please. You know who he was. His nickname was Carlos. I just need to know his real name."

"It doesn't matter, Camara. I'm sure that snake in the grass is probably dead. And if he is alive, he would probably never help you. In fact, I'm sure he isn't alive, because if he was, he would've been in your pocket a long time ago. You know he was the one that kept Faith in those drugs."

Cam sighed. Aunt Mary could be stubborn, but today she was just not budging. "Please, Aunt Mary. I really need to know who he is. And if he's still alive. If he isn't, then it's not going to hurt me, now is it?"

The phone went silent, and Cam overheard Yolanda Adams in the background singing, *The Battle is Not Yours.* Finally, Aunt Mary replied. "I believe his name was Charlie. Charlie Bonds. He liked to call himself Carlos 'cause he thought he was cute. Like he was Spanish or something, but he was nothing but Black."

Aunt Mary went on and on about Carlos being a slick-haired devil, while Cam quickly Googled his name. The results showed up instantly, noting her father's checkered past. She started to click on a link to a newspaper article about her father when her Aunt said something that gave her pause.

"Just promise, whatever you do, promise me that you won't invite that criminal into your life. Nothing good will come from it, believe me. Once a snake, always a snake. A serpent don't ever shed its skin."

She didn't want to lie to her aunt. She was tired of lying. She wanted to be completely honest with at least one person in her life, so she said, "I'm sorry, Aunt Mary, but I can't promise you that. If Carlos, I mean, if my father is alive, I need to talk to him. He might be able to help me."

Once again, the phone was silent, as Yolanda took them to the bridge in the background. "Well, I'll pray for you, child. 'Cause you're going to need it. He may be your father, it's true, but he can't mean you no good. I never wished anyone dead, but in this case, I hope he is. Not because I don't want him to help you, but I just don't believe that he will and I don't want you to be disappointed. You've been through enough."

Cam tried to change the subject, and but didn't get anywhere. Aunt Mary droned on about Carlos and how he had ruined Faith's life, so

Cam decided to end the call, with a promise to contact her again within the week.

As soon as she hung up from her aunt, Cam Googled her father's name again, looking for pictures, and was disappointed when none were found. She thought back to the photo album her mother used to keep, and the fading Polaroids of him taped inside. It made her sigh. She was more than sure that if Aunt Mary still had those books, she had cut Carlos's pictures out of them.

Using *USA Peoplesearch*, she was able to find current information on her father. She didn't want to, but had to use the credit card Randolph had given her to pay for the record search. After charging $19.95 to the Visa, the search engine indicated that Charlie Bonds, a/k/a Carlos Bonds, was still alive. His last known address was Lewisburg Federal Penitentiary.

She ordered a criminal background check on him for $49.99, and it listed his charges and convictions. He was currently doing a bid of 15 to life on narcotics charges in Lewisburg. A quick search on Mapquest revealed that Lewisburg was about 170 miles from Philly. Cam now knew what the third phase of her "Operation Cam" plan would be. She had to go to see him. The challenge would be figuring out how to get there.

Besides getting there, she had to take a quick tutorial on prison culture. She was smart enough to realize that she couldn't just waltz into the prison; she knew that there were certain criteria and rules. As she downloaded the regulations guide, her phone rang. It was B. Real. She hadn't had time to think about his offer, so she sent his call straight to voicemail. After a few seconds, she listened to his message.

"Yo, Tru. It's B. I'm here to tell ya, ma, you're song's gettin' mad love. It's on fiyah. The hits have been off the charts, an' the link was shut down for a while yesterday 'cause of the traffic it was gettin.' Yo, I know ya busy, an' that's whassup, but yo, holla at me. I really wanna work wit' ya. At least get ya back in the studio an' get ya videoed or somethin'. Plus, I wanna send ya stuff to some of the major labels. Hell, it's just a matter of time before they come knockin' anyway.

"But for real, old man Sandler here at the studio is gassed about havin' ya work outta here, so I'm sure we can work out somethin' if ya stacks is low. Call me, okay? I told Sandler and my boys that ya need to stay on the DL, and

they're cool with that. Are ya in Witness Protection or somethin'? Never mind. Whateva. We got your back. Peace."

She listened to the message again, and saved it in her mailbox. If her music was creating this much buzz, B. was just going to keep at her until she responded. And he was right. The industry always had people making the rounds on the Internet, searching for new talent. But, she wasn't beat about it. B. might've been hyped about it, but Cam knew that her song was just one of millions flooding YouTube with potential superstars. Some probably just as talented as she was. And she didn't expect her rough works to get very far.

But, it made her smile to know that a young, vibrant cat like B. was hyped about her style. She didn't know much about him, but was planning to find out. She hoped she could trust him. She also knew that before she did anything, and before things really got out of hand, she was going to need help. Industry help. And there were only a few people that she could rely on. Or even trust. And those were Jamie, Rashad, and maybe Big Mac. But, before she did anything, she needed to have a face-to-face with her father. And what he had to say might change the course of her life.

After completing her plans for her Reconnaissance mission to see her father, Cam reviewed them one last time before tucking them into her cover notebook. She had so much to do. Layers upon layers of things to do. To see her father, she would first have to get placed on his visitor's list. Check. She had already called his Unit Manager, saying that she was his cousin and wanted to visit. Now she just needed a fake ID in the name of Mary Bonds, which shouldn't be too difficult to do in the city of Philadelphia.

To get to Lewisburg, she would have to take a five-hour bus ride. The schedule showed only a few return buses, so her time there would be pretty limited. She'd be on a tight schedule, but what else was new? She still hadn't figured out when she was going. She would have to wait until she found out Randolph's schedule for the following week.

Confident she had done everything she could, she settled in and prepared for her fiancé's return from work. Guilt was eating away at her insides, so she decided to put all of her Cam issues away for the evening and focus on her man. She loved him with all her heart and knew that she was more than lucky to have found him. If she could forget everything but him tonight, perhaps it would give her the strength to endure the difficulties that lay ahead.

And she did just that. She ran down to the gym and stored her backpack, then ventured over to the open air Italian Market and picked up a bouquet of roses and assorted flowers, two nice Porterhouse steaks, fresh herbs, baby spinach, two giant potatoes, and strawberry gelato, and headed home. She even splurged on a chilled bottle of Prosecco, and stopped by Victoria's Secret. She purchased a sensual chocolate brown negligee, silk robe, and matching slippers.

As she arrived back at the apartment, the doorman greeted her with a smile and helped her with her bags. She texted Randolph to hurry home, and started dinner by preparing the potatoes for the oven, and concocting a marinade for the steaks. She set the table, trimmed and arranged the flowers, and removed a few rose petals for later use.

She then took a nice hot shower, as warm as her still recovering skin could tolerate, and scrubbed away the filth and lies clinging to her body. She sprayed on some of his favorite perfume, *Light Blue,* then slipped into her new sexy teddy. She also started to run a steaming hot bath for Randolph, sprinkling some rose petals in the water and others on the bed.

Lastly, she removed the blank card she had picked up from VS and wrote, "To the man I love. Thank you for loving me." She placed it in the pocket of his bathrobe. She found a cool jazz radio station on the microstereo, and waited for his arrival.

Greeting him with a long kiss, she removed his bag from his hands and his clothes from his back. She then led him into the bathroom, where a steaming bath awaited him.

In between his bath and their candle-lit dinner, they reconnected. Not only did she find out his schedule, but a few more of his secrets too, like that he was ticklish on the back of his neck. And they shared their dessert in bed, sipping wine, feeding each other spoonfuls of ice cream, and making love. And for a few hours, her mind was still, focused on something loving, sure, and positive.

And those thoughts accompanied her on her clandestine trip to Lewisburg a few days later. The bus was filled with all types of women, old and young, quiet and loud; ride or die chicks going to see their man, locked up, doing a bid.

She had gotten her ID through someone at the gym, and had purchased a long, chestnut brown wig for the trip. After finding out she had clearance from her father's Unit Manager, she bought the bus ticket. Before she left, she made sure she had enough extra cash to add to her father's book. She had read somewhere that putting money on an inmate's commissary book was expected of visitors.

So, as she maneuvered through the strict security measures at the penitentiary, she tried to remain calm and blend in. *This is something I have to do,* she kept telling herself, even as the metal gates clanging behind her threatened to send her right out the door. But she pressed on. She would not be deterred. Not even by her better judgment.

Passing cleanly through the Ion Scan machine, the machine that detects and identifies the presence of controlled substances, she was directed to the visiting area, where she took her seat at the glass enclosed booth number 14.

Taking a few deep breaths, she tried to lower her heart rate, and pasted a nonchalant look on her face. She wasn't sure how she was going to react when she saw him, but she was trying her best to play it cool. Everytime the guards brought out an inmate, she turned, searching each man's face as they approached. Finally, after what seemed an eternity, Carlos came out. As he approached the booth, she immediately recognized him from the pictures in her mother's photo albums. He was still handsome, just older and visibly worn. His face had hardened and aged, and the fine hair her mother had been so captivated with was now salt and pepper, but still wavy and full. He was of medium height, normal build, the color of dusty honey, and had a slight pauch in his midsection.

He sat down, and simply stared at her. His eyes misted over, and he blinked. After a few moments, he picked up the phone, and motioned for her to do the same. She picked up the receiver, and held it. She could hear him breathing on the other end, but he didn't say anything. He couldn't say anything. She opened her mouth to say hello, and he interrupted her.

When he spoke, she saw that he had a few key teeth missing.

★

He held his hand up against the glass. "I don't believe it. It's been a long time. It sure is good to see you," he said. "I was hoping that what I had heard about you wasn't true, Baby Girl." His voice crackled over the phone.

Cam took a deep breath. "How, uh, how'd you know?"

"You're the spittin' image of your momma, God rest her soul. That was my baby. She used to call me 'Boo,' ya know." A tear had trickled down his cheek as he spoke.

Tears welled up in her eyes, too, yet she steadied her voice. "You don't seem too surprised," she said.

"Bein' incarcerated numbs you to a lotta things. Bein' surprised can get you hurt, so I try not to let too many things sneak up on me. But, I've also learned a lot, too. Mainly, that you don't always believe what you hear. But, you go along to get along. It doesn't change if you got faith and you believe."

She placed her hand up against the glass, and measured it against her father's. His hand was large and brawl-scarred. A sense of relief radiated from his hand through the thick glass.

"I didn't know what to expect, so I—"

"*Shhh*," he said, eyeing the guards. "I know you probably haven't been to the pen before, and it's only a little like what you've seen on TV. Around here, they hear everything, and they watch everything too. And you're the first relative I've had up here in a while. So, I know everybody's wondering who you are," he said.

She took the hint. She had to be careful not to blow her cover, even if she wasn't even supposed to be alive. It was never publicized who her father was, but dealing with Heywood had taught her that nothing was impossible to know. If you have the right connections.

Carlos continued. "I asked God to give me a second chance. I've blown those too, but I always, always asked Him to help me make a few things right. You were one of them, Mary. I just hope you can forgive me." His eyes shone with sincerity.

323

She had a million questions for him, but didn't know where or how to begin. He sensed her anxiety, and tried to help by taking a fatherly stance.

"Look, something's got you where you are right now, so I know you must need my help. And I need to help you, too." He lowered his hand, and she followed suit.

"I need to know what happened that night with my mother. Why was she doing what she was doing, and who was she doing it for?"

Carlos filled in all the blanks. He told her what happened that night, and who orchestrated the whole deal. Using initials like Kay for Kevin, he told her about Kevin and his backdoor deals, and about how Eff (Faith) had found out about them. He told her that Ach (Heywood) was involved from day one, using Eff to get next to her. And how they had set Eff up that night, to shut her up.

His voice was escalating, and he took a few moments to calm down. Evidently, he had played and replayed those moments in his mind for many years, and was just waiting for the day to get it all off his chest and conscience.

He inhaled deeply and glanced around. "I'm sorry about all that, Baby Girl. I really am. I'm sorry that I wasn't more of a man about mines, and never told you or said anything, but they did me in, too. They shot me up, but I guess my tolerance was a lot higher. When I woke up, I was in the lock-up on some bogus charge, an' I didn't remember shit. I was told by that fake-ass attorney of mine, Kay, that if I ever said anything, they had evidence to make it look like I had somethin' to do with Eff's death. So he pleaded me out, and let me do time."

"Wait a minute. Kay was your attorney?"

Carlos nodded. "Yep, he was me and Eff's suit. Courtesy of the big dog."

"The big dog? You mean he was Ach's too?"

"Naw. I said the big dog, not that worm-filled puppy of his.

"See, I was kinda confused when this all went down. I was told that I had to get ghost, and never contact my baby girl again. Kay relayed the message, an' I thought it was comin' from the big dog. And so, I hate to say it, I did it. I punked out. I tried to save my own sorry ass instead of doin' the right thing."

Cam was shocked, and couldn't repress her expression. "But, why?

Why'd they do it?"

"That dude Ach ain't shit. Look at him. He ain't got no street cred. He's a sucker. He's a backstabbin' punk who ain't man enough to face his. At least Tee was a man about his."

She quickly interrupted him. "Tee? Who's Tee?"

Carlos glanced around and scratched his chin. "There was this cat that he worked for. He's the big dog. Hell, we all worked for him. He ruled everything under the *moon*. Everything. He had so much clout, he could even command the weather. Storms, hurricanes, typhoons, and tornados. You're a smart girl. I know you know what I'm talkin' about."

Her head was spinning. If Kevin was supposed to be working for Typhoon, but allowing Heywood to call the shots that got her mother killed, he really was a lying two-faced, backstabbing, deceitful bastard. Now that she thought about it, Kevin probably even helped Heywood break into his uncle's office and steal those files.

Her father's blunt disclosure shook her. She nodded, not having any idea that they all worked for Typhoon. But, Carlos made it clear that he didn't think that Typhoon ordered the hit on Faye. He thought that was all Heywood's doing.

"I've always wanted to make that right, too," he said. "I just know how this cat Ach rolls, and he's crossed a lotta lines and messed over a lotta folks to get where he is. See, I'm old school. I believe in doing things the right way. So, I've been waiting a long time for this opportunity, and I just want a chance to meet this cat. And let him know that there's one brother out here who's not afraid to step to him."

Cam blinked. She was happy to know that her father had her back, but what could he really do behind these steel bars?

"I think Tee might be able to help us. There's some real interesting stuff Ach is doing that Tee might be interested in. I just don't know where he's at."

Carlos was a quick study. He caught on immediately. "I can find that out. I don't care if the Associated Press don't have it on its wire, the jailhouse wire has it. I can get that for you."

"Cool," she said.

"Just let me handle this, Baby Girl. I owe y'all this, at least. I'm gonna do what I can do, and make it happen."

"Don't do anything that's going to come back on you," she said.

"Don't worry. I'm up for parole in three years, and I'm determined to do the right thing to stay legal. I'm talkin' about doin' what I need to get right morally," he said with a wink.

That night, she tossed and turned in bed, unable to sleep. She was sweating and grinding her teeth. She was beginning to fray around the edges, and it was beginning to show.

She had rushed back to Philly, and had gotten off her mark. Her carefully executed plans had blown up. On the way home, the bus experienced mechanical difficulties, and the driver had pulled over onto the shoulder of the road, where they waited almost two hours for another bus to arrive. Already upset from the events of the day, being late, nervous, and hungry did nothing to improve her mood. Cam grabbed a taxi at the bus terminal, and too late to do her planned "stop and drop" at the gym, brought her backpack up to the apartment, arriving just before Randolph.

She ordered Chinese, one of Randolph's favorites, and tried to at least be a pleasant dinner companion. She pasted a smile on her face, and listened to Randolph talk about the events of the day while she pushed the food around on her plate.

When they finally went to bed, sleep once again eluded her. She replayed the events of the day in her mind, finally meeting her father, what he had said, what he had meant. And then her thoughts turned to Heywood and the last DVD she had seen. Cam groaned, remembering the young girl in the video. Suddenly, she shot straight up in the bed. She did know who the girl was. The youngster on the tape was her old lighting man Billy's niece, Stephanie, the one that she had met right before the accident.

chapter thirty-eight

"JUST FIND out what ya can, Duck. An' do it like yesterday," Heywood snarled, closing his cellphone. Looking out his office window, he could almost feel the thick blanket of humidity and fog that was summer in Midtown. He pressed 'play' on the remote of his Bang & Olufsen Beosound stereo system hanging on the wall, and replayed the track.

Ever since Duck had updated his iPod®, he had been enthralled by *Miss En You*. He had to find out more about that voice. "Tru Talent," he said aloud. She had balls to call herself that, and he liked a ballsy chick he could break. She had talent, though. She definitely did have some chops.

She was raw, her production was bootleg and base, but the voice was incredible. He heard hints of brilliance in her, and while he wanted to dismiss her as a wannabe or copycat, he couldn't. There was something compelling about that voice, and he had to have her. But before he put forth any effort, other than running Duck through his usual motions, he needed to find out if she was a heavenly voice with a hellish face. He didn't care how well the chick sang. If she even remotely resembled a schnauzer, she wasn't gonna get jack from him.

Word on the street was that this new artist was getting mad hits on YouTube. Heywood had Duck working every angle to get next to her, but there was nothing to get. Not yet.

He even had Rae sniffing around to see if she could find anything on Tru Talent. Even the usually super resourceful Rae came back empty-handed.

Heywood listened to the track for the umpteenth time, and tried not to sway to the hypnotic rhythm and the vocalist's command of the melody. He felt something that he hadn't felt in a long time. It was inspiration. It was desire. It was a rush of adrenaline; it was intoxicating. He had to have this Tru Talent. She could put him on top again. She could restore his status as a mega superstar. And he knew that if he was feeling it, his peers were too. He just needed to get to her first.

There weren't too many opponents to be concerned about. Noah was now a non-issue, and he didn't have to worry about too many of the older cats beating him to the punch. And if any of these indy label cats came with, he'd do his normal thing. Throw a little cash their way, sign them to a binding contract, and squeeze the life out of them. Either way, he was going to win. But, he had to play his cards right.

Now that she was in contact with her father, the pieces of her puzzle were coming together. She had put money on his books so he could purchase phone cards and other incidentals. However, his first call to her was to let her know that although her appreciated it, he didn't want her money. He said that he had saved a lot, and wanted to use his own money to help her. She was pleasantly surprised to hear it, but Aunt Mary's warning caused her to still be a little skeptical. He was her father, and he seemed like he genuinely wanted to help, but she wasn't sure if she could trust him. She had misjudged Allison's character and trusted Allison, and look what had happened. For the moment, Cam was just going to have to wait and see.

But, B. was living up to his word. He said they weren't answering the phones or responding to voicemails or email, and they had stacks of messages about her. He said he didn't know why she had to stay under the radar, but he was going to do everything he could to keep her there. He would do anything to get her signed.

He had polished up her track, and like he said, her song was getting mad play on the 'net. He really wanted her to do more recording, and at least make a video of her other song, *Trick Bag*, but she was reluctant and afraid.

B. Real wanted to keep the momentum going, and thought *Trick Bag* might be even bigger than *Miss En You*. After much negotiation, Cam finally agreed to make the video, but only as a silhouette behind a white screen. B. had been right. The video became an Internet sensation. And, as she could have predicted, with the interest, came the haters.

"She's a fake it 'til you make it."

"She's a poser. An auto-tuned heifer."

"She's a gimmick. She's a Milli Vanilli."

"The reason why we ain't seen her is because she weighs 600 pounds and looks like The Creature from the Black Lagoon."

Eventually, industry moguls were asked to weigh in, and Heywood was the first to call her a phony. He was coming out of M2, in Chelsea, when a reporter from TMZ mentioned Tru. "Who?" he said, feigning ignorance. "Oh, her. Until I see her sing, all she is is smoke an' mirrors," he said. "Poof," he said, holding his hand out and blowing into it. His antics delighted the onlookers.

"We gotta prove 'em wrong, Tru," said B.'s message. "Ya gotta let 'em know you're for real. That you're the real deal."

Cam listened to the message and knew she had to get help from someone. And the only person she knew she could rely on, outside of her aunt, was Jamie Tee.

This time when she asked her Aunt Mary for help, she readily obliged. The plan was for her to contact Jamie's mother, under the guise of having Jamie make an appearance for Cam's youth foundation. His mother, being a good church mother like Aunt Mary, leaped at the opportunity to have her sinning son do something that was spiritually grounded.

Aunt Mary arranged everything. Jamie was either going to come to town or she would meet him somewhere. Jamie's mother liked the idea of having him come to DC, so the plan was to meet at Cam's house, in the studio, so they could hash out the details. It took a few days for Jamie's mother to confirm the date, but she did. Jamie would be in town the following week.

Cam made her way down to Maryland, and hid out in the studio until Jamie arrived, sans entourage, with only his assistant, Que, in tow.

After a brief tour of the main house, Aunt Mary asked Que to stay behind and keep an eye on a pot she had cooking on the stove, and led Jamie out to the studio, where Cam was hiding in the bathroom.

"This is really nice, Aunt Mary," Jamie said as he stepped into the studio. "Cam must've really loved this place. It almost feels like she's here." He walked across the floor, the legs of his Armani jeans falling stylishly down his inseam. Wearing an oversized cream colored linen shirt, Jamie was elegant and polite, but seemed a little subdued.

Eyeing the recording booth and equipment, Jamie sat down at the keyboard and started to play. Aunt Mary closed the door behind them, and adjusted the temperature. "Yes, it is like Camara is still here, Jamie," she said, and walked over to where he was sitting. "Can I get you something to drink?"

"No ma'am," he said, and hit a few chords. "I'm fine."

Aunt Mary reached in her pocket. She wanted to make sure she had her smelling salts with her. "Jamie, I brought you here because I needed to talk to you about something." She slid in beside him on the bench, with her back to the keyboard. She reached over and touched his hand. "I want you to know that Camara loved you like a brother."

Jamie nodded, and hit a few more chords, unable to speak.

"And there's so much that's happened since my baby went down to that island. And Camara always knew she could rely on you, no matter what."

"I know, Aunt Mary. I just wish I could've done more for her. I can't tell you how much I wish I could've stopped her from going down there. I just wish there was something I could do."

Aunt Mary reached for his hand. "There is, child. There is. Sometimes God gives us a second chance, and that's why you're here today. To do something Cam wanted you to do. But first, I want you to play something for me. Can you play that gospel song you sang that first night we saw you?"

Jamie struck a few more chords, trying to find the right key. "Sure. Anything for you, Aunt Mary. What was it? Was it *Goin' Up Yonder?*

Aunt Mary shook her head, and glanced toward the bathroom. "No, it was *How I Got Over.*"

Jamie smiled at her and started banging out the opening. He started at the top, and went through the first verse. When he got to the chorus, his mellow tenor sounded as smooth as butter. *"How I got over, o-ver, my soul looks back and wonders, how I got o-o-ver."*

Aunt Mary was swept away, her body swaying as she stood. She positioned herself behind him and started the one-two-one church clap.

Pumping up the last verse, Jamie raised the tempo. Moved by the music, the words and their meaning, he was really feeling the message. Tears were streaming down his face, and when he hit the chorus and sang, *"My soul looks back and wonders,"* Cam joined him from the kitchen.

"How I got o-ver!" she sang, and Jamie's hands dropped down on the keyboard as she appeared from behind the kitchen doorway. He leapt backwards, where a waiting Aunt Mary caught him under his arms.

"Oh no! Oh Lord! Jesus!" He shrieked, staring at her as if she was a ghost. He tried crab crawling away as Aunt Mary clung to him. She had plenty of experience assisting the saints in the church when they caught the Holy Ghost, so this was nothing new.

Cam kept singing. *"I will sing, hallelujah, I'm gonna shout, trouble over, I wanna thank Jesus for all He's done for me."*

Jamie kept shouting, and practically speaking in tongues. As Cam approached him, he screamed, tears streaming down his face. He fainted, and Cam and Aunt Mary lifted him and carried him to the sofa.

"Good thing I got my smelling salts," Aunt Mary said, as they struggled to carry the still twitching man

Even with the salts, it took Jamie a minute to come to and come together. Aunt Mary applied a cold compress to his forehead, and held the open bottle of smelling salts under his nose. As soon as he opened his eyes, he coughed and shouted, "Cam!"

Cam held his face and kissed his cheeks. "Yes, Jamie. It's me," she said, tears choking in her throat.

Jamie, tears streaming down his face, clutched his chest. "Camara. Girl, you almost killed me," he sputtered, and then grabbed her, hugging her tightly to reassure himself that she was real.

They sobbed in each other's arms, and Aunt Mary set a glass of water down on the coffee table in front of them, and excused herself. "I'm just going to go tell Que that you're okay, and that you want him to go on back to the hotel. I'll tell him you said you'll call him later, all right?"

Jamie nodded, his eyes riveted to Cam's face. Finally, after crying and snotting and messing up each other's clothes, Jamie shook his head, his face full of disbelief. "Camara. How did you?" He cut himself short. "What happened? Where have you been? Oh my Lord," he said. "I need something to drink. I think I'm gonna pass out again."

Cam brushed his cheek with her hand. She leaned forward and handed him the glass of water. "Jamie, I'm so sorry I had to do this to you. But, I didn't have any other way. I'm sorry, but I didn't mean to scare you like that."

He gulped down the water, and blinked. "*Shee-it,* I need some Henny right about now. Whew, I gotta take it down a thousand," he said, and then turned in his seat and faced her. "Cam. Now listen, Miss Girl. What's going on? What happened? I ought to slap you senseless for not letting me know you were okay. You know I'm your boy. Damn.

"I can't believe it. Look at you. You look so good. Especially for a dead girl. Tell me, what the hell happened down there in Montserrat? Nobody ever said nothing. Not a word. I always knew something wasn't right about that whole thing. I mean, if everybody thinks you're dead, and you're not, then who the hell got buried? And whose funeral did I sing at?"

Cam looked him in the eye. "Jamie, I'll tell you everything, I promise. But, I need your word. You have to help me. I would've called you, but I didn't know what to do. I just need you to promise me that you'll help me, and not betray me, Jamie."

Jamie placed his hand over hers and nodded. "I swear, Cam. You're like my little sister. I would never do that to you."

"Thanks, Jamie. You don't know how much that means to me," Cam said. She then gave him a brief rundown of what happened to her at the volcano, and where she had been since. She told him about Marisol, and tried to explain how she thought her identity had been switched. But since she still had no real idea, she couldn't explain that part very well. "I didn't know what happened, and it wasn't like I could just come back and find out. Especially if my death wasn't an accident."

"You mean the accident wasn't an accident? I knew something foul went down."

"I know, right? I just felt that someone might have tried to kill me. And I needed to know who."

For the next hour, Cam went over everything she had learned, thought, and done since the accident, and Jamie was understandably astonished. She didn't tell him everything she knew about Heywood, and didn't say a thing about her break-in or her father. Even though she loved Jamie, she just wasn't sure. As proven before, people that couldn't stand Heywood later found themselves under his spell. She didn't want to find out later that Jamie was under Heywood's control, too.

Jamie pulled a cigar case from out of his coat pocket, and pulled out a fat blunt. "I hope you don't mind, but this is all a little much for me. I need something to bring me down." He pulled his lighter from his other pocket, and lit up. Inhaling deeply, he shook his head and held the smoke. He blew it out slowly.

"Cam, this is some serious shit you talking, you know. I don't mean no harm, but it really sounds like that damn Heywood is behind all this. I knew his ass was lying when he was poppin' off that you two were engaged. Pu-lease. I knew that was some bogus shit."

Jamie went on, blaming Heywood for everything from the mortgage crisis, to the falling U.S. dollar, to being the cause of the new strain of Swine Flu. He was being his usual animated self, and it was a welcome relief for Cam.

"But, for real, Cam, Heywood's a shady bastard. Now, I have my own reasons for feeling like I do, 'cause I know he's done some shysty shit to some folks, but he usually covers his tracks real good. Do you have any proof that he might've set you up? Proof that's not just going to walk away or get paid off?"

"I think so. Well, at least I think I can get it. I might need your help, though."

"That's a given. You got that. Anything you need, you let me know. I swear, I wanna get that son of a bitch too. Since you died, I mean left, Heywood's really been showin' his ass. Our paths have crossed a couple of times, and he's been wildin' out for real. More so than ever. I mean, he's always done some foul shit to his artists, but now I even heard that he's behind trying to get my boy black-ballled and what not." Cam frowned, and asked him who he was talking about.

"My producer, Noah. Noah Parker. I think he was just gettin' on the scene when you, uh, left. And Heywood's been out to get him for a minute, talking about how Noah was trying to steal his shine. You know, folks kill me with that 'crabs in a barrel' mentality. Like there isn't enough for everybody. Anyway, rumor has it that Noah was up for the head job over at APB, and Heywood was pissed, even though he kept grinning in Noah's face. And he must have done something, something mighty serious, because Noah backed out even before they asked him.

"Anyway, now, I don't know it for sure, but that's what the word on the street is. And it kind of makes sense. Noah's not talking to no one, not even me about it. He's been on vacation for the last month, and there's talk he might even resign or even get out of the industry." Jamie pulled on his joint. "Whenever Heywood's involved, it's never nothin' nice."

Cam sighed. It was all making sense now. Evidently, Heywood either made that tape or had somebody make it, and was using it to blackmail Noah out of the business.

"That's a shame, Jamie, but you know what? I don't put anything past Heywood. Nothing."

"Me either, Boo-Boo," he said, toking and blowing smoke. "Me either."

"You know, I'd really like to help Noah, but you just can't tell him I'm alive. In fact, you can't tell anyone, Jamie. Even if we do have non-disclosures with them." Jamie nodded, and she continued. "And I really want to make Heywood pay for what he's done to me, if I can. That's why I need your help. But, I have to do it the right way. And I think I might have an idea as to how it can be done."

And that idea was Tru Talent. But first, she had to bring Jamie up to speed on the other events in her life, including Randolph. When she mentioned that she had a man, Jamie laughed, and commented about how she had picked up weight in all the right places, and how her hips had spread like she was getting some on the regular.

They laughed, and then she told him about her journey back to reality, and now Tru Talent, and how she thought she could work that to her advantage. He had heard of her and B. Real, but really hadn't heard any of her music. Jamie was down for anything that would take Heywood down, and was willing to play any position she needed, including making Tru his new protégée.

Jamie finished his blunt, and called his assistant. "Que? I'm gonna need to spend some time here with Miss Mary. Take the night off, and I'll holla at you in the a.m."

Jamie and Cam stayed and talked, hashing out their plans for Heywood and Tru. Without going into a lot of detail, Cam said that she might be able to help Noah, but only on the DL, and Jamie said he didn't care how low she had to go, just do what she could. The poor man was in ruins.

Aunt Mary cooked, the first real home-cooked meal either one of them had in a long time. Enjoying a sumptuous meal of baked salmon, macaroni and cheese, and kale, they laughed, ate, and worked, and Cam relaxed completely. Randolph had a double-shift at the hospital and wouldn't be home until the following afternoon. She and Jamie had plenty of time to reminisce and plot their next moves.

EARLY THE next morning, Jamie's limo picked them up at Cam's house. He had sent Que on to Philly by train, so that they would have some privacy during the ride up to Philly. Cam was on her way home, and Jamie and Que were booked at the Four Seasons in Center City for the next few weeks. Jamie cleared his schedule, and was ready to begin work immediately as Tru Talent's mentor, using his industry connects to amp her name and image.

Jamie's first call was to his boyfriend Gary in California, and Jamie had him procure the services of Jon D., one of the best theatrical make-up artists in the business. Things started falling into place quickly. Jon D. was in New York working on a movie, and would be only too happy to work with Jamie's new client in Philly. Jamie also called his lawyer, and, pulling a page from Heywood's book, requested that he draw up a version of the N-Snip, where they were guaranteed confidentiality in any of their business dealings.

Cam, so thankful Jamie was in her corner, felt the darkness lifting. The sun was rising as they crossed the Delaware Bridge, and Cam, normally not superstitious, decided it was a good sign. She felt like she was crossing a bridge to a new life. And when she switched on her phone to check her messages, she heard her father's voice. In code, he reported that he found Tee, and asked her to call him. Cam was elated.

The elation, however, was fleeting. When they reached Philly, Jamie dropped her off around the corner from her apartment. They planned to meet later that afternoon at the recording studio, and go over some more details. Before she got out of the limo, he kissed her on the cheek.

"Cam, I still can't believe I'm looking at you, talking to you. I always thought you were an angel, but now I know you are. The proof is right here, sitting right next to me."

Cam practically skipped home, flashing the doorman a bright smile as she passed him on her way to the elevator. When she placed the key in the door and unlocked the deadbolt, the door was pulled open from the inside. Randolph was standing there, her poor, exhausted Randolph. She would never forget the look on his face, or in his eyes. A terrible mixture of fear, hurt, anger, and disbelief.

"Marisol! Where have you been?"

chapter thirty-nine: side b

SHAYE BARRELED out the door, cursing wildly and nearly knocking the 275-pound Duck on his big ass. Heywood laughed, chalked up his cue stick, and licked his lips. With his toothpick dangling out of the corner of his mouth, he started laughing so hard, he had to take the toothpick out so he wouldn't swallow it.

"Whassup with Shaye?" Duck asked, glancing back at the tornado that had just blown past him. "Is she heated or what?"

Heywood, no longer laughing, eyed his shot. "Aww, she'll get over it. She's just bent out the frame over somethin' that ain't really none of her damned business."

"Oh, word?" Duck said.

"Yeah, she was eavesdroppin' while you an' me was conversatin' 'bout that Tru chick, an' she tried to call me on it. Like she gotta right to do that shit."

★

Their conversation had been brief. Duck had reported on Jamie Tee's surprise announcement that he was mentoring Tru Talent. He knew Heywood would not be pleased to find out that they were planning an interview with Wendy Williams, and that Tru was going to perform live from an undisclosed location.

Heywood told Duck to get his ass over to the penthouse, pronto. He was beyond furious. He didn't know if he was angrier that Wendy had the exclusive interview, or that Tru had hooked up with Jamie. Whatever. Tru, whoever that bitch was, was going to be his. Both Wendy and Jamie better watch their backs.

"Can ya believe Shaye had the nerve to black on me? She tried to say that she couldn't understand why I was chasin' after some Internet hack, when I already had her on the roster."

Duck glanced at Heywood, and then turned away. "Yo, uh, Heywood, Imma grab a brew. Ya down?" He quickly walked over to the mini-bar and removed a Corona.

Heywood tilted his head toward Duck. "Did ya hear what I said, Duck? That bitch blacked on me over some bullshit."

Duck inhaled, and forced a smile. "Yeah, that *is* some bullshit."

Heywood eyed the table, then turned his attention back to Duck. He was trying to decide if he wanted to go for the #7 in the corner pocket, or take his stick and whack Duck in the mouth. "I get the feeling ya agree wit' ol' girl. Come on, be a man 'bout yours. Ya disagree wit' me or what?"

Opening his beer with his bare hands, Duck took a deep gulp. He had been down this road before, and had a good idea where he was going to end up. But, the time had come for him to say something. He had swallowed a lot from Heywood, and had lost himself and who he was for the roller coaster ride he'd been on since joining Heywood's inner circle. It was time to pump the brakes. He was ready to get off.

Duck cleared his throat. "Well, Wood. She does have a point. She's been around, an' she does have some skills. An' she's down wit' you an' ya program. Seems like that should count for somethin'."

Heywood chewed on his pick, and stood up, holding his pool cue. "The only point Shaye has is the point of my dick in her ass. That's it. Now, if she was holdin' it down like this chick Tru seems to be, then maybe she could be my bottom bitch. But she ain't, an' if she don't want to play her position, an' stay in her lane, then she can get the fuck off the road, ya feel me?"

"I feel ya," Duck said, and then downed his beer. Normally, that's where the conversation would end, but today, he wasn't having it. He was fed up with the way Heywood handled his people, and had been for a long time. He was tired, so tired of watching and sometimes helping Heywood use, abuse, and discard loyal, talented folks. His nephew Parsley was just one of them. He'd brought the kid in, but had been unable to protect him. And now that Shaye was making waves, he knew she'd be out the door for real, soon.

"But on the real, Heywood, I'm gonna be a man about mines, at least today. I think it's fucked up the way you treat yo' peeps, man."

"Duck, seems like we been havin' circular conversations lately. An' Imma tell ya like I told ya before, ya don't like it, there's the mutha fuckin' door, partner," spat Heywood, still chalking his cue.

"An' believe me, I ain't beat about that Tru bitch or no other bitch for that matter," he said, chewing on his pick. "If she's workin' wit' that fuckin' Jamie, then she ain't got no talent, an' she ain't got no brains."

An icy silence filled the room, and both men stared at each other. Duck folded his arms across his massive chest.

"I dunno, Heywood. Jamie seems to got her back, for real. I hear he's really ridin' wit' her, gettin' her in front of the right folks. doin' it all up right. An' hell, word is that he's gonna get her signed wit' Noah."

Heywood sucked his teeth, took his shot, missed, and let out a string of obscenities that ended with "Fuck!" Hurling his cue onto the table, it cleared most of the remaining balls.

He was fuming. There was no way he was losing to Jamie. Or Noah. No way. This was Duck's fault. Duck's lame ass was coming up short and talking slick again. There was no way Jamie should have gotten to Tru before him. No way.

"I got Noah covered. His ass'll back down, no doubt. It's that fucker Jamie. Who told his ass he could get in the game? He ain't got no game. *Shee-it*, he's barely hangin' on hisself, an' now he got time to be mentorin' somebody?" Heywood raised his eyebrows. "I don't believe it. Somethin's up. An' Duck, ya betta find out what it is. An' if ya fuck this up, we won't have this conversation again. Cause yo' monkey ass'll be outta here."

Duck sighed and reached for another beer. "All I know is that the interview is happenin' tomorrow night. On YouTube. That's all I know," he said through clinched teeth.

chapter forty: side a

"WHERE HAVE you been?" he asked again. His voice was strained, and his body was nearly shaking with rage. She had never seen him like this.

He grabbed her arm and pulled her inside their apartment. Closing the door behind him, he was still in his scrubs, with a five o'clock shadow and heavy bags under his eyes. "Marisol? Answer me. Where have you been?"

She didn't know what to say. She felt like a cornered animal. What could she say? Should she tell him the truth? How could she tell him the truth? Should she just keep lying? Where could she begin? She didn't even know which of her lies had come apart. "What are you talking about, Randolph? I've been out."

"I know. The doorman told me you were out. Where were you? I've been worried sick about you. I called and texted you. What's going on? Are you cheating on me?" His voice cracked with pain and fear. "Tell me the truth?"

That damned doorman, she thought. *And to think, I just smiled at him.* "Cheatin'? Why would you ask me that?" She said, reaching for him. He pushed her arm away from him, and held up an envelope and two pieces of paper.

"Because of these, Marisol," he said, throwing the papers at her. "You paid to search for someone on the Internet, using our credit card, and then I find a receipt for a bus ticket to Lewisburg. And then you don't answer your phone all night. What are you doing? What's going on? Who do you know in that prison?"

Swallowing hard, she searched for the right words. Where did he find that receipt? Had she gotten that sloppy? Randolph deserved the truth. It was right on the tip of her tongue. But she was in too deep. She didn't want to lie again to him, but right now, she had no choice. The lies rolled off her tongue, just as the tears rolled down her cheeks.

"When I, uh, went back home, I found out that I had a relative 'ere in the States. But he's in jail, an' I was ashamed to tell you. But, he is me family, an' the only that I got 'ere. So, I looked 'im up an' went to see 'im. I didn't tell you 'cause I was shamed."

Randolph shook his head, like what she was saying either didn't make sense or didn't answer all of his questions. He started to reach for her, but stopped himself.

"Well, uh, I hear you, Marisol. But, this doesn't add up. Why didn't you tell me, huh? And where were you this morning? And last night?"

She wiped her eyes, and cleared her throat. "I went to DC. My relative, Bonds, has children there that he thought were bein' neglected. He asked me to go an' take a check on 'em.

"I know it sounds crazy, an' I probably shouldn't have done it, but he is me blood. An' his children too. An' when I found out about 'em, I thought to me self that 'ere's me family. When we get married, at least I'll have someone on me side of the church."

Her chest heaved with exertion and emotion. She hated herself for telling him only a half-truth as much as she hated the part that was true.

Randolph's arms fell by his side, a sad, resigned expression on his face. He carefully selected his words. "I'm sorry, Marisol. I can't imagine what it must be like for you here, with no family. I just wish you had told me." He reached for her, and drew her near.

"Trust is everything, baby. And I don't want you to think that I don't trust you, because I do. I was so worried about you. Afraid that something had happened to you. I didn't know what to think, and I'm sorry I jumped to conclusions like that."

"I'm sorry too, luv. I really am. I didn't like keeping it from you, an' it's my fault, Randolph." Her admission only made her feel worse, and she started crying again. She couldn't hold back the tears. "I'm so sorry."

Randolph kissed her forehead, and sniffed. Tears of relief filled his eyes, and he wiped hers. "I'm sorry I lost my temper. But, I thought that something had happened, and that I had lost you. Or that you were seeing someone else. Playing games with me." He hung his head, and pressed his face into her hair. "I love you, and I don't know what I would do if I ever lost you."

Cam started sobbing uncontrollably, the stress of lying to the man she loved and living alternate lives crashing in on her. She was afraid, afraid she had lost the trust of this wonderful man. Afraid that in the process of finding herself, she would lose the most important person in her life.

"I don't know either," she wheezed, in between sobs. "I don't know what I would do if I ever lost you." She really didn't.

Later, lying next to him, a restless Cam forced herself to remain still and breathe evenly. Randolph's mind might have been eased, but hers was on overdrive. Was any of this worth it? Worth all the lies and sneaking around? What was the point? Why was she doing this? When would she be able to tell him the truth? Would he ever look at her the same way again? Could they have a life together? When was this charade going to end?

Cam was totally confused, her loyalties to Randolph, her aunt and grandmother, Jamie, her charities, and her singing career all operating at cross purposes. She remembered that when all of this started, before the accident, all she wanted to do was to "be me." That's still all she wanted.

She realized that she couldn't be herself until everything was sorted out. There couldn't be a new life until her old one was in order, and that included a life with Randolph. She had to keep lying to him. Now that she was out as Tru, the ante was up and the stakes were even higher, and Heywood was even more dangerous. She admitted to herself that it might be a cop-out, reasoning that she was protecting Randolph from Heywood, but it was a rationalization she could live with, at least for now.

Perhaps she had gotten a little lax, but now that she knew the door-man was keeping tabs on her, she was going to have to tighten up her game. From now on, she would tuck away her laptop inside her gym bag whenever she left the building. She wouldn't give the doorman anything to report. Anything. And it will be a cold day in hell before she smiled at him again.

With so much at stake, she couldn't risk blowing any of her covers. She had to work harder to be Marisol, the person Randolph was in love with. She needed to keep his mind off her erratic behavior. She needed to be a better fiancé. She decided to tell him that she'd love to meet his family at Thanksgiving, hoping that everything would be settled by then.

She also had to concentrate on the arrangements she made with Jamie. With Tru's career taking off, she knew things were only going to get worse before they got better. And speaking of worse, there was Heywood. Once again, she had to ask herself, how far should she go to get him? Was she endangering herself? Her family? Randolph? And now Jamie?

Hours later, she was still concentrating on pretending to be asleep when Randolph left for the hospital. When the door of their apartment closed, she ran to the window, waiting to see him walk down the street. As soon as she did, she jumped into the shower, dressed, and grabbed her athletic bag. Bolting out the door of the building, she ignored the doorman as she ran past him and down the street. She was pressed for time. She had to meet Jon D., the makeup artist, at Jamie's hotel, and they had to get to the studio by seven o'clock.

After signing one of Jamie's new N-Snips, Jon D. was stunned to dis-cover his new client was Starr, one of his favorite performers. He was elated to be working with her. She presented him with an unusual request. She needed him to create a new face for her; one that the gen-eral public would not recognize.

On the ride to Philly, she and Jamie had decided that Tru needed to give a live performance that would be broadcast on the Internet. The performance would heighten interest in her as an artist, prove to naysay-ers that she was a real talent, and 'bait the hook' for any future dealings with Heywood. With the new face, Cam would perform in the small

Philly recording studio, with B. working the boards and Jamie in the house for moral support and to make sure everything went as planned. The icing on the cake would be to have the voice, Wendy Williams, do the exclusive interview. That would really draw Heywood's ire.

Jon D. was a gifted technician. He was able to quickly craft a mold of her face, a seamless mask that modified her appearance just enough to make her unrecognizable as Starr, or Marisol, for that matter. Virtually undetectable, even at close range, it gave her a different nose and a slightly darker complexion. As long as she wore a wig and stayed out of bright lights, she would be fine. No one would ever suspect that she was wearing a mask.

And while Jon D. worked his magic, so did Jamie. He called Noah and left a message for him, telling him he had someone he needed to hear. Someone who might be huge, and who would get him back in the game, in a big way.

As a personal favor to Cam, Jamie also called Rashad, and turned him on to Tru. Jamie added a little flourish to the story, and claimed that since he had done such a great job supporting Starr and leading her fan club, he was a perfect candidate to take charge of Tru's burgeoning fan base. Rashad was happy to be remembered, and vowed to help any way he could.

He also put his assistant, Que, on the job of building Tru's star power, and overseeing the creation of a signature look. Working with Jamie's personal team of stylists and hairdressers, Que created a new image for Tru. Her signature "look" would be a stylish hat; she would wear a different one with every ensemble. She would never be seen without one.

Que reached out to every media contact in his Crackberry who could create some buzz about Tru, from Jamie Foster Brown to Patty Jackson to Flo Kennedy to Necole Bitchie, to Natasha at theYBF.com. Since there hadn't been a hot new superstar for a while, his contacts were hungry, eager to be in on the ascent of a new star. And it all worked. Tru Talent was born, and Jamie was the proud obstetrician who delivered her.

B. Real and his production team, all with signed N-Snips, were waiting for them at the studio, awed at the idea of meeting and working with Jamie Tee. This was one huge step up for them, going from local Philly wannabes and underground artists to a real live international star. They were ready on their end, and, with Jamie's connections, the video link had been connected with the encrypted Skype technology so Jamie could dial Wendy at the designated time.

He had faxed a list of questions to her, and, to get the exclusive, she had agreed to stick to the script. They would broadcast for ten minutes, then fade to black.

The interview went off without a hitch. Wendy did her part flawlessly, and Jamie provided his rehearsed, yet charming responses. Tru was up in the cut, wearing a hat that provided coverage for her face, but let everyone see that she was a real, live, breathing person.

After greeting them and her audience, Wendy went into her spiel. "So, tell me, Jamie, how did you find this new talent? Come on, you can tell me."

Jamie smiled. "I actually heard her on YouTube, just like everybody else, and was blown away."

"Right, right," Wendy said. "Kudos to YouTube. Now, Ms. Tru. Tru Talent. Is that your real name?"

Cam laughed and dug into her thick B-More accent. "Naw, Wendy. But, that's what I am. Tru Talent."

Everyone in the studio broke up at that, and even Wendy chuckled. "I hear you, sister. Is that a Baltimore accent I'm hearing?"

"Yes, ma'am," Cam said.

"Now, Wendy, you know I told you we're not going to discuss a lot about Tru's background. There's plenty of time later for all that. We're just here to set the record straight. To stop the rumors about my new protégée."

"Straight? You, Jamie? Really? Right. Okay, 'how you doin.' But that's for another time. We really want to know about Ms. Tru, Jamie. Being an enigma and a big secret is part of her draw, but so is that voice of hers. We want to know who she is. Where she's coming from. Come on Jamie, share."

"I'll share this, Wendy," Jamie allowed. "Tru is the real deal. And I'm going to do all I can to promote her, and get her put on so that the world can see her gifts. That's what I want to share."

"An' I want to share this," Cam said, standing up and taking a cordless mic from one of the crew. B. Real started the track, and Cam, or Tru

Talent, belted out *Trick Bag*, putting every rumor about her talent or existence to rest.

After the performance, Jamie, energized and getting calls about his new client from all over the world, flew to New York to continue fanning the flames of interest. Cam, however, was drained. She found the low of the previous night and the high of performing difficult to assimiliate. Jamie told her to lay low, play her position, and finish tying up her loose ends.

And she had plenty of loose ends to tie up. In his message, her father tipped her that Typhoon was in the McCreary Penitentiary in Kentucky. She had to get to him to let him know that Heywood was cooking his books. Her father said he'd try to get the word to Typhoon through his jailhouse connects, but she still needed to provide proof. The proof from Heywood's ledgers.

How was she going to get those to him? Cam knew her traveling and disappearing days were over. She could never go to Kentucky, especially with Randolph now clocking her every move. And, even if she could go, she could never get on Typhoon's vistor's list and she didn't want to. Her father had warned her that Typhoon was being watched by the Feds. Then it dawned on her. She remembered reading in the rules and regulations for visiting Federal prisons that only clergy and attorneys were allowed to see prisoners at will. While she couldn't get anyone to play his attorney, she could get someone to play a clergy member. That someone had to be Aunt Mary. And that was going to be a very hard sell.

chapter forty: side b

TRU'S APPEARANCE on YouTube and the Wendy Williams Show created a firestorm. Jamie's phone rang off the hook, and his voicemail was maxed out. Labels were sniffing around to try to get their hooks into the next best thing. Jamie told Cam he felt like they were in a shark tank, and she was the meat. Everyone wanted a piece of her.

Everyone but Noah. Convincing him to take on Tru hadn't been easy. Jamie called and called, pushing him to get back in the game, injured or not. He was a warrior, and Tru was going to take him to the winner's circle, no doubt. Noah was reticent at first, but Jamie could sense that he was becoming more intrigued every time he called. When Noah finally agreed to come to New York to meet Tru, Jamie was ecstatic.

Ensconced at the Waldorf Astoria, Jamie's rooms looked like command central. Que had rented or purchased computers, flip charts, telephones, fax machines, and copiers, and one or both men were working the phones constantly.

"Jamie!" Que called excitedly, holding his hand over the handset. "You'll never guess who's trying to reach you."

"Who?" asked Jamie. He had already gotten calls from publicists, agents, producers, and even record execs. Que had screened them all, but had never acted like this.

"It's Kennard Heywood, Jamie. His rep's on the phone, and Heywood wants to holla at you."

★

Heywood had no choice. He hated even the idea of calling Jamie, but he had exhausted every other option. He wanted Tru, but couldn't get any information on her. Even with all his sources, he couldn't find out which studio she had broadcast from, and that bitch Wendy Williams wasn't giving up anything. Mad and frustrated, he was blocked at every turn. Jamie was it. His only avenue to Tru, so he had to go down that road. He decided to play it cool, and not let Jamie know where he was coming from.

"Hello," Jamie said, not trying too hard to mask his gloating. "This is Jamie."

"Yo, Jamie man, this is Heywood. What it do?"

"Excuse me?" Jamie said, and tried not to laugh. He could tell Heywood was trying not to black.

"Yo, Jamie. Let's talk. Real talk. I wanna know whassup up wit' yo' new artist."

"Who?" Jamie put his hand over the handset and tried to control himself.

Surprisingly, Heywood kept his calm. "Tru. Tru Talent. I heard her, son, an' she's really got some chops. I'm really feelin' her, an' I wanna see if we can make some moves."

"Make some moves like what, Heywood?"

"Like gettin' her signed to Kennetic Records."

"Well, Heywood, that sounds interesting, but lots of labels are interested in Tru. My phone hasn't stopped ringing. What are you offering that these others aren't?"

"I can make her a star, baby. Ya know how I do."

"Exactly, I know how you do. And I don't want that done to her. Hell, I have a lot of options to consider. My boy Noah's interested in her too, and he's willing to let me continue working with her. And keep a stake in her."

Heywood sucked his teeth. *How dare this mutha fucka try to play me,* Heywood thought. "Oh, so ya tryna get in the game, too, huh Jamie? Ya tryna run with the big dawgs or what? Well, I don't know if ya boy Noah's gonna be able to help ya out on this one. Rumor has it, he ain't tryna stick around too tough."

"Rumor has it, huh? Well, I have it on good authority that if he lands Tru, he could give a shit about rumors or anything else. He'll be on top, showing everyone who's really running things in the industry."

"Yeah, yeah, well, that sounds like a nice dream, but I'm dealin' wit' reality. Now, ya can sell yo' girl on a dream, or ya can give her some reality. Kennetic Records can do that, believe that. If ya can prove she can really sing."

"Didn't her performance the other night prove that? I'm sure you caught it. The girl can blow."

"Yeah, I saw bits an' pieces. I want to see the real thing."

"No can do, Heywood. That's part of the appeal. No one's seeing Tru until the time's right. Part of her allure. It's our marketing strategy. Don't you see how the public is just eating this up? Waiting to find out more, to hear more?"

The cash register in Heywood's head rang. "Yeah, as long as she ain't anotha Milli Vanilli. I don't purchase nothin' sight unseen. That ain't gonna happen."

Jamie shrugged. "Then I guess it won't happen then, because that's the only way it's going down. Trust me, when it comes to folks being interested, I'm not getting any static from anyone else over the concept."

"Whateva, Jamie. This betta not be some fuckin' bullshit, ya heard?"

"So, what are you saying, Heywood?"

Heywood gritted his teeth. "I'm sayin', ya play ball with me, an' I'll make it worth ya while." Jamie pressed him on just how much worth was his while. "I'll, uh, I'll give ya two million cash up front, if ya can deliver her to me."

Jamie blew through his lips. "Pu-lease, is that all? What about Tru?"

"Aiight, aiight," Heywood said. "I tell ya what, I got an idea. Let's make her debut a phenomenon. It'll be so big that *Cirque de Soleil* will look like some grade school production. Ain't nobody gonna be able to top it in years to come, ya heard?

"It'll be an international, pay-per-view concert. On New Year's Eve. Get her the right songs, the right production, get her the right hype, man, we'll sell the fuck out. Then we can get a big tour scheduled, an' make sure she hits all the big markets."

"Hmmm," Jamie mused. "Whoa, pump your brakes on the tour talk, Big Baller. Let's get this debut nailed down first. Now, the way I see it, two mil ain't gonna be nothin' but a drop in the bucket for you. Tell you what, I'll consider having Tru do the concert, if you give me five mil cash, have a lineup that can bring it, then we'll have Tru close the show, got it?"

Heywood took major issue with taking direction from the likes of Jamie, but he knew he'd make that $5M back on the sponsorship alone. Not to mention that he'd get ten-fold from the sales. "I'll think about it," Heywood said.

"And I want ten percent on the back end. And if Tru's going to head-line, then I want on the bill too. I have to be the act right before she comes on."

Heywood snorted. "Yeah, okay, Jamie. Sound like you might be dreamin' now. So, if ya want all this, ya gotta give me somethin'. Tell me, who ya workin' with?"

Now it was Jamie's turn to snort. "Now, now, Heywood. You know better than that. Until we have a deal, you'll never know. Believe that."

"I'll get back at ya in twenty-four, Jamie. Real talk," Heywood said, and clicked off his phone.

chapter forty-one

AUNT MARY'S knees were knocking as she walked through the vistor's gate at the McCreary correctional facility, clutching her bible and toting a bag of smaller bibles to distribute to prisoners. It had taken Cam almost a week to convince her aunt to make the trip, practically begging her to do what she could not do herself.

She felt awful asking her aunt, the poor thing had been through so much because of her, but she had no one else to turn to. Aunt Mary had been stubborn as a mule. Even after Cam told her how Carlos had come through for her, she still wouldn't budge. Cam had tried every avenue she could think of. She appealed to her Christianity, her humanity. Nothing worked. She talked about her mother, Faith, but got nothing. Finally, Cam had to roll the tears of desperation. There was no one else she could trust. That did it. Aunt Mary agreed to go. She had never been able to say no to Cam, and she didn't now. Cam thanked God she had been blessed with a guardian angel like Aunt Mary.

But Aunt Mary didn't agree easily. She had never flown, and didn't want to. But, catching the bus or being driven to Kentucky wasn't an option. It would take far too much time, and time was of the essence. Finally, Aunt Mary agreed, and Cam tried to prepare her for what she needed to do.

Through his connections of cons and guards on the take, Carlos had gotten word to Typhoon that Heywood was playing him, and that Kevin was in on it. Knowing that Typhoon wouldn't believe just any information coming through the jailhouse pipeline, Carlos promised to send irrefutable evidence, as soon as Typhoon got a little religion from the Saints of St. Mary's Baptist Church.

Yes, there was no such place of worship, but they agreed that Aunt Mary should use a fictional name so that her real church would not be associated with Typhoon. So, she donned her black skirt suit and missionary cap and Cam hooked her up with one of the churches who regularly visited McCreary. Once her name was added to the missionary list and to Typhoon's visitor's list, it was just a matter of waiting until she could get up enough nerve to make the trip.

When she landed, the other missionaries met her at the airport and accompanied her to the prison. They knew the drill and security routine, but the sheltered Aunt Mary was shook. It took her a few moments, and a lot of prayers, to ready herself for the visit.

But, she did it. After the guards checked her bags, and even the bibles for drugs and weapons, she passed out the small bibles to the other missionaries, keeping the large one for Typhoon.

The missionaries were led into a fairly large room ringed with guards. Several tables and chairs had been set up in the middle, occupied by the inmates who had been waiting for them. After introducing themselves, the missionaries sang a few gospel songs, read a few bible verses, and prayed. At the end of the prayer service, each of the inmates, under the watchful eye of the guards, had an opportunity to speak privately with the missionaries. And Aunt Mary spoke to Typhoon.

"Hello, Miss Mary," said a fully bearded Typhoon, now graying at the temples. A ruggedly handsome man, his milk chocolate face was still smooth, and he still had the air of authority, even in his prison jumpsuit. He was unable to extend his hand to her because he was shackled, hands and feet, to the table where he was sitting, so he nodded courteously.

"Hello, Tyrone," Aunt Mary said, returning the nod.

"I understand you have somethin' for me," he said.

She handed him the bible across the table, his arms only able to extend so far. "I do. It's the good book, and instruction on how to read it. That's what I'd like for you to do. Read it, and really focus on the Book of Psalms. I hope you'll find strength and knowledge there." There was measured caution in her voice.

"I thank you, Miss Mary. And I want to tell you that I'm sorry about Faith. I didn't have anything to do with her passin', ma'am. I promise you."

Mary took a deep breath, and nodded. "Maybe not directly, son. But you know in your heart that by your acts, deeds or direction, others have been hurt. Some innocent, some not. But, I'm not here to judge you or condemn you. I'll pray for you, but you need to ask the Lord to forgive you."

"But will you?" he asked, as he stretched his fingers out toward her, and pointed the bible reader at her. "And will He?"

"I already have and so has He," Aunt Mary said, as she stood and started collecting her things. "Now, you just have to forgive yourself. And try to redeem yourself. And you can start by taking responsibility for your actions. And if you have the opportunity, try to do the right thing. Right the wrongs you have done."

That evening, in the solitude of his cell, Typhoon opened the bible, specifically the Book of Psalms. Neatly glued in the pages of that chapter were several copied pages of ledgers, with entries that clearly showed that Heywood was gypping him. Ripping him off. And proof positive that the forked-tongue Kevin was in collusion with him.

chapter forty-two

SHE FOLDED the clothes and carefully placed them in her oversized checkered dollar store tote bag. Doing laundry was the only way she could get out of the house when Randolph was around without raising too much suspicion. They were leaving soon to visit Randolph's parents, and he had taken his car to the service station to get it checked out before they hit the road.

Cam had a lot to do while her laundry was running through the cycles. She had to check her messages and return phone calls. On her list were Jamie, Aunt Mary, B. Real, and her father.

Jamie's message had been urgent; he wanted her to call as soon as possible. Aunt Mary let her know that she had just returned from her mission, and that everything had gone well. Her father had just checked in, letting her know that the chickens were coming home to roost. Apparently, Typhoon was going to handle things on his end.

She returned Jamie's call, and learned that he and Que had hired another assistant just to work the Tru inquiries and media attention. They had a website up, TruTalent4Real.com, with just her silhouette, a snippet of her song, and the words, "TRU… BELIEVE… Coming Soon." The site, stoking the fires of intrigue, was becoming a viral sensation.

The number of daily hits was off the charts.

Jamie also told her about Heywood's call and his sneaky offer, and her wheels started spinning like the commercial dryers in the laundromat. She didn't want to get anywhere near Heywood or his business again, and needed Jamie to convince her.

Jamie was back in Cali, chilling poolside at Gary's Malibu beachhouse, and basking in the warm, nearly tropical weather.

"Jamie, I don't know. How can I appear on television, pay-per-view, for Heywood? I don't think I can do that."

"Cam, you gotta do it. It'll work out. You got your face, and I'll make sure that you're deep with security. I'm not going to let him even get close to you."

"That's what you say, Jay. But I know Heywood. You're going to have to keep everything under wraps. Otherwise, he'll be all in it. He's a master control freak, you know."

"I know, but I got this, Cam. Trust me, I know how Heywood makes his moves. I'll make sure he won't even see you until the last minute. And if he tries to strong-arm me, I'll pull out and mess up his rep. And he doesn't want that to happen."

She wasn't convinced. "You know he'll start following you. He'll put people on you."

"And I'll give him a show. But my show is not going to include you. I'll run their asses ragged trying to keep up with me. And all the while, you'll be doing your thing. Trust me, I got your producer and studio and their crew on lock. Nobody's going to say anything. This is their chance to get put on. They want to work with you. They'd be fools to ruin this opportunity to bubble by talking. No doubt.

"So now, really, all we have to do is work on the music. Trust me, we have your boy right where he needs to be. Thinking he's in control, but really getting controlled."

Jamie continued, telling her about the money, and how Heywood had called and pretty much offered the moon if he could sign Tru. Cam removed her last load of clothes from the dryer, and started folding.

"That's what I'm afraid of, Jamie. Heywood'll do just about anything to get what he wants. He's already done that."

She knew it wasn't going to be that easy, and for Jamie's sake, she still hadn't told him everything that she had learned about Heywood or how she had learned it. She had to protect herself and Jamie. If he knew everything about Heywood's connection to her mother's death, Typhoon, and those sordid videos, she didn't know what Jamie would do. And she didn't want to take any chances.

After she agreed to take Heywood's offer, Jamie told her that Noah, while extremely leery of working with Heywood, was down for the plan. She told Jamie not to worry, that she had Noah's back. Jamie pressed her, but she refused to tell him what she was talking about. No one would ever know. Since it looked like she and Noah wouldn't get a chance to meet, she decided to drop the envelope in her backpack at the FedEx counter on her way home. Already addressed to Noah at his home address, the envelope contained the video and the following note: "Enclosed is the only copy. You no longer have to fear retribution. From a Tru Believer."

"This is wonderful, Randolph," she said, as his sporty British Green BMW 540i tooled through the picturesque Pennsylvania countryside. The warm colors of fall caressed the roadway, and with Lalah Hathaway playing in the background, she was feeling relaxed and in a comfortable space. Though her nerves were still frayed, she and Randolph were finally on their way to the Poconos for Thanksgiving with his parents.

Today, she was feeling upbeat. Still raw from the aftermath of her trip to DC, she had focused on their relationship over the past weeks, making it her number one priority. With Jamie taking over the logistics of Tru, Cam could afford to slip back into the role of devoted fiancé, a role she treasured. She made a point of being present, not only in body, but in mind and emotion. She was home whenever Randolph was, planned romantic afternoons and evenings, made his favorite foods, and loved him. Randolph more than deserved the attention, and he reveled in it.

Cam knew she wouldn't be able to keep this schedule up for long, as the New Year's concert was approaching and she had to work on her music, but, as always, timing was everything. She would be able to use the upcoming holiday season as a pretense for her absences, and knew Randolph would understand. She only hoped he would be as understanding after the concert.

Randolph's mother had agreed to keep their Thanksgiving dinner small, immediate family only, so her future daughter-in-law wouldn't be overwhelmed. Only his parents and sister would be there. However, even that had given Cam pause. Randolph had mentioned that Robin was a free spirit, a hip-hop head, and Cam was terrified she might recognize her. It was a stretch, but it was possible. Cam said her prayers anyway, and hoped that her concerns would be for naught.

And her prayers were answered. She thanked God when she heard that Robin had a last minute change of plans, deciding to spend Thanksgiving in South Beach with friends. Randolph was disappointed, but at the end, all Cam had to do was speak with Robin on the phone, and they had a nice, if stilted, conversation.

Their visit with the Williamses was very pleasant, and they graciously accepted her into their lives. Cam felt genuinely sorry for putting Randolph's parents off for as long as she had. Randolph's mother Pat was kind and endearing and treated her like a daughter. His father Frank was a larger, grayer version of Randolph, with a big hearty laugh. Upon meeting his future daughter-in-law, he gave his son the head nod of approval, and gave her a warm fatherly hug.

After helping Randolph's mother clean up after their delectable holiday meal, everyone sat comfortably around a roaring fireplace, sipping coffee, while Randolph's parents entertained her with stories of his childhood.

Being around a functional family unit was something she had never experienced, in any of her identities. After meeting his parents and looking through all of the family albums and momentos, she appreciated Randolph even more. She could clearly see where he acquired his morals and strong character. And even though no one was perfect, and the Williamses didn't pretend to be, they were a family unit who loved and cared about each other, flaws and all. And that was as near to perfection as she had ever seen. Being around them made her feel loved and secure. And gave her an idea as to how she would really want to live her life, if given a chance.

She actually hated leaving them, and clung to her future in-laws as they loaded up the Beamer with luggage and foil-wrapped leftovers. Randolph was quiet on the way home, at a happy peace, content and proud that his family approved of his future wife.

Cam was quiet also, contemplating and deep in thought. She made a difficult decision; she made a promise to herself that she would not break or negotiate. She would not enter into the New Year with lies in her heart or on her tongue. Whatever had to be done was going to get done this year, and she was going to get all of her issues resolved immediately after the New Year's concert. If they weren't resolved, she would just accept them and move on. No more lies. No more deception.

She realized that she was making a major commitment to herself. A commitment that was contingent upon variables that were out of her control. But she was going to do what she had to do. Now that all of the plans had been set into the motion, and the major players given their marching orders, she was determined to take back her life, effective January 1, 2009. And she meant that.

She had already accepted that she had no concrete proof that Heywood had orchestrated her death. However, she did have proof that he was involved in and had avoided punishment for many other horrible acts. She didn't want his blood on her hands, but she had folks involved who could make things happen. And if they did, then so be it. The chips were going to fall where they may, and her conscience would be clear.

Jamie was working it out for her, baiting Heywood and keeping Tru's name on the tip of everyone's tongue. On a handshake, Heywood had agreed to give Jamie the $5M on the night of the concert, if he could additionally guarantee that Noah would be front and center. Heywood wanted to watch Noah's face when they announced that Tru was signing with Kennetic Records. Check.

Her father was still doing his thing. Check. Typhoon had been given everything he needed to do his thing. Check. Noah had regained his footing, and was working out what he needed to do. Check. Rashad was amping Tru, promoting her beyond their wildest imaginations. Check. The concert was going to be held at Madison Square Garden, and attendance at the pay-per-view special had sold out in less than 20 minutes. Sponsorship had reached record rates. Check. The number of subscribers who had pre-paid for the event had reached astronomic proportions. Check, check, check. It was all working out.

★

After Thanksgiving, Cam was back on her hustle and grind. Randolph was extremely busy at the hospital, and she was able to get her production on. Still working closely with B. Real and select members of Jamie's production team, she was able to put the finishing touches on the songs she would sing at the concert.

Between Thanksgiving and Christmas, she logged countless hours finalizing the intricate details of the concert and its production. She and Jamie selected the songs and their arrangements, in addition to working the band, choreography, stage, and set design. No expense was spared. The set actually included a replica of the Times Square ball drop. Jamie also added extra personal security, extra venue security, and extra EMT personnel.

To keep everything top secret, Jamie practiced with the dancers separate from her, for she couldn't wear her prosthetic and perform the routine. She learned it alone first, then, when she joined the dancers, performed in front of a well-placed screen.

Jamie's stylists worked out her outfits, finding the hottest hats and matching ensembles from the best designers and labels. It was both daunting and thrilling to find herself back in the groove and better than ever before. As her deadline loomed, Cam was a virtual machine of efficiency; checking and re-checking every step of her plan.

She had a few specific requests for Jamie, mainly that he make sure that Rashad was there, and that he bring most of her old crew back, including Billy, her lighting technician, Sonya, her backup singer, and Big Mac. She wished she could look forward to finding Necy, Torrie, and Allison in her dressing room backstage, but those days were over, at least for this concert. Even loving them as much as she did, she couldn't take the chance that Necy and Torrie had taken Allison's path and joined Heywood's camp.

Amidst the concert preparations, she planned and executed a quiet, romantic, drama-free Christmas celebration just for the two of them.

Although it wasn't their first Christmas together, it was the first time she would have to make it special. They bought and decorated their first Christmas tree, attended church together, talked to Randolph's parents and Robin on the phone, and opened presents. It even snowed, and was a lovely day, one for the memory books. Cam hoped it was the first in a long lifetime of special Christmases with him in their own home.

Since Randolph was scheduled to work over New Year's, she told him that, if he wouldn't mind, she wanted to go to DC to visit her cousin's children. She would leave early enough during the day on New Year's Eve to avoid the crowds, take the children to church, stay in a downtown hotel, and travel back on New Year's Day. He agreed; he realized that her family was important to her, and he was glad that she realized that it was important to him that she share with him.

With Christmas over, the next few days were a blur. Jamie was again in Philly, posted up at the Four Seasons, commanding every moment of her time. He wanted a flawless execution, and they practiced and rehearsed until she was ready to drop from exhaustion. Their mutual quest for perfection reached a level of nirvana.

The day before New Year's Eve, they met one last time to run through their set. Pleased with the final production, at the end of the rehearsal, they held hands and prayed. It was a seasoned performer's ritual. There were no rehearsals the day before the show. You rested and got your head right, and the next time you stepped foot on the stage was for your sound check.

Cam and Jamie reviewed their plans for the last time, confirming all times and logistics. The drop-offs, hand-offs and pick-ups. They even had a Plan B, just in case things went south. Jamie was going back to the Waldorf, and his road crew was going to handle the equipment and set-up at The Garden. Jamie had arranged for a car and bodyguard to pick her up at the studio at noon, and deliver her to the Waldorf's back entrance, where she would chill in his suite until the performance.

Jamie would handle the sound check at four, keeping her away from The Garden, and then they would come together to the concert. He had already spoken to the hotel concierge and manager about the specifics. When they left for the concert, they would also leave from the back entrance. Jamie had hired look-a-likes who would make their grand exit from the front entrance at the same time they would be making their get-away in the back. It was a perfectly plausible plan, and a great way to engage the paparazzi.

They hugged and parted company. Cam made her way back to the apartment, iPod® in her ear, vibing with her concert playlist. She arrived home, completely drained, but excited. After grabbing an orange, she took a quick shower, changed into sweats, and fell fast asleep into a deep slumber.

Soon, however, her nap was interrupted by sounds coming through the bedroom door. Sounds of Randolph and another woman.

chapter forty-three

SHE SCRUNCHED her nose, wiped the sleep from her mouth and eyes, and then glanced at the clock. It was 10:45 p.m. She blinked. *I must be dreaming,* she thought. *Why would he bring someone home at this hour? Who could he be talking to?*

The floors creaked, so she couldn't just jump out of the bed, but she strained her ears to hear what they were saying.

The woman laughed, a big throaty laugh, and Cam heard Randolph chuckle. She listened to the sound of ice clinking into glasses, and then to the stereo, which was tuned to a local hip-hop channel, Power 99 FM.

"*Shh,* turn that down," Randolph said. "I told you, Marisol's asleep in there."

Oh God. Is he having an affair? No way, she rationalized. What the hell was going on?

"Robin, just turn it down. She's tired."

Uh-oh, Cam thought. *It has to be his sister, Robin. Unbelievable.*

"Oh, okay, Randy," she said, her voice carrying under the door. "What's she doing asleep now? It's only ten-thirty. Damn. You said she wasn't working, so what's she doing to be so tired? Sexin' you down 24/7?" She continued talking, but Cam couldn't decipher her words.

With the stereo up, she cautiously crept across the floor, and pressed her ear against the door.

"She's probably tired from working out," he said, pointing to her gym bag. "See that? That's a gym bag. You know, that's what you use when you spend time in the gym."

"Whatever. Why couldn't you have gotten with somebody with a little flavor? You go all the way down to the islands and bring back an old dry piece who's asleep at ten-thirty. What kinda shit is that? You supposed to come back with a bangin' broad, one of those hot, fiery island gals," she said, popping her fingers. "Hell, you could've got a tired church girl right here. You didn't have to import her. And you certainly didn't have to sponsor her." She took a long drink from her glass.

"That's enough, Robin."

"That's enough," she mocked him. "When am I going to meet her? I stopped through just to meet her, you know."

"I know you lie. The only reason you stopped here is because you were on your way to New York, and you didn't want to spend money on a hotel room for two nights."

Robin took another sip. "Okay, you got me. But, you know I'm just a struggling teacher. And I can't help it if my funds are limited. By the way, you think you can help a sista out? Break me off a couple of dollars?"

"Yeah, I can break you off some free advice. First off, no one told you to spend an arm and a leg going to New York, Robin," Randolph said, sounding like the older brother that he wasn't.

"You wouldn't understand. This concert is history in the making. An event like this happens once in a lifetime, and I wasn't about to miss it."

"Yeah, you're right, I wouldn't understand. I don't know why you would spend that kind of money on a concert, of all things, particularly when you don't have it."

"Because, knucklehead, this chick Tru Talent is the bomb. I know you don't know anything about that, but get with the program. She's the next best thing, you'd better recognize.

"So, go in there and wake your girl up. She can always go back to sleep. I want to meet her now, because I've got to rise and shine in the morning, so I can get my hair done in New York before the concert. One of my girlfriends from Atlanta swears by the Dominicans, and I can't wait to see what they can do with this mess. So, I've got to be out of here and in the cut before that traffic gets crazy."

Cam jumped, and scampered back into bed. *Oh shit,* Cam thought, *She's going to the concert. My concert.* Suddenly, she had to use the bathroom, but couldn't with Robin out there. Her heart started palpitating. What was she going to do?

Thankfully, Randolph stood his ground and did not wake her up. She waited until he came to bed and fell asleep. And then, just to be sure, she waited even longer for Robin to fall asleep on the sofa. Unable to hold it any longer, Cam slipped out of bed, and tiptoed over to the door. When she heard Robin snoring, she quietly opened the door, and dashed over to the bathroom, keeping the light off while she did her business.

Relieved, she hesitated before she flushed. She didn't want to, because it might wake Robin, but she could not flush, either. She sighed and pulled the handle, and quickly rinsed her hands. Then she waited to see if she had disturbed her future sister-in-law.

She tiptoed back across the room, reaching the door without making a sound.

"Hey girl," Robin's groggy voice called from the couch. She sat up and looked at Cam in the darkness. Cam hesitated, more worried about being discovered than ever. She figured she might be okay, as long as Robin didn't turn on the lights.

"Hey Robin," she responded, laying her island accent on extra thick as she slowly turned her head. "Welcome. I thought that might be you."

Robin reached for the lamp, but Cam quickly waved her hand. "No, no don't do that. Please don't turn on the light. I didn't mean to wake you up. We can speak in the mornin', okay?"

Robin yawned, her wild curly mane stretching out in every direction, and fell back on her pillow.

"Okay, cool, see you in the morning."

"Goodnight," Cam said, and hurried through the bedroom doorway.

"Yeah, goodnight. And y'all try to keep it down in there. It's not proper etiquette to be screwing in a one bedroom apartment with paper thin walls. Trust me, I know," Robin said

Cam closed the door, and slid back into bed. Randolph turned over and threw his arm around her waist. "So, you met my big sis, huh?" he asked, nuzzling his face into her neck.

Yeah, I met Robin, all right, she thought. *The problem is, I don't want her to meet me.*

★

Once again, her guardian angels were out in full force. Both Robin and Randolph rose early the next morning and left while she played possum. He had to report to the hospital for his double shift, and she overheard Robin say that she was getting an early start on her road trip to New York.

Oh well, Cam thought. *I'll have to try extra hard next time I see her. Robin probably thinks I'm a lazy broad, sleeping 20 hours a day and marrying Randolph just to get a green card. What a horrible first impression. Oh well.*

Free to get her day going, Cam grabbed the notebook from her gym bag, placed the empty glasses into the dishwasher, and tossed Robin's linens into the laundry basket. She was ready to review the day's plans. It was after 8:00, and she needed to store this bag, pack an overnight bag for her pretend trip to DC, and make sure she didn't leave any evidence behind.

There was a rap on the door. Not expecting anyone, she quietly walked over and peered through the peephole. It was Robin, talking on her cellphone.

Cam panicked, and started backing away from the door. She couldn't pretend not to be there, for Robin had just left. She ran into the bathroom and called out, "Who is it?"

"It's me, Robin."

Uh-oh, Cam thought, *she sounds irritated.* Cam scrambled under the bathroom sink, looking for something. "Oh, Robin. I'm sorry! I'll be right there," she called out, pulling out her faithful jar of cold cream, and slathering some on her face.

Collecting her nerves and throwing on her robe, she took a deep breath and walked back to the front door and opened it. Robin's eyes bucked when she saw her. "I'm sorry, Robin. I was in the bathroom."

"*Hmmph*, you sure do spend a lot of time in there," she said, her voice frosty as she brushed past her with her luggage. She dropped her bags and immediately collapsed on the sofa. She sighed. "Jesus, I need a drink." She typed in a quick text on her phone, and glanced at Cam.

"Sorry 'bout that," Cam said. "What happened?" she asked, eyeing Robin's bags. *Oh no,* she thought. *What the hell am I going to do now?*

Robin stretched, stripped off her Banana Republic wool coat, and then flung her feet onto the sofa. "My car got towed. That damned Philadelphia Parking Authority. Then, I go to the impound lot, dragging this big-assed bag, and they try to hit me up for almost $400 worth of charges." Her phone chirped, and she glanced at the screen.

Multi-tasking, she fired off a text message while still speaking to Cam. "Somethin' about old parking tickets. Some old bullshit. Whatever, I'm not paying it. I don't have the money, and I paged Randy, but of course he didn't respond. I can't get my car, so I don't know what I'm going to do."

Cam thought about offering her the money, but then she knew that both Randolph and Robin would question why she had $400 in cash. Forget it. It would create even more questions about her. She would still have to leave, using her DC trip as an excuse, but didn't want to have to deal with Robin until she made her getaway.

"That's really unfortunate, Robin. I know how much you were lookin' forward to your trip."

Robin eyed her suspiciously. "How'd you know?"

"Um, Randy told me," Cam said. *Oh boy, I really have to get away from this chick.*

"Well, if I don't hear from Randy soon, I may take the Chinatown bus. It's only $25 each way, and I can swing that until brother man comes through. Yeah, that's what I'll do," she said, and sat up. "I just need to let my peoples in New York know that my plans have changed." She fired off another text. "So, now that I've got that settled, I think I'll have that drink."

Climbing off the sofa, she sashayed into the kitchen, opened the freezer door, and reached in. She removed a half-empty bottle Absolut

Vodka, and poured some in a glass from the dish strainer. She offered Cam a drink, but she declined.

"Y'all have any juice? OJ or grapefruit? It doesn't matter." She opened the refrigerator door and removed a small carton of orange juice. "Ahh," she exhaled. "The breakfast of champions."

Cam watched in silence as Robin fixed and sipped her drink. After a few swallows, she changed the focus from her drink to Cam.

"So, Marisol, we finally get a chance to chat for real. Not just those little pleasantries we share on the phone" She walked back over to the sofa, and plopped down. She patted the seat beside her. "Why don't you sit down and tell me all about yourself?" Her cellphone chirped again, and she looked at the screen. This time she didn't respond.

Cam checked the wall clock and almost groaned. It was approaching 9:00 a.m., and she had done nothing. "Well, I, uh, I'd really like to do that, Robin. But, I don't know if Randolph told you, but I'm, uh, gettin' ready for a trip to DC. To see me relatives for the holiday."

Again, Robin patted the seat beside her. "I think you have time. I know I do. That bus runs every hour on the hour, so I won't miss one. And I'm sure you can get another train if you need to. Why don't you run in there and get that junk off of your face so we can talk?"

"I have to keep the cold cream on me face for a while every day. My skin's still recoverin' from the burns," Cam lied.

"Oh, I'm sorry. Randy said they were pretty bad," Robin said off-handedly.

Robin looked at Cam's ring and commented. She asked about her past, about their wedding, and about their plans for the future. She grilled her, and Cam knew that if she was in Robin's shoes, she would act the same way. She would want to know who this mystery woman was. But then again, she could tell Robin was suspicious by her tone and questions. She really tried not to be upset about the questions. But she was upset about the time slipping by.

At 10:00, Cam decided enough was enough. Robin's time was up.

"Well, um, Robin. I hate to have to interrupt, an' I wish we had more time, but I really have to get goin'. My cousins are expectin' me, an' wit' the holiday an' all, the trains are sold out," she lied. But, this time, it didn't bother her.

Robin sighed. "Oh that's right. I forgot about the holiday. Jeez, I hope the buses aren't sold out. I hadn't even thought of that." She glanced at her cellphone. "Oh shit. I didn't know it was almost ten. I forgot about my hair appointment. I need to get my ass to New York so I can get my wig tightened."

She reached for her purse and removed her cellphone. "Okay, I've got to make a few calls, Marisol. Book this bus ride an' what not. And see if I can slide my appointment. So," she said standing and giving her a weak hug, "I'll probably be outta here by the time you get out of the bathroom." She checked her shoulders to make sure Cam hadn't gotten any of her cosmetics on her.

"Okay, Robin. It was nice finally meetin' you," Cam said, and started walking toward the bathroom. She went inside, closed the door, and clutched the sink.

Robin stared at the closed bathroom door, and squinted her eyes. She made several phone calls, and decided to repack. Since she was not taking her own car, she would only take the essentials. Rolling her bags over to the window, next to Cam's gym bag, she quickly transferred several things from the larger bag to the smaller one.

With the sound of the shower running in the bathroom, she grabbed the handle of her suitcase, and turned to pick up her coat from the sofa. Her suitcase caught the strap of the Cam's gym bag. It tilted over, and the wedding notebook fell out. Robin reached down to unhook the bag, and noticed the cover on the book.

She glanced at the bathroom door, and slipped the book into her own bag. Putting the gym bag back where it had been, she called out, "See you later, Marisol," and grinned, practically running out of the apartment.

Certain that Robin was gone, Cam dressed in a flash, gathered her personal accessories, and tossed them into a small overnight bag. Her nerves were on a razor's edge. After countless months of sneaking and scheming, she was finally putting the final pieces of her puzzle together.

And the picture was being revealed. She was overwhelmed with the prospect of performing at such a huge venue after all these months. But it was in her blood. She lived to perform. And tonight would be the performance of her lifetime.

She had to get focused. Instead of getting her chi and meditation on, she had spent the morning being raked over the coals by Robin. But, now she had time to regroup. She was determined to get it together.

chapter forty-four

"YOU'RE MY attorney, an' I need to see you today."

Kevin cleared his throat, and scratched his head. He folded his arms over his stomach, which was churning uncontrollably, and started to rock back and forth. "Well, uh, Tyrone. It's New Year's Eve. I don't even know if I can get there today."

"Oh, you'll get here, Kevin. This is about my appeal. My freedom. One of the rats who testified against me is willin' to recant. So, I don't care if you have to flap your wings and fly like the bird you are. I don't give a fuck. All I know is that you betta be here today," Typhoon hung the phone up with a loud click.

It was after 9:00 a.m. on New Year's Eve, and Typhoon was summoning him to Kentucky. And he was mad. For some reason, Kevin didn't think a witness was recanting. It just seemed a little off because normally, Typhoon let his other attorneys handle matters like this. But, with his money dried up, perhaps Kevin was his only resource. Maybe.

But, then again, maybe Typhoon was really angry about something else. Maybe, he had found out about Kevin feeding him Heywood's lies, or maybe Heywood had made good on his threat and set him up. He stood and started pacing around his filthy condo, kicking the discarded shoes, papers, and clothing that were in his path.

He reached for the pack of cigarettes on his cluttered kitchen table and cursed when he found it was empty. The weather in DC was threatening, and that would only make travel even more difficult.

No matter what, he had to go. After all, what could Typhoon really do to him from behind that glass? Even if Typhoon had the inside dope on Heywood, Kevin would just tell him the truth, then go underground if he had to. As he paced and scratched, he decided to check the flights, and make plans to disappear after his meeting with Typhoon.

"Yeah, girl. I'll holla at ya when I get to the Big Apple," Robin kee-keed into her cellphone, holding a McDonald's bag while she waited for the attendant to load her suitcase into the bottom of the bus. The terminal was crawling with people, early New Year's Eve celebrants who were getting a jump start on their liquid festivities before they even neared Times Square.

She huffed when she heard the announcement that the 11:00 bus to New York was running late. She sat with her feet on her suitcase, and folded her arms across her stomach. "This shit better hurry up and get here," she said to herself.

She finished off the Egg McMuffin, then reached into her purse and pulled out the notebook.

"Well, Little Miss Marisol. I guess you'll have to amuse me while I wait on that raggedy-assed bus to come. So, let's see what's really good with you," she said, and flipped open the pages.

chapter forty-five

"I'M SORRY, Jamie. It's all my fault. I've had a hell of a morning," Cam said, as she looked out the limousine window onto Schyukill Expressway, where traffic was almost at a standstill.

"Well, Miss Girl. Today is not the day for the drama," he said. "You had me worried sick about you. I didn't know what had happened."

"I know, I know," she said. She barely had time to get into her Tru Talent gear before meeting the bodyguard and limo at the studio.

It was after 1:00, and the weather was threatening snow, traffic was in a snarl, and she was stuck, over an hour away from New York.

"Well, don't sweat it," Jamie said. "We'll work it out. I've got everything under control here. Worse comes to worse, I'll just meet you at The Garden, aiight? We'll be good to go."

"Okay," she said. "I'll call you with my ETA when we get a better idea." She hung up, with her heart still racing. She needed to chill, so she reached in her gym bag and removed her iPod®. Something felt strange to her. "Oh my God. Where's my notebook?"

★

"Attention all passengers waiting for bus number 458, going to New York City.

It'll be arriving in ten minutes. Please prepare for boarding."

"Oh God, what the hell is this?" Robin said aloud, as she read the passages and entries in the notebook. She swallowed, and nudged the half-blitzed white guy who was sitting next to her. "Excuse me, but what did the announcer just say?'

"I dunno. I think he said somethin' about the bus to New York coming," he said, taking a sip from his flask.

"Fuck that," Robin said, reaching for her phone. She flipped through a few more pages of the book, and then quickly texted a 911 to Randolph. "I've got to get the hell outta here," she said, and dialed her brother's cellphone. "Listen, Randolph. This is an emergency. I need you to meet me at your house. Right now. I'm serious. Call me back, as soon as possible!"

"Robin, what the hell's going on? Is everyone all right? Is it Mom and Dad?"

When he hadn't returned her texts or phone calls, Robin had frantically called the hospital, requesting that Randolph be given a note in the operating room. Thankfully, he had just finished a procedure when he received the message, and as soon as he was able, he turned the patient over to the OR nurse. He had run out of the room, pulled off his mask, and called Robin on her cellphone.

"They're okay, Randy."

"Is it Marisol? Oh God, is she okay? What happened?" he asked, his hands shaking.

"Randy, I'm sorry, but I couldn't wait. You need to see somethin'." she said.

"See what, Robin? Do you realize I had to leave surgery? This better be important."

"Just come home, Randy. Just come home."

He slammed the door. "I need to see what, Robin?"

She held the wedding book toward him. "Are you out of your mind?

I was in surgery, for Christ's sake. And this is one of the busiest nights at the hospital. I hope you're not playing some kind of game, Robin."

She opened the book and shoved it in his face. "I'm not playing any games, but it looks like your girl is. Look at this."

chapter forty-six

"LOOK, JAMIE. I hear ya girl hasn't made it to the sound check yet. What the fuck's up wit' that?" Heywood was sitting in the barber's chair in his penthouse. He had just received the report from Duck, who was down at The Garden making sure Heywood's acts were doing what they were supposed to do, and being his eyes and ears.

Heywood was busy primping, getting ready to fulfill his duties hosting tonight's highly hyped and publicized event. Wearing only a wifebeater and boxers under the satin barber's cape, he eyed the Tag Heuer on his wrist as a flurry of personal attendants, including Allison, brought in wardrobe and accessory suggestions, and did his bidding.

"Yo, Jamie. It's after four, nigga. Ya betta not be tryna to play me close. This shit is ya ass."

Jamie was at The Garden, working out the final details for the performance, including the sound check. "She was never coming to the sound check, Heywood. Where'd you get that idea? Look, I got this. She doesn't need to worry about these little details, it's all good. Plus, I'm saving all of her energy for the concert. So, don't be beat about it, Heywood. She'll be there. You have my word."

"Ya word don't mean shit to me. This is my rep we're talkin' 'bout.

That's what's really good."

Jamie repeated what he had just said, and then added, "Just be sure to have your end of the deal, Heywood, because I'm gonna deliver what I promised. I want my ends."

Jamie hung up and called Cam. She was close, on the New Jersey Turnpike, getting ready to take the exit for the Lincoln Tunnel. "Good. I'll be back at the hotel in a few. Meet me there, girl," Jamie said. "Just like we planned."

Everything had gone as planned at the Waldorf, and they arrived on time at The Garden. She was in her full Tru regalia, and Jamie and their entourage surrounded her as she blew past Duck and the other Heywood people in a blur.

Duck immediately called Heywood to let him know Tru had arrived. "I'll be right there," Heywood said. "Just keep an eye on her."

Jamie whisked Cam into their extra large dressing room, and posted two mammoth bodyguards at the door with specific instructions not to let anyone in but Que.

"You okay, Miss Girl?" Jamie asked. He handed her a single rose. She grabbed him and hugged him, whispering, "Jamie, you remembered!" in his ear.

"Miss Girl, I can't tell you how happy I was to order that rose for you today. I never thought I'd be able to do that again."

"Jamie, do you know how many things you've made possible for me to do again? I can never, ever thank you enough." They released each other from their bear hug, and he grabbed her hands.

"The pleasure was all mine, Cam. And I mean that." Jamie lifted her hand up. "What, what's this?" He asked, pulling her hand toward his face.

"Oh damn, I forgot to take my ring off," Cam nearly shrieked. "Oh no."

"You're engaged? Say what? Why didn't you tell me?"

She tried to pull the ring off, but it wouldn't budge. "With so much going on, I just couldn't even think about it, Jamie. I'm sorry."

"Was that the something that was going on this morning?"

She nodded, and Jamie, shook his head. "Missy, you have too much goin' on right now. We'll talk about that ring later. Right now, put Miss Cam away so we can get Miss Tru together. It's her time to go out here and show out."

She made a fist and with one hand, and gripped it with the other. "I'm scared, Jamie. I really am. I don't think I've ever had stage fright before." She shook her fingers like they were cold.

"Don't worry, Baby Girl. It's gonna be alright," he said and then there was a knock on the door. One of the huge guards stuck his head in. "There's someone here from Mr. Heywood's team who wants to see you, Jamie."

Cam's eyes stretched and she gasped. Jamie, moving towards the door, patted her on the arm and winked. "Say a prayer, Baby Girl. I got this. I'll handle this."

"I don't know if I can handle this, Robin," Randolph said as he flipped through the pages of the Wedding Book. The pages were filled with new clippings, dates, times, names, events, everything. Everything related to this Camara or Starr. He was almost sick to his stomach.

Robin stroked his arm, and sighed. "I'm sorry about all this, Randy. But you needed to know. This is some crazy shit, right here. Who is this woman? And why does she have all of this shit on Starr? She's nuts."

"I don't even know who Starr is," he said quietly, staring blankly at the pages. "Who is she? And why would Marisol have all of this information on her?"

"I don't know, bro. But, from what you've told me, Marisol was burned around the same time Starr was in her accident. Maybe she knows somethin' more about it. Whatever it is, it's not cool. It seems a little scandalous to me."

"I can't believe this. I don't even know who Marisol is. I don't know what to believe. None of this sounds like her. I just need to call her," he said, and reached for his phone.

Robin snatched the phone from his hands. "There's no point, Randy. What are you going to say? We need to try to figure out all we can before she brings her ass back from DC. That is, if she really is in DC. Hell, for all we know, and from what you told me, she's probably holed up with that con out in Lewisburg. That's probably not even her cousin. I hate to say it, but it's probably her man." Robin curled her lips. "I tried to warn you not to fall for the first broad that put it on you."

Randolph sighed, tears of anger and hurt filling his eyes. Robin softened. "I'm sorry little brother. But, I'm here, and we'll figure it out. I mean, I hate to think that she put the Santoria on you just to get a green card, but it's looking pretty suspect right now. I'm sayin', I don't know if this chick is some psycho or murderer or a black widow or what, but if she was down there when Starr got killed, and she has information about it, then she needs to come clean. And come correct. And I'm going to stay with you until she does."

His eyes brightened, and he sniffed. "You'd do that for me?"

"Of course I would."

"But, what about your concert? I don't want you to miss that. Why don't you just go on, I'll be alright."

Robin's eyes glinted. "Look, you don't have to be back at the hospital until tomorrow night, right? And we need to get somewhere where we can really think this thing through. So, now, hear me out on this one. Why don't you and I go ahead and catch the train to New York? I'll miss my hair appointment, but so what? We'll talk on the ride up, and you won't be here looking at her stuff and getting all in your feelings because this is you all's little love nest."

"Robin, I can't do that. You know I don't like crowds like that. I can't go. I can't."

"Yes, you can. Listen, I'm your big sister, and I'm pulling rank. I say we go, comb through all this bullshit you've been going through since the voodoo doll, dame of darkness entered your life, and we'll figure her ass out. And have a better time in the process. You can even go to the concert with me. That'll really take your mind off things until you get back."

"The concert? I thought you said it was sold out?"

"You know how I do. A sista had some connects, and I had an extra ticket I was going to scalp. But, for you," she said, and tapped his hand, "I'll sell it to you for face value." She nudged him, and he tried to smile, but couldn't.

"Look, Randy. I know how serious this is for you. But, right now, I want to do what's best for you. And that's clearly not sitting here, waiting for her ass to come home. So come with me, and I won't take no for an answer."

"I don't want to ruin your holiday, Robin."

"You won't, because I won't let you. Your alternative is that we order the concert on Pay-Per-View, and you sit here with me until her ass comes home. But, I know you don't want to do that. So, it's a plan, right? We'll go through every page of this book and we'll do what we got to do when we get back tomorrow. We'll handle it, okay?"

chapter forty-seven

"PAY-PER-VIEW," Carlos said, as he slipped the guard two $100 bills through his cell door. "I want you to order that concert tonight for me an' a couple of my buddies. One note's for you, an' the other should cover the cable."

The guard shoved the money in his pants pocket and nodded. "Alright, Bonds. I'll be back for you after lights out."

"Lights out, Kevin," Typhoon said as he walked into the private visitors' area. Typhoon was seated at the long steel table. The area was monitored by the guards, but they couldn't listen to their confidential conversations.

"Huh?" Kevin said as he slid his briefcase onto the table. His brow was sweaty, his suit was wrinkled, and his shirt collar was soiled. "What do you mean?" He asked as he sat down across from his client.

"Just what I said, Kev," Typhoon said, holding the bible Aunt Mary had given him. "See, that's what they say when the day's over, time's up, it's a wrap. Lights out." His voice was even and deliberate.

"See, I've seen the light," he said, touching the bible. "It's come to my attention that you've had me on some real bullshit. Talkin' up an' cosignin' shit that just ain't true. Tellin' me my money was funny an' that the Feds were on to my overseas accounts. I just wanna know why you did it an' for how long?"

Kevin started stammering. "I, uh, well, it wasn't me, Ty. It was Heywood. It was his idea, not mine. He threatened me. I knew I shouldn't have, but it wasn't like I did anything to you. Really."

Typhoon stroked his chin and fingered his book. "Really? See, where I come from betrayal is worse than just about anything. I thought you knew. But, you know what? This book here has really enlightened me. I wanted to look in the eyes of my Judas, hear what you had to say, an' let you know that I know that I forgive you."

Kevin swallowed and blinked. "Are you, you serious, Ty?"

Typhoon stood up and smiled. "I do. In fact, I want you to have this," he said, and slid the book in front of Kevin. "Read it in peace," he said, and motioned for the guards to come and return him to his cell.

Kevin glanced at the book, and back at Typhoon, who was walking toward the exit. The guards opened the heavy door, and Typhoon walked through the doorway.

"Is that it?" Kevin called after him, and Typhoon stopped and turned around. "No, it isn't. Happy New Year."

Another guard waited as Kevin quickly opened his briefcase, and shoved the bible inside before following the guard back out through the winding hallways to freedom. As he approached the Ion Scan, Kevin placed his briefcase on the belt and stepped through the unit. The lights and buzzers sounded, and the guards instructed him to step to the side of the room.

They frisked him, waving a hand-held scanner over his body. They then told him to open his briefcase, and removed everything, including the bible Typhoon had just given him. Opening it, they instantly drew their weapons and told Kevin to place his hands above his head. Inside the book, in a neatly cut-out section, was a half brick of cocaine.

HEYWOOD STEPPED out of the shadows, and peered around Jamie's shoulder. "So, I don't even get an introduction?"

"Nope," Jamie said. "You got my money?"

Duck appeared and handed Jamie a briefcase filled with bills. "I don't need to count this, do I?"

"I don't think ya can count that high," Heywood sneered.

"I guess I'll learn tonight, huh?" Jamie asked, weighing the case in his hand, and then he turned to walk away.

"I don't want no shit outta ya, Jamie," Heywood warned. "Now, I'm gonna make the announcement that Tru's gettin' signed wit' my company right before she does her grand finale, ya got that?"

Jamie stopped and nodded. "At midnight."

"Word," Heywood said. "That'll work. Just make sure she don't fuck up. Or that's yo' ass."

"Yeah, mine indeed," Jamie said.

★

At 9:00 sharp, Heywood commanded the stage and the show went off exactly as rehearsed. Hyping the crowd, he did what he did best. The showman, the ringmaster, announced the acts and titillated the audience with a promise of "major news" he was going to break at the stroke of midnight.

With each wardrobe change, Heywood was more and more in his element. He was better than P.T. Barnum. The Master Ringmaster. Minor acts like Shaye and Casbar opened the show and did their thing, while the headliners got ready backstage.

It seemed like the entire world was either present or tuned in. Noah was sitting in one of the luxury skyboxes, courtesy of APB Records. Heywood knew exactly where he was, so he could be sure to see his face when the announcement was made.

In Lewisburg, Carlos and his crew of buddies and guards were huddled in the recreation room. He was beaming, happy for Cam and elated he had contacted Typhoon. He had just gotten word that Kevin had gotten pinched at McCreary.

Kevin had been locked up immediately. It was the weekend, and a holiday, so booking was slow and the guards took their time making the proper notification. And because he committed a felony on Federal property, he was taken into the tombs until he could be processed. There, the guards slipped him an 8-ball of pure cocaine, and he overdosed. Kevin was gone, lights out, before the New Year even began.

Aunt Mary and Jamie's mother were watching the concert together, clutching their bibles and saying prayers for their children.

Rashad and Big Mac were front and center in the VIP section, noisemakers in hand.

After spending the train ride up poring over every page of the book, Robin and Randolph were on their way to The Garden. New York was jammed and crawling with revelers, and she was trying her best to keep her brother's spirits lifted. She wasn't being very successful, but was glad that he wasn't pining away alone, in Philly.

They finally made it to The Garden, and waded through the crowd until they found their seats. They were up near the sky boxes, in the nose-bleed section, but they were there. Randolph hated every minute of it, but Robin was determined to pull him through this devastating situation.

chapter forty-nine

THE COMEDIAN Mike Epps warmed up the crowd after Casbar completed his set, and right before Jamie hit the stage. Because he and Cam were sharing the same set-up with only lighting changes, managed by Cam's former lighting tech Billy, there would be no delay between his set and hers.

He and Cam were watching the program from the closed circuit television, and monitoring everything that was going on. Cam was getting jittery, so she and Jamie held hands and prayed. "Father God, protect us," he said, with his eyes shut tight. He squeezed her hand tightly. "Annoint us."

"Please, Father," she prayed, not wanting to release his hands.

"It's gonna be okay, Baby Girl," Jamie said. "Now, let Big Daddy get out there an' do his thing. Watch me shine."

After Mike cracked his last joke, the cameras zoomed to Heywood, who was watching the clock and keeping the momentum going.

"That's a funny brotha. My man, Mike Epps, everybody!"

The crowd went wild. "It's 11:05, an' that means ya got less than an hour before ya experience the performance of a lifetime. I'm talkin' history, baby. Or should I say 'herstory.' At midnight, ya girl Tru is gonna bring it, an' take ya into the next year. But, before she comes an' blows this mutha up, we got Mr. Magnificent himself. My man, the incomparable Jamie Tee! Jamie Tee!"

The lights went down, and a spectacular lighting show erupted. Jamie was lifted onto the stage from a lower platform, and launched into the first of his string of hits.

He sang his favorites, his hits, and his ballads. He floated, he glided, and he emoted. He wowed the crowd with his precision dance steps and tireless energy. He was truly Mr. Magnificent.

Cam watched him from the monitor as he worked the crowd with ease, playing to the audience and to the cameras. As he neared the end of his performance, Que knocked on the door. "Tru, you ready girl?"

She took a deep breath, and looked at her image in the lighted mirror. She wasn't wearing the mask, but she had on her signature hat, dark shades, and a full wig effectively covered her face. With her full, curvaceous body, she was safe. No one would mistake her for Starr. The the midwaist top and tight low-rider pants she wore clung to her hips and heightened her sex appeal like she never displayed when she was Starr.

"This is it, girl," she said to her reflection in the mirror. She touched her necklace and looked at the bracelet for strength. She stood and braced herself. "I'm ready, Que."

Jamie finished his last song, a cover of Larry Graham's *One in a Millon You*, to a roaring audience, then strutted off the stage to his first hit, *Fired Up*.

Billy brought the house lights down, and Heywood provided commentary in the darkness. "An' now, the moment you've all been waitin' fo' is here. She's here. The next true recording star of Kennetic Records. Yes, it's really true. It's Tru. Tru Talent!"

And the crowd went wild.

Watching from the wings, Jamie shook his head at Heywood's lying ass. And when Heywood joined him on the side of the stage, Jaime let him have it about not sticking to the plan.

"Hey, Imma do me," Heywood responded. "This is my show, my money, an' Imma do things the way I want 'em done. I thought ya knew."

Jamie rolled his eyes and shook his head. "It's always all about you, isn't it?"

"Always," Heywood said with a smirk.

The band hit the first keys of Tru's hit *Miss En You*, and the crowd went beserk.

To playfully mock the earlier rumors about Tru being mere smoke and mirrors, they created a live illusion. All five performers on stage were identically dressed, and the fog machines were working overtime, and mirrors lined the stage. One by one, each woman stepped through the fog and started singing, each pretending to take the mic as the real Tru.

It drove the crowd wild. Finally, the real Tru stepped up, hit the first note of the song, and it was on and poppin'.

She was in her element. With her rich voice, she worked the tempo and rhythm of the song with expert style. Heywood watched the performance from the wings in an almost altered state.

Tru never spoke, just worked the crowd with her expert vocal skills. At the end of her first number, she uttered a short "Thank You," before starting her second number, the upbeat *Trick Bag,* and the crowd was mesmerized.

Robin was standing on her feet, totally in awe. She swayed from side to side, sipping on a cup of generic white wine from the concession stand. Randolph sat glumly in his seat, his chin resting on his hands.

In between sips of her wine, she reached down and tapped her brother. "Damn, this chick is good. Randolph, are you watching? She can really blow."

He just stared off into the crowd, his eyes never even focusing on the widescreen that showed the performer on the stage.

★

As the clock approached 11:57 p.m., it was time. Tru decided to speak. With the band playing a little light music from one of her new songs in the background, she said in her fake Baltimore accent, "Thank you, thank you so much. Thank you for welcoming me into your world."

"I know everyone thought I was a fluke, but I'm for real."

The audience clapped, stomped, yelled, and wolf-whistled.

"I know we're about to do the countdown, but I had to get somethin' off my chest," she said.

"I want to thank the two guys who have made this all possible. Jamie Tee," she said, and blew a kiss in his direction, and the camera panned to him. "And Kennard Heywood."

On cue, one of the mirrors on the stage swiveled, revealing a high-back chair, almost a throne. "Heywood? Would you please come out and join me on the stage?"

Heywood, caught a little off guard, was easily guided onto the stage by two of the stagehands, and seated on his throne. He was King of the World, and he was enjoying every minute.

Tru walked across the stage, and continued talking. "They say that when God closes one door, He opens another. How many of y'all know what I'm talkin' about?" The crowd screamed.

It was 11:58 p.m., and the ball lit up. She cued the band, which started playing Luther Vandross's *Superstar*.

Then she signaled Billy, and he darkened the stage and focused two spotlights. One on her, and the other on Heywood.

★

She started singing, *"Long ago, and oh so far away,"* and abruptly stopped. The band took it back down, and the camera zoomed in on her. It was 11:59 p.m., and the ball started dropping.

"It was long ago, and oh so far away that my life changed," she called out. "Thanks to this man," she said, pointing to Heywood.

The ball continued to slowly descend. It was 50 seconds to midnight. She removed her hat, and the crowd went wild again. "You see, this man changed my world, people."

Forty seconds to midnight. The crowd was howling, on its feet and screaming.

"And see, sometimes change can be good."

Thirty-five seconds.

"And sometimes it's not."

Thirty seconds. People in the audience who were counting down stopped.

"I want you to know that I'm happy to be here, but this is a rough business. I'm sorry that I had to do some of the things I had to do to get here," she said, with her accent slowly fading.

Twenty seconds.

"But I had to," she said, removing her shades. "To protect myself."

Fifteen seconds.

The camera split the screen, with a close-up of her on one side, and Heywood on the other. A hush fell over the audience.

Ten seconds.

"Because this man wanted me dead. Either by his hands or by his deeds, he left me for dead in the islands."

She snatched her wig off, revealed her face to the world, and the audience gasped.

Heywood's eyes bugged and he fell out of his chair. "What the fuck?!" he hollered, looking like he had seen a ghost.

The clock struck midnight and the ball burst and sprayed confetti on the stunned audience. People passed out, howled, cried, and screamed.

Security fought to contain them, and EMTs flooded the area, trying to reach some of the ailing revelers. Shouts of disbelief filled the air, and television screens all across the world were filled with the faces of bewildered and frightened fans.

Eventually, the bewilderment melded into shouts, anger, and threats. All directed at Heywood.

"What the fuck?!" Numerous people in the crowd screamed in unison.

"That mutha fuckin' Heywood. He fucked over Starr? He betta not sleep," somebody else yelled.

"He's a foul son of a bitch."

"Bitch-ass nigga!"

"Get that rat-faced bastard!"

The reaction across the world was mass hysteria. The Internet blew up, and word spread in rapid succession.

In the wings, Allison cried tears of shame, joy, and relief.

In the skybox, Noah watched the events unfold with cool confidence and composure.

In Lewisburg, Carlos and company cheered, high-fived, and gave each other pounds and fist bumps.

In McCreary, Typhoon watched with a look of redemption on his face.

In DC, Aunt Mary and Jamie's mother did the holiness dance.

In the orchestra pit, a confetti-covered Rashad threw his hands up and screamed.

In Montserrat, Mr. Davies hastily made plans for another leave of absence, and the old man with grey eyes smiled.

In the stands, Robin dropped her drink, and it splashed all over Randolph's pants. "Un-fucking believeable," she said. "That's Starr!!"

Randolph was jarred from his altered state when the wine hit his legs, and he jumped. "Who? What's wrong, Robin?" Then, glancing at the widescreen, he leaped out of his seat. "What the hell? Marisol! That's Marisol!" He yelled, and grabbed Robin's arm.

★

"I'm sorry I had to pretend, but I hope you understand," Tru, or Starr continued. "A lot of stuff went down that I don't completely understand. I've been through the fire and I am blessed and highly favored. And understand this. I'm Starr and I'm here to stay, baby!"

The camera cut to Heywood, who was scrambling to his feet and attempting to run off the stage, away from the booing and hissing audience. As he rushed into the wings, a stunned Duck, Parsley, and a number of his groupies, wannabes, and artists were standing there.

"Yo Duck, get me the fuck outta here," Heywood snapped, nearly hyperventilating. His face was ashen and drawn.

"Yeah, uh, Heywood, about that," Duck said, stepping aside as two men in suits, holding suitcases, stood behind him.

"Mr. Heywood?" One of the bespectacled men asked, and Heywood glared at him.

The man in the suit handed him a bunch of folded papers. "Mr. Heyward, this is a subpoena. You are hereby notified that the IRS is freezing your assets and placing liens on your properties."

Heywood snatched the paper from his hand, and spat on the floor. "Fuck. On what fuckin' charges?"

"Underreporting of income and tax evasion," the other suit said.

"Duck!" Heywood shouted. "Get my attorney on the phone!"

On cue, Duck handed him a phone. On the other end was one of Heywood's attorneys, who confirmed that everything had hit the fan. In addition to the IRS, agents were also on their way to arrest him on charges of possession of child pornography, child endangerment and abuse, and even rape.

"What?" Heywood screamed into the phone. "I ain't catchin' a case fo' no one. Who the fuck's bringin' charges against me?"

"Billy Lewis. It is my understanding that he allegedly has evidence that you had sexual contact with his underaged niece. So, as your attorney, I'm advising you to get out of town until I can get things settled."

The color drained from his face, and Heywood hurled the phone against the wall.

"Duck, I said, get me the hell outta here."

"Heywood, man, I would, but when word got out that your assets were locked, the limo booked," Duck said.

Jamie, listening to all this in apparent astonishment, put his arm around Heywood and said, "Man, this is fucked up. I hate to see you out there like this. I'll hook you up with a limo. At least for tonight."

Heywood gritted on Jamie, but didn't decline his offer.

"Come on, Duck. Let's get the fuck outta here."

As arranged, as Heywood left, Big Mac and his detail whisked Cam off the stage, shielding her from the cameras, the media, and the onslaught of peers and fans. As she passed the lighting boom, Billy called down to her, "Thanks, Starr!"

She smiled. She had given Billy his niece's tape so that he and his family could levy charges against Heywood, and get counseling for his niece.

She paused to hug Noah, who had descended from the skybox to give her a hug. "I know we never met before, but I thank you, Starr. You really came through for me, and I'll never forget it. I can't tell you how much I appreciate it."

She embraced him tightly, feeling his relief. "You're welcome Noah. You didn't deserve what happened to you anymore than I did. I'm just glad I could help."

"Well, I'm going to help you too, Starr. All I can. I'm really looking forward to working with you."

As she walked through a swarm of admirers and backstage well-wishers, another loud commotion was brewing in the corner. Big Mac quickly whisked Starr into her dressing room, where Jamie awaited, and then he took up his usual post at the door.

chapter fifty

JAMIE KISSED the side of her face, and smiled. "You did it, Baby Girl."

"We did it," Cam said, and forced a smile. Jamie's makeup artist was nervously trying to help her refresh her makeup, but Cam waved her away. "I'm okay," she told her. "I know it's been a long night, and you really don't have to do this. I can do this myself, okay?"

Jamie looked at the makeup artist, and nodded for her to go. "Why don't you check with Que to see if anyone else needs your help, alright?"

"Will do," said the girl, scurrying out of the dressing room. Jamie turned to Cam, and looked at her like she was crazy.

"You don't get it, do you Miss Missy? What's up with that, 'I'll do it myself,' shit? You're Starr. You're a star. You betta act like you know. You know this is you. This is who you are. This is what you do."

"I know, Jamie, but it's a lot to get readjusted to. You know it's been a minute since I've been in the game. So while it's old, it's still kinda new to me, too.

"But, believe me, I thank God to be back. But I guess I've come to realize that I have a lot more to me than just being Starr. A lot more that I still have to get figured out."

He pointed at her ring finger. "So, would this be one of the things you have to figure out?"

She nodded, and he continued. "So, you gonna tell me about that now? And him?"

Cam smiled and shook her head. "I really don't know what to say, Jamie. I really don't. You're right. I've got to figure that out."

At the moment she got the word "out" out of her mouth, they heard a huge commotion outside the dressing room.

"He needs to see her," a vaguely familiar female voice screeched, and Cam jumped. Big Mac's voice was muffled in his response, but the female voice only escalated, and Cam could make out only bits and pieces of what she was screaming.

"What the hell's goin' on out there?" Jamie asked, turning his head toward the door. "Don't tell me that's the stalkarazzi tryna swoop down on you now. They know the deal. Que already told them that there were no interviews tonight. We're going to do major press tomorrow."

Cam's eyes widened. She didn't want to tell Jamie what she was thinking, but she was pretty sure the screaming voice outside belonged to Robin.

"What's goin' on?" Big Mac asked the other security men who were trying to hold Robin back. "You know we don't let visitors back here to the dressing room. What is it? Do they want an autograph or what?"

Robin puffed up. "No, sir. No we don't. We need to talk to her."

Cam looked sadly at Jamie, and with a quivering voice said, "I think my time for figuring things out is up."

"What? You what? But, that's a chick out there. Don't tell me some chick gave you that ring."

Cam shook her head and stood up. "No, that's my fiance's sister. I guess now she knows who I am."

"Aww, *shee-it*," Jamie said. "More drama? Cam, girl, we gotta get you on the bill with Mary J. Blige. *No More Drama*. Wooo, what you gonna do?"

She wiped her eyes, and checked herself in the mirror. "I'm going to let her in. I can't run from this anymore."

Jamie stood up, and gave her a hug. "Okay, girlfriend. I'll give you some privacy. But, I'll be waiting out in the limo for you, okay? And I'll make sure Big Mac's right outside if you need him. Sista girl out there sounds like she's trippin' or a little full or somethin'."

She hugged him back, and took a deep breath. When Jamie opened the door and gave Big Mac the go-ahead, Robin barged in, snapping pictures with her camera phone, while Cam smiled nervously. It wasn't until Randolph stepped in the doorway, wearing a down jacket and a cloak of vulnerability, that her reality was really checked.

Her eyes locked into his and the pain he conveyed with one look rendered her speechless. The toll that her months of deceit had inflicted on their lives was etched on his face. Her knees buckled, and she grabbed the salon chair for balance.

"Um," Jamie said, "Is this your fiancé?" his eyebrows rose, his eyelashes fluttered, and he smiled coyly. "Nice to meet you," he said, and extended his hand.

Randolph's eyes never left Cam's. "Nice to meet you too," he mumbled, and quickly shook Jamie's hand.

"Wow, I don't believe this. Starr, I mean, Marisol, I mean, I don't know what to call you," Robin cheesed, and flicked her hands, talking a mile a minute. She was staring at Cam like she had never seen her before, and clearly, her earlier hostility had been erased and replaced with a new star-struck groupie persona.

Cam could barely breathe. Her lungs were on the verge of collapse, and her heart was beating a mile a minute. She had to stop her foot from tapping.

Jamie, still holding the door, quickly sized up the situation. "Um, Miss Sister Girl?" he said.

"Robin," she gushed, and gazed at him like a smitten schoolgirl. She whipped out her cellphone and took a quick picture of him.

"Would you like to come join me in my limo? We have a couple of parties to attend, and I'd love for you to join us."

Robin's eyes flashed. "Love to, Jamie Tee. I'm right there with it," she grinned. She turned to Cam. "Well, I know we met, but it was nice seeing you again. I'll, uh, see you later, I guess?" She placed a hand on

Randolph's arm. "Be easy, Baby Brother. It'll be okay," she said, and sashayed out of the door on Jamie's arm, still chattering a mile a minute.

Safely in the limo, Heywood was almost foaming at the mouth, while Duck looked nonchalantly out the window. Enraged, embarrassed, and just outdone, he was a madman.

"Why don't you have a drink, Heywood? It'll calm ya nerves," Duck said, and poured a glass of Stoli Elit and orange juice. Duck pulled a beer from the fridge, opened it, and took a sip.

"Fuck," Heywood cursed, and nearly swallowed the drink in one gulp. "Just get me home. Take me the fuck home. That fuckin' bitch. She's a witch. She's the devil. How the hell did she do that? I know I, uh, well. Shit. What the hell? How'd she do that shit? I don't know what the fuck she's talkin' about. Tryna scandalize my name. She ain't got shit on me."

Heywood finished his drink, still raving and erratic. "Get me a blunt, Duck. Gimme, get me, somethin'. Now." Heywood's words were becoming slurred, and he waited for Duck to hand him a joint that never came.

He became more and more woozy, and eventually passed out. The limo driver lowered the privacy window, and Duck nodded. After a few moments, the driver pulled over on a side street, in front of a lone man standing by a streetlight. It was Noah. Duck opened the door and stepped out onto the slushy street, and Noah slid in. As Duck gave him the pound, Noah handed him two DVDs, and they both nodded in silence. Duck flipped his collar up, and disappeared down the snow-covered sidewalk.

"The piers," Noah said, and the driver pulled off.

Heywood woke up, his head was splitting, his ass was burning like he had been sitting in a pool of fire, and he was overcome with the desire to wash his hands. He blinked his eyes, trying to focus.

He was sitting up in a chair, with a seatbelt across his waist, in what appeared to be an airplane seat. He looked around, and realized he was on a Cessna, a medium-sized private jet.

He stood up, and nearly tripped over a briefcase. He kicked it aside, and looked up and down the aisle. Then he looked out the window. He couldn't tell where he was, but it looked like he was sitting outside of an airport.

The cabin was empty. A movie was playing on the monitors. He was wearing the same clothes he had on during the concert. Was he dreaming?

His mouth felt like cotton, and his throat was parched. He needed to wash his hands. He buzzed for the flight attendant, and his eyes gravitated toward the screen. It looked like some kind of porn flick, except it was all dudes. Heywood crinkled his nose. That wasn't really his flow, but he was slightly intrigued.

It looked like a bunch of dudes running a train on some guy. Heywood leaned forward to get a better look, and he nearly knocked over his tray when he realized the dude getting piped down was him. And he was wearing the same clothes he had on.

"Hey! Somebody! What the fuck! Cut this shit off!" he bellowed, and pressed the attendant's buzzer again. This time, the side door of the plane opened, and a rush of arctic air blew in, along with a team of gun-carrying DEA and FBI agents wearing bulletproof vests.

"Mr. Kennard Heywood? Heywood? Put your hands up. We are agents of the Federal government, and you are under arrest." He stated the charges, and started reciting the Miranda Rights.

One of the agents swooped down and picked up the briefcase Heywood had pushed aside. He opened it, and revealed rows of cash. It was some of the same cash he had given Jamie earlier that evening.

Heywood's face dropped, and he raised his hands. "What the hell?"

Another agent glanced at the movie screen, nudged one of his coherts, and they were barely able to contain their laughter.

"Money laundering, conspiracy narcotics, and drug charges," the lead agent said, cuffing him and leading him to the airplane's exit door.

Outside on the tarmac, a huge crowd of papparazi waited with cameras poised. Ready to capture the low point of Heywood's life. He hung his head in shame and tried to shield his face as he shuffled past the agents unloading and opening crates of weapons and drugs.

★

"I'm so sorry, Randolph. I just don't know what to say. I really don't."

He just stared at her, blinking his eyes and shaking his head. "I don't either, Maris-, well, Starr."

"Please don't call me that. I don't want to be Starr to you. My name is Camara."

Randolph grunted, and emitted a nervous laugh. "You don't want to be Starr to me? Well, I don't know who Camara is, either. But, you're certainly not Marisol."

The moment she had acted and re-acted in her mind a million times was finally here, and it was nothing like she thought it would be. The hurt and pain in his face was a million times worse than she could ever have imagined.

"I'm sorry. I never meant to hurt you."

"You're sorry? You never meant to hurt me? I'm completely devastated. I'm engaged to a woman who doesn't even exist."

She glanced down at the floor, and tears sprang to her eyes. "I know. I wanted to tell you a thousand times, but I didn't know if you would understand."

"And you thought that lying to me would be better?" He grunted. "*Hmmph*, clearly not the right choice." He folded his arms, and shot her another look of hurt and anger.

"It's the truth. I wanted to tell you. I just didn't know what to say. For the longest time, I didn't even know what happened to me. And honestly, when you met me, I thought I was Marisol. I really had no memory."

"That's convenient."

"That's the truth. And I was wrong for not telling you. Dead wrong. But, there was no easy way to deal with this. When I found out that Heywood was responsible for everyone thinking that I was dead, and that he was manipulating my estate and trying to destroy my family, I couldn't take it. It wasn't safe for me to come back as Starr. He might've tried to kill me or my family. I—"

He cut her off, and his bravado both stunned and intrigued her. He had never acted so bold before, and while it frightened her, she kind of liked it.

"Yeah, uh, Robin tried to tell me about that whole video thing. I still don't get it. Who was this guy? Is this someone you were involved with?"

Cam sighed. "Yes, unfortunately. But, that was a long time ago, and whatever we had was over. Long before I ever got injured."

Randy's eyes dropped. "I see. I still don't understand why you just couldn't be honest with me."

Cam sighed. "Because, I wasn't being honest with myself. Before the accident, I really wanted to leave it all behind. I was actually going to take a break from the industry, and just spend some time doing me. But, then, when I got injured, and when I woke up, everyone called me Marisol. I really didn't know who I was. I didn't know what to do. Everything I had was gone. I was truly all alone in a foreign country, with a scarred body and no future. I thought I was an orphan, until my memory came back. Then it was worse, because I did have a past and a family, and I couldn't have them.

"And then I met you, and you were so very sweet. And kind. And genuine. But I was afraid. It wasn't like I didn't trust you, I just didn't know you. And as I got to know you better, and I started finding out more things about the accident, I just got too scared to tell you. I was scared that I might lose you."

He dropped his arms, and fidgeted with his ski jacket. "That sounds too convenient, Maris-, I mean Camara. You've had me at a distinct disadvantage since I met you. Everything was a lie. Your accent, your name, who you are, I don't even know who you are. I know nothing about you."

"I am who you think I am. I'm the woman who really loves you. I'm just not from the Islands, that's all."

"It's not that simple. You can't just live a lie like you did, for months on end, and then turn it around overnight. Even if you think you had good reason to do what you did. And you can't say that you love me, because although you may know me, the me you know doesn't know you. And I can't love someone I don't know."

Tears falling freely from her eyes, Cam wiped her cheeks, her engagement ring glinting as she moved her hands.

"You know how you feel about me," she whispered through her tears.

He caught a glimpse of the ring, sighed and dropped his head. "I don't know how I feel."

"I guess you want your ring back," she said, and tried to pull it off her swollen finger.

"I don't know what I want. But, I'm sure that means nothing to you. Hell, you probably laughed when you saw it. You being used to all the big "bling" and what not."

"Bling doesn't mean anything to me, Randolph. It never has."

"I wouldn't know that."

"What matters is that you gave the ring to me, and what it represents. That you loved me enough to want to marry me." Cam took a step forward, and gazed into his eyes. "Look, I know I was wrong, and I know we come from completely different worlds. But, our worlds were different as Marisol and Randy too. But, we found a way to love each other, then."

Randolph stepped back. "That was then. Under completely different circumstances."

"Your heart is still the same. My heart is still the same," she said, still advancing towards him.

He continued stepping backwards. "It doesn't matter. Too many things have happened that will never make any sense to me. And I don't know if I'll ever allow myself to understand it."

"That's your head talking, Randolph," she said, pinning him up against the wall. "And you are a brilliant, beautiful, compassionate man. But, this isn't about what you think. It's about what you feel. The heart wants what it wants, and our minds have very little to do with it." She drew closer to him, and placed her hands on his chest.

He stuttered. "That sounds like a movie or something. Not my life. I don't live like that. I live in reality, and realistically, I can't deal with this. And I don't know if I ever will."

"I don't know if I can either. But, I know I want to try." She slid her hands up his chest and cupped his face. "I love you, Randolph. I really do. If I don't know anything else, I know that."

"I don't know," he said, his arms remaining rigidly at his side. He looked at her full in the face. "I just don't know if I can ever trust you."

"I know. And I know that if you give me a chance, I'll try to earn your trust. But if you really don't want to, I'll have to understand. But, I would ask you for one request, though. Just one."

He reached for her hands, and tried to remove them from his face, but she held on. "Just kiss me, and let your heart decide," she said.

★

Their lips met, and she kissed him like she had never kissed him before. As a free woman, a woman with no secrets, with no heaviness on her heart. A woman finally open to and willing to surrender to her emotions, and to give herself as she never had before.

At first his lips were reluctant, but after a few seconds, he yielded. He took her in his arms, slammed her up against the wall, and kissed her like he had never kissed her before. Overcome with passion and emotions, the energy that crackled between them erupted. There was no sense in denying what they shared, no matter what their names or titles were.

After kissing softly, roughly, violently, and finally, gently, they parted, leaning against the wall, locked in a tight embrace. Both of their chests were heaving, and tears were flowing.

"I do love you," Randolph said, his eyes misty and red. "I can't deny it."

"I love you too," she said, wiping her lipstick from his mouth, and the tears from his face.

"I just don't know what we're going to do," he sighed. "But, I guess we have to try. I can't make any promises. All we can do is take it one day at a time."

"That's all we can do. I just can't imagine my life without you. Whatever my life is going to be."

chapter fifty-one

WITH ROBIN happily ensconced in the celebrity world and making the rounds with Jamie, Cam and Randolph were seated in the back of their Maybach limousine, heading back to Philly.

They were content, in a comfortable silence, as the limo snaked through the Lincoln Tunnel. She laid her head on his shoulder, and sighed. He wrapped his arm around her, and stroked her hair while he gazed out the window into the starry, snow-kissed night.

She wasn't sure what she was going to do. Returning to the life of a superstar wasn't necessarily what she had wanted, but it was who she was. So, despite how it happened, she was back on the scene. But, at least now, she wasn't alone. She had someone who really loved her, and someone she could really trust.

To the world, Marisol was gone, Tru was no more, and she was Starr again. And the world was expecting her to shine. But, for the moment, she was Camara, and the most important thing to her was being with Randolph. She only wanted to be by his side as they started their tenuous journey together down this unknown path.

As the limo found its way to the New Jersey Turnpike, she found herself drifting off, and for the first time in a long time, she wasn't afraid of her dreams or having anymore nightmare. She was content; her heart and mind were finally at peace.

There was a comfort in knowing that at the end of her present trip, she would awaken in a familiar place, fully aware of how she got there. Without lugging the baggage of lies and deceit with her. And for the moment, that was more than enough.

epilogue

"I'M SO *sorry, Marisol," she thought to herself. "So sorry that your life ended so soon and that I had to use your name. It's yours again, girl. God bless you."*

And she smiled, thinking of Marisol. Cam was at that moment heading back to Marisol's island, along with the balance of the money from Heywood's suitcase. Jamie had set it all up. The money would be used to make Marisol's dreams come true for other island girls. The Marisol Kent Scholarship Fund would enable several Montserrat girls every year to attend school in the United States. Cam had her work cut out for her now. In addition to her other charities, she planned to make substantial donations to the Luis Eduardo Aybar Burn Center and the University Hospital of Lausanne.

ACKNOWLEDGMENTS

I GIVE all honor and glory to God. I thank Him without ceasing.

To my family, my parents, Lee & Frances; my sisters, Linda & Lynette, my brother-in-law, Monty; my nieces and nephews, Portia, Brandon, Mickey & Morgan; My cousins Mary Brown, Yolande' Brown, The Fergusons, The Kennedys, The McIvers, The Mumfords, The Lakins, The Palmers, & The Woods . . . thank you all for being who you are to me.

To my extended family: Mildred Boykins, Butch & Phyllis Fisher, Vivian Gaunt, Ida Hutchinson, Tee Johnson & Rev. Kevin O'Bryant.

A special thanks to Nicky . . . it's been a long journey, but I promise that the destination will be incredible!

Special thanks to Maggie Nelson & Lauran "Starr" Walker. Thanks so much for the support and inspiration. Without you, this would not have been possible.

To my brother and sister friends: Alan Agho, Rodney Akers, Renee Anderson, Dywane Birch, Mia Booker, Brenda Brown, Cissy Carter, Earl Coleman, Mike Graham, Robb Jackson, Lisa Jeffress, Barbara Lewis, Eugene Lowe, Val Matthews, Meryl McDuffie, Tanya Mena, Brenda Miller, Ros Murphy, Sheila Murchison, Greg Parrish, Val Robertson, Trina Savage, Doc Smith, Pat Sugick, Louis Thomas, Ros Vinson, Nichole Winborne, Kelli Wynn, and Sebrena Woods-Ofei. Thank you for the laughter, the love and the good times.

TO MY other moms, Mrs. Pat Buck and Dr. Sandra Newsome. Thanks for always thinking of me and mine. You are very special, and I really appreciate your love and support.

To the wonderful staff and residents at the Villa Rosa Nursing Home. The love, support and kindness you showed my grandmother will never be forgotten. A special thanks to Kathie, Shirley, April, Al, Elaysha, Danielle, Dania, Michelle, Portia & Sharnay.

My editor Lee Ann Knapp: Thank you for being so generous with your talents and gifts. I will never forget it.

To my agent, Sarah Camilli: Thanks for always keeping me in your thoughts and concerns.

To all of the book clubs (Just Friends, The DIVAs, STAR, etc.) and readers who have kept me in their thoughts. I hope you have room in your bookshelves for this. Thanks for your patience and support.

LaVergne, TN USA
26 July 2010
190882LV00003B/1/P